"It's best never to be at a loss for wishes," Jesse bantered. "Out with 'em."

"I wish to know who I am. Even more," she hesitated, studying his handsome face, "I wish to stroll out under the moon on this perfect night and forget that I've ever forgotten."

"Your second wish! I can make that one come true." He handed her the bottle and glasses and swept her off her feet. His mouth brushed hers.

"I am perfectly able to walk," Lorena said, putting her arm around his neck.

"So what?" Jesse answered.

The garden at the side of the large house was hidden from the avenue by a high, brick wall covered in English ivy. When Jesse put Lorena down, they touched along the length of their bodies causing a tingling need. Lorena felt a rush of delight when she and Jesse moved toward each other, neither one equal to the task of preserving physical distance between them. Jesse drew her to him hard. She raked his glinting hair, black and smooth as satin in moonlight, back from his brow. Her hands fluttered to his broad shoulders and her body flowed to his as they kept their profound, long kiss alive . . .

Books by Joyce Myrus

TENDER TORMENT

ANGEL'S ECSTASY

ISLAND ENCHANTRESS

SWEET FIERCE FIRES

DESPERADO'S KISS

BEYOND SURRENDER

LOVE AND GLORY

TEMPTATION

MASTER OF MOONLIGHT

LOVING JESSE

Published by Zebra Books

LOVING JESSE

Joyce Myrus

ZEBRA BOOKS
Kensington Publishing Corp.
http://www.kensingtonbooks.com

To my sons, Richard and Noah

CHAPTER 1

Lorena Reed stood on the corner of a wide and busy New York City street that ended a block away at the South Street docks. From the spot where she had been deposited by her traveling companion and instructed to wait, she could see what appeared to be a dense forest, and was actually the masts of ships docked and riding at anchor in the harbor. She heard the calls of scavenging sea gulls, shouts of stevedores and draymen, and the steady tolling of buoy bells riding the swells off shore. To hurrying passersby, several of whom glanced her way, Lorena appeared somewhat out of place in the simplicity of her country attire, yet cool and composed amidst the chaos of a bustling, unusually warm spring afternoon, April 1, 1865. She was not quite as serene as she looked. She had been standing alone, with her carpetbag at her feet, occasionally fanning her face with her hat, for nearly two hours.

Near the docks, sounds of hammering, of steel wagon wheels on cobblestone, and the calling of workmen—from the warehouses, sail lofts and coopers' works—mixed with the cries of street peddlers and the raillery of sailors, newly ashore. As the day wore on, the din grew louder with passengers arriving in a steady flow to board ferries and seagoing ships. The reek of refuse, floating in rivulets of melting ice along the curb, and of steaming horses and their droppings became more pungent as the temperature rose. Just after the noon hour was struck by a nearby church bell, Lorena decided to continue her vigil in the shade of a build-

ing across the way. When she lifted her bag, a pair of weath-
ered, scruffy men detached themselves from a group of
boisterous seamen loitering nearby. The two came toward
Lorena, boldly looked her up and down, grinned at each other
and stood one on either side of her.

"Lost are you, girlie?" one man asked.

"Need a place to stay the night, mebbe?"

"Thank you, sir, but no. I am waitin' on . . . on a friend, a
guide to . . ." She flushed, at a loss about how to proceed.
Well-mannered, taught to respect her elders, as these men certainly were, and not inclined to judge books by their covers,
Lorena hesitated. Not altogether naive, she decided the unsa-
vory sailors offered more of a threat than kindhearted
assistance.

"Ain't she the polite and shy country girl?" one of the men
said. "No need to be timid with us, miss. We'll be pleased to
guide you to wherever it is you've a mind to go," he told
Lorena. "I'm Able-bodied Seaman Roger Truckett. This
here's me mate, AB Will Swisby, both of the frigate *Howard
Wister* out of Liverpool." Swisby appropriated Lorena's bag
and Truckett grasped her upper arm. She tried to shake him
off.

"I have been raised up mannerly as you say, but I've never
been timid. I have no need of your help, thank you." She said
this more crisply, her heart beginning to pound.

"But I've a need, dear, if'n you do or not," Swisby answered.
"Don't be skeered. Just come along quiet and polite now, as is
your natural bent, and let us show you about the ship. No one's
aboard but a junior officer on watch so there'll be no one to
grumble about us inviting a female for a bit of a visit."

"And if that female is still aboard when we haul anchor in
at dusk or dawn, dependin' on the tides and the captain's business dealings, no one'll be the wiser." Truckett smiled,
showing a few yellowed teeth between wide gaps of gum.

"And if this stowed-away female stays quiet and obliging,
she'll be aboard still when we reach Jamaica," added the one

called Swisby. "If she's not obliging, and quiet . . . well, the sea's deep and vast, she'll discover."

"What? Quiet and . . . ? My friend will be here at any moment. She'll raise a hue and cry if I'm not to be found where she left me," said Lorena in a controlled, incredulous tone.

"I doubt that, dear. The lady what left you alone on *this* street corner was no friend. Swisby will back me up on that, aye, Swisby?"

"Unhand me and my property," Lorena ordered in a firm, loud voice, "before I call out for help now." With all her might, she tried to tug the handle of her bag from Swisby, and free herself from Truckett's hold, but to no avail until, quite suddenly, a look of dread came on Truckett's face. As suddenly, he let go of Lorena's arm, her carpetbag came free in her hands and she reeled backwards not, as she had expected, to go sprawling in the street, but to fetch up against a bulwark of solid support.

"May I help you with that, ma'am?" a cool voice inquired as the two sailors edged off, then turned and ran. Lorena looked up over her shoulder with a grateful smile into a pair of menacing, if weary, black-fringed blue eyes, hard as bullets, under a dusty and battered Yankee cavalry hat. The officer looked so fierce she knew at once why her would-be abductors had fled at the sight of him. He was tall and very slim, too slim Lorena decided, though he was broad enough through the shoulders to carry plenty of sinewy muscle when he was hale and hearty, which was not his condition just then, despite his threatening demeanor. Lorena was acquainted with self-assured, uncompromising men of this variety and, despite his glowering expression, she was not intimidated. Quite the contrary.

"You were raised up in the Carolina Piedmont, suh!" she exclaimed with obvious relief. "I know your way of speakin'. It's just barely southern-tinged but I can tell. If you say a few words more, I'll likely be able to name the very town where you were born. I knew a teacher—in school—I've been to school, really, and the teacher I speak of had the gift of music and tongues. He told me how to do that, figure out where a person comes from if it's anywhere in or near North Carolina, not too far afield of our mountain, leastways. He taught me to read, to write and, his favorite part, speak with perfect diction, he called it, so as no one could tell where I come from. Unless I want a person to know. I don't usually bother too much about that, diction—I mean. I like folks to know I live on the Mountain. I'm proud of that. Well, anyways," she blushed, "I have no call to prattle at you so, nineteen to the dozen. Do please tell me what Hester Potts told you about escortin' me the rest of the way or even part of the way home. I won't chatter at you, I promise. Hester must have told you how she was to accompany me herself, but something come—came—up when we reached New York. I told her I could manage the rest of the way on my own but she insisted on going off to look for a guide for me, someone also journeying south. That'd be you and I am well content. Hester's kind of bossy."

"North Carolina was my infrequent place of residence. I'm headed there now, or as soon as the armies have passed through and the peace comes, but, no, ma'am, I am not sent by any Hester Potts. I've been watching you for a time, from across the way, is all. I was leaning against that lamppost, waiting for a friend, and I conjectured you might be getting tired, as I was, just about now. Or uneasy. Those tars had long been keeping an eye on you, as I had."

"For a very different reason, it seems, ah . . . Lieutenant? I see your insignia. Whatever are *you* doin' in a Yankee uniform soundin' kinda sesech?" Lorena hesitated, her hazel-hued eyes searching the man's weary, intense face. Stark cheekbones, high beneath dark blue, bullet-hard eyes, were particularly prominent in a thin face darkened by some days' growth of stubble. He swept off his hat to reveal shoulder length, matted black hair.

"I have this tunic on loan. I'm . . . Soldier Sparhawk, Battery F, First Rhode Island Light Artillery, at your service. I'm *Mister,* rightly. Even more precisely, just plain Jesse Sparhawk, now the war's coming to a close, and I've been, well, not quite mustered out of the army, merely removed from front lines fighting."

"As good as over?" Lorena repeated, almost breathlessly. "Oh, my! Oh, my gracious and goodness be thanked!" She clasped her hands beneath her chin and did a lively little tap dance in place. "I hadn't known the end was all that close. Thank the heavens it is." Sparhawk nodded in profound agreement.

"There's a bit to go still," he said. "The main Reb army under General Lee must be defeated and Richmond taken. Even after that happens men will go on warring for a time, in fruitless skirmishes between Fed and Rebel units. It will take days for officers to receive the news. And even after the peace is proclaimed from one end of this land to the other, there's some who'll never quit." Jesse scowled, appearing dark and dangerous again, then bemused to see something of his own anger and threatening temerity mirrored on this pretty girl's face. There was a fury in her akin to his own, he realized. He wanted—had to—know why.

"I'll ask you the question you just posed to me: Why is a young lady from the South—you—standing alone and waiting so long, on a New York City street corner? As soon as you speak to a Yankee, you could be taken for a spy, you know, accused of counting ships or taking note of supplies being loaded. It's happened before, accusations based on no more than a lilt of the tongue," he said.

"Your drawl, turning on and off as it does, would make you as much a suspect as I—of being a secret agent but for your uniform and your injury," she answered.

"Perhaps, but this spy business is serious. People are on edge. Just late last year, in November, agents led by three Rebel officers, used Greek fire—turpentine and phosphorus—to try to burn down the city. They lit up ten crowded hotels and also Barnum's Museum. The fire department was right on the job. There was little damage but emotions ran high and remain so, even as Confederate armies, outnumbered now, are falling back."

"*Falling back,* in North Carolina? Are they fallin' back in North *Caroline*? You know so much, Soldier, about the fightin'. Do tell me, please, if you know anythin' a-tall about what's occurring there at home," Lorena implored.

"I was in North *Caroline* with my Battery, but not since earlier in the hostilities. Right now, some of General Sherman's troops are skirmishing around Snow Hill. Sherman's headquarters are at Goldsboro, in your—our state. That's all I can report, except that Joe Johnston and his troops are in the western part of Carolina, but information doesn't come out of the hills any too swiftly. I can tell you that the next important battle is shaping up under General Grant, against Lee and Pickett. President Lincoln has made use of his telegraph office in Washington for some time now; he's just been to meet face-to-face with his generals and senior staff at City Point in Virginia. They're confident now, planning the peace."

"You sound almost as if you had been there, too, you knowing so much, Mr. Sparhawk." Placing a hand on the crown of her bonnet, she looked up into Jesse's face again.

"I've just come from the army offices on State Street, near the Battery. There's a telegraph machine there. I learned that the significant fighting right now is at a place called Five Forks in Virginia. I . . . I *should* be there," Sparhawk growled, fierce and furious again, "but as I've told you, I'm out of action. For a time."

"Oh, but you are injured, Mr. Just-Plain-Jesse Sparhawk!" Lorena said, her large, round eyes and her voice at once soft and brimming with concern. The soldier's left coat sleeve hung empty, his arm beneath his jacket held to his chest by a grimy strip of sheeting rigged as a sling. "I should be the one offering you assistance, suh. May I help?" Lorena asked as he swayed on his feet, the scant color that had been there, draining from his lean face. He reached out to steady himself with his good hand on her shoulder.

"Thank you kindly, but I'm about well now, as the surgeons tell it. They've done all they can. Use of my arm may be forever lost to me. Maybe not. But I'd not give a tinker's damn about being winged if they hadn't shot my mount out from under me. I was hit. He was killed, a great, noble animal."

"I am sorry for your loss, Mr. Sparhawk. But I must disagree with you and the doctors. It does not appear to me that you were just 'winged' or that you're 'about *well*'! It's my pure good luck those two ruffians didn't know your actual strength, or lack of it," Lorena replied. "When did you last et . . . *eat* last?"

"I've not had much craving for food. Thank you kindly for inquiring." The vestige of his drawl, stimulated by hers, became more pronounced.

"Is it hunger or money you've not had much of?" she asked, glancing about for a place where they might find nourishment and shade. "Hester insisted on holding my folding money, forty Yankee dollars, for safekeeping. I've only a bit of silver in my pocket but it's enough to feed us both somethin', over there." She pointed across the congested intersection at an eatery with a few chairs and tables set out on the wooden sidewalk beneath an awning.

"I am meeting a friend here shortly who will see to my needs. I've money enough for food, more than enough I assure you, thank you kindly ma'am, just the same." Sparhawk's hard expression gentled and he attempted a grin. It was more a wan grimace than a smile as he looked intently, with focused curiosity, at Lorena. The frayed brim of her straw bonnet had allowed the sun to scatter a spray of freckles over her small nose and rounded cheeks. The bonnet's crown, though, was encircled by a new yellow ribbon that trailed down her back beside a long, thick braid nearly the same color, though of a paler gold. An unadorned, much mended dress of blue homespun gently followed the discernible swells and curves of a dainty figure. "You *are* a mite of a thing to be taking charge of me so promptly. Tell me now, how did a wisp of a southern girl come to be alone in this northern city? You're all of eighteen, I'd guess. Will you also tell me your name?"

"Lorena Sue Reed, of Reed Mountain Laurel. I turn *eighteen* come Friday, on the fourteenth of April," she answered with restrained pride.

"Truth to tell? You 're from *Reed Mountain?*" Jesse asked pointedly, narrowing his fatigued eyes. "That's a remote, out-of-the-way place, the Reed Mountain Valley. I'm even more curious now, to learn what you're doing here, alone."

"I'll be pleased to explain, soldier, soon's we're seated over a meal," Lorena answered authoritatively. He relaxed some, and almost smiled.

"Well, and will a proper young lady of the Carolina Highlands set herself down in a public, big city saloon with a man, a *strange* man at that?" By then, Jesse's face had gone chalky pale and he swayed on his feet. He passed his good arm to rest over Lorena's shoulders for support even as he tried to keep his tone bantering.

"From the first word you spoke—the way you spoke it—you were not a stranger to me, Mr. Sparhawk. True to southern form, even weak as you are, you came to my rescue and now, I think you're funnin' with me. That, or flirtin', suh?" Lorena smiled. He chortled and then a look of incredulity came to his eyes.

"The sound of my own laughter is something I haven't heard of late," he explained. "Thank you for that. Yes ma'am, I've been known to flirt in my day, Miss Reed. That seems a long time ago now," he replied before a shadow of anger and despair flitted over his face. "Well," he said recalling himself to the moment, "you're a straightforward young lady, one who . . ."

"Who values propriety, yes. But I have passed nearly two years up north in the state of New York, at Seneca Falls."

"Where there's a large infirmary and convalescent camp for Yankee war wounded. You were working there, I take it?" he asked. Lorena slowly nodded, hesitated, and then went on.

"Seeing what this war has done to so many boys and men, changes one's understanding and, also, there at Seneca Falls, I spent long hours in the company of women, helping to nurse the wounded, some lonely strangers to them and some their own men. Some of those women were very modern; suffragists, they are called."

"And they told you females are the equal of males in all things?" Sparhawk asked, beginning to understand what accounted for the mingling of worldly ease and simplicity he found in this backwoods southern girl.

"Not equal in all things, but in many, equal enough surely to have a voice in the future, and to vote and to get in out of the sun on a hot day, to take food and drink, even at a public establishment. If we go there, before you pitch right over with fatigue, to the Forrest Spring House," she read the sign she had been eyeing, "we shall be able to keep a look out for Hester and refresh ourselves at the same time. Forrest Spring, indeed!" Lorena smiled. Jesse lowered his arm from about her shoulders, stood on his own a moment to test his balance, then hefted her bag. She slipped her arm through his to steady him if the need arose.

"Will you tell me, after you've eaten, how it is you heard of my mountain, Mr. Sparhawk, and how *you* come to be here in this New York City, as alone as I am, and wounded and still chivalrous as ever a Southern man could be, rescuing me from ruffians and carrying my bag with your one good arm?"

"First, you must tell me somethin'. Is that a wedding band you're wearing?" he asked, looking down at her small hand resting on his sleeve. Lorena nodded, silent, her full lips drawing tight. "But it's not on your ring finger." She shook her head no and was silent. "Well," Jesse continued, "I'm sure your husband will be joyful when you and he are both home again to your hearth. Will you tell me another thing?" he asked. She shrugged and didn't nod, just squinted her eyes a little and shook her head tentatively. He took her cue and quickly dropped the subject. "Who else is waitin' on you?"

"I'll tell you, but only if you come along to eat this very minute."

"Yup. Sure will."

"I'm on my way home to help my mamma. Only young Frank is at home now—one brother was lost to the war and I haven't heard about my Daddy for some time. My mamma's been working too hard, running the place. Trying to. She needs me and my earnings, to buy a plow and a mule, if there's any of them things to be found, to replace what was took by the Rebels and the militias—taken . . ." Her rosy face went a shade pinker with embarrassment. "When emotion overcomes me, words betray me. I really have been taught to talk in a proper and grammatical manner but I lapse into my cradle tongue when . . ."

"When you're agitated?"

"Or when I'm feelin' real easy with a person, one or t'other."

"I really like your cradle tongue," Jesse reassured broadening his own slight drawl to put Lorena more at ease. "Was it difficult for you to learn to talk, ah, proper?"

"See, when I was a little baby girl my mamma killed a wood tick that was walking on my leg. She used a book to do it, the Good Book, to thwack that tick and you know what that means!"

"I'm afraid I don't know," Jesse shrugged, smiling again.

"As everyone in *our* valley is aware and I've been told all my life, that was a special sign, a good omen. It meant I could learn to talk good—I mean speak well, and to use proper words. They all of them at home give up a lot, 'specially my mamma, so I could go to the school most days they had it instead of me working about the household chores and in the field. Maybe I'd become a teacher myself someday, Daddy conjectured, in the holler school, or even down in the village, and maybe I'd be something of a lady, too. Then, while I was gone from home up north to Seneca, helping the nurses with their patients and tending my . . ." She abruptly turned away from Jesse. "While I was gone, the vigilante Rebs rode into the valley and *terrible* things came to pass. I was not there to help my kin when they needed me!" Her tone was profoundly sad and also angry.

"You *were* helping and comforting someone most dear, who needed you, and others, too, at Seneca Infirmary. I don't know what one girl could have done to change things in the valley. If you've been away from your home for two years while the war's been raging, how do you know what happened exactly, in Reed Valley? I'm aware folks in the mountains

were short on wool and corn and hogs, of course, but they're
a tough lot, your kith and kin. They may be, very likely most
of them are, all right," Sparhawk suggested, trying to put the
best face on the possibilities. "What do you say we go eat
now? We'll both feel better after a meal, I reckon."

"Isn' that just what I've been tryin' to get you to do from
the start?" she said with exasperation.

Sparhawk scanned the traffic, looking for an opportunity
to cross the street. His strength appeared to ebb further.
Droplets of sweat gathered on his brow and streaked down his
ashen cheeks. He leaned even more heavily against Lorena
who feared he would crumple beside her and she too gauged
the passing vans and lorries, certain she must quickly get him
to a chair in the shade. When they stepped off the curb,
Lorena led Jesse through the flow of traffic.

"Have a care! This man is one of our brave and noble
wounded!" she called out, lifting her hand and bringing an ice
wagon, a hansom cab and a private carriage to a stop so she
and Jesse could cross without excessive haste and no danger
to life and limb. By the time they reached the opposite side of
the street, Sparhawk, his step faltering, was putting most of
his weight on Lorena's shoulders as she led him toward the
nearest empty table—where he more slumped than sat, in the
first chair he came to. He rested his brow on his arms, which
he had crossed on the table top, as a heavyset man in a white
apron hurried to their aid.

CHAPTER 2

"By me faith, I been seeing a lot of these poor fellows nowadays, just out of the army, hurt and too weak to stand for long, and bony as stray dogs. Some's actual heroes, just sent on their not-so-merry-ways from the Soldiers' Depot Hospital there on Howard Street. Same as if they was shirking Belfast beggars," said the aproned man. He handed Lorena a cool, damp cloth. "I keep them chilled napkins handy in a tub of the ice water, and when I seen you pair headin' my way . . ."

"Thank you kindly," answered Lorena, wrapping the cloth, like a scarf, about Jesse's neck.

"I'm Bud."

"Thank you kindly, Bud. Iced water, please, to drink and a glass of something stronger. My daddy's own brew would do no end of good now."

"Irish whiskey it'll have to be," Bud shrugged, and poured. "Yup, a lot of lads come down here to the harbor seeking a boat to get south of New York or find a ferry going up to Boston. Where's your young officer from, Miss?"

"I'm not precisely sure. He was fighting for the North and talking sort of south, like Carolina. We've only just met," Lorena explained and then added, "He's not my officer." Her perfect diction and the quality of voice, which seemed to convey a suggestion of regret, prompted Jesse to lift his head to search Lorena's eyes. He found them averted. He then emptied, in a long series of gulping swallows, the tankard of water Bud had set down.

"Feeling better, son?" asked the man. "Have a go at the whiskey. Then let's start fattening you up some, so that your lady won't be able to count your ribs next time you and she—" Bud paused, blushed scarlet to the roots of his carrot-red hair, and then asked, "How would some home-cooked food suit you two? We got a fish stew simmering, ready now, beefsteak ready soon."

"Home cooked?" Lorena asked skeptically.

"I know this saloon ain't a home, strictly speaking, but it's me own wife, Mrs. Ryan herself, in the kitchen and it's the only kitchen we got, so that's home cookin', ain't it? See, we live in the alley back behind this place. We built a good little shanty, small, but tight. It keeps off the rain, don't it, nearly as good as the soddie shack we left in County Claire?"

"Is this your place, Bud, Forrest Spring House?" Jesse asked.

"This is not a forest, nor is there any clear spring hereabouts, and you'd not be likely to find neither one nor the other in this part of city. Nor is it any more likely a poor man like meself could own an establishment such as this. Some distant day, I hope to head out to your great west, to farm that rich soil I hear tell of. For now, me and Lara, me wife, we're obliged to stay here. Course, if the proprietor of this establishment should offer to give it to me, which is as likely a happenstance as snow falling in hell, or New York in July, I'd not turn down the gift, understand, forest spring or no spring. That'd be fine by us. Lara, and me, we ain't got a pot of our own, not to cook in nor anything else. No, sir. But we *are some* better off than the hard laboring Irish in New York. Our hours are long but the workin' is easier here than diggin' ditches for a dime a day. Me and Lara are payin' off a debt. Not our own," Bud was quick to explain. "Lara's brother got himself in money trouble. We settled his debt and so saved his miserable life, keeping the cops and the thugs, both, off him. We work here by special arrangement, so to speak."

"Only a pittance of what you earn stays in your own pockets," said Jesse. "Am I right? You've indentured yourselves for Lara's brother and here we're fighting to end slavery." Bud nodded, his head tilted to one side, shoulders lifting in a shrug. His smile was resigned.

"That's a long tale, more'n twice told. I won't bore you with it 'cept to say we know when we'll own our freedom again, and then Lara and me will head west, and no one none the wiser. Well, we must feed up this officer here, right miss? Before he vanishes all together. What'll it be?"

"Bring on everything, Bud," Lorena said, "stew, steak, potatoes, the best Lara has. This officer and I, why, we're so hungry—we might—*could* eat a horse. Each!"

The sun, well into its afternoon decline, sent low bright rays along the narrow, usually shadowed, canyon of the street on which The Forrest Spring House looked out. The buildings, set shoulder-to-shoulder, rose five and six stories tall along narrow sidewalks bustling with workers as offices and shops shut down. By the time the tavern filled with other customers, Jesse and Lorena had already devoured oysters, fish stew, steaks, potatoes with gravy, dressed cucumbers, hot rolls, and ice cream. She had had a glass of claret, he several glasses. They both felt far better than they had before—their troubles, for the moment, put aside in the pleasant afterglow of food and drink and easy company. As dusk came on, candlelight glowed rosy on their faces and danced, reflecting on refilled wineglasses.

"May I have this dance, ma'am?" asked Jesse languidly and they waltzed to an old Stephen Foster ballad, his sound arm about her waist, her hands set upon his shoulders, her golden braid and skirt, his long hair, flying as they whirled. A melancholy-looking fiddler accompanied a sweet-voiced child's rendition of *Open thy Lattice, Love.* It was a song that always tugged at the heart strings and it now affected both young dancers with a formless sweet longing to which neither gave words. Jesse's shoulders curved forward protectively, as if to envelope his partner. "This tune brings to mind more peaceful, bygone days." Lorena nodded, her head up-tilted, her eyes smiling into his. When a man at the bar requested the livelier *O Susannah,* the couple danced a gallop that left

Lorena weak with laughter and Jesse rather short winded but buoyant. They came near to flirting, which almost at once seemed to quell Lorena's easy laughter. Jesse's pallor returned and the dark rings around his eyes attested to his exhaustion. They returned to their table in silence. To recapture their lighthearted mood Jesse asked what he considered a neutral question, in an easy drawl.

"Now, Miz Lorena Reed, after we've been here dinin' and chattin' and dancin' through the shank of the afternoon, are you able to tell, by my way of pronouncing words, where I was born and raised?" Her eyes lit and danced at the challenge.

"Suh, where you were born and where raised were not one and the same place. I know you did do some of your early growing in Carolina. Not the mountains or even in the foothills. I'd venture to say . . ." she paused, teasing, keen to keep him hanging on her every word.

"Well, out with it!" Jesse laughed, "Unless your claims are merely a charming little amusement, a conjurer's trick or a party game. If you guess wrong, I won't bite or even glare, I promise."

"Why, I do *not* have to guess. I *know*," she insisted with mock indignation. "Your first baby words was spoke somewhere north and a mite east of Reed Valley. There!" Lorena replied pleased by the look of appreciative surprise he offered. "I see in your countenance I wasn't wildly off."

"You have me just about right, actually," Jesse answered with admiration. "I first saw the light of day near Albemarle Sound, in the Carolina lowlands, not all that far, as the crow flies, from Reed Valley, but a world away. I admit you do have a charmed skill with words—speaking and listening. How, exactly, did you know my precise provenance, if you don't mind tellin' me your secret?" At that, Lorena tilted her head to one side and studied Jesse thoroughly from his blue eyes to his scuffed boot tips. He just shrugged, winked and waited, basking, it appeared, in her perusal.

"No secret to it," she eventually said. "See, there's a cluster of clues, besides merely talkin', that a person hardly knows he's giving and I was just generally reacting to. Though you happen to be too lean just now, your shoulders are broad enough to carry considerably more weight and muscle. You have the graceful height and, doubtless, the same strength, when you're fit, as my male kin in Daddy's line who are of Scots ancestry. There are many such in North Carolina. And those eyes of yours, so dark a blue with, now and again, a slant of gray when the light shines just so. Deep-set eyes they are with dark brows above 'em. Your cheekbones are strong. I have seen features resembling yours on many a Reed mountain boy. I mean, not all put together on one face, just not arranged so . . . pleasingly as yours. Your nose is finely formed, narrow and a mite hawkish, rather like those of my uncles on Mamma's side, who came up from the lowlands two generations past, maybe from Albemarle, to settle in the hollows away from crowds to live their own way.

"Your mouth though, gave me pause," Lorena puzzled, her eyes lingering on his lips, her own lips pursed. "Your mouth is so . . . full and invi . . . interesting. I mean, that is not the sort of mouth I ever recall seeing on any Carolina man. Be that as it may, it wasn't only your way of pronouncing words that helped me to determine your homeplace, the direction of it, leastways." During Lorena's inspection and description of his features, Jesse was amused by her self-confident inspection and forthright narration of what she was seeing.

"You are not a diffident or coy young woman, are you, Lorena? You've just looked me over and evaluated my physical traits as though I were horseflesh up for auction at the Raleigh Fall Fair. Would you care to check my teeth? I've got them all!" Lorena looked abashed and she did blush before she giggled.

"I . . . I am . . . I do some sketching. I've gotten used to staring hard at what subjects interest me. It's not real polite, I know, and I do beg your pardon."

"No need. I admire your straightforwardness. I just might take up sketching myself. It would give me a fine excuse to gaze at my leisure on pretty faces. Like yours. I'll start in right now to try my hand and eye at drawing." Jesse smoothed his linen table napkin and took a lead pencil from his breast pocket. "Turn your head aside and raise up your chin a mite, if you please." Lorena complied and Jesse quickly did a profile of her smooth brow, touched by a stray lock of hair, her rounded cheek, her straight nose a little upturned. Her lips were puffed and seemed in profile pursed, as if for a kiss. Her long, slender throat was graceful. How utterly lovely she is, he thought, staring. "How are *your* teeth?" he asked with a raffish smile. She turned to face him.

"I, too, have got a full set as you can see." She broadly grinned to exhibit them. "Oh, but what will Bud say, you drawing on his table linen that way?"

"Bud," Jesse called gesturing the man to their table. "Add the cost of this," he waved the napkin, "to the bill, please." He exhibited his work, then folded the napkin with his good hand and tucked it into his pocket. "Also, if you would, please send a full plate and a cold draft to the coachman there," Sparhawk requested pointing at an elegant rig parked nearby. "The poor man's been sitting up on the bench there half the day."

"How can you be callin' him a 'poor man' drivin' a rig and pair that fine? I know horses, as many Irishmen do."

"I know," nodded Jesse.

"That groomsman on the padded bench is earning enough to feed *you*. His employer should pay for his supper anyways, not a poor down-at-the-heels soldier, such as yourself, if you pardon me saying so. Right behind that one, see, there's a drayman been wiggling on his hard perch near as long as the carriage driver been sitting pretty up on his upholstered seat. Feed the other as well, why don't you, if you're so well-heeled, soldier?" Jesse drew a fistful of dollars and coins from his pocket and dropped the lot on the table. There was a flat gold locket which he hurriedly took back.

"Feed both men, Bud. I've enough money here to share some and . . ."

". . . and tomorrow you'll be bust and unable to feed your own self," Bud preached.

"I'm feeling generous, even celebratory, this evening what with the war winding down and a pretty lady at my side. And thank you kindly, Bud, for your concern," Jesse added as the waiter offered him an open box of cigars. He selected three, trimmed them, gestured with two toward the drivers on the street and put one in his own mouth. Bud held a long match at just the right angle as Jesse turned the *maduro* in his lips and puffed it alight. Lorena's attention fixed once again on his mobile mouth. Watching her watch him with a curious look in her eyes made Jesse laugh again, a matter that did not escape him. Glad as he was, he cautioned himself to have a care not to let her take too strong a hold of him, this backwoods charmer who well might have a husband, maybe even a passel of young ones, as she would say, up in her beloved mountains. Although warned, he threw caution to the wind, for the moment at least, and went on flirting with her.

"Would you care for a sip of this cigar, Miz Reed? That's what you do, you know, to get the most pleasure of it, sip slow." He did, exhaled a smoke ring, and ran the tip of his tongue over his lips. There was a glint of a tease in his eye, the jump of a smile muscle at the right corner of his mouth.

"Thank you kindly, but no thank you. While *you're* at that sipping, do tell me what occurred after you were born near Albemarle Sound."

"My father had himself a big drink of mountain dew and, no doubt, smoked a cigar not unlike this one."

"Jesse Sparhawk, you are funnin' me!" It was Lorena's turn to be amused and she produced a throaty giggle

"Me? Funnin' you? Of course, I am. You want to know where I spent my formative years, is that it?" Lorena nodded with an indulgent smile as if dealing with a winning, evasive child. "North mostly, in the State of Rhode Island and Providence Plantation, with my mother's folks, until I grew old enough to be sent south to my father on his plantation."

"You were raised by your mother's folks, not by your mother

or by your father?" she asked, compassion in her voice. "Were you orphaned young?" He shook his head indicating not.

"My father, Guthridge Sparhawk, was kin to one of the great families of North Carolina, the Collinses. He was a Reb to his bones. My mother was of the New England Hart family, she a fierce Abolitionist from a long line of freethinkers. She fell in love, despite herself, with a slave-holding, chivalrous southern gallant. She thought she could change him, that, for love of her, he would free his chattels. Some, not many, slave owners did, either giving manumission all at once or gradually through legal documents, over time. Mary Hart Sparhawk could not convert her adored husband to the Abolitionist cause."

"She left your Daddy and took you away with her, to Providence?"

"Yes. Brokenhearted, Mary went about her life's mission, which was to do good works and better the world. She did better the world, some." Jesse turned away, puffed his cigar and was silent.

" 'To be good and do good is all we have to do' President John Adams said to his daughter, in a letter. 'There all honor lies,' he told her. How did Mary Sparhawk do good and change the world?" said Lorena.

"She traveled to the first women's rights meeting, nearly twenty years ago, at the town where you've just been, Seneca Falls. You, yourself, Lorena, were impressed by the ladies who reside there, still working for the same causes—women's equality, temperance, and abolition. They'll go back to battling for the female vote right after the war. That's a sure bet in my view. Well, my mother kept a journal where she wrote down many of her thoughts and hopeful plans. Before she passed over the following year, many of her ideals, which she shared with the others, of course, were adopted by The First Women's Rights Convention. She saw them printed out, as part of The Declaration of Sentiments drawn up at that 1848 gathering. Mary Hart Sparhawk was one of the writers and signers of that document. Now she's part of history, though she's unlikely to become as famous as her ancestor, Roger

Williams, founder of Providence. He did that after the Quakers 'ejected' him from Plymouth. Mary was always gratified to be of his line."

"You're proud of her. I hear it in your voice," Lorena said before the smile went out of her eyes, replaced by that intense determination Jesse had seen earlier. "I also will do good by upholding the honor of my kin so that my children may be proud of me one day."

"I didn't mean to plunge you back to reality just yet, Lorena, by mentioning Seneca and reminding you of your hard times there."

"Reality may not be evaded for long, no matter how distracting the company one keeps," she said, somberly.

"I would not for the world bring you sadness. I have found great pleasure and relief in your sweet company today. My own troubles fell away during these shared few hours and yours, I hope, did as well. You saved me, with your liveliness and warmth, from my brooding self, the only one I've known of late. I realize I need not court darkness and anger to accomplish what I must, settle a matter of honor. I will be forever in your debt, Lorena Reed. You've broken the spell of gloom that has been holding me in thrall." His smile was heartfelt, almost bittersweet. "It happens, I've heard said, that a chance meeting may change a person's life forever. Do you suppose that's possible?"

"Not just possible. It's a certainty. Why, that actually has been so for me, more than once," Lorena replied. "Meeting you, for instance."

"Meeting me—what?" Jesse encouraged.

"Meeting you saved me from being kidnapped by hooligans. But remember one thing, please. Now we're quits."

"Quits? Absurd! But why would you even think so?" he asked, obviously annoyed but also let down.

"Quits. Even. I mean there's no debt between us," she insisted. "We've helped each other today."

"Ah. I understand. But whether I'm indebted to you or no, I'll see to it you reach your home safely. It just so happens,

I'm going your way." His face hardened. "The fighting is nearly done for most. But I've still got a piece of work to do before my war is over. A matter of honor."

"As do I," she answered, anger simmering just below the surface. "A matter of honor of my own to tend to."

"Tell me," Jesse requested, tilting his chair back.

"Little Brother, that's Frank, sent me a letter by the hand of a Yankee who had escaped from Andersonville prison. The man was being guided through our valley, north to the Yankee lines by Clay, that's Big Brother, and by Clint Reed."

"Your husband?" Jesse asked carefully. She didn't answer at once and when she did the reply was neither yes nor no.

"My cousin, twice removed, on Daddy's side," was her reply, so succinct it precluded further questions on the subject.

"Go on telling about your matter of honor."

"The salt ran out altogether, the slaughtering season I left," Lorena replied."They had no way of preserving what little meat there was, even for that winter comin'. The boys and Daddy used to do some trappin' but they couldn't shoot nothin', what with the sesech listening and looking for 'em."

"When North Carolina was the last state to join the rebellion, as you know better than I, most men in your hills sided with the north. I've known a few fine Union soldiers from those mountains. And others, not fine," Jesse said, his dark look claiming his handsome features. "The sesech were merciless up in some of the highland hollows."

Lorena's eyes grew huge and angry and the sadness in them wrenched at his heart.

"If ever there was a place in this world where no man among 'em would answer the sesech call to arms, it was our valley. Little Brother's letter told how the Confederates, the regular army and vigilantes, came hunting through our hills for so-called deserters like my brother and my cousins and didn't find them. The younger men had taken to the woods to fight for our way of livin' free, and for the Union of States. One particular Reb, a man from Taylorville, not far from the valley, shot down some old men and boys, right in our own barnyard. He aimed a rifle

straight at my Old Granny Heth and missed and shot off a hank
of her hair instead of her old gray head. Brother Frankie was
fourteen then, and they mostly let him be, but not his friend,
Drury Sicklear. That boy was but fifteen when they done for
him." Lorena's eyes glazed with angry tears. "I might have done
something if I had been there, and I *will* do something now to
uphold our honor. Frankie will help me. He's near fifteen now,
old enough to avenge Granny and Clay and Clint." She had pronounced the last of her list of names with such care, Jesse was
nearly certain it was her husband she spoke of. "Brother Clay
has not been seen or heard of since that day. They came down
out of the hills when they heard the shooting, to defend the old
folk and children. Clint got away. The sesech took Brother,
maybe for the Confederate Army, or maybe to string him up in
the woods. His bones could be out there somewhere, swinging
yet, all alone." Her lips compressed into a tight line. "I have got
Frank's letter right here," Lorena touched her bosom, "where
it has been this long year. It's the last word I've had from home.
I must get back there and soon!"

"So must I. I've been through your valley." Jesse's voice
was a harsh whisper. Lorena sat up very tall in her chair, lifting her head sharply, not pressing him for details. He would
tell her, or not, in his own time. That time came at once.

"I was one of those escaped Yankee prisoners, Lorena, who
was guided through your woods and steep passes toward Tennessee, by a mountain man who was no such thing. He was,
in truth, a Confederate vigilante spy. Of the three of us he was
supposed to be leading to 'safety', I'm the only one who survived to see justice done."

"I understand," she nodded. "I thank you kindly for your
offer of protection and I welcome your company on my travels
because it's going to be a long, long walk. We neither of us have
money to pay fare on a train or boat or hire a horse, not unless
I'm soon able to find Potts who promised to safeguard all my
money," she said more brightly, displaying the innate optimism
which overtook her at the slightest excuse. "Oh, where *is* that
Hester?" she sighed looking urgently looking about.

"Is Hester Potts any relation to you?" Jesse asked.

Lorena shook her head 'no.' "Hester came to Seneca Falls some weeks ago, from Canada, to search the infirmary for a lost soldier," she said. "She didn't find him there so she was returning to, well, going south, is all I know, all she said. She told us at length of the bread riots in Richmond in '63. She told of the sesech president, Jeff Davis, braving the mob to stop the looting. We supposed she was headed through the lines to go back there. However, it seems New York City was as far to the south as she was actually going, and so she went off to find a traveling companion for me for the rest of my journey." Lorena's voice trailed off and she was unable to repress a sigh as she looked out at the street turning her head from side to side.

"A Southern lady returning from Canada? That makes me uneasy," Jesse said, knowing that the country to the north was a haven for Confederate conspirators. "Do you really suppose she's coming back with your money?" he asked calmly.

"I never considered otherwise," Lorena answered. "She was wearing a black dress but with a bright red bonnet just so that I could pick her out easy in a crowd."

"I noticed a tall woman in a black dress and red bonnet, as I was making my way to South Street. She was around the corner, engaged in deep talk with those sailors who later accosted you. Her red hat with a white rose pinned to it caught my eye. I never saw her face but it seemed unbefitting a woman in so stylish and elegant an outfit should be involved with those two."

"She is not all that elegant," Lorena replied a bit testily. "It's only that her maid, who remained at Seneca, is clever with tacky fabric and mouse-nibbled laces. Your description fits Hester, but surely it was happenstance she was with those men. She might have been asking directions or . . ." Lorena glanced from the tabletop at which she had been staring, to look quickly at Jesse. "You suppose, I read in your eyes, that she had a connection with them," she said, then sipped some water to conceal her distress.

"Happenstance or no, money changed hands," he answered

reluctantly, and then blew a series of smoke rings as if to divert a little girl on the verge of tears.

"I am loath to say I never warmed to Hester, but I would not have suspected the woman—or anyone—of such deceit. My money is lost for good and all, I fear. She's duped me, hasn't she?"

"So it seems. I'm sorry," Sparhawk said. Smoke rings were no longer appropriate. The matter was too serious. Besides, Lorena was not a little girl about to cry. She was a resolute young woman trying to puzzle out her situation.

"But why didn't she just . . . just run off with my savings?" Lorena wondered. "Those men were trying to force me to their ship, to kidnap me. Why would Hester pay good money, my money, to have someone make off with a penniless fool like me?"

"I doubt she did. I think it was the men who paid Hester Potts," Jesse replied with chilling ferocity.

"Paid *her*? I don't believe I understand," Lorena answered slowly, even as understanding began to dawn.

"You're not too far from Mott Street and Pell, the city's China Town. There's long been talk—more than talk, about opium and white slavery. It happens, Lorena, that people vanish from city streets, men shanghaied for boat crews, women to be used in brothels, or sold into servitude on the Barbary shores of North Africa. Others are preserved in a condition of maidenhood to be sold in harems if they are young and pretty, as are you, at great profit to the sellers. Some women, and men also, found to be well-connected and well-to-do, are offered for ransom. And then there are the lucky ones who turn up months or years later, alive, in some West Indies harbor town."

"Lucky ones? Perhaps," Lorena whispered, appalled. "Some girls captured in the west by Cherokees are so shamed they don't ever want to be 'saved.' But . . . but, look!" she exclaimed urgently, pointing across the street. "There she is! Hester, in her red bonnet! Hester!" she called, abandoning Jesse and dashing headlong out into the road.

"NO!" he shouted, standing, knocking over his chair, and

starting after her as the lorry, which been standing for so long
at the intersection, started up at speed when the well-fed
driver shouted and cracked his whip, spooking his horses. The
out-of-control wagon careened directly toward Lorena until
Jesse, using both arms, shoved her forward out of the way of
the horses who instinctively tried to swerve to avoid running
her down. That maneuver, as the lorry sped by, sent a barrel
flying from the open tailgate and rolling toward Lorena. She
heard Sparhawk's furious shout, her own scream, and then
she knew nothing more.

CHAPTER 3

Lorena's eyes slowly opened, her head, which ached awfully, rested on Jesse's knee as he knelt beside her, his jacket thrown over her as a makeshift blanket. Despite the spring warmth, she shivered as she looked from Jesse's drawn face to that of another man crouching beside her, a black bag open beside him as he waved a cloth doused in ammonia beneath her nose.

"Why, you're wearing a stovepipe, like Mr. Lincoln's," Lorena mumbled weakly, with a slight smile. The heavy, florid man had a fringe of bright-white hair showing around the edge of his black hat. He nodded benignly and patted Lorena's hand.

"Thank the powers that be, Lorena, that you're conscious and able to speak," Jesse said tensely.

"Sir?" was Lorena's response.

"Come, Lorena, there's no need for formality," Jesse admonished kindly. "You've been addressing me by my given name since high noon and here it is half after five. This venerable mountain of a man at my side is a doctor and my good friend, the person I was waiting for when you and I met. I present Dr. Benjamin Longworth."

"Call me Doc Ben, young lady," the physician instructed in a deep rumbling voice. "You gave us a scare, unconscious as you were for the past . . ." From his vest pocket, the doctor extracted a gold watch on a gold chain long enough to traverse his substantial girth, and clicked open the case. ". . . Twenty minutes. Now that you're coming back to yourself, my prognostication is you'll recover quickly. You're young, and healthy." Lorena began to sit up, but at her first move she gasped at a sharp pain in her chest and gave up her efforts. Only temporarily, she told herself.

"What's happened to me, Doc Ben? Where am I?" she asked, taking care not to breathe deeply.

"There's concussion, no doubt, and a cracked rib, perhaps two, but after a few weeks in bed and good care and feeding, you'll be on your merry way, good as new. That fool of a wagon driver thought he'd done you in, you dashing into the road and him speeding along a crowded street in an over-loaded vehicle. When a barrel came loose from the tailgate, it sent you sprawling, Jesse tells me."

"Wagon?" Lorena questioned. "I don't rightly recall it or a barrel either. I cannot stay about here any longer, Doctor. It has taken me far too many days as it is to make my way this far, and I've still not got where I'm goin' to . . . going to . . . going . . ."

"Be sensible, Lorena," Jesse implored kindly. "You are not in a condition to make the long, arduous journey to North Carolina. Doc Ben has offered you a room in his home rather than placing you at Bellevue public hospital. He tends special patients such as you at his private clinic."

"Why am I a 'special' patient, sir, an ordinary girl on her way . . . ?"

"You're special because I say so and because my good old friend, Doc Ben, insists. Don't fret in your thoughts. I won't leave on my own mission without you. I'll wait for you as long as need be and I'll see you safe home to your own hearth, as I promised. My search will end with the same result no matter if I find my foe today, tomorrow, next month . . ."

A police officer pressed back the small, jostling crowd, which had gathered. One among the gawking onlookers was a tall dark woman dressed in black, wearing a red bonnet. Lorena's dazed eyes flicked over the peering faces above her, searching for a familiar one. She found only strangers, though she wondered why she felt unsettled by a glimpse of bright red as a tall woman snatched off her hat and turned hurriedly away. Jesse noticed Lorena's fleeting frown and followed the direction of her eyes but by then Hester Potts and her hat had disappeared.

"You'll wait, suh, for me? But, why?" Lorena asked Jesse with bewilderment as the fine carriage parked across the street, drawn by its matched pair of bays, pulled up near them. "Whoever you are, wherever you're going, you're wrong about my destination, suh. I have only just come from . . . ? Where? I must be gettin' on to the soldiers' sanatorium at . . . Seneca? Is there a place of that name or have I imagined it? There was a Roman philosopher of such a name, but is there a town and a hospital? I *am going there.*" She fingered the stripes on Jesse's tunic and a look of outraged determination on her face was so strong and unambiguous, it took Jesse and the doctor off guard. The two men exchanged concerned looks.

"Something's not right here, Ben," Jesse told the doctor, mouthing the words over Lorena's head as he continued to hold her against him. The older man nodded before shifting his full attention back to the nearly immobile but tense patient now covered with a soft blanket provided by Bud Ryan.

"Now, young woman, I am the doctor here and I will decide when you'll be up to traveling," Longworth scolded with simulated sternness, taking a pen and pad from his bag. "For my records, I need certain information about you. Understand, my dear?"

Lorena nodded, moving her head only slightly.

"Where have you traveled from, my dear and why do you need to go to Seneca Infirmary?" the doctor inquired cautiously.

"I . . . I don't know the answers to them . . . those questions. I do know I should be getting on in a hurry!"

"Is there anyone we should try to notify of your accident, someone expecting you?" the doctor asked.

"No sir, not a soul on earth is expecting me, not that I am able to recall, but I have a strong feeling someone may be wishing hard to see me."

"Would that be a brother . . . your husband?" Jesse asked. Lorena, confused and troubled, attempted to move, then tried to hide the pain the action brought her.

"I don't have a husband. Not . . . yet."

"How do you know?" was Jesse's instant, sharp response.

"I don't know how, but I do!"

"Enough of this, distressing the patient with idle chitchat Jesse, and she lying here in the street. We must get you to bed, young lady," grumbled Ben. "Your full name, please?"

"I'm Lorena," she said. "I think. That is what this gentleman I'm holding on to called me." Jesse's eyes narrowed but he said nothing more, just watched her face more intently.

"So it is *Miss,* my dear?" the doctor continued, pushing his sliding spectacles back up his broad, sweaty nose. "Tell me your age, Miss Lorena, and the date of your birth, if you are able?"

"I was born at high noon on a sunny day. I forget what day and which month, but I know it's good luck to be born in the sun at high noon." Lorena took a deep breath and winced.

"Who told you so?" inquired Jesse. "Can you hear a voice in your mind saying 'It's good luck'?"

"No," she answered reluctantly, feeling that somehow she had disappointed this weary-looking, handsome stranger in whose arms she found herself cradled, in the middle of a city street. Tall houses rose on either side but she couldn't tilt her head to see their upper reaches.

"Tell me, what is the year now, and what is the name of the President of our great battle-scarred Republic?" asked Longworth.

"You must be teasing me, Doc Ben, to ask such simple questions, even if I am a simple girl from . . . from . . ."

"Go on," Jesse encouraged. "What makes you think you're a simple girl?"

"By the look of my homespun dress," she smiled slightly. "The year is eighteen and sixty-three. Mr. Lincoln is trying to save the Union from being torn asunder." There was a moment of silence as again Jesse and the doctor traded worried looks. "I must go now, north to Seneca. I must be of help. Do you gentlemen know where that is? Will you direct me to Seneca, please?"

"I'd be honored to be of service to you any way I'm able," said Jesse. "I'll take you there myself, but first, you must mend. What help could you be—so rattled you don't know your own name, and injured besides—to whoever it is awaiting you up north?" Not pausing to hear her answer, Jesse lifted Lorena with one arm under her back, the other under her knees. He stood, hardly aware that his injured arm was serving him, and Lorena, well.

"Take me there, yourself!" Lorena said before she lost consciousness again, her head dropping against his chest.

"Pain has made her faint away. That's a benevolence in our human nature. It appears, however, that her plight has solved one of your problems, Jess," Doc Ben said. "The waiter informed me you saved her life by pushing her out of the wagon's path. Your infirmity was primarily in your head man, not in your sinews. That 'inadequate' left arm of yours, of which you wrote to me, has the ability to move after all, when you need to make good use of it."

"So it seems. That puts me in debt to the lady twice over at the least. She's cured me and brought me back to life today, in a way. I *will* repay her," Jesse promised as he gently placed Lorena beside him on the upholstered carriage bench.

"To the doctor's house on Fifth Avenue, Sergeant," he ordered the driver, the man to whom he had earlier sent a meal. "Go as carefully as you are able. Avoid the ruts and ditches as best you may, please, Mr. Nicke, for the comfort of our injured passenger. "

"Yes sir, Colonel Sparhawk!" was the brisk reply from the military groom who saluted smartly, climbed to his seat and touched his whip to the lead horse's flank. The carriage began to roll with barely the slightest joggle.

"I think you're becoming a faith-curer now, Ben, telling me my medical condition was all of the mind," Jesse said. "What of her injury and *her* mind? How may I help her?"

"Faith-curer, psychographist. Call me what you will, my

young friend. She'll require all the care and kindness you have to offer. And patience. Besides concussion, she may have a cracked rib, perhaps two, which a few weeks in bed will mend. More serious, she is unable to clearly remember the past two years of her life. I suspect she has no will to recall some painful occurrence. She's avoiding thoughts, such as the name of her home, which might remind her of whatever it is she'd rather forget. An injury to the head such as she suffered will, in many cases, cause amnesia and no two patients are alike. That's well known in the medical profession, and beyond, particularly since the advent of war injuries. How long her condition will persist—that's not predictable. I theorize that to attain a cure, she must recover the lost years. You're the only one who knows anything about her at all, now."

"That isn't much, Doc. Her speech pattern has changed. There's not much left of her backwoods southern sound. She told me that when she was uneasy, she spoke the Queen's English as she'd been taught. "

"Blows to the head have been observed to precipitate altered patterns of speech, Jesse," the doctor said in his deep, gravelly, most serious tone, "I realize you were only passing through when you asked me to look at your arm. Now, I say, remain here in New York with our pretty patient. That should be no hardship as you seem to be rather fond of her, hey? You'll also be my guest until your strength, and hers, return," the doctor pronounced.

"And then?" Jesse asked cautiously as he passed his right arm about Lorena to support her against his shoulder.

"You or someone must guide her, slowly of course, on a journey of discovery. Start with her recent history, the place where you and she met, let us say. Eventually, take her home, if you can find it."

"I can find it."

"Don't blurt out that, or any other, bit of information until I evaluate her case more thoroughly. Over considerable time or maybe overnight, reality, I'm almost certain, will manifest itself. It usually does." Doc Ben took Lorena's hand and snapped open his gold watch to measure her pulse. "A mission of mercy suits you better, Jesse, than one of retribution. A vengeful mind may become mean and small. That's not your style, son."

"I'll get my quarry, no matter what, if later rather than sooner. Bet on it." Sparhawk's look was ferocious and determined. His tone was ice, which melted with his next words. "I will stay with Lorena and do as you prescribe to help her, Ben, even if I'm not so sure I want her to remember her past."

"What's this?" said the doctor with a lifted bushy white brow. "Not want her to recall who she is? Why ever not?"

"I would not knowingly delude her, but the mind's devilish sometimes, as you're only too well aware. It dabbles with yearning as well as forgetting."

"She's forgotten. Are you the one yearning, or are you planning to dabble?"

"I'm not *planning* anything, Doc. Fate works its wiles."

"You've a reputation for doing the same, working wiles. This little country girl won't have a chance against an aficionado of seduction such as you, not once you shine the full light of your charm upon her. Jesse, you've one mistress at least, that I know of. Maud Wharton has done some rather public yearning, since you've been away."

"Maud yearns only in her own best interests. She's charming and beautiful. She and I agreed to 'dabble' a while. I would not toy with Miss Reed. I intend to marry her." The carriage rocked over a displaced cobblestone and Lorena moaned. Jesse held her more securely.

"Are you implying your intentions are *that* certain and serious, man, that you've fallen in love?" Longworth marveled at the idea with comic disbelief. "You *are* in a bad way, my good man. How'd that happen so quickly, to you of all men?"

"Don't know," Jesse shrugged and grinned appearing boyishly discomfited. "I've heard it happens that way, instantly, to some. I don't know beyond all doubt if love's what it is. That's yet to be determined. I need to find out."

"How?" Ben demanded.

"I've a variation of the Cinderella story in mind. I want to give Lorena everything a poor mountain girl has never had—fine clothes, elegant surroundings, an education in art and music and the like. She shall have drawing lessons. She has a fine, unpolished talent. When her memory returns, she'll be free to make a choice not offered to many young ladies. And if she does not recover?" Jesse turned to gaze out the window as the carriage turned a corner.

"You say you'd not toy with her, Jess, but what you propose sounds like a dangerous game to me. If you want her," Ben said in his deepest, most authoritative voice, "woo her but only after you and she both know who she is. Then, take your time. Win her playing fair and square. As Cinderella's prince you risk making her a stranger in two worlds—her own and yours."

"She did say she was proud to come from the Reed Valley, naturally. But city life, trips abroad, studying painting with a talented master will have their appeal."

"She's not a blank book. Appealing as it may be for you to anticipate being her Pygmalion, she's not, as was the mythological Greek sculptor's creation, an ivory statue brought to life by love. Lorena Reed has a life of her own. The very first thing you need to find out before you put your rags-to-riches scenario into action, my friend, is whether or not she's already wed, or if she has commitments, plans, obligations, and the like. Then, over time, you will be at liberty to discover if you are really in love with her, and if she could love you. Have the answers before you jeopardize your heart and hers on a wish and a gamble. Be warned. Lost memories have a way of returning, in part or in full, days, weeks, even years later. Now give me a moment's quiet while I measure her pulse once more," the doctor said peering closely at his watch in the gathering darkness. Then he rummaged in his bag and came up with a long, narrow, tin case.

Ben reached forward to undo the top few buttons of Lorena's dress. He withdrew a much-folded bit of yellowed paper that showed at the top of her chemise. He passed it to Jesse who tucked it into his pocket with the napkin sketch he'd done earlier. Lorena stirred, lifted startled eyes to Jesse then glanced at the doctor.

"You needn't be frightened. Don't move about, my dear. You'll be more comfortable if you don't and I shall be better able to listen to your innards. Do you recognize the marvelous instrument I have in my hand?" Longworth asked, opening the tin case and withdrawing an object with metal tubes to which he attached an ebony funnel at one end, then little round ivory objects at the tube tops. Her eyes grew large and round and the doctor went on speaking in a low steady monotone to calm his patient. "This, my dear, is a stethoscope."

"I've seen one before," she mumbled. "Will we soon be there, wherever you're taking me?"

"Ssh," Ben hissed pleasantly and nodded once. "I'll do the talking." The doctor hung the instrument about his neck and carefully set his hands to either side of Lorena's face beneath her ears and he tilted her head from side to side. "That hurt?"

"Not unbearably but yes, it does. Doc Ben, I wish to know . . ."

". . . About my stethoscope? A most important advance in the practice of medicine. The first one was made by a Frenchman, Dr. Laennec in Paris . . ." The doctor was turning Lorena's head from side to side now. "Good. You have reasonable mobility, considering. Where was I? Ah, Laennec. In his day, thirty some years ago, a medical practitioner—squeeze my hand, there's a strong girl—a doc had to press his ear against a patient's chest to listen to sounds of the heart and lungs. Well, faced one day with an amply bosomed young lady, poor Laennec was embarrassed by the intimacy of putting his ear to her chest. A game he had played as a boy, with a hollow log . . . lift your arms, a little bit higher, if you're able . . . ah. Well, necessity being the mother of invention, my dear, shy René snatched some papers from his desk—twenty-four pieces exactly, and rolled them into a tube. He placed one end upon the lady's heart and set his ear to the other and, lo and behold, the auscultation—that's listening to the sounds from within the chest—was louder and clearer than he had ever before heard using the ear to the chest method. He soon made a tube of wood . . . then of metal and, one thing led to another, then to this, the most modern scope available." Longworth dangled it in front of Lorena's nose. "Your eyes are focusing well," he observed.

"I'm not as ill at ease with the ladies as was Dr. Laennec, so without further ado I will look at your ankles . . . and grasp each one briefly. Do not be discomfited. Jesse will close his eyes." Jesse did, still holding her against him.

"So . . . so . . . fine. No swelling. There's more about Laennec's tube, if you're interested." Lorena nodded while he felt all around her neck. "One thing led to another," the doctor rumbled on, "and, a few years ago, my colleague here in New York—Dr. George Cammann—perfected a bi-neural model, a device enabling physicians to listen with both ears at the same time." Longworth set a little ivory ball in each of his ears, adjusted a hinge, slipped the ebony disk into Lorena's loosened chemise and pressed it to her chest. He listened intently as he moved the disc from place to place. "Your heart sounds splendid, my dear, strong and steady."

"If only the human heart, Lorena, could be fathomed as easily as it now may be heard," Jesse mused, but by then she had fallen asleep.

CHAPTER 4

Lorena supposed she was alone when she next awoke. Her head ached and a deep breath was impossible, so tightly bound and tied was her rib cage. Through long windows, sunbeams slanted into the room, the light filtered by white, flower-embroidered gauzy curtains moving in a breeze. The air was cool and smelled of spring. She could glimpse new little green leaves on the tree branches close outside and hear the sounds of trotting hooves on the cobble stones of the street below. The bed in which she found herself was made up with sheets of pale-yellow silk and piled with pillows of softest down, in embroidered cases. She was covered by a warm and virtually weightless blanket-throw of a deeper yellow, woven as if of spider webs and generously fringed. A silver bell, shaped and engraved as a walnut half, its handle a stem decorated with a leaf and floret, rested within reach of her hand. She extended her silk-encased arm and lifted the bell, charmed, before she hastily restrained the clapper to stifle a clear, melodious ring, which seemed loudly out of proportion to the daintiness of the shell. As she did, a figure which had been hidden in a wing chair facing the window sprang up, a tall, slender man who turned toward her, one hand in his pocket, the other extending toward her.

"How are you feeling now, Lorena?" he inquired kindly in a caressing and mellow, most comforting voice, she thought. With his back to the light, his face was hidden until he approached the bedside, lifted her hand and brushed it for a moment to his lips. "Do you know where you are? Do you know me?" he asked.

"Should I, sir? I think I do not. I do wish I did," she answered breathlessly, not only because of her bindings. With a hint of the bantering sparkle which had so captivated Jesse Sparhawk the day before, she gazed at his face, finding it near to perfect—strong-jawed, sculpted, with elegant, yet totally masculine features. "Do sit, sir. You seem not altogether well yourself." He was too thin, too pale and dark shadows ringed his midnight-blue eyes, she noted, while also admiring his blue-black shining hair raked back from his brow. He pulled a chair close to the bedside and again took her hand.

"We have met. There was a street accident. A heavy barrel rolled from the tailgate of a speeding lorry."

"And struck us. That accounts for it, then, your disabled left arm and your pallor and my paining head and ribs. Forgive me for not recalling you or your name, sir. Do you know mine? I hope I've not put you to trouble."

"How does 'Lorena' sound to you? There's a song soldiers sing in the evening by the fire, about a girl of that name."

"I'll take it," said Lorena, "for now."

"Good. You have not put me to trouble, Lorena. Your doctor says such lapses as you are going through right now are not unusual after a blow to the head. I wasn't injured in the same accident that put you here. My arm, which is nearly healed, and my pallor as you describe it . . . was . . . are the effects of a war injury." He waited for her response.

"Ah! You're a soldier. I recall your tunic jacket covering me, after the accident I suppose. Your name . . . it's Warbird, or some such. You were just discharged from an army hospital, though you are not well at all, owning nothing but your name and the clothes on your back, such as they were. Am I right?"

"Somewhat," he answered. "I'm a soldier, that's true."

"The embroidered lounging coat they've given you here suits you far better than a scruffy uniform . . . Lieutenant. You must be a patient here as I am, I think. Yes! There was a large man with us in the street, leaning over me as I rested against you. He was a doctor with a stovepipe hat such as the President wears, except the doctor's was askew. Is all that so?" Lorena smiled nervously, awaiting an answer. Jesse grinned and nodded with boyish pleasure.

"There! You're already beginning to recall your recent past at least. Actually, my name is Sparhawk, though Colonel Jesse Warbird has a nice ring to it. What else comes to your mind? Thoughts of your travels, home or family?" She shook her head no. "Your accent, *your way with words,*" he said with particular emphasis and a hopeful pause. She didn't recognize the phrase as he hoped she would. "Your way with words gives little hint of your native locale or background but for the way you say 'sir' as 'suh' sometimes." Jesse again waited for her response. Lorena's smile melted away. A haunted look replaced it.

"No thoughts come," she said. "Take your pick of suh or sir. Are you not able to tell me any more about myself? Can you give me even a hint that may jog my mind? Was there nothing upon my person of significance? A calling card or letter, perhaps a purse, by chance?"

Jesse had been cautioned by the doctor not to reveal too much too fast and risk disturbing the patient profoundly if not permanently. He fingered Frankie Reed's letter in his pocket, and justified his failure to produce it as a necessary deception of omission, not an out-and-out lie.

"Your dress, chemise, and the rest of your attire have been removed, for washing and so on. Not by me," he was quick to add. "A nurse saw to your comfort. You had a piece of luggage. It's been misplaced I'm told." Lorena drew herself to a sitting position, grimacing slightly, and Jesse thumped and rearranged the pile of pillows behind her. She sank back gratefully, fatigued by the effort.

"Oh, who am I, Jesse Warbird? And where am I, in which town or city? Why am I . . . where?"

"Before I even attempt to answer your questions I must first tell you that on doctor's orders you are not to move about much, not at first, not until the possibility of concussion is ruled out.

Also, you are forbidden to brood or worry. Doing any of those could slow your recovery. You are in the home of Doc Ben Longworth, in the city of New York, where you will remain until you are able to continue your travels. In the interim you will be attended by the finest practitioner in New York, who has a particular expertise with head injury. You will be served the most nourishing of foods and tonics, nursed, pampered, fussed over, also entertained and amused, the latter mostly by me, and also by Rachel and Robert Longworth, the doctor's twin off-spring. They are of an age with you, I would venture to guess. How old are you?" Jesse asked casually but with a narrowing of his eyes that alerted Lorena to the importance of her reply. "Do you happen to know?" he gently pressed.

"Eighteen or near to it," she answered. "I don't know how I know so, but I do." He frowned. She was about to turn twenty before the mishap. "Do you play poker, Jesse War-bird?" The inquiry took him aback and gave him greater cause for alarm about Lorena's mental stability.

"As it happens, the answer is no."

"Good. Your eyes reveal your thoughts too freely. You have a most expressive face. You'd never win. Why is my age so significant to you?"

"It's a tool to help resolve who you are and to help you get well sooner."

"I'm a traveler, you say. Are you a traveler as I am—or was, until I got this bump on the head?"

"Actually, I'm going your way, is all, so . . ." Jesse paused again, poker-faced this time, to hear her rejoinder.

"And which way might that be?" Lorena asked eagerly.

"South." He said the one word firmly. "There is, or was, a family plantation I must see to, and I've other business to take care of. I'll be your guide and protector."

"But why do I need a guide and protector?"

"You don't even know who you are, that's why. Even if you did, you'd require, as all decorous young ladies do, someone to look after you—carry your bags, hire horses and the like, even after you're mended." He gestured at her prostrate, aching form. "And if that's not enough reason for you to accept my protection, please realize it's dangerous now for anyone, particularly so attractive a young woman as you, to move alone through war-torn countryside," he insisted.

"Prettiness is in the eye of the viewer of course, but what has led you, knowing nothing of me, to think me southern? Or decorous?"

"It's the way you pronounce 'suh', ma'am," he winked.

She shook her head, puzzled.

"I have an inkling I ought to go . . . north. Soon. Does that make any sense to you at all?" she asked.

"Inklings are useful. They may lead to certainties." He leaned to adjust her pillows again, using two hands this time and then he held a glass of water to her lips. She sipped, gestured it aside and, without a moment's forethought, as if it was the most natural thing in the world to do, she raised her arms to enfold his neck and draw his mouth down to hers, finding the pleasure of her action more compelling than the tenderness in her ribs. Jesse, bemused though not displeased, found her kiss sweet and cool and fresh. It was open-mouthed, tongue-thrusting, long and delicious for them both. "A kiss may be as helpful as an inkling," he murmured. "A kiss or two or more may lead to . . . certainties."

"May I kiss you again?"

"Doc won't believe this," he smiled leaning toward her.

"Believe what?" she asked in a whisper after a series of short, exploratory kisses.

"Believe . . . how well . . . how active his patient is." They kissed again.

"Do women often do this with men they have an inkling they favor—kiss them, to make certain?" she asked.

Jesse experienced her innocence as endearing and humorous. His laugh rolled softly as he hugged her to him. She yelped, feeling as if she had taken a cupid's blow straight to the heart. Jesse assumed it was her ribs again.

"Sorry!" he whispered as he tenderly eased her down. "Um, yes, they do, women, kiss on an inkling. Some, some women do," he answered with a bit of a stammer and a fierce blue-eyed stare that could have been seen as either threatening or passionate or both.

"Oh, I've upset you," Lorena lamented. "Is it not respectable to be setting my lips to those of a man I don't know? I must be a mischievous flirt, perhaps even a forward sort of a woman. What do you think?"

"I think you're making yourself up as you go along. It could be you're a perfectly upright young lady freeing the high-spirited girl within her. Perhaps she's the one you've always wanted to be but were duty-bound to hold in check. Since you have no idea who you are, you're at liberty to be flirtatious, mischievous, altogether forthright. I, for one, find you delightful. No one'll be the wiser."

"When we met, Colonel, was I subdued or vivacious?"

"We didn't have much time to get to know one another, but in a short while I found you kind and brave and generous. You wanted to buy me a meal even if it took your last cent. You were outgoing . . . lively . . . anything but diffident. And probably respectable and proper." He winked.

"Sounds to me more as if I were a veritable tart, taking up with a strange man on the street," she bantered, not without a hint of uneasiness.

"Now, listen, Lorena! You have *never* been a 'tart', neither yesterday nor today. It's perfectly plausible that this *is* the Lorena—or whoever—you've always been, that your customary free-spirited nature, your actual and true personality, is showing itself now, charmingly intact. That's good." He grinned. "I like you exactly as you are."

"You do?" Her heart swelled with an astonishing emotion. It took her off guard.

"Why are you staring at me, Lorena? Would you like to draw my picture?"

"Your eyes. I'm staring because they're so dark blue, with slants of gray when the light shines at an angle . . . and also because of the configuration of your brow—strong and prominent. You've hollowed cheeks and carved cheekbones right up under your eyes and your eyes are deep placed. I seem to recognize your sort of face, but your mouth, though . . ."

"Yes, go on," Jesse encouraged with contained excitement, recalling her words of the day before. He moved away from the bedside to the window and stood unmoving, his nerves a bit taut, a tall, strong, silent silhouette in profile in the golden sun. The moment passed and Lorena returned to the previous subject under discussion, her identity.

"Do you think you'd still like me," she half teased, "if actually I'm a combination of the two types of women you describe, duty-bound and devoted, yet also too forthright and something of a tart?" She giggled though her question wasn't as frivolous as she tried to make it sound. She wanted him to really, *really* like her. It mattered a lot.

"I have no doubt your company would delight me, that I'd feel friendship and affection for you, any way you are at all. Remember, though, that whatever we discover about you, Lorena, do not, under any circumstances, vex yourself," Jesse commanded, folding his arms across his chest. "It's against doctor's orders. It might cause you a setback. Now, let's follow another clue you've given me. This concern you have with demureness, let's call it, or lack of it. Could it be a result of your upbringing? Do you have an inkling about it?"

"Yes. Only an inkling. I mistrust it," she said, her voice jagged when she drew him toward her and they kissed again, longer and deeper. "Do I know you better, Warbird, than I know I do? Have I trusted you before? Should I now? "

Jesse laughed. It was a sensual, low, seductive sound before his head dipped again. Their mouths were closed, softly touching, barely brushing. His breath came rasping, hers restrained because of her ribs. He forced her lips apart and worked his firmly against them, his tongue sliding and curving, on the offensive. She didn't stint, not with her mouth at least.

"Lorena, as what seems to be your true self becomes known to you, to us," he whispered against her brow, "no matter what you hear or discover about yourself or me as we move on together, never mistrust me! Promise that." He was intense now. She drew away, uneasy, and turned her face aside.

"You sound . . . possessive, almost jealous. But we met only a short while ago, you say. And briefly. Why this urgency and entreaty? How can I swear to blindly trust you if I don't know you at all?" she asked. "I also have a feeling that it's dangerous to trust a stranger, that I've done so before with dire results."

"You will get to know me and come to trust and rely on me, without question, above all others. There'll be no dire results," he said confidently. "I will care for you and never knowingly do you harm. That's a pledge. Understand?" His promise seemed as much a warning as an assurance. Lorena took it as a challenge of sorts.

'Who are you, really, Warbird?" she whispered, wanting to kiss him again, trust or no. "You could be a stage actor by profession. Your gift for high drama is striking." He laughed again, low in his throat.

"Who, in actual fact, knows himself? Possibly, I'm your true love," he suggested genially. Her heart jolted. He was kissing her lips and reading her mind.

"Bravo! Oh, well played!" was her answer and she comically rolled her eyes heavenward. When he rested his hand upon her breast, enticing her nipple to firm and erect, he arrested her laugh and captured her full, serious attention.

"Do you happen to know, Lorena, whether or not you're a virgin?" he asked, his eyes holding hers as the dark dots at the hazel centers widened and spread like drops of ink. The surrounding fringes of her thick lashes gave him the sensation of drowning in black-eyed, yellow daisies.

"I haven't even an inkling," she sighed. "What do you conjecture, Jesse?"

"We'll both find out, soon," he whispered, his breath warm against her brow. "At an auspicious moment. Not just yet. You must follow doctor's orders now not to move about too much or overexert."

"So, kiss me more, if you will, suh. That's a pleasing activity requiring little exertion and it's more or less painless to the ribs, unless one is too tightly clutched. I think more kissing is likely to give me inklings, one way or another, about my past experience."

"And about your future. I'll provide you more than inklings when you're better."

"All better? That long?" she jested and he bellowed a laugh.

"If I have some qualities of a dramatic actor, you could well be a comedienne, Lorena! No, not all better, but somewhat. It's well and good you find kissing a pleasing mild pastime. However, it's one that often proceeds to greater exertions. We must have a care. One of these days, if you like, maybe we will try more strenuous, more fascinating diversions. Do you have an inkling of what I mean?"

"Well . . . yes, as a matter of fact. I'm not ignorant, I find, of the doings of birds, bees, mares, stallions, men and women, together, but I don't know if I know so from observation, hearsay or firsthand experience," she replied. Again, Jesse exploded with hilarity and then they laughed together, and would have been hard-pressed to say which of them looked more eagerly forward to her recuperation and the kissing they would do in the interim, starting at once. But a knock at the door wrenched them apart.

"Jesse! I could hear your laughter downstairs in my study! I've not known you so cheerful in a good while," Doc Ben rumbled, laughing himself in accord, filling the doorway with his great girth. "This young woman is a tonic to you, and you to her, by the look of things. You're using that left arm. Good! Good! How are you, my dear?" he inquired of Lorena.

"My head throbs, my ribs hurt a bit, I don't know who I am or where I'm going and I have an inkling that I've never been happier in my life. How do you explain it, Doctor?"

At that, Doc Ben, beaming, lumbered into the room, pushed forward, only because he permitted himself to be, by a small crowd which flowed around him and spilled toward Lorena, to surround her bed. Two small spaniels leaped about, yapping.

"I shall explain your prognosis as best I can when we are alone as doctor and patient. This is a more social occasion. I will present to you, one-by-one, your well-wishers, each of whom will be involved in your care and amusement. First, here is my dear Mrs. Longworth, Molly my wife and lady of this house, which she runs with precision. She'll see to it you'll want for nothing."

Molly Longworth was robust, crowned like a queen with elaborately arranged blond hair. She had arrived in the room attired in a fashionable, full-skirted silk walking dress of lustrous gray silk with pearl buttons big as sparrow's eggs running up the bodice. An elaborate white lace collar extended over her shoulders. She smiled dutifully, hastily, and extended a wide hand encased in a bulging, buttery soft white kid glove.

"Any patient of Ben's is a patient of mine. I'll be in to see you after my morning calls are made. Certainly before teatime. Until then, you've the staff and family at your beck and call. Get well soon," she burbled, patting Lorena's cheek. *Auf Wiedersehen, au revoir*!" Her many gold bangles jingled pleasantly as she fled the sickroom, the spaniels following close on her heels.

"We'll soon get you back on your feet," the doctor's daughter promised in a no-nonsense manner which suited her appearance. "I'm Rachel." Lorena was impressed by Rachel's striking dissimilarity to her mother, in both costume and conduct. The girl's dress was buff brown in color, unadorned, plain as a penitent's. Her pale red hair was pulled taut into a bun at the crown of her head and there was not even a pretense of a smile when she none-too-gently shook Lorena's hand. She had eyes round and hard as not-quite-ripe blueberries.

"We don't know who you are. That's a challenge to us all, to gather information. It will be a true life game of Blind Man's Buff and I already have a clue. Your coarse hand reveals you have never been a lady of leisure." Lorena nodded. She felt somehow that Rachel was right. No matter if memories hid in the recesses of her mind, her feelings, she realized, didn't lie.

Rachel's brother, her similar-appearing twin—he too had red hair and pale skin—was his sister's contrary in personality and dress. His riding jacket was elegant to the point of dandyism; his mustaches were drooping and waxed, his hand smooth as satin when he took Lorena's.

"She might have been a lady of comfort and ease who undertook sporting pursuits—riding, sailing, and shuttlecock. Hey, Lorena?"

"Shuttlecock?" she asked with a lift of an eyebrow. "I'd wager I've never even heard of it before."

"Oh, too bad!" answered Robert with childlike disappointment. "I'll teach the game to you," he brightened, "soon as you're allowed out of bed. We, all of us, are here to lift your spirits high."

"I'm here for more than fun and games," interrupted a tidy, tight-lipped little woman with equine features—a squared chin and wide set eyes in a long face framed by a nurse's white headdress. She removed a red-trimmed, navy-blue cape from her shoulders, folded it neatly over a chair and took up a pitcher and basin from Lorena's bedside table.

"Everyone out," she said unceremoniously. There was no discernable response except from the gardener and the doctor who said, "Now, now Mrs. Horton, a moment if you please, dear."

"I'll leave these posies to be put in water, miss. More tomorrow," the gardener said. He was a man of middle age and middle height with faded yellow graying hair, gray eyes and a complexion to match. Standing pressed against a wall near the door, he might well have been invisible but for his armload of freshly cut daffodils. He thrust them at the ladies' maid before he withdrew like a shadow fading. The girl curtsied.

"Ethel Hope. I'm to serve you, miss," she told Lorena, peering through the flowers. "That was Hamson. Pardon him. The man's never been comfortable indoors."

"He's grand with horses however, and his horticultural knowledge is prodigious," Doc Ben interjected. "We've the grandest garden in the city!"

"It's important I speak to this young lady about the incident," a young man who had come wandering in after the others said to no one in particular. His Irish brogue seemed under control except for a rare word or two. He stepped forward, bowler hat in hand, his dark hair ruffled, thick dark brows furrowed, looking nearly as uncomfortable as Hamson had, though he looked more colorful than the gardener in an ill-fitting, loud-checked sack suit. A shiny eight-pointed star was revealed when he flapped open his jacket.

"A secret copper?" Jesse asked, affable and interested.

"Bright as my copper shield is, I'd rather be called a shadow, sir."

"Star Police is how the newspapers used to refer to your kind. Were you especially good at the job of uniformed patrolman or are you politically well connected in Tammany Hall?" Robert Livingston inquired with a faint sneer. "May we know your name?"

"Ryan Q. Runion, sir, called Q. by most, so's not to confuse me with my uncle. I was never a patrolman, sir."

"Ha! I told you so," Robert gloated. "And your uncle is . . ."

"Superintendent Ryan X. Runion," the young man replied, letting it be known by his chary expression and brusque omission of 'sir' that he was not to be trifled with. "Now, it's necessary that I ask the lady a few questions."

"As must I. I'm an attorney. My card." Yet another man, a new arrival, spoke, then extended his calling card to the doctor. Jesse intercepted the transfer.

"*Walter Schuyler, Esquire*" Jesse read. "I know you by reputation. What are you gentlemen doing here?" he asked.

"Miss Reed's accident may ha' been no such thing," announced Q. "I work Five Points and the docks, keeping an eye on known thugs and other shifty looking specimens. I observed you scare off the pair of sailors bothering the young woman, Colonel. Later, the same young woman is bowled over, by coincidence, by a barrel? My uncle, Ryan X. Runion, has read my report. He has a strong suspicion there were deliberate attempts on the lady's life, sir. I agree."

CHAPTER 5

There was a rumble of displeasure from the doctor and a squeak from Miss Hope who nearly dropped her armful of flowers. Everyone in the room turned to Lorena. Her response was a careful, casual shrug of one shoulder and a lifted brow that didn't quite hide her anxiety. "Sorry. Can't help you," she said trying to appear calm though her nerves tingled. Jesse knew her bravado was hiding a sense of dread stirred, perhaps, by a formless memory of her encounter with the sailors. His doubting smile in her direction, involving one corner of his mouth, was intended to defuse the threat and ease her mind.

"Anyone, a person a little under the weather in particular, would be distressed by that blunt bit of specious conjecture, copper. I saw the *accident,*" he said with pointed emphasis, again for Lorena's benefit, before turning from her to show his scowl to Q. with whom he was in complete agreement. "We'll step out into the hall, gentlemen," he said striding to the door.

"Have a care what you say in the lady's hearing," he said glancing from the policeman to the lawyer who had hurried after them. "I agree with you and your uncle, Q., but Miss Reed must not be involved just yet. She'll be safe here and, once she starts getting about, I won't let her out of my sight."

"I've incarcerated the lorry driver," Q. reported in a loud whisper.

"I've been retained to defend him," said Attorney Schuyler in a low voice. "My client tells me he was paid to merely throw a fright into Miss Reed, that he had no intention of running her down. The loose barrel really was an accident, my client says."

"Who retained you?" Jesse pressed. "Not a hard-up lorry driver who was well into his cups at the time of the event. Whoever it was hired your client to 'put a fright' into Miss Reed, and the individual paying your fee, is one and the same scoundrel, I'd guess."

"I'm not prepared to say. More precisely, I am unable to answer your questions, sir, for I do not know the answers. And if I did know, I'd not be obliged to supply you with the information you request. I will say this: A sum of money and a letter was delivered to me by a messenger, a ragged paper boy, who dropped a package at my feet and vanished back into the anonymity of the streets."

"Anonymity? Applesauce! We plainclothes fellas," Q. said, "ain't called shadows for naught. We're everywheres. I likely know your paper boy already, merely from my daily observations on the sidewalks and byways of the city. I'll need a few details—age, hair color, distinguishing features, and such. You, Mr. Schuyler," the policeman went on, guiding the attorney with a hand on his elbow down the stairs to the hall. "You know the law, sir. You *are* obliged to answer my questions."

"Q.," Jesse called softly, from the top landing of the spiral staircase that overlooked the entry hall. "When you're off duty, I've an unofficial task I'd like you to take on for me."

"Yes sir, Colonel. When and where? Anytime after midnight, say two, three in the morning?"

"How would the Forrest Spring House suit you? Good," Jesse responded. He watched as the two men left the Longworth house.

"Enough of this ruffle and to-do, disturbing my patient," Nurse Horton was proclaiming as Jesse stepped back into the room. "All out. I mean it. It's time for me to attend this young woman and see to her medications. All of you—go. If you please," she said with a bored air. "Yes, yes, even you, Doc Ben, for the time being. You know the discipline."

"No one but me contradicts Mrs. Horton and, this time, I'm

not going to." The doctor moved swiftly for a man of his size toward the hall. "She has worked with me—except when she was off tending our brave wounded at Washington—since her career began and that's many a year ago. Lorena, there's no one better, no one, at the nursing profession."

"Well, not *that* many a year," Mrs. Horton sniffed, shooing people to the door and from the room with flapping hands. Jesse was the last to comply with her orders. "No exceptions, not even for you, Colonel Sparhawk." The nurse said this adamantly, but with obvious affection. "Just look at you, if you please! If you don't need as much tending as this child in the bed here, I'll be pickled. Lord, you're thin as a reed!" Lorena looked from one to the other, and then pulled the beautiful sheets up so that only her eyes were visible when she spoke Jesse's name.

"Have you remembered something?" he asked.

"I think so. Reed. It's my name. So is Lorena. Lorena Reed. You knew. You didn't tell me." Her tone was accusing.

"Better this way, for you to do this on your own. What else came to your awareness with your name, Lorena Reed?" He took her hand.

"What else do you know that you're holding back, War-bird?"

"Oh, not much."

"You asked me to trust you, but how can I?"

He looked pained. "In truth, Lorena, we have only just recently met."

"Where?" she asked in a whisper, her eyes widening. "When? And the sailors Q. spoke of?"

"We met near the South Street docks, downtown in New York. The sailors were obviously annoying you. I sent them packing and then learned you were intent on traveling south at once. So was I. Now you can't travel just yet and I've changed my plans. Trust me now? Good," he smiled when she nodded, though somewhat tentatively.

"More so. But I feel lost . . . lonely."

"Lonely? In this household, it's impossible to be lonely. In a day or two you'll be seeking a quiet corner of your own. Lorena, you'll be safe and happy here, I promise." He kissed her hand before Miss Horton could wave him away with a tea towel. "I'll be back as soon as this female tyrant lowers the bars," he smiled as he quit the room, closing the door after him.

"There!" the nurse said in quiet triumph. "Now, I'll just lower the window some," she told Lorena, "and then, your bath. I know you're looking forward to that, my dear."

"Miss Horton, was it terribly hard, nursing our wounded?" Lorena asked hesitantly.

"*Our* wounded were men of both North and South. Our New York City poet, Walt Whitman, was also a nurse. He most eloquently described the heartbreak of the job in a copy of his notes he sent to me about a particular patient we both had cared for. He was a boy of barely nineteen, from Baltimore. Death had marked him but he lingered some weeks. Morphine hardly eased his pain. Whitman was very good to the boy, visited him daily, soothed him, held his hand. One day the child said to Walt, 'I hardly think you know who I am—I don't want to impose on you—I am a rebel soldier.' That brought the poet close to tears and of course Mr. Whitman was quick to assure the boy it didn't matter one iota. Soon after, in another ward not far from the boy's, the poet found the young man's brother, a Union officer. They were both wounded in the same battle, found each other after a four-year separation and both died in a northern city. Such a thing boggles the mind and sears the heart." Nurse Horton paused, and then said, "I think it unwise for one in your condition, Miss Reed, to dwell on such things."

"I have a deep need to know of these things, but perhaps not just yet in such sad detail."

"We won't talk of them again, until you're stronger."

Lorena, inexpressibly affected, nodded her agreement.

Horton, as she was called by one and all—Lorena would not learn her first name for months—leaned out the window a moment. Her attention was captured by a tall woman wearing a very attractive red bonnet, who was crossing Fifth

Avenue to hail and climb into a hansom cab, which then headed downtown. I must make a bonnet like it, she thought, already picking through her remnants basket, in her mind, for a white silk rose.

"So. Doc Ben told me that you, Lorena, are doing exceptionally nicely at recovering, what with your courage and age and strength in your favor," proclaimed Horton after Lorena's bath in the deep porcelain tub in the small chamber off her room. The water, scented with oil of lilac, had been kept wonderfully luxuriously warm by the constant addition of pitchers of steaming water brought by Miss Hope, the ladies' maid, scuttling back and forth to the kitchen. When the plasters on her ribs were suddenly and briskly stripped by Horton without any warning, Lorena yelped, more in surprise than pain. Instantly there was a sharp rap at the bedroom door.

"Have a care with that patient, Horton!" Jesse called, "or I'll have to tend to her myself."

"And he would, too," giggled Ethel Hope, "whether you was decent or not."

"Not on *my* watch, he wouldn't," Horton huffed with indignation. "Hold your horses, Colonel," she called loudly, in a shrill voice, then told Lorena in an authoritative but sympathetic tone, "Better to forget about biting the bullet and just get the plasters off quick, I've found. It keeps the patient from unnecessary worry about the coming twinge. Soak a few minutes longer to dissolve the last of the paste."

Lorena soon stood to be wrapped head to toe in warmed towels and directed to the dressing table in her room to watch in the mirror while Ethel combed and brushed her long hair, which had darkened from yellow to deep gold by damp. Lorena, doing nothing, felt ill at ease.

"Miss Hope, you needn't . . . it doesn't seem right somehow for you to be . . ." Lorena blushed and stammered, "I'm certain I should be doing my own hair. I'm not a child."

"What? And do you want to put me out of a job?" giggled Ethel, a very round and curly person of diminutive height and ample energy. "I'm a lady's maid and you're my lady of the moment and that's that, if you don't mind. I'm called 'Ethel' usually."

"Thank you, Ethel," Lorena nodded. "Whether I'm a genteel lady or not, I'll save your position by behaving as one." Ethel again applied her skills to the job at hand and when Lorena's hair was smoothed straight back from her brow it was captured and held in a high horse tail by a pink ribbon Ethel produced from a pocket of her apron. She draped a white silk wrap about her lady's shoulders then tied the sash. The door knob rattled.

"It seems the Colonel is reluctant to have you out of his sight, Missy," Horton grumbled. "Shall we make him wait or give his heart instant ease by inviting him in?"

"Oh, by all means give him ease! He has been most attentive and kindhearted to me, hasn't he?" Lorena answered. Her imploring tone and yearning little smile didn't escape Horton's sharp eye. "I do so wish to thank him for his help and concern. A moment, Miss Horton," she added when the nurse had her hand on the door knob. "If I happen to discover that I have a bit of money of my own, a gift for Jesse, Colonel Sparhawk, would be in order. As soon as I'm permitted to get out and about I'll see to it. Tell me please, Mrs. Horton, where his interests lie, so I may give him something suitable to his tastes and also special, a bit out of the ordinary."

"Thank him, by all means, Missy, but have a care. Ladies are high on the list of his many and varied pursuits, though I'd venture to guess his collection of fine books is somewhat larger than the string of broken hearts acquired." Lorena was a little disconcerted and very annoyed at this bit of information gratuitously provided by Horton and determined not to give the nurse the satisfaction of showing it.

"Oh, dear," Lorena sighed. "Handsome and winning as he is, poor man, women must pursue him mercilessly. Give his heart ease at once if you please, Mrs. Horton," Lorena sighed. "Invite him without delay!"

"One thing Jesse Sparhawk is not, is poor," sniffed Horton, thwarted in her attempt to stir a touch of agitation.

"Pay her no mind," scoffed Ethel. "It's a favorite pastime of Horton's, goading folks with a bit of a prick here and there. She doesn't mean anything by it, do you, Hort? It's her way of getting to know you." Horton jerked open the door and marched out of the room as Jesse entered. He took no notice of the nurse, but went directly to Lorena.

"Doc has revised his diagnosis of your condition, Lorena, for the better," Jesse smiled, pleased with his news. "He'll be back any minute now to fill in the details."

"Bruised ribs, my dear, not broken!" Doc rumbled happily. "That's why you are able to move about so freely. Much preferable, I need not say. You do not appear to be experiencing the dizzy headache usually associated with concussion. If you suffered one at all, a concussion, it was mild. So, Lorena, you may dance at the ball two nights hence—in moderation."

"If my concussion was mild, where's my memory, Doc?" she asked.

"It'll be along," he assured her. "Until it comes back in part or in full, follow your feelings, as I've told you before. Now, I will listen to your heart, my dear." His stethoscope dangled about his stocky neck as he rummaged through his bag for it. Horton returned just in time to come to his rescue and he frowned as if her help was a blot on his competence. "Thank you, Nurse, but I'd have found it myself, sooner or later," he growled, and then gave the nurse a wink and an appreciative pat on the shoulder. "Now, where was I? Ah, Lorena. The instant you feel even a mite dizzy dancing at the ball, you are to find a chair at once, even if you're in the middle of a romp. Even if you're in a romp with me!" With his always-surprising portly man's agility, Ben pantomimed a dancer whirling a lady in his arms.

A pattern of clouds like the ribs of Goliath were banding the sky, stars showing between them when, later, at her open window, Lorena looked out on Fifth Avenue below just as Horton had done. It was nearly midnight. A hansom cab passed now and then and, less frequently, a private carriage, its hood down, the horses' slow hoofs clicking on cobbles, moved lazily by, conveying jewel-bedecked women and their attentive escorts in evening dress. Lorena heard not too distant muted city sounds nearly as enticing to her as a siren's song. The spring wind was generous in its intoxicating sweetness. She was unaware that it stirred her now as it often had before on a wilderness mountain slope on just such spring nights as this, carrying then as now an elusive offer of love. But though she had known this very breeze, she had only a sensual memory of it. The touch of wind on her cheek made her heart swell and ache for something she could neither name nor put a human face to until she let Jesse Sparhawk invade her thoughts. She was all at once awash in conflict. She needed to stay with him and learn beyond doubt if he was, as he'd jested, her true love. But the spring night seemed to be letting her know it was time to move on, to redis-cover her life's mission, to learn who she was and what her destiny required of her. She would have to do both, she decided, but in which order? If she stayed with Warbird, she might never know what she had lost. She probably wouldn't want to. If she left him now, he almost certainly would not be waiting for her if, or when, she came back to him. She was at a crossroad. Ide-ally, her two journeys of discovery should be combined. Realistically that was improbable. One truth would likely over-whelm the other.

The mantel clock, bisque porcelain scrolled in gold, struck twelve with a dainty double chime.

"It's a day closer to my birthday now," she told the moon, which raced along with fragmenting strands of clouds, "and I don't even know who I am."

There was a quiet knock at her door. She opened it to look up at Jesse Sparhawk holding two stemmed glasses in his left hand, a bottle of champagne in his right, offering her a bold, winning smile. At the sight of him she was no longer certain she had a choice of which road to follow. As swiftly, Jesse felt the intensity of her conflicted emotions and waited for her to speak.

In a glance he appreciated even more fully than he had before her extraordinary natural loveliness, heightened by the color and style of her garb. Below her very small waist, a crinoline and several petticoats supported a bell-shaped skirt of red silk with contrasting trim and ruffles. The bolero jacket revealed white lace at her wrists and the close fit of the shirt-front bodice. Her golden hair, smoothed back from her face and looped at her nape, brought into clear relief the perfect features of her face. She was not merely pretty as he had, of course, known. She was a lovely woman who would mature into a great beauty, one who could, if she so chose, claim a prominent place in New York society merely with the perfection of her appearance.

But she was much more than her beauty, he knew as she twirled about in front of him.

"This is Rachel's outfit," said Lorena, "not brand-new but never worn! Rachel delights in agitating her mother with her insistence on plainness, Horton says. Horton says Rachel would wear sackcloth if she could, to remain unnoticed and rile her mother who is anxious to marry her off. Apparently, Doc's daughter will accept the offer of one man only and no one but Rachel, probably not even the man himself, Horton reports, knows who that is. But Molly has the dressmaker come often so that Rachel's high-style wardrobe will always be up to the fashion minute. There's a roomful of new gowns, nearly my size. The sash on this one draws in the waist to my dimensions. Oh, I've been babbling at you, nineteen-to-the-dozen. Sorry. But anyway, do you like me in it, Jesse?"

"Of course," he said flashing his incomparable smile, pleased by her use of the odd phrase—nineteen-to-the-dozen—that she had used before the accident. "You're a storybook princess come to life, a new doll just unwrapped from tissue. Let Rachel have her things. You shall have your own and they will be exactly your size. We'll visit the most exclusive shop on the Ladies' Mile tomorrow. Now," he said, the wonderful smile back again when he turned to close the door behind him, "Turn round for me once more."

She did, with a laugh, and as she came full circle, Jesse was in her path, his arms open to gather her to him. He kissed Lorena softly, then framed her face in his hands and kissed her again, harder, deeper, her lips softening and parting. "You really do know how to kiss, don't you?" he whispered, his two hands nearly circling her waist. "Shall we go a little beyond kissing to discover what else you know, to test the waters?"

"And if I find myself out of my depth?" she questioned, all aglow, eager to jump into the shallows at least.

"I'll rescue you, throw you a line, set you safe ashore," he said in a smoky voice as he undid the hooks on her blouson bodice, and then slipped it and the little silk jacket from her shoulders. Her high breasts, concealed only by a flimsy chemise, were perfectly rounded, the pink tips standing under the gossamer fabric. Jesse leaned to kiss her lips again, gathering her breasts in his hands while his fine fingers teased her nipples harder and even more erect.

"Jesse!" she gasped, wonderfully stunned by the sensations darting through her body. He took a step back, and then raised the chemise over her head. "Jesse?" she said again, and to his delight, did not cross her arms before her to hide her loveliness.

"You *are* quick to take fire. You're also more perfect, from your small waist up, than any woman I've ever set eyes on. You should have been painted by Leonardo. You should be painted by my friend Orlando Johnson. After we visit the dressmaker, we'll call at his studio. Now, shall I toss you that safety line, Lorena? Have you been tested enough—for the time being?"

CHAPTER 6

"First, I wish to see you also, at least as much as you have seen of me, else our test will be inconclusive," Lorena said, shrugging charmingly. Jesse grinned at her with interest and admiration when she extended her hand to remove the jeweled studs of his shirt front, dropping each, as it came free, into her skirt pocket. She stood on tiptoe to peel off his shirt, and then touched his smooth bare skin, tracing her fingertips from the waistband of his trousers up over his flat stomach and ribs, lingering at a pectoral muscle before coming to rest on his shoulder. "A few pounds more on those ribs and you'd be rather perfect," she drawled, throaty and slow, her eyes warm with appreciation.

"*Rather*?" he complained, jesting gruffly. "Soon there'll be no 'rather' required. Just you wait and see." She leaned forward to set her lips to the declivity at the base of his throat. Her long lashes drifted down over her eyes when his mouth found her erect, hard nipples. She laced her fingers behind her head, lifting her breasts higher. He grew more vigorous with his tongue and worked softly with his teeth, further lifting her nipples. She stroked his black-satin hair, kissed his shoulder, then felt herself drawn against his hard chest as it moved and chafed against the tender tips of her breasts. He deftly undid the bow of her skirt sash. With his help fighting her crinoline, she stepped out of it—leaving on the floor a white, upright cage beside the bright, silk pool of her skirt. He lifted her in his arms and carried her to the bed, mumbling what seemed to be an affectionate oath. His eyes were at once both fiery and soft as he set her down and loomed over her. His hand, resting at her ankle at first, traced up her leg beneath petticoats, following a silk stocking to its top. He peeled it down, fingered it off, and traced the smooth skin of her instep and her naked ankle. Then his hands started back up the firm calf of her leg until he reached her knee. Her eyelids fluttered under his gaze. Her full lips parted, her tongue roamed over them and she breathed deeply. She wasn't going to resist him at all, Jesse realized, but neither did her body move or arch to his caresses. Her parallel legs hardly parted. He stopped, cold. Lorena felt lovely, though diminishing billows of piercing sensation coursed through her.

"Jesse?" she questioned sitting straight up when he walked away from the bed and reached for his shirt. "What's wrong?" He found an amazing expression in her beautiful, half-lidded eyes when he allowed himself a look at her.

"Not a bloody thing!" he said in a roared whisper, feeling as he never had before, ready and hungry for a beautiful woman and conflicted about taking her. He wanted Lorena as she clearly did him but he was almost sure she was a virgin and he was unwilling to compromise her honor.

"Lorena, all the girls I've had before—women rather— were . . . well, sophisticated, experienced ladies-about-town— many towns—New York, London, and Paris, more."

"How is that . . . relevant . . . now?" The naiveté of the question strengthened his notion that he had taken her further than any man had done before.

"Leaving those women when the time came or interest waned, has always been painless for me. If any of them ever cried, it was after I'd gone. For me, ending liaisons has been, by prearrangement, uncomplicated. From the start, the *dénouement* was a pending certainty for both players. It was only a matter of time." He was leaning an elbow on the mantel, shirt front open, toying with the clock. It struck half after the hour. For an instant Lorena was silent, furiously so.

"Are you requesting such an agreement from me?" she

asked. "I'd consider being a 'player.' Doc said to follow my instincts." Jesse couldn't suppress a low laugh.

"No, Lorena. You're another matter entirely, no plaything." His eyes ravaged what he wanted to touch and taste and pleasure. Instead, he brought her her clothes.

"Why's that?" she pouted up at him. "You, sir, are causing me to disobey doctor's orders. And please do not laugh at me!" Her expression was that of a sulky, sassy little girl. Her full lips were perfectly positioned and pursed for a kiss and her eyes flashed with a challenging glitter. She was playing the naughty child so well he briefly considered positioning another part of her anatomy over his knee for a sharp little lesson in manners. That, however could have unpredictable end results, he punned to himself.

"I think your virginity is intact. We have already gone further than you've ever been before," he said. "I won't take a maidenhead from any woman—except the one I make my wife. Save yours for your husband, or your true love, at the least. Now, where are my studs?" She didn't respond to his last question.

"Ah, you think I'm virginal. You don't absolutely know."

"A man can't absolutely know without pressing the matter." He stood close over her, his hands set in fists on his narrow hips.

"Why not press the matter, then marry me or not as the situation and honor, of course, demand?"

"That might not be . . . appropriate.

"Knowing what you do of me, and I do not, do you think it will ever be appropriate for us to be together?" she asked.

"I can't say," Jesse shrugged. His eyes were stormy, his voice caressing. "What of the other Lorena, the girl neither you nor I know right now?"

"I was worried about her earlier. Her dilemma is solved at this point, her priorities and mine are perfectly clear. Warbird, I have more than an inkling I may have fallen in love with you. I need to find out for a certainty." She was in his arms at once, hers folding about his narrow waist beneath his shirt, he gently drawing her against him, raising her chin so he could set his lips to her brow.

"Not now, Lorena. Not *yet*," he said in a throaty voice, setting her away from him. Her pique vanished as quickly as it had come.

"Of course, not now," she agreed, beginning to collect and put on her scattered clothing. She retrieved Jesse's shirt studs, one by one, from her pocket and replaced each. With her standing close, he was enwrapped in the fragrance of the lilac scent she had just dabbed on, after she had brushed her golden hair and looped it again in a coil. He sat in the wing chair watching her at the dressing table, his long legs stretched before him, crossed at the booted ankles, enjoying the intimate easy moment. Jesse was charmed.

When they were both dressed, she smiled at him—all softness and warmth. He was both glad and a mite sorry to see her sensible self again. He'd quite enjoyed her feisty display. Moreover, he recalled having told her that he was sure to *like* her when her true personality took hold. That was proving true, a self-fulfilling prophecy, though the word *like* he was finding was something of an understatement. That made him edgy. So did the different yet simultaneous feelings, she stirred in him—a man who knew his own mind and was never ambivalent.

Rising on tiptoe with the grace of a dancer to just brush his lips with her own, Lorena knew she could be patient. Whoever she'd been, whatever she'd done before still mattered immensely, of course, but what took precedence now in her heart was trying to make certain that the rest of her life would unfold with Jesse Sparhawk beside her forever.

"It's almost your birthday, Lorena Reed. Make a wish now," he said. "Not the obvious one."

"Drat!" she laughed. "You've denied my first predilection, but luckily I have others."

"It's best never to be at a loss for wishes," Jesse bantered. "Out with 'em."

"Of course, I wish to know who I am. Even more," she hesitated, studying his handsome face, "I wish to stroll out under the moon on this perfect night and forget that I've ever forgotten."

"Your second wish! I can make that one come true." He handed her the bottle and two glasses and swept her off her feet. His mouth brushed hers.

"I am perfectly able to walk," Lorena said putting her arm about his neck.

"So what?" Jesse answered.

The garden at the side of the large house was hidden from the avenue by a high, brick wall covered in English ivy. In the light of a glowing moon a brick walkway wound beneath crabapples and between beds of crocuses and daffodils. Welcoming white marble benches formed a half circle around a burbling fountain. When Jesse put Lorena down, they touched along the length of their bodies causing a tingling need. Lorena set the bottle of Veuve Cliquot and glasses under the cold water of the fountain cascade and felt a rush of delight when she and Jesse moved toward each other, neither one equal to the task of preserving physical distance between them. Jesse drew her to him hard. She smoothed his glinting hair, black and smooth as satin in moonlight, back from his brow. Her hands fluttered to his broad shoulders and her body flowed to his. They kept a profound, long kiss alive until Jesse abruptly broke it off.

"Oh, blast!" he growled, striding toward the fountain.

"Jesse, we must be together. We must let intuition and nature rule, be straightforward, so that everything will be crystal clear between us. I put myself in your hands, but I accept all responsibility, no matter what the outcome may be because I think I love you. I've already told you I thought it a possibility." Her large hazel eyes were so warm and beautiful they quite took his breath away. He brought a hand to his brow in a gesture of bemusement. "You, think? You had better be damn sure about love, little girl, before you let impulse rule." His hands set on his hips he then threw his head back and laughed affectionately. "You are a persistent romantic, aren't you?"

"So it would seem," Lorena speculated, showing a provocatively sweet half-smile. "Tell me, Jesse; have you any inclination at all to fall in love with me? And don't laugh, please. I'd find your amusement patronizing."

"You're loveable, no doubt about it. I'll not deny it or that I could fall in love with you, but what if . . . ?"

"Forget what if. Love conquers all. It makes everything permissible." She mirrored his stance, hands on hips.

"Even if you have a husband and a passel of babes back home?"

"Oh, how could that be if, as you presume, I'm a virginal 'little girl'?"

"You've a point there," he acknowledged, "but you didn't tell me, when you might have before your bump on the head, whether you are free or spoken for." He was walking around the fountain in long impatient strides.

"I wonder why I didn't tell you," Lorena seriously pondered trying hard to jog her memory.

Jesse fished the chilled wine bottle from the well of the fountain, popped the cork and poured them each a bubbling glass full. He raised his to Lorena. "In the event I'm not here that evening, happy birthday to you, in advance."

"Not here? Then, where?" Her voice and expression showed keen disappointment.

"One never knows. Now, allow me to complete my toast. I drink to you and to our discovering if we're free to 'be together'."

"That gives me a very special reason to learn all about myself pretty quick. Will you give me a hint?"

"If I recount what I know about you, only because you told me yourself and, remember, it wasn't much, I'll be going against doctor's orders again. Doc worries that the sudden shock of reality will set you back, that you may never really accept yourself or who you are."

"Knowing me even a little, do you concur with his dire prognosis?"

"I think you're stronger than that," Jesse admitted, "but Doc's the expert."

"Well then, lacking particulars, we cannot talk further about me. You must be our subject of conversation," she told Jesse. "Start with where you were born, and then tell me . . . oh, whatever you'd care to." Her voice was husky, mischievous, and faintly tinged, he heard, with yearning. Jesse set one elegant booted foot beside her on the bench where she had settled after fluttering, glass in hand, like a lovely small bird. She shifted about from one vantage point to another seeking the best view of the moon. Its light now fell full upon her, but only lit one side of Jesse's handsome face, sharpening the angles. The other side of his face was hidden, almost mysteriously, in shadow.

"I was born in North Carolina, ma'am." He waited for her to react. She did.

"Know what?" she said with excitement, springing to her feet. He nodded. He knew. "So was I! Born in North Carolina. It's just words to me now. You must show it to me on a map, if you will. Oh, we must go at once to find . . . ?"

"To find you, Lorena?" he said placing his hand along her cheek.

"And you, too," she answered.

"Me? I'm not lost," he replied with a twitch of a smile.

"No? Then you've lost something. I see it in your eyes. Shall we search together? When?"

"Soon." He watched her pace, almost dance, along the path around the fountain, clasping and unclasping her hands, her rounded hips swaying subtly beneath her tiny waist, her eyes alight under the moon. Her manner and expression were exuberant, her carriage and posture elegant, almost regal. "Calm down," he laughed, capturing her on her third circuit and setting her back on the bench beside him. "What else do you want to know about me?"

"You? Oh, of course. I am not the center of the universe, am I? Tell me when were you born."

Thinking she might, perhaps perilously, become the center of his universe, he urged himself to have a care. "I entered the world on the tenth of July in the year of eighteen and thirty-six. I don't know the time of day."

"That does make you a young colonel."

"Not really. In time of war, promotions arrive with undue speed. You do know about the damndest little details, Lorena, military ranks of all things, and not about the big ones. Don't worry. You will. You've made a good start, with North Carolina." He held her hand—he had no choice—as they sat shoulder to shoulder in the moonlight, leaning into each other.

"I was dispatched from the Capitol at Washington, to Providence, as a lieutenant, to muster Battery E of the First Regiment of Rhode Island Light Artillery into the Federal Army. I have property near Providence. I knew many of the volunteers and their families. When their last goodbyes, perhaps forever, were being made, I promised more than one aged parent and young wife to look out for their sons and husbands, as well as one could be looked out for in war. Emotions ran high that day. The loving relatives filled their soldiers' haversacks with cakes and pies, pairs of socks, handkerchiefs by the baker's dozen, needles and thread and buttons, and Lord knows what else. Bottles of ink and portfolios of writing paper, pipes, tobacco, and of course they also carried regular army rations from the quartermaster. Those weighted men marched through the streets of Providence, cheered every step of the way, to the Fox Point wharf. They took ship to the roar of saluting cannons." Jesse went silent, lost in thought. With a hand on either side of his face, Lorena gently turned his head to look into his eyes. She knew she had studied them before—hard, cold, fierce—but in another face, it seemed to her, one ravaged and bearded beneath a battered hat brim.

"You've a dark, mysterious side I think, Jesse," she said, shivering a little, not with chill, as clouds began to drift over the face of the moon. "You're keeping too many secrets. If you reveal one to me I'll carry some of the weight of it and your heart will be less burdened."

"I'm a spy. I trust you never to tell a soul." He winked.

"Be serious!" she complained and his mood shifted suddenly, an awesome rage on his hard face, blue eyes dark, determined.

"There were two soldiers among my brave and loyal men who lost their young lives to a traitor. I'm responsible. I'm going to avenge them. Is that serious enough for you, Lorena?"

"I am sorry, Jesse!" she said despairingly. "I didn't mean to ruin your pleasure in the evening by pressing you so."

"You haven't ruined anything," he offered, changing his tone and demeanor, bringing her hand to his lips. "I know what I must do, exactly where my obligation lies. It's something always in my mind, just below the surface. I will do what I've set out to accomplish. I no longer let bitterness dominate my every waking moment, thanks to you. So, here's another happier secret. Remember the ball they're all preparing for? It's to be a birthday party for you."

"That's not a secret, Jess," Lorena said before she set a kiss on his cheek. He found her easy spontaneity delightful. "Rachel and I are going to choose an evening dress for me, from her collection."

"You'll be beautiful, I know. Now, it's time for you to retire. You have to be rested and lively for the new day. I've some business to attend to."

"Business?" she echoed with disappointment. "What might that be at this time of night?"

"There's still a war on. Confederate Secret Service agents are persistent in planning their sabotage. There are plots afoot to kidnap and murder the President. There have been since the war began. Poisoned candy was delivered to him even before his inauguration and there was a credible threat to blow up the inauguration platform itself. Last year, a Kentucky doctor sent Mr. Lincoln a 'gift' of six exceptionally elegant dress shirts that had been taken from yellow fever victims. Trunk loads of patients' blankets were being shipped to Federal soldiers in Virginia and North Carolina."

"What happened?" asked Lorena with a horror-struck expression.

"We discovered the scheme in time but Doc tells me the yellow fever can't be passed on that way anyhow, though it's not known how it *is* spread. A spy like me must keep about his devious affairs." He stood, drew her to her feet, touched her lips with his before he turned on his heel and strode toward the gate. "Go inside directly, understand?" he called over his shoulder as the latch scraped, and then clicked shut. Lorena stood a moment feeling abandoned, until Mrs. Longworth's two little spaniels appeared, racing across the garden to chase each other, yapping, around the fountain.

"Have they scairt you, miss?" asked a man stepping silently from the shadows of the carriage house. Hamson, the gardener, tipped his cap. "They stay here with me most nights. Sorry for the bother."

"No bother, no bother at all Hamson. What are their names?" Lorena asked, indicating the dogs.

"Mrs. Longworth calls 'em Cupid and Psyche. Too fancy for my taste. I just call 'em Jack and Jill."

"Ah. So will I call them Jack and Jill," Lorena said to fill the awkward silence. "Hamson, thank you for the flowers."

"We've a conservatory, a glass house. There'll soon be more flowers, and herbs as well, some of 'em exotic. That's Mrs. Longworth's name for 'em. To me, they're all beautiful; Nature's gift each in its own way, even the scraggly weedy ones."

"Ginseng. It's just called 'sang' by some folks. I just remembered that, Hamson!"

"Yes," the gardener replied. "It grows wild in the southern hills. Sorry I don't have none in the glass house."

"Will you show me around the glass house one day?" Lorena asked. "Perhaps something else will come to my mind." The gardener nodded, shyly turning his eyes away from her face.

"I'd be pleased to give you a tour, Miss. You're prettier than the prettiest flower, Miss," he said, much to Lorena's surprise. She smiled. He blushed. The silent pause that followed Hamson's unexpected compliment was filled this time by the sound of hooves and carriage wheels, which stopped, apparently, in front of the Longworth house. One of the spaniels tore off to the gate and wriggled under it. Lorena ran after him.

"Jack! Come back, Jack!" she called flinging open the garden gate to see the spaniel nipping at the feet of a splendid, pure white trotter hitched between the shafts of a white cabriolet with its hood raised against impending rain. The horse had begun snorting and dancing and flinging its head about and a man, muttering under his breath, leapt from the carriage to soothe the animal and deflect the dog's unwelcome attention.

"Whoa, Jupiter, whoa," he said calmly, then "Go home! Go home, Cupid!" Jesse ordered as a woman's beckoning slim, white-gloved hand extended from the carriage. Lorena was taken aback and, in quick succession, expressions of surprise, dawning enlightenment, disappointment, and anger flitted over her upturned face.

"His name's really Jack, Colonel Sparhawk," she informed Jesse curtly.

"I told you to go to bed," he said. The woman to whom the gloved hand belonged alighted from the carriage and stood, glittering with gold and diamonds, under the corner gaslight. The gardener arrived at the gate. No one moved for a long, odd moment until Hamson whistled softly and he and the spaniels were gone.

"Mrs. Wharton, may I present Miss Reed." Jesse scowled at Lorena.

"A pleasure," said Mrs. Wharton, showing scant interest.

"Indeed," answered Lorena, superficially cool but intensely interested.

"Goodnight, Lorena," Jesse nodded curtly, then handed the elegant woman back into the carriage and followed in after her. The horse pranced away from the curb. Only Lorena remained, confused, angry, and alone on the deserted street. When she finally moved she headed not toward the Longworth house or garden gate but down Fifth Avenue, in the same direction the carriage had gone, all unaware of the dark-clad figure moving south also on the other side of the street.

CHAPTER 7

The moon was hidden. A fine mist turned to rain. Before Lorena had gone far she was damp and chilled. She kept walking, though she had no idea where she meant to go, feeling as if drawn by some unknown force. She passed several blocks of elegant Fifth Avenue mansions, quiet and dark in the small hours but for the odd light of an insomniac, she supposed, or of a student here and there in an upper story window. She glanced left then right along each deserted side street she crossed looking, she acknowledged, for the stylish gig in which Jesse and his Mrs. Wharton had ridden off.

Fool, she admonished herself, to be chasing after a man, no matter how well he kisses, who abandoned your company for that of another woman. But I do need the walk, Lorena reasoned, after my day of inactivity. It just didn't feel tolerable to her, doing nothing. Well, not exactly *nothing,* she giggled and blushed though she was alone, when her memory evoked Jesse's visit to her room. Nothing useful, leastways, her inner voice carped. He ain't with you now, is he? An' if'n he was, then what? Lorena came to a sudden full stop beneath a lamppost, taken aback by the drawl and jargon she heard in her thoughts. "That must be *me* talking to myself, *the* actual girl I used to be!" she said aloud, then pivoted about to face in the opposite direction, sure she had heard footfalls behind her. She saw no one, only shadows between the circles of light beneath widely spaced lamp posts. "Get a hold of yerself, girl!" she said and clasped her hands and laughed. "She's . . .

I'm . . . coming back!" Lorena exclaimed, striding on with a new bounce in her step. "Oh, but whoever I was, I do hope she and I will both love Jesse Sparhawk just the same when I find her." But what if she doesn't love him? Lorena pondered, again slowing her pace. I mightn't want to happen upon her too soon and have to become her again all at once, not until I know about true love and Jesse Sparhawk. It was then she reached a street corner. The avenue opened out into a wide, square park, trees and plants at the center, residences bordering it on four sides. Washington Square, a street sign informed her. She hesitated to decide which way to proceed.

Gaslight lamps illuminated the fronts of the narrow graceful houses. Their iron-railed stone steps led to brass knockers, gleaming out of the dark, on double doors with traceried glass transoms. In a tree-shaded, dim area on the far side of the spacious square, a white cabriolet and white horse at a hitching post, the animal blanketed against the rain, took shape as Lorena's eyes adapted to the dimness. She began moving in that direction and then heard, without doubt this time, a scuffle of feet behind her. Uneasy, she looked over her shoulder to see a couple approaching across the deserted square, apparently bent on overtaking her, that or coincidentally following in her footsteps. A bow-legged man with a peaked cap pulled low on his brow, moved with a lumbering, nautical gait, scuffling to keep up with a tall quick-stepping woman shrouded in a hooded cape to keep off the light rain. As the distance closed between them, Lorena felt a chill of sharp panic and considered bolting in Jupiter's direction, calling for help. Someone, hopefully Jesse, who must be in one of those houses, would hear her. But she remembered that Jesse was with that Mrs. Wharton and, as the lesser of two evils, she turned to the pursuing couple and waited, standing her ground, reasoning that they very likely were just folks out for a walk as was she. When they were within a few feet of her, there was a shout from the opposite side of the park.

"Run, Miss, run!" Lorena and her stalkers all responded with equal alacrity, sprinting in three different directions. The slow, lumbering man tossed something shiny into a flower pot before he stumbled and sprawled, cursing colorfully. There was the warble of police pea whistles and the sound of running feet scraping cobbles. Surrounded, the fallen man was pulled to his feet by three uniformed officers of the law. Lorena didn't look back and so saw none of this. Breathless, her dress now wet through, her hair tumbled and bedraggled and clinging to her brow and cheeks, she reached the white carriage and clambered into it to get out of sight. She talked softly to Jupiter who danced a bit in place but made no further objection to her presence.

The door of the house where the horse was hitched flew open. A housemaid in a black dress, white apron and cap, stepped onto the landing and peered about.

"Oh, la!" she said on seeing the police lanterns and activity across the way.

"Whatever is the disquiet at this time of night, Julie?" asked Mrs. Wharton, also appearing on the doorstep still gowned and bejeweled as Lorena had seen her earlier. Jesse, in shirtsleeves, a brandy snifter in hand, followed her from the house and headed off toward the center of activity where the three policemen, their nightsticks upraised, and Q. Ryan, the plainclothes shadow, had someone surrounded.

"Roger Truckett off the *Howard Wister* out of Liverpool, *just* taking a stroll, enjoying me land legs before we put to sea," the man with a gap-toothed smile was explaining.

"So, why'd you try and run off, sir, and where's the fleet-footed lady who was sharing your no doubt charmin' company?" questioned Q., flashing his copper badge.

"We thought you men was footpads, naturally, at this hour," Truckett shrugged and kept on grinning.

"And I suppose the young woman you've been skulking after for blocks, while I was shadowing you, thought the same of you and your friend—that you were out to rob her."

"How's one ever to know what any young lady's thinking?" grumbled Truckett, dispensing his false good humor. "I ain't been skulking, just strolling. Oh, blimey, it's him again," the

sailor groaned, dropping his head as if to hide when Jesse
came forward, snifter in one hand, and a four-inch blade with
a scrimshaw handle in the other.

"You've lost your weapon, Truckett. He's lost his weapon,
Q. I found it in the planter there. I was about to be on my way
to our meeting at the Spring House, but with this new development, I'd prefer to see you at the station house tomorrow,
after this man has been questioned."

"Do you know this sniveling sneak, sir?"

"He's one of the louts who tried to make off with Miss
Reed at South Street. Why are you here now, Truckett?" Jesse
waited for an answer, his eyes so piercing and fierce the sailor
blanched before he scowled belligerently.

"You're lookin' some slicker than when last we met, soldier. Why do you keep turning up in me way like a bad-luck
albatross around me neck? I was only trying to help that
pretty little individual keep off the wicked waterfront streets.
Me and me mate only meant to help, see, and then you
showed up looking all wrathy and bad-tempered."

"Trying to help? Don't make me laugh, limey. I've a
wicked sense of humor. Since she got free of you, you've
been trying to reclaim the 'goods' you 'bought.' Right?" Jesse
asked and gulped some brandy. Truckett looked longingly at
the snifter.

"I could do with a drop meself just now, soldier."

"Could be these police officers will consider your request,
after you give them the truth," said Jesse.

Truckett shuffled his feet, rolled his head from side to side,
and looked at the sky. "Okay, this is the meat of the matter. I
have a right to her person or a obligation to get me investment
back. Now, gimme a swig, fella?" Jesse handed over the glass
and watched Truckett lap up the last dregs.

"Your *investment*," said Jesse in a ominous tone that went
unrecognized by the indignant seaman for what it actually
was, the veneer of a near-murderous fury.

"Yeah, me and Swisby give a gold piece each for 'er, none
of your worthless Yankee greenbacks. She's quite the comely

prize, the little miss you took from us. Course, I'll let you have her, soldier, for the right price."

"Even at the cost of a few gold coins, you got yourself quite the good pennyworth, Mr. Truckett," said Jesse calmly now.

"We gotta make a profit, as much a one as we'd a got if we did our business with somebody else. You seem a chap who'd take a proper deal when it's offered, and take pleasure in the merchandise," he added in a lecherous cackle.

Jesse walked a few feet away, set his repossessed brandy glass on the edge of the nearest planter, sauntered back to the group of men in the center of the square, and struck Truckett a pair of stunning two-fisted blows, one to the nose, which generated a jet of blood like a whale spout, one to the chin, which dropped the man to his knees. "Officer, help! Save me! Protect me, from this murderer," he cried before he fell forward, unconscious.

Lights were coming on in several nearby houses when Jesse handed over the knife he'd retrieved from the planter. "You'll find it fits his empty holster, Q. I think you'll also find the name his accomplice is using at the moment is Hester Potts, a tall dark-haired woman, with a weakness for red bonnets."

"Accomplice at what, sir?" one of the uniformed men asked. "What are the charges?"

"Attempted kidnapping with conspiracy to do mayhem, menacing, plotting murder. Also sedition. This man's working hand in glove, though he might not know it, with a notorious Reb spy, the woman who got away. In which direction did she flee?" Jesse asked.

"West. We've lost her by now, Colonel. Miss Reed ran that way," Ryan gestured.

"Miss Reed is in the neighborhood?" Jesse was both dismayed and delighted. "Do tell? I hadn't realized she was at the center of this episode. It's the second time they nearly got her. The willful sprite is supposed to be safe and dreaming right now, in her bed at Doc Ben's."

"What is Miss Reed's role in this?" Q. asked. "It might help the case if we knew."

"Can't say. Don't know," Jesse shrugged. "Neither can she, in her amnesiac state. It's a real thriller, gentlemen, better than a penny dreadful novel. Thank you for coming to her rescue. I'll take steps to see she doesn't wander about again without an escort, at least not until all the villains are caught and this puzzle is solved.

"I'll leave you all now with some good news; President Jeff Davis, with his staff, has fled the Confederate capitol city. The Rebs burned the arsenals and storehouses of Richmond as they withdrew. The city has been abandoned to Federal troops!"

Jesse found Lorena curled half-asleep in the carriage, wrapped in a knit shawl forgotten by Maud Wharton. He untied Jupiter, sprang up beside Lorena and raised his hand in farewell to Maud and Julie. While her mistress kept to the shelter of the doorway, the parlor maid came skipping through rain puddles to hand up his jacket, which he put on, and an oilskin, rain cape, flannelled on its inner surface. This he wrapped about his passenger.

"Oh la! A foul night, *monsieur*. Is there more I do for you now?"

'No, Julie, and *merci*. Go inside. Tell Mrs. Wharton I'll get back to her as soon as . . . soon enough." He waved to Maud Wharton who returned his gesture before the door closed upon the two women.

"Lorena," he whispered as he worked the reins so that the horse rounded the Square and trotted north on Fifth Avenue. "I'm taking you home."

"Good," she answered more asleep than awake, her teeth chattering with cold. "To whose home? Is it far? I'm cold."

"Mine. It's a bit of a drive," he answered. "Get close to me now, as close as you are able, to share my warmth until I can warm you properly, through and through."

* * *

After a ride of what seemed at least half of an hour, with many turns and twists, the horse and cabriolet were taken charge of by Sergeant Nicke who was waiting at a carriage house on an alley behind a totally dark brownstone building. Jesse guided Lorena, sheltered in his oilskin cape, through a small garden and into the chilled house where no fire burned. No gaslight illuminated the way when Jesse, without a false step, led his guest by the hand through dark rooms.

"Welcome to my humble domicile, Lorena," he said quietly on reaching the foot of a spiral staircase below a skylight several stories above. In the gray light falling to an entry hall from above, she could make out the stenciled walls of a vestibule, sheet-shrouded chairs, a covered round reception table, and tall inner French doors with panes covered in drapery. At only one edge of a pane, a slant of gaslight from the street was allowed to fall on a thick rich Turkey carpet. "The place has been closed up, more or less, since I went off to war."

"Why?"she asked. "Tell me, now that you're home, why keep the house shuttered and dark?"

"I hadn't intended to remain in New York at all, or to show myself alive and quite well, in public, but to go on with ah, certain inquiries incognito. Then you and Doc changed my plans." Lorena bumped into him when he stopped before a door on the second floor landing and released the door latch. Inside, he lit one candle, which sent light and shadows dancing about a high-ceilinged, elegant, welcoming room. There was a high, pillow-piled mahogany bed with porcelain medallions of Greek figures set into the headboard. Bedside tables held Limoges pitchers and basins. A pair of open-arm chairs, the backs decorated with medallions to match the bed, was set at a breakfast table near the draped windows. A gentleman's leather armchair faced the fireplace and marble mantel. The room was faintly redolent with the spice-and-lime scent of Jesse's East India cologne. He poured cognac into a pair of snifters and warmed them over the candle flame.

"From the outside, this house appears closed and deserted,

with no lights visible, no wisp of smoke rising from the chimneys. The nature of the work being done here, my work, prevents us lighting a fire, on the hearth, anyway," he explained, flashing a boyishly chagrinned, flirtatious smile.

"Is this your room?" she asked. Superficially at least, she ignored his suggestive *double entendre*, and gazed all about her, everywhere, except at him. She was edgy. She didn't precisely know why, not that she'd yet admit that to herself, and so she stood shivering, sipping, then gulping, the brandy, his rain cape pulled close about her until he virtually unpeeled it from her grip.

"My room, my bed, yes," he nodded. Attentive to her apprehension, he kept a slight distance, not wanting to panic her. "Lorena, you're soaked to the skin. Get out of those wet things before you get ill."

"Yes," she answered, and with cold, unsteady hands, she fumbled awkwardly at her hooks and sash. "But what are you doing?" she whispered when he opened a folding pocketknife and came toward her.

Deftly, he applied the blade to layers of her wet, clinging clothes until they lay in a beribboned heap at her feet. He intended to look away until she was warmly concealed in quilts, but her eyes, innocent and trusting as a child's, sought his. What he read in them was an invitation only a woman could offer. She was perfectly made, slender and curved, her fawn-toned skin wet and glistening in candlelight, her high breasts rising and falling with every deep breath.

Lorena saw his eyes take fire. Her lids fluttered when, in confusion, she dropped her own eyes, her whole body trembling more dramatically with more, now, than cold. He enfolded her in the long, rain cape again, its inner, flannel-side dry and warming as he pressed it to her. He toweled and touched everywhere, ran his hands over her shoulders, down the full length of her back before his hand slid inside the cape lingering at the swell of her breasts. They both felt the tips rise and become firm. Pliant in his hands, she let his touch move along her hips and thighs and down her slim legs.

"Don't be afraid," he said before his mouth touched hers.

"Of you, Jesse? How could I be when it seems I've known you forever though it's just two days, almost three, since we found each other?" He nodded captivated, before he flung back the down quilt on the bed and, relieving her of the cape, set her there. She pulled the quilt up to her little nose, her beautiful, questioning eyes peering at him over the edge.

"You better close them," he suggested. "Now I'm getting out of my wet things."

"But I've already seen half of you exposed," Lorena answered and didn't close her eyes.

"Suit yourself," he said and shrugged, his low laugh reminding her of a stove roaring into heat. He turned his back to her and began to strip wet garments from his lanky body. Flexed long muscles stood in his solid thighs and flanks. His hips were narrow, his shoulders wide, his rippling contours as she remembered them until he turned to face her. He heard the catch of her breath before she lifted the quilt inviting him with a sleepy smile to share *her* warmth. He moved toward her and she saw glistening rain drops still caught in his gleaming black hair when she shifted the covers away. He knelt above her, imprinting in memory the perfect contours of her young body, his fierce eyes caressing each finely wrought turning and smooth swell. When he flicked back his hair, he sent a shower of raindrops along her creamy, warm length. She shivered and then, where the drops had fallen, Jesse's mouth followed, moving with excruciating slowness, hardly touching her, brushing her lidded eyes and the smooth arch of her throat before taking ravenous possession of her parted lips. Her slender body shimmered into motion when she half rose alarmed at what she was feeling and Jesse traced the lilting curves of her breasts first with his hand, then his tongue.

"Has anyone ever told you . . . told you the tips of your breasts are like new spring berries? And more tasty."

"I don't really know if any one has." Her voice, which had gone throaty and warm, was silenced by the sensations sweeping her while his hand traced the joining line of her thighs, parting them, invading the muscled passage between.

Do you think you're ready to do this? I think you are, but . . ." His voice flowed over her like warm honey, "we don't know what we'll discover." She shuddered at the shocks of pleasure his sensitive hands caused and she arched her body to enclose his. He straddled her hips and slid slowly tentatively into her until he came up against the fragile barrier, the obstruction he had fully expected to be there. And he breached it, with strong, steady pressure as her sheathing narrowness gave way. He moved into her with steady pressure, until in one stronger thrust, he broke through. But for one head-to-toe shudder Lorena showed no sign of pain and she made no protestation. To the contrary, she sought Jesse's mouth, her arms went about him and she moved with him freely and gave herself to him completely.

Hours later, when a pale light began to appear at the edge of the draperies, Lorena was still sharing Jesse's body heat, now from head to toes, her rosy hips curled back into his hard body beneath the down quilt. They were like a pair of perfectly matched spoons, she mused happily, more asleep than awake until he spoke into her ear.

"What was it exactly you said earlier," he mumbled, "that's even more relevant now than yesterday, given this new state of our affairs?" He lit the candle on the bed table and leaned on one elbow to look into her face. His disheveled hair, a dark storm, was falling over his brow. She raked it back for him with a caressing hand. "You said, Lorena, 'Why not press the matter, then marry me or not, as the situation and honor demand?' Those were your words, more or less?"

"Mm. Yes. And apparently we know I am not now nor ever have I been, a married woman."

"You soon may be. Honor will be served." He smiled broadly.

"You inferred I might already have been spoken for, wed,

even mother to a 'passel' of babes. Recant, Sparhawk unless you still credit any of that?"

"It seems unlikely—no, impossible, that any man legally wed to you wouldn't have enjoyed his prize. Until me, you were virginal as the winter moon." There was an ephemeral trace of uneasiness in his eyes he knew and he hid them, nuzzling in Lorena's silken hair that was fragrant with the scent of lavender. "Though stranger things have happened," he ventured, kissing her shoulder. "I wouldn't want to make you a bigamist."

"Ah, but making a faithless wife of me was acceptable, I take it. Well, and now I'm either a confirmed tart—worse, a fallen woman or I've made a cuckold of some unsuspecting fellow. But don't you give the matter another moment's care, Colonel Sparhawk. In the circumstances, you've no responsibility for any of it."

He was sensitive to the bravado she tried to convey and the anger she tried to conceal but mostly of her disappointment as she held her breath, waiting for his rejoinder. Before he found the right words to say, she said sighing, "I won't hold you to your obligation, you know."

"What obligation?" he asked blankly, trying with minor success to look grim until he broke into his rumbling, low, hot laugh.

"To make me your wife, now that . . ."

"Be still!" he commanded and set a hand over her mouth. He looked hard and what seemed to her awfully long into her eyes. And she saw in his eyes the precise moment at which he jettisoned his last modicum of doubt. He rolled her above him and basked beneath the laughter in her eyes. She was sure she could hear him thinking, *She's mine to lay claim to, and I'll do just that.*

"By taking you to wife, Lorena, I won't be fulfilling any damn obligation, you heah? It'll be mah pleasure, ma'am, ah am sure," he added in his best drawl. "As you come to know me better you'll understand I value honor, perhaps above all else."

"Above love?" She stirred in his arms.

"Love and honor are the noblest of instincts. It's not one or the other for you and me to choose between. Love and honor are in harmony for a man who knows his own mind as I do."

"And your heart?"

"Hearts may be a problem, for some. Love's not logical and the mind strives to be. But I know my heart and mind. Do you know yours?"

"I know Lorena's. She absolutely believes, in her heart, in love at first sight. Her mind's going along. Lorena might be more cautious about giving her heart away in a day, but she'll get used to the notion. We'll tend to that, Jesse."

"Be my wife?"

"When?" Lorena laughed, sitting over him.

"Oh, before supper, if that suits you." He answered casually as if replying to an offhand inquiry about the weather or time of day. "After we pay a visit to the *couturier*."

"That suits me, rather well, I think. Do you mean before supper, today?"

"Oh, perhaps tomorrow. Soon." Lorena kissed Jesse's mouth and tasted and claimed and invaded it, while he moved his hands over her before he went into her again, easily this time, smooth and deep in one thrust. She rode, moving her body gracefully, with no haste, pleasuring them both until neither could hold on any longer. After awhile they lay, bodies joined motionless. Lorena, enfolded in Jesse's arms, raised her head that had been resting on his chest, and whispered.

"We could disappear into this shut-up house of yours for days on end and no one would ever be the wiser."

"That's a captivating idea," he grinned. "I'd enjoy nothing more than hiding out with you forever, but now that I've been seen all over town, I'll either have to disappear again at once or open this place soon, with great fanfare and celebration, before I bring my dazzling bride to her new home. I think I had best show you around, after you've dressed of course, just to be sure everything meets with your approval."

CHAPTER 8

"The bathing chamber," Jesse showed Lorena with a flourish. "The *salle de bain,* in French, which some ladies find a more genteel description."

In the paneled room was a zinc tub, sleek and shiny, encased in dark mahogany. A washstand held a round marble basin fitted with brass faucets with porcelain handles. In a mirrored mahogany cabinet above it, the door open, were Jesse's pewter-backed brushes, a bottle of cologne, a straight razor with scrimshaw handle, a pair of gold cuff links, gold collar stays, and a single pearl earring. Jesse dropped the jewel into his pocket, closing the cabinet. He proceeded with the tour, opening a closed door within the bathing room to reveal a water closet. Lorena reached up to a dangling brass chain.

"It's not yet ready to use," Jesse explained. "I had an English engineer come and build this for me. They're somewhat more advanced with their creature comforts than we are, but as soon as this war is over, there'll be time and resources and laborers to proceed. Water, heated below stairs will be pumped through pipes into these fixtures and that'll do away with hauling water from the kitchen or fireplace."

"I shall be delighted with such a system and take perhaps as many as two baths a day! What needs doing to make it work now?"

"Better drainage systems. These are poorly sloped because most so-called plumbers are metalworkers who make ill-fitting pipes and know nothing of hydraulics or sanitation, and that,

Doc will tell you, is of greatest importance. New factories making war supplies and cotton have brought thousands of people to the city to work and they are crowded together in tenements without water or decent means of disposal. There have been almost daily front-page reports of neighborhood outbreaks of illness in every American city. Among Doc's wide interests is the public's good health. He knows a lot about hydraulic engineering. As this work advances so will healthiness."

"Oh, the pot in the closet with the tank and chain do you mean? How . . . modern."

"A godson of Queen Elizabeth I is said to have put a flushing bowl in one of her castles over the River Thames, but it worked badly and inspired jokes and the Queen refused to use the device. Or so history suggests. You'll enjoy all the conveniences, I think, when you're lady of the house," musing on the contrast of up-to-the-minute New York with her backwoods way of life.

"This is better than all the golden chamber bowls of the French Court," replied Lorena surprising them both with this bit of knowledge. "But I can't help wonder about the earring?"

"I'll return that to its owner," said Jesse, "and that's an end to it."

"And end to what?"

"A gentleman doesn't kiss and tell. It's finished." Jesse brought her hand to his lips. She withdrew it.

"Lorena, jealousy doesn't suit you, you know? You've no cause for it, I promise." His very worried little boy expression melted her heart.

"Sorry!" she exclaimed more or less shaking off her unease, her smile open and bright as ever. "If you tell me it's over, what right have I to ruminate?" With a hand beneath her chin he set his mouth to hers, gently and with a sweet tenderness.

"None. Let me show you my library," he said. Lorena readily agreed, though, despite his assurances and her wish to believe in him, she harbored an unease. He had not directly answered her question, not with words, at any rate. Oh, but what right or reason had she, she silently remonstrated, to pry into his past when he had taken her with no questions asked. Of course, there was no one to ask them of. He had no alternative but to take her at face value, so to speak, or not take her at all and it was too late for that.

The library was a comfortable room with a vaulted ceiling embellished with plaster medallions, a simple brass chandelier hanging above a reading table at the center of the room, though now light came from only the few discreetly placed candles Jesse had lit. Glass-doored mahogany bookcases, fitted with brass hardware and scrolled decorations, lined the two long walls of the room. At one end, there were French doors which opened on the garden, Jesse explained. Now, they were heavily draped with brocaded lime satin that concealed lights in the room. At the opposite end of the library, a fireplace with mahogany mantel was dark and cold.

A candle in hand, Lorena roamed the length of a bookcase which held encyclopedic works, dictionaries in several languages, fiction by modern popular novelists—Balzac in French, Hugo in English translation, Dickens. Also Emerson's essays, works of Hawthorne and, in several volumes, Gibbon's *Decline and Fall of the Roman Empire*. In locked cases were what looked to be very old volumes—ancient herbals, alchemical tomes, illuminated day books, and books of hours.

"While I'm hiding away with you here, I'd not lack for something to read," Lorena quipped. "In idle moments, I mean."

"You won't have many of those if you're hiding out with me," he said.

"Really, Jesse, this is an inspiring library. One could acquire an excellent education right here. 'A fine book retains its beauty forever.' I heard that, or read it, though I don't know where." In an adjacent music room she examined a piano, made by Gibson and Davis, and also a harp. When Lorena sat to pluck the strings, to her great wonder and Jesse's, she played the notes of Mozart's delicate *Andante in C*.

"I think your harp might need tuning, though I've no idea how that's done, nor do these pedals seem at all familiar though the music seems to come as by magic from a distant place to my fingers," she offered, bemused but not displeased.

"This is a concert harp made by a fellow name of Sebastian Erard about fifty years ago. The pedals, operated by these hooks, change the string's length and vibrating frequency. There's a pedal for each of the seven notes and each pedal has three positions. I think you've played an earlier version of the harp, one without levers. That distant place you talk of as the source of your proficiency is your own head and your heart. You've talents we've only just begun to uncover."

"Uncover, quite literally," she laughed, recalling the night just passed before she turned away from him, giddy with sensual memory that gave instant rise to lovely responses.

"Why are you blushing? Don't hide it. It's charming, that high color in your face but . . ." He was behind her, his arms enfolding her, his lips at her nape.

"Imagine what we've learned together in only a few short hours. You *were* an innocent, we now know, one with a natural aptitude for love. We also have found that you play the harp. What more could a man desire in a wife?"

"The harp takes practice and dexterity." Lorena's voice was low when she rested her head back against his shoulder, felt his lips nibbling first at one ear, then the other, one hand at her breast, his other arm drawing her back to feel his body rising hard against her.

"So does love, take practice." He, too, spoke softly, fighting her petticoats to clear his way. He set his hands on her hips, she her palms on the gilded curve of the harp, the vital movement of their joined bodies eliciting deep breaths from Lorena and reverberating random musical sounds from the quivering harp strings.

A short time later, they went hand in hand, Jesse leading the way, down the back stairs to the "English" basement.

"It's called that because this house is built on a small hill," Jesse explained. "The front room is somewhat below the plane of the street, but the kitchen here at the back opens onto the garden."

"It's rather like a ship's galley," Lorena commented. The room had long zinc counters with drawers beneath and glass-fronted cabinets of china and glassware above. There was a huge sink with faucets, as in the bathing chamber, waiting to be linked to a water supply. Copper kettles and cauldrons, shiny even beneath a layer of fine dust, hung from the ceiling and there was a modern hooded, cast-iron coal stove with not one but two ovens.

"Ship's galley, you say? Is there anything you don't know?" Jesse asked with a humorous grin. "I'd not be surprised if you find among your temporarily misplaced experiences a sea journey. What do you think?"

"A river boat, perhaps? Look. What's there?" Lorena pointed at a streak of light under a door just off the kitchen.

The room they entered was a brightly lit office, well hidden, its one small, high, basement window covered in black fabric. A telegraph was clicking furiously. A man with his back to the door made marks on a sheet of paper—dots and dashes. All along the walls of the hidden room, charcoal sketches and photographs of men and women were tacked, with names carefully scripted in large letters below.

"Hamson!" Lorena exclaimed to the man on a ladder adding a new picture to the gallery.

"Mornin', Miss," he half smiled as if chagrinned to have kept a secret from her. "Colonel Sparhawk here? He'll explain."

"I do hope so!" Lorena answered when the "coachman" Nicke and none other than Robert Longworth stood at their paper strewn tables in deference to the arrival of a lady and their commanding officer.

"This is a hidden center of command, Lorena. We hunt Confederate spies and sympathizers operating in the North or in Canada, though we've tracked a number of them into Dixie."

Jesse explained. "Only a very few Union officials know we exist."

"We work under Colonel Sparhawk," Nicke, the Morse Code specialist, saluted smartly.

"We've had quite a number of impressive successes, even triumphs, but of course, our work cannot be generally known now, and probably never will be," said Robert Longworth, his small, round, brown eyes glowing with pride.

"And I'm proud to report, discreetly, to General John Adams Dix," said Jesse, half sitting on the edge of the table. "The general is in command of Department of the East, with headquarters in New York City. The man was a fighting hero of the 1812 war, but now is thought to be too old for active military duty. He deals with newsmen and the public."

"And that's as tough—no, tougher—than going into battle I suspect," Robert said laughingly. Then he asked, "So Jess, are you recruiting the lovely Miss Reed to our clandestine unit?"

"In a way, yes, I am, soon as she's up to it."

"I am ready and able, sir, to do anything I can for our cause." Lorena spoke with heartfelt intensity.

"Almost ready. First, we must get you attired and after a bit of training, we'll launch you, probably in New York society, but perhaps in our nation's capitol. There's work to be done in both cities." He looked over some dispatches, signed a bank draft, and then, leading Lorena to the door, paused to look at the newest sketch posted on the wall.

"Have we no name for this woman?" he asked Hamson. "She seems vaguely familiar."

"To me, as well," Lorena said staring fixedly at the long, unsmiling face beneath a brimmed bonnet.

"No name yet, sir," Hamson replied frowning. "I seen her with the lawyer, Schuyler, who's a known Confederate under-cover agent, of course. That's why I described her to Orlando, so he could do the sketch, sir. It's not exact, but close. She may be harmless but I'd rather know than take chances."

"Jupiter and the carriage await you without, Sire," Nicke said in parody of a coachman. "Need me to drive?"

"Thanks, Nicke, no," Jesse answered before ushering Lorena out through the kitchen and quickly, through the garden to the waiting carriage.

"Why, Jesse, we are just across the Washington Square from the house of your friend," Lorena noted, with some unease, as they drove past the Wharton house moments later. "You and she are neighbors as well, as well . . . It seemed we drove quite a distance last evening, before we arrived at our destination."

"It is over, Lorena. Mrs. Wharton and I will remain friends and neighbors of course. And I never come directly to my humble abode no matter where I start out. She has no idea of the underground work going on, almost literally, beneath her nose."

"You are early. The shop's not even open yet. Been up all night?" asked the woman who unbolted her door to Jesse's pounding, her voice a low purr.

"In a manner of speaking," he replied and grinned. He and Lorena had come from his house where they'd passed the night, not up precisely, but not asleep either. "We saw the 'closed' sign in your salon window downstairs, but I knew you'd be hard at it up here and welcome us to your workrooms. I've a job for you, Ann, a sizeable order. Outfit this lovely lady, Miss Lorena Reed. Lorena, this is Mrs. Overton, New York's fashion authority." The seamstress nodded and extended her hand. She looked Lorena over precisely taking measurements by eye that would be confirmed by tape measure, though Ann Overton was rarely off by so much as a quarter inch in her visual evaluations.

"Same as for the others before, Jesse?" asked Ann waving them in, her movements languorous, conveying a great lack of energy. She barely stifled a yawn though whether of sleepiness or boredom Lorena couldn't be sure. The seamstress was a woman nearing thirty with very dark hair already shot through with steel gray streaks, swept up from a small, composed, oddly beautiful face. There were faint dark circles beneath her world-weary brown eyes, and her small mouth turned down at the corners, giving her a perpetually dissatisfied expression. Her dress was of rich, dark, feathery wool so light and softly woven it moved like silk and heightened the elegance of her tall, willowy figure.

"You make it seem I've brought gangs to be gowned by you. There was only one or two before. And Rachel Longworth, of course, as a favor to her mother. For Lorena, please do your very best, Ann. I'll stay a while, to help choose patterns and fabrics." At that, a lackluster spark of interest came to the woman's eyes and she nearly smiled, Lorena thought.

"My assistant will help you to undress, Miss Reed, down to your chemise and one petticoat. Leave your things in my bed chamber, please," the dressmaker instructed.

Lorena glanced at Jesse on her way out, and then left him with Ann in the neat, elegantly comfortable atelier.

The bedroom of the seamstress's apartments, which doubled as a changing space and design studio was done all in gold, dusty pink, and shades of rose, the flocked wall in deep red, the darkest color. The pink silk drapery of a crown-canopied sleigh bed was askew revealing a clutter of empty cups and glasses, books and papers amidst a pile of silk pillows. The room was lit by many flickering candles and lamps. The air was heavy with the fragrance of roses from at least a half-dozen wilting bouquets and their dropping petals and from open scent bottles on a marble-topped dressing table with gilded lyre legs. The surface was strewn with Dresden jars and bottles and porcelain boxes of lotions, creams, and medicinal salts. There were many brass candlesticks on the marble mantel, Oriental temple jars, snuff boxes, and framed pressed flowers set on little brass easels. The window and window seat, done in mauve velvet, overlooked the street and, near it, was a lace-covered round table piled and littered with bolts of fabric, unreeling spools of bric-a-brac and ribbon, scissors, pins, patterns and sketches of gowns, fans, hats, and shoes.

"She's to have 'at homes' and morning dresses, at least two, riding suits, a dozen dinner gowns, as many ball gowns, tea dresses, petticoats of Chantilly lace, embroidered chemises of cotton, bed gowns and chamber robes, wraps of the finest . . ."

"Yes, yes," Ann Overton interrupted Jesse with a jaded look. "I know precisely how to attire your new friend," she said and smiled archly. "I've done the job before for your paramours. This one seems rather young. That's no business of mine, of course but . . . who is she?"

"It's no business of yours, Ann," Jesse said amiably, "but I couldn't tell you if I wished to because I'm not certain *who* she is, nor is she. Result of a mishap that befell her. I could be prince to her Cinderella, or knight to her royal sleeping beauty." Jesse shrugged happily. "I'll play either part. I've been spellbound by her breathtaking charm." He clipped and tasted one of the cigars Ann kept in supply for gentlemen and she leaned toward him with a light. "We met two days ago when I came to the aide of a damsel in distress—Lorena. I only know she's unlike anyone I've met before. Different."

"Oh, of course she is," Ann answered with bland cynicism. "Love at first sight and all that. May I offer you a sherry, Colonel, while you observe Miss Reed's fitting? I'll take her measurements first thing."

"I know her measurements."

"Of course you do, as do I, for different reasons of course. We'll confirm our sightings with the tape."

"She must also have traveling suits, at least one a tartan plaid."

"Of course she must," Ann mildly agreed.

"And the *bashlyk*."

"Ah, yes. Now I begin to understand. She is different, for you, this girl."

"Of course she is," mimicked Jesse with a large, forced yawn as, Lorena, a pink wrapper covering her chemise, emerged from the changing room.

"Tea, Miss Reed? But first, see this," Ann said as, with a lazy flourish she took a garment from a large tapestry bag and displayed it in full at Lorena's feet. The white velvet cape with deep fringe and scarlet satin trim spread out for yards. "A great rarity carried from the court of the Russias by a ship's captain who sold it to Jesse at a magnificent profit. I've held it here for safekeeping at the request of the Colonel until he chose the woman on whom to bestow such a rarity. Now we're fortunate. See how it drapes and falls from your shoulders perfectly with no need of alternation."

Jesse watched with pleasure as Lorena pranced and twirled before the looking glass then hurled herself into his arms.

"Rather better than a glass slipper," Ann nodded. "I shall design a gown to do it, and you, justice, Lorena. The dress will be shot-silk *crêpe de Chine*, wine red, glorious with your coloring and the *bashlyk*."

Prancing again, Lorena asked her audience of two, "Should it have white boots or red?"

"Both," they both answered at once, to Lorena's amusement.

"I'll leave you ladies to your swatches and sketches, but only for an hour, mind," Jesse said. "We've one more stop to make today, Lorena, before I deliver you home to Doc's to get prepared and rested for tonight's event at the Longworths'. There's a ball tonight, Ann, a celebration of Lorena's birthday and of the fall of Richmond to the noble triumphant Army. We'll be toasting Lorena and General Grant well into the small hours of the morning."

"Ann, may I ask you a question?" Lorena began when Jesse left and she stood with her arms extended at shoulder height.

"He adores you," said Ann moving about with her measure and making notes on her cuff. "Is that the answer you were looking for?"

"That's lovely, but I was going to inquire about Mrs. Wharton." Lorena made a half-turn.

"She adores him. Beyond that she's something of an enigma. Very cool, very private, never engages in gossip. She lived abroad for years with her husband, in England. She returned alone soon after the war began and has selectively cultivated as friends only a few in New York, Jesse and Molly Longworth among them. I don't know what she's up to."

"Up to?" Lorena inquired.

"A poor choice of words. She's merely a mite guarded. Jesse knows her better than anyone. Ask him." Ann yawned broadly and went down on her knees to measure the distance between Lorena's waist and ankles.

"I did ask. He's closemouthed about her in a gentlemanly way. Did he adore her, also?"

"Turn," commanded Ann. "Jesse has always been capable of great, though short-lived tenderness and, naturally, women respond to him. He's handsome, charming, a man of the world and he has a quick energy, an appealing, boyish restlessness about him. He tires of a thing, once he's mastered it, and moves on to other challenges. You and he have just met, he informed me. You've plenty of time yet." Ann said this last with a faint smirk and a sideways glance up at Lorena. "Sorry," Ann offered. "That was cruel of me, but I'm a poor loser."

"You, too?" asked Lorena in barely more than a whisper.

"Oh, long ago. Long ago. He also told me you were ah, *different* was the word he used, so stop looking so troubled."

"I can't," answered Lorena. "I was already concerned that it has all been so easy, too easy, for us, more of a fairy tale than the true romance of a real couple falling in love. Now, with what you've just told me about Jesse, I know my concerns are not unfounded."

"Only time will tell," purred Ann with her crooked smile. "Oh please do put down your arms this instant. It's making me tired merely looking at you."

CHAPTER 9

"How remarkable it must be, Lorena, to have forgotten every moment of your life and be able to begin again," said Rachel Longworth. "I almost envy you, I'm afraid, though envy is a deadly sin." A few hours after her visit to the dressmaker, Lorena, wearing an evening dress of flowing red silk, was again standing stiffly in front of a cheval mirror. This time she was back in her room at the Longworth mansion while Rachel, who was perched on a high stool, tucked and pinned a collar of a complimentary shade of magenta lace along the *décolletage*.

"Envy me?" questioned Lorena. "But I want nothing more than to have all the memories of my former life returned to me. In a way, I'm thoroughly lost and may be forever, despite finding Jesse. And all of you, of course," she quickly added. "I have an unease deep in my heart and soul and a loneliness though I don't even know what for. Is that what you're 'almost envying,' Rachel? Why on earth?"

"Because you may start all over again, fresh, new, unburdened by past blunders and regrets, by hapless, hopeless loves or by your family and the stale, dull hopes they have for you. You, Lorena, may be whatever you choose to be. That's what I wish for. You are newly created, perfect, and complete as the Greek goddess, Athena when she sprang from her father's mind, empowered with wisdom and beauty. *That* is the freedom you have. I long for it."

"Rachel! Hopeless love? Serious blunders? How many

could there have been in your young life?" Lorena took Rachel's hands in both of her own.

"There's been only one hopeless love, but it was my true one. And I've more than a few dumb blunders to my credit," the girl answered with a wistful smile. "It's just too late for me to be anything but mildly happy and that only when I forget myself for a time, in good works." Lorena peered at the girl in sympathetic disbelief.

"Which good works in particular help you to lose yourself, little Rachel?" she asked.

"Comforting half-orphaned, fearful children at the foundling home, reading to them letters of advice from their concerned fathers on far-flung battle fields. I escort groups of children to rallies where we are all fortified and uplifted by patriotic speeches and music. We hold fairs and musicales to raise money for the soldiers and their babes at home. Of course, Horton and I knit, pull lint, and roll bandages at Soldiers' Aid Society meetings."

"Rachel, you're as free as I am, perhaps even more so. I have no past, though it may return to haunt me one day. You are the keeper of your history and mistress of your future. Whatever your ambition, there is nothing but yourself to keep you from fulfilling it."

"But there's Mother to be taken into account." Rachel circled about Lorena, her small, blueberry-colored eyes probing every fold and drape of her own as yet unworn red evening dress. "It's a fine fit on you, Lorena. Not as perfect as your own Ann Overton creations will be when they're made, but just lovely. On you," Rachel commented.

"It would be on you, also. Your mother seems to have burdened you with all sorts of lovely things. Do go on about her, Rachel," Lorena said.

"Mother has found me yet another suitor, the fourth or fifth since my eighteenth birthday. I no sooner reject one than she produces another bore."

"Oh, pshaw!" Horton interrupted. The nurse was hidden in the big wing chair facing the window, knitting and watching the flow of pedestrians and horse traffic on the avenue. "Doc Ben has promised you'll never be forced to wed no matter how many eligible men Mrs. Longworth recruits. And, to boot, you have your own independent fortune, Rachel."

"Which I may not control *until* I am wed so there will be a man to advise me in financial and property matters. The terms of grandfather's will are clear and another restraint upon my freedom."

"Oh, this is so *boring*," complained Robert Longworth who half reclined upon a chaise alternately watching the dress fitting, paring his fingernails, sipping from a glass of sherry wine and tossing tidbits from a bowl to the impatient spaniels. He and Lorena had exchanged greetings with veiled acknowledgment of their earlier encounter in the concealed basement room at Jesse's. "You may not control your fortune, Rachel, until you've attained the ripe old age of thirty, eight years hence, or have a child—whichever comes first. The matter of marriage is not specifically mentioned in Grandfather Opdyke's will."

"Oh, you are so wicked, Rob. Just a gadfly, a trouble-maker," Rachel affectionately complained to her brother. "Are you saying I may just go on to reproduce—society and decency disregarded?"

"You pride yourself, sister, on your unconventional opinions. Women's rights and free thought."

"Look at this," said Rachel taking a much-folded sheet of paper from her apron pocket. "This may be my solution."

"A broadside from a Shaker Village?" Rob scoffed, smoothing the page. "If you go off to live a simple backwater life in a closed society, what need would you ever have of your inheritance? More important, what will become of me without you, Sister?"

"Become a member with me," Rachel answered. "Read what is offered. Perhaps, Lorena, the simple life will appeal to you also." Rob cleared his throat and began.

" 'A Celibate, Religious Community,' " he read with stentorian formality. "They've already lost me, Rachel, I'm afraid."

"Just read on, clown," Rachel insisted.

" 'Basic Principles of the Shaker Order—Virgin Purity. Peace. Justice. Love.' " It goes on to seriously ask members to live celibate, and to be non-resistant pacifists, temperate in all things, and to share all their goods and wealth with the community. Attend to this: 'One must be noble, selfless, and very good to become a Shaker.' That certainly does not describe me, Sister."

"Not yet, but you could change. The group also espouses 'equity of the sexes, equality in labor and property.' That eliminates rich and poor. All have justice, freedom of speech, and will be treated with kindness. True Democracy!"

"Be calm and quiet, Sister, while I read on, lest you swallow the dressmaker's pin you're holding at the ready in your lips." Rob got up and went to stand at the window assuming the exaggerated stance of an orator, one foot forward, head high and Lorena marveled at how well the secret agent played the slightly ludicrous and self-absorbed gent about town.

" 'Golden Rule! Life of the Spirit! Love Thy Neighbor!' Oh, right," said Robert in a skeptical aside. " 'Purity in thought and speech . . . simplicity in dress.' Perfect for you, Rachel, but my wardrobe would not do. Oh, and hear this. The broadside also deals with practical issues: 'Beautiful, comfortable community homes. Daily manual labor for all according to strength and ability . . . opportunity for intellectual and artistic development.' " Rob sat on the window seat continuing to read in a more interested, moderated tone of voice. " 'Sanitation, Health, Longevity.' And this of particular significance to me, 'Freedom from debt, worry, and competition.' " He paused to look at his audience of three, his sister, rapt, Lorena, inquisitive, and Horton as usual, the doubter. She turned her chair to face the group.

"They shan't last, these Shakers," said the nurse, knitting rapidly, a sock taking shape beneath her flying fingers to complete her fifth pair of the day to be sent to Union soldiers.

"Shakers have thrived in America since 1776. They recruit very effectively. There are many communities now in many states," Rachel argued. "Women and men are *equal*. They call each other Sister and Brother."

"So do we, Rachel," Robert teased.

"Won't last," repeated Horton. "I've read of their founder, Mother Ann Lee, and her 'Shaking Quaker' dancing and singing to disrupt proceedings in churches of Manchester in England where she was born. It seems that she was frequently jailed for disturbing the peace, and that during one of her jail stays, she had a vision telling her that the Shakers must go to America. She and seven others did. They were blamed, because of their peculiar behavior, for nearly getting their ship sunk in a storm. Then they were given credit for saving the ship by bringing down divine intervention. They disembarked to preach pacifism here in New York on the very eve of the Revolution and got in trouble again."

Rachel said, "I think Shaker ways and revelations might help jog Lorena's memory. Through exuberant dance, people go into hypnotic trances, and also there's channeling—direct revelation from other worlds."

"Oh Rachel, really!" sniffed Horton. "These people have been known to rock buildings and awaken whole neighborhoods. They dance, twist, tremble, shake of course, and gyrate themselves into trances and . . ."

"Sounds great fun, actually, Horty," Rob offered.

". . . And just happen to rouse a few souls from the beyond, they claim." Horton, in mid-speech and high dudgeon, would not be interrupted. "Now we have commonplace 'parlor spiritualism' in some of the best homes, table rapping and the like, thanks in good measure to Shakers. They are sincere believers, I suppose, but now there are field tricksters everywhere, exploiting the weak and lonely. Is that what you suggest for Lorena, Rachel?"

"Dancing would be fine, but as for all the other, I think I'm not suited," Lorena commented and flushed thinking of her un-celibate time in Jesse's arms and unwilling to renounce that particular pleasure in the future.

"I'll call you 'Sister' more often, Rachel," said Rob. "Be content with that. Sorry, but I could not possibly join the Shakers, with or without you. Celibacy and wardrobe aside, I am no pacifist. Sometimes a man must fight for his beliefs." Rob's brown raisin eyes glinted with fervor. "I wished to fight for the Union, to go into glorious battle against the Rebellion with my eyes flashing and my sword upraised. My mother forbade it."

"You were but fifteen and small for your age when the fighting broke out," Horton chided.

"Yes and when I was seventeen and grown somewhat taller, Father bought a substitute to go to war in my stead. I could have run away and joined up, but here I am." His expression was sheepish and downcast. "That was during the riots of '63. Do you remember hearing about that, Lorena? No matter where you were, you'd have heard about the New York City draft riots of that summer."

"Oh, it was a truly calamitous time!" Horton said. "I have been witness to many events, seen many things in my day but even I was actually in a state when I looked from my boardinghouse window onto Lexington Avenue and saw a huge mob of men, women and even children rushing by, all of fiendish appearance, shouting, waving clubs, and throwing stones."

"Riots?" Lorena frowned, unsuccessfully probing her mind for a clue. "When? Why here in New York? I do *not* recall the event," she said, irritated with herself. She had assumed Rachel's place on the tall stool. Rachel had gone to sit beside her brother. When she took hold of Robert's hand, Lorena felt a twinge of heart and a pang of loss. Had she a brother somewhere, she asked herself, who now mourned her loss? Thinking of Jesse, she wasn't sure she wanted to know. In a way, Rachel was right. With no past, there could be only the future.

"Union ranks were thinned, by 1863, by death and desertion. Volunteers alone could no longer, as in the past, be counted upon to man the guns," Robert explained to Lorena.

"Abe Lincoln proposed a Draft Law, the Federal Enrollment Act, which was passed by the Congress, calling up all northern men to fight. Every man between twenty and thirty-five years of age was supposed to go for a soldier. Those unmarried, between thirty-five and forty-five were also to see battle. Many a man who could pay, such as I—Father paid really—was exempted. That was one of the causes of the riots."

"There were still volunteers of all ages and incomes in '63, but not enough," Rachel amended. "The draft lottery most affected poor laborers, many of them immigrants—factory workers, railroad men, shipyard employees, machinists, ironworkers, German street sweepers, and Irish ditchdiggers, hard working men mostly, with families to feed."

"By eight o'clock of the July morning of the first draft lottery drawing," Horton took up the story, "the workers, who feared freed slaves would come here to take their jobs, were streaming in a mob along Eighth and Ninth avenues, closing shops, factories and construction sites and collecting more of their ilk to join them. Many carried aloft crudely lettered 'NO DRAFT' placards."

Horton, Rachel, and Robert had stopped what they had been doing to relate the details of a shared, dreadful experience. They seemed to be vying, as if each needed to outdo the others in offering details. Horton's narrow horse-face paled and the twins both flushed with high color as memories flooded their hearts and minds. Lorena and even the spaniels were motionless, so compelling were the events described in voices freighted with emotion.

"It went on for five days," said Rachel, wringing her hands. "The New York militias were on the battlefield at Gettysburg fighting for the Union. There were not enough police officers to disperse the mob. On the first day of the riot, in the early morning, when I heard loud cheers from the street, I supposed it must be news of some great victory. In wondrous excitement, I hurried downstairs to get particulars, but soon found that the shouts came from the rioters. The summer heat was intense, which didn't help. The beer-besotted rowdies burned draft offices, the black children's orphanage, and the *Tribune* offices. By dusk, fires burst forth everywhere, and by dark it seemed the whole city was ablaze. I counted from our own roof eight fires in close proximity."

"Sister and I, dressed as servants, slipped into the streets," Robert related.

"Rob took notes of all we saw," Rachel nodded.

"So foolhardy, you two," snapped Horton. "Endangering yourselves like that." Then she added, as if not to be outdone in the telling, "Even the tracks of the Third Avenue Rail Line were ripped up."

"We shouted with the best of them, hey Rachel?" said Rob. "Particularly when anyone took notice of us. Needless to say, we were unable to impede any of the violence. Uniformed military officers on leave in the city, a colonel among them, were shot down in the street, black people and white were hung from lampposts, police officers were beaten up and killed, stations ransacked. Hearing the guns firing and shouts of those hurt gave me a slight inkling of the terrors of war." Robert held his head in hands.

"Those were dark and wicked days in New York." Rachel sighed deeply. "Our New York militia soldiers were rushed back here after the battle ended, and then the riot came to a quick end. There were a thousand killed or injured by then."

"I've never seen the like I don't suppose."

"I hope you never will, Lorena," Horton said closing that subject. Ever practical, the nurse asked, "Will you be able to maneuver in that outfit?"

"I've a question," said Lorena as she slid off the stool and began moving gracefully about the room not once tripping on the train of her gown. "If the riot was two years ago as you say, it must have occurred in '61. July of 1863 has yet to come. Why are you all looking at me as if I were daft, which I am, of course, in a way but . . . ?"

"Doc will go into that with you, the matter of your daftness," Rachel replied a bit sharply. "Close your eyes, Rob," she told her brother, "while I take this dress from Lorena. The ball is but a few hours off. I must get the alterations stitched, and the patient must have some rest." Rob covered his eyes with his soft hands and, to gratify Horton's unflattering misgiving about him, stole a glance through parted fingers. He saw only a camisole and pretty petticoats, no revelation to a young man with a twin sister.

"Robert, you rascal! Turn away at once!" Horton hissed. "Why did you not simply go off and join the army, young man, as other boys did?" she asked. His expression was remorseful.

"I'm spineless," he said. His sister went to his side and took his hand. "I lack the courage of my convictions."

"Blather," said Rachel. Horton appeared momentarily to pity him.

"Buck up, boy," the woman said, her equine features firmed again with indignation. "I cannot abide self-indulgent vacillators so do not go on in this self-castigating manner."

"Do not speak so of yourself, Rob!" exclaimed Lorena. "I know you to be a noble and courageous defender of your cause. Know it in my heart . . . of course," she added, relieved that his expression had not changed an iota even though she had almost given him away.

"Thanks for the avowal of confidence in me, Lorena," Rob shrugged. "Ah, here's father now. Father, Rachel's been telling us about Shakers. Seems they have a serious interest in health, longevity, and sanitation."

"And in dancing until the rafters shake, my boy! Just my cup of tea!" roared Doc. "Richmond's fallen, in our hands and burning yet again. Our ball tonight will celebrate that victory *and* Lorena's birth anniversary." He began to hum a waltz under his breath at first, then louder and louder before he tugged the reluctant Rachel into the role of partner.

"They do dance divinely together," Robert said without the least hint of sarcasm. Rachel, her head held high, was darkly aglow, Lorena decided. Robert then bowed before her.

"I don't think I know how to dance, not this way," she worried.

"Ladies are led by their partners. Trust me," he replied, and she was soon whirling in Robert's arms to the sound of the doctor's offbeat and off-pitch humming of *Ring, Ring the Banjo.* Partners were exchanged. Robert danced with Rachel and Doc took up the repeated chorus of hurrahs in *Marching Through Georgia.* "New song!" he huffed, "written by my friend Henry Clay Walk in praise of General Sherman's March to the Sea! Through Georgia. Hurrah!" he bellowed jubilantly over and over as the others, even Horton on her own, turned careful circles in place and laughed. Lorena had never before heard the nurse snort and snicker, and she found the sound not unlike the whinny of a horse.

So caught up were all the dancers in the dance that none noticed Jesse step into the room and look on the comic scene at first with amused surprise, then fixedly at Lorena with something like a *voyeur*'s pleasure. Her profile was lovely, the curve of her throat, the tilt of her head, charming. She moved with grace and danced without a misstep, even to decidedly odd musical accompaniment in a makeshift, comic setting.

"Charming and pretty as you are, my dear," Ben roared at Lorena as if, in fact, there was music to compete with, "I doubt I'll get to claim a dance with you later, what with all the young officers Mrs. Longworth has invited. It's one of my Molly's particular contributions to the war effort," Ben shouted on, "keeping young fellows on leave entertained with social gatherings, to remind them of more congenial, ordinary days. This ball has been planned for weeks, my dear, weeks, and luckily has coincided with your birthday. And Richmond's demise." He hurrahed a few more times until he began to gulp for breath then retreated until he had backed himself onto the dressmaker's high stool which threatened to a collapse under his weighty bulk. He coughed and laughed, tears of hilarity streaming from his eyes, until his son and daughter began to harmonize in singing the old folk ballad, *Barbara Allen.* Horton then engaged Ben in a less strenuous slow dance until he drew her against him. She at one tried to break free of Doc who was obviously reluctant to relinquish his hold. When he did, the nurse snatched up her knitting, holding it before her like a small wall and set briskly to work.

"No young officer but me will have a turn with you this evening," Jesse said to Lorena, not entirely in jest, though his wondrous smile broke over her like a warm wave as he claimed her for a go around then and there. "I demand every dance, every quadrille and polka and mazurka and waltz, of course," he added and set his hand at her waist.

"I've never done any of those dances," she laughed playfully. "You'll just have to teach me as we go along!"

"Don't I always?" he asked forthrightly, the seemingly innocent, pleasant question a trigger to amazing feelings in Lorena. He of course knew exactly how evocative his query actually was. When he drew Lorena close, her eyes were at the level of his uniformed shoulder. She hid her blush against it and viewed in her mind's eye all of his anatomy, uncovered, as she had seen it, felt it, tasted and touched its sleek reality in the small hours of the morning. Her magical hazel eyes were meltingly soft when she raised them, seeking his stare which she found deep sea blue and seductively fierce. Her mouth, slightly open, was a pink and ivory promise to Jesse and she seemed, all at once, the source of a lovely light between them. The twins' voices ceased. The dancing ended. They all stood as they were. The significance of the moment, the incontrovertible awareness of love, was lost on no one. Lorena was feeling little need just then to discover her past. She wished with all her heart to get on with her future with Jesse.

"Doctor, will *you* tell me, please, which year this *is*?" she asked unexpectedly, turning to the large man, keeping hold of Jesse's hand in a gentle, beseeching caress.

"Ha! That's *my* question for disoriented patients." Ben slapped his knee. "Are you suggesting I'm a touch barmy, young lady? I'll admit to absentmindedness, yes, but I've got my Horton to help me keep my wits about me. Oh, but Lorena my dear, you're seriously posing that question," he said. The flirtatious, whimsical, singing clown vanished on the instant and professional Doctor Ben Longworth reappeared with his usual temperate professional authority and kind concern.

"The is the momentous year of 1865, Lorena. It is that which will see the end of the War of Rebellion and the birth of the reconciliation and forgiveness in our United States, which Mr. Lincoln so wishes for and will implement. You, Lorena, have lost the two years just passed. Amnesia has not taken your *joie de vivre* or your vibrant style, my dear. You are generally knowledgeable of the workings of the world. You seem to have no means, perhaps no wish, to recall those years. Quite the opposite. You're avoiding links in your thoughts—home, family, even what year it is—which may remind you of whatever it is you'd rather, or need to, forget."

"Spineless of me." She echoed the words, used earlier by Robert, with veiled self-doubt.

"That's a description that will *never* portray you," insisted Jesse vehemently. "You can't control your thoughts totally no matter how brave, strong-willed or determined you are. Be easy with yourself, Lorena."

"Jesse is correct," Doc interjected. "We are not always masters of our secret selves. Sometimes precisely the reverse is true."

"Doc Ben is a specialist when it comes to the workings of the mind."

"Now Jess, I'm more a therapeutic buff than a specialist," Ben rumbled modestly. "That does not mean I use magnetism and hypnotism, both of which I hold in low esteem. Any physician working with such methods damages his scientific career and medical practice. But I am fascinated by the relationship between thought and action, force and weakness, what is being called the 'field of consciousness.'"

"Ben is applying all his knowledge to your case. I'm helping, too, I hope, in my own way, of course." Lorena and Jesse exchanged a private look. His smile was warm, encompassing, and wonderfully possessive, almost a touch wicked. She smiled back at him with matching mischief in her eyes.

"I thank you both," Lorena answered. "I cannot promise that my patience will hold under the medical practice of slow self discovery. One day, before long, I may have to ask you to tell me all you know, everything I told you, Jesse, of my past. Will you?"

"If Ben would agree, or at the least does not object."

"My brilliant, old friend, Dr. André Talbot, who will be joining us this evening, is a proponent of the mind-altering method of direct suggestion to a patient in the waking state, as opposed to the time cure or even hypnosis. That's not appropriate for everyone, bear in mind. Talbot's technique is termed 'psychotherapeutics.' It might be useful for you to consult with him. You have a good head on your shoulders, despite the bump it took. In the meantime, Lorena, follow your instincts. They will not mislead you. Take pleasure in every moment, and what will be, will be."

"I absolutely, positively agree, Doctor, with all you say, especially about instincts," she told Ben though she was looking directly at Jesse.

CHAPTER 10

In a guest room turret of the Longworth mansion, the rays of a warm, spring dawn slanted down through a lead-filigreed skylight, waking Jesse from a nightmare of bursting cannon shells. Sensing movement very close by, he flexed upright to a sitting position, his hand flashing under a pillow to his Colt revolver. Then, the lethal tension changed to longing at a view of Lorena languidly gliding toward him. Sunlight, through her sheer wrapper, outlined each beautiful curve of her slender form.

She pursed her lips, passed her tongue across them, raised her hand and blew him a kiss. And then she smiled, suggesting considerably more than the ingenuous innocence she had offered only days before. She pressed a palm firmly against his chest. He understood. He lay back—still.

Her flaxen hair, with its scent of lavender, the preferred fragrance at the Longworth mansion, cascaded down her back as she glided over his body. He kissed her, this time flicking his tongue. Then she was astride him, raised up on her knees; her round and firm, smooth and pink bottom teasingly in view in the cheval mirror opposite the bed. She eased down on to him rocking backward and sliding forward, while his hands gripped and probed and they moved perfectly together.

"Now, Lorena, now!" he sighed in a smoky whisper.

"Yes, Jesse, now!" she answered still moving with him without restraint.

And now, not for the first time, Lorena experienced his

power—not just a sigh or a tremble, nor a mere moan from her but an momentous paroxysm that, impossibly, seemed to last forever.

Later, curled to him tightly she whispered, "I feel like a goddess, Jesse, to bring you to such a state, strong as you were and then, quiet as a helpless—little boy, almost. And by the look of your soft eyes and that stifled yawn, a sleepy little boy.

"Sleep a while now, Jesse. Later there's much to do. This is Friday the 14th of April, the evening of Doc Ben's dinner to celebrate our victory and the surrender of General Lee at Appomattox and my birthday, or so he calculates."

"That's right, your birthday. All the more reason to celebrate again." He stifled another yawn and managed to ask, "Why are you going? Stay with me a while, birthday girl. In fact, stay forever." She kissed his lips and protested, "But, I must go now. Mrs. Montespan, no Madame Montespan, Mrs. Longworth's French cook, has promised to show me something of what she calls the "culinary arts.' She says, Doc Ben is a gourmet and that he always expects something called *haute cuisine*. I'm sure you know all about it and someday perhaps you'll be pleased that I do, too."

Jesse smiled and murmured, "Gourmet . . . *haute cuisine*, indeed. As for General Grant's triumph, like every Yankee soldier, I'll long remember and celebrate it, as I will your birthday."

Still lingering a moment, she smiled down at him then said, "Sweet dreams, Colonel," as she arose and silently left.

"The entree that the Doctor has chosen and which is the most important part of the dinner, at least, its the central part, is *Rôti de Veau à la Parisienne avec Fonds d'Artichauts à la Barigoule* and since I believe you do not speak French, as regrettably so few of your countrymen do, I will translate. You are to dine upon Parisian veal roast with stuffed artichoke hearts," said Madame Montespan.

"Madame, I mean to learn about cooking and to learn

French also. I might add that I don't suppose somehow that we served *haute cuisine* at home, wherever that is." Lorena sighed faintly.

"Mademoiselle, we here below stairs have, of course speculated a good deal about our doctor's charming patient. Servants cannot resist to gossip of the 'quality' they wait upon. There has been every suggestion from chambermaids to valets for your cure. 'Try giving her sugar loaf and morphine six times a day, oil of cinnamon and spirits of lavender, poultices at the back of the neck, startling you with another good bump on the head to get your brain back in place. Someone, the laundress I think, says you are like a somnambulist, a sleepwalking princess waiting for the right prince to revive her with a kiss." Lorena blushed, though refrained from explaining that she had been rather well kissed recently and repeatedly.

"Ah," said Madame with a canny smile, "you are most pink in the face. If the heat is too much for your delicate constitution, I suggest you get out of this kitchen at once. Otherwise, start to whisk the bowl of egg whites over there and keep at it until they stand high and are stiff as your crinoline. Then I will show you one of the most valuable tricks of my trade, *ma petite*, one that will serve you well someday I know. Oh and by the way, *petite*, here's my best advice to further your recovery. EAT."

"With aromas coming from your kitchen, Madame, that recommendation will be easy to follow and much preferable to another bump," Lorena laughed glancing about the cavernous kitchen built below the fashionable upper floors of the federal-style mansion.

"My staff has been made . . . how you say here . . . is made much depleted by the manpower demands of the War and also the new jobs to be filled on steamships, railroads, and telegraph stations, but especially in the ready-made clothes factories nearby. Make in a factory uniforms for soldiers, *bien sûr*, and dresses for shop girls *peut-être*, but not for ladies such as Miss Rachel who prefers them to *couture*. But of course, no one asks me what's right, except about cooking, of course. Come now, just bring your bowl and keep at it, to meet my staff of helpers. They make up for their small number with their enthusiasm for the Union victory and by frequent surreptitious sips of rum. *That* they do not think I see, but nothing escapes the keen eye of the frugal manager, *nést-ce pas?*"

A skillful, bustling group of assistants filled the air with sounds of chopping, as others silently salted, rolled, and marinated, even as more provisions arrived in a steady stream from the quays and marketplaces surrounding the city. The meat, fish, and garden produce, all the seasonings and spices, the *bouquets garni*, were arranged on a long, freshly scrubbed-and-bleached table where Madame Montespan and each of her helpers had his or her own *mise en place*.

"Yes. It's a French term meaning everything to be prepared and the tools to prepare with, are arranged just right and ready to be plucked, pounded, roasted, rolled, scalded, *sautéed* or whatever. It is just like a fine portrait painter who has all his colors mixed and arranged on a palette before taking up the brush," Madame rhapsodized. But, then, observing Lorena's intense expression, the Frenchwoman took pity on her pupil and in an effort to be less grand and more friendly like the citizens of this new country she had chosen, she quipped, "All the French phrases in the world do not make for a hill of beans. Really, what matters to the culinary *artiste* and to the diners at the table are the aromas of the food, its colors, and its taste. Or as the English say, 'The proof of the pudding is in the eating'." Then, more to herself than to Lorena and not expecting an answer anyway, she murmured. "I wonder if they are black or white, those hills of beans?"

She was interrupted in her reverie by the boisterous arrival of Doc Ben. "*Bonjour, mon amie*, and a good morning to you, Lorena. You look lovely as usual and so early in the morning at that. Now, Madame, how does it all go? Do you have everything you need?" he inquired. It was a rhetorical question only, the answer apparent in his reactions as he sampled a rich, chocolate-brown sauce, daintily pressed one of many loaves of rising dough, and lowered his head down to the very rim of a simmering pot of marinade. With a mischievous grin he dipped a ladle into the rum barrel and gulped it down, shaking off its biting aftertaste.

"So, Lorena, what do you think of it all, this exuberant, precise preparation of a properly called 'French Dinner'?"

It was not a casual question directed to a simple girl. The Doctor knew his patient better than that. He had observed and chatted with her at length during her rapid if not yet complete convalescence and he knew her to be quick of mind and determined of spirit even if not very sophisticated by the standards of cultivated New York society.

"Doctor, it is too soon for me to declare a judgment. It's all so new, and strange. I don't think I have ever seen anything like this . . . except the preparation of a goose and of a suckling pig. Of all things to remember!" she laughed. "I'm particularly struck by the copious amounts of butter Madame Montespan is using."

"I must say, that *is* an interesting observation. It touches on the essence of French cookery—the necessity of fats—butter, oil—generally olive oil and lard. Garlic and salt and pepper play their large part but butter is the most important ingredient of the Madame's cuisine. There is the story told of a Frenchman who traveled widely in foreign countries. On his journeys he had trouble finding the butter that he required for his tasty style of dining. Ingeniously he solved this problem by getting milk from a cow, or a she-camel, or a ewe—which one came most readily to hand wherever he happened to find himself. He would fill three-quarters of a freshly washed wine bottle with the milk, cork it carefully and attach it to the neck of his horse. When his day's journey was ended he broke the bottle to find a piece of butter the size of his fist.

"A good story, don't you think, perhaps even true, but no matter, it makes the point. A Frenchman will not give up his butter, no matter what!

"I wish I could join you now, Lorena, to learn more from Madame Montespan. She is one of the many treasures we have received from France but my Surgery awaits me. Lorena? Those may be the stiffest egg whites I ever have seen," he teased. "*Au revoir* until this evening."

The cook, elated and more outgoing as a result of the doctor's visit, continued her lesson with enthusiasm. "You may put down your bowl and listen. Now I will explain the plot of our feast, Miss Lorena. It's more usually referred to, of course, as the *menu*. I've written it out on this slate so that everyone involved always knows what steps to take. Notice how the plan is contrived so that there is variety, contrast yet harmony of texture and color. Notice how the meal develops from liquid to solid, from cold to hot, and through all the flavors from savory to sweet."

"Pardon me, Madame, but what is this very first item, '*Soupe Geminy*?'"

"Ah! It's a very special favorite of mine. I have a personal history associated with this dish. In the spring of 1860, I was at the *Café Anglais* in Paris working as an assistant to that marvelous chef, Adolphe Duglere when he created this elegant sorrel soup and dedicated it to the Governor of the Banque de France, Comte de Geminy. Chef Duglere predicted his great new soup would spread to be enjoyed by *tout le monde*—the whole world. For all I know it has. In any case, I brought the recipe with me to New York. Besides sorrel leaves, which I cut into thin strips with my scissors, it is made of bits of bread, fried in butter, which I place in the bottom of the soup tureen that is then filled with a mixture of hot stock, egg yolks, cream and then garnished—sprinkled, that is— with fresh chervil, which Hamson the gardener grows in all seasons in our glass house. The chervil must be minced fine. You must watch this evening for the smiles appearing on the faces of the guests. Doctor Longworth, he knows a good thing, and that is why he is designated a '*gourmet*.'"

"How did he become so, I wonder?"

"Well, it so happens that there was talk about him in the kitchens of the *Café Anglais* when I was employed there once, twenty years after my apprenticeship. It was said that the young Doctor Longworth, a student of the great Doctor Dupuytren, Napoleon's personal physician, often dined at the café where he met and was smitten by Madame Chevreuil, the wife of the cafe's founder. As is frequently the case in my country, especially in Paris, an older woman takes a younger man as a *protégé* and maybe," Madame winked at Lorena, "even as a lover, especially if he is as handsome and as brilliant as I remember Doctor Longworth to have been. And still is, of course."

Lorena nodded, observing Madame mincing chervil rapidly and steadily as she talked.

"Besides, all French society was fascinated then by Americans. They still remembered the exciting American Ambassador, Benjamin Franklin. So Madame Chevreuil, in her passion for Doctor Longworth, did everything she could to please him; she even arranged for him to be tutored in his free moments by Duglere, who was the most celebrated chef in Paris in his time.

"But you'll learn more of the Doctor's tastes when you dine with him and his guests later this evening, that is, if you have something to dine on. A chef must concentrate in order to create, a difficult task at best in this madhouse of a kitchen. So, now I suggest that you make a copy of the menu for yourself. When you finish, I'll ask you to leave. Come back another time, any other when we're not so busy, to go on with your lessons. Who knows? Perhaps you too have the makings of a great cook?"

Lorena did as suggested. In a beautiful, trained script she copied the full menu, which listed even the wines. She did not write with chalk on slate, but with a stubby, very soft, black-as-coal pencil on a neatly trimmed piece of dead-white butcher's paper.

A là Francaise
(French Dinner)
Friday, April 14, 1865

Aperitif Amontillado (Spanish Sherry from the Palomino Grape)

Soupe Germiny (Sorrel Soup)

Veuve Cliquot 1860 (Champagne)

Rôti de Veau à la Parisienne avec Fonds d'Artichauts à la Barigoule (Parisian Veal Roast with Stuffed Artichoke Hearts)

Pommes de Terre Noisette (Potato Balls in Butter)

Clos Vougeot 1846 (Burgundy from Philippe, in Rue Montorgueil)

Profiteroles au Chocolat (Cream Puffs with Chocolate Sauce)

Café (Dark Roasted from Ethiopian Beans)

V.V.S.O.P. Grande Fine Champagne (Very, Very, Superior Old Pale, from the Cognac Region)

Menu in hand, Lorena left the kitchen after unsuccessfully attempting to offer a parting thanks of appreciation. But the cook was intensely concentrating on the preparation of a brown sauce. Lorena, who was herself absorbed in the menu, set off to find someone to tell her about the wines, of which she knew nothing. She was not unfamiliar with the taste of whiskey and beer. She preferred, she suddenly recalled, the bourbon of her native Carolina mountains. More and more frequently, sounds and smells and images appeared in her memory, like a toy jack-in-the-box opening in some corner of her brain. She stood without moving halfway up the steps, remembering a whiskey made in a still according to the old ways of Scotland. But not of barley, she could hear her grandfather grumble as he insisted she taste the pale liquid he brewed, that burned like fire in her mouth and throat. She had never had barley-made whiskey, which, the old man, a patriarch never to be contradicted, proclaimed far superior in taste. Barley, he had lamented, did not grow in their part of America. Lorena did have a sip of Irish whiskey at The Forrest Spring House where she and Jesse had gone the day they met. The liquor had seemed to instantly revive him, weak and pale

as he had been then. As for wine, the claret she had with Jesse
on the same occasion was her first experience of it. By now,
several days later, they had shared many firsts, she mused
with her tell-tale blush, and was relieved that this time there
was no one there to see it. However, she set off at once to find
Jesse and see if there was a little flexibility in his day's schedule. She'd enjoy his company right then, she decided, however
brief the meeting might be. She was disappointed on reaching the turret room to find him already gone and consoled
herself with thoughts of the gala evening ahead.

"Colonel, I've laid out your things. The invitation says
eight o'clock and black-tie except for officers on active duty.
You are going as an officer, I assume, and with your sword?"

"Yes and yes, Nicke. I am going as an officer, my full rank
and full-dress blues and I will wear my sword. In addition, set
out my derringer. The surrender has occurred but I don't think
there will be any peace. Southern sympathizers may not give
up without protest. I want you to stand by with yours eyes
open, even at this dinner among friends.

"Permit me to say, sir, my eyes are always open."

"Yes, I know the agent who never sleeps in the Intelligence
Service that is Ever Watchful," Jesse grinned pulling on his
close-fitting breeches. The Sergeant brushed down the regu-
lation senior officer's single-breasted frock coat and then ran
a soft chamois over the fourteen front buttons, the ten back
buttons, and the yellow shoulder boards of the cavalry and
their gold eagle insignia. The Colonel put on his own white
linen shirt and then buttoned on a high, white, lightly-
starched collar around which he dexterously tied a soft black
bow knot. He pulled up his suspenders, and slipped into a
vest. Around his waist he wrapped a sash trimmed with gold
embroidery. He waited for the sergeant to aid him with the
gleaming black boots of a horseman.

Sergeant Nicke, who had joined the army to escape life
on the farm, was, as a result of his enlistment, a skilled valet

having served at the start of the War in the retinue of Samuel Chase when Chase became Secretary of Treasury. Later, seeking adventure the young Corbett Nicke joined the cavalry. Very soon a representative of the War Department, acting on the recommendation of Secretary Chase, recruited him into a clandestine unit of the Army Intelligence Service. He became a spy, part of a team led by Jesse Sparhawk, who at the time was serving on the staff of the Union's finest cavalry general—Phil Sheridan. In keeping with Army tradition that ordained that soldiers and officers did not fraternize, the Colonel and the Sergeant maintained a certain formality, though either would give his life for the other, if circumstances required.

"The Report, Sergeant."

"Yes sir." The Sergeant read while the Colonel sat rocking in an armchair and puffing on a cigar.

United States of America
Washington, District of Columbia
War Department
Army of the Potomac
To: Staff Intelligence Officers, All Union Armies
From: Major General Anthony Akers, Chief of Intelligence
Subject: Rebel Assassins and Kidnappers
Classified: Top Secret
Date: April 11, 1865

The War Department has declared a state of extreme danger and proclaims that no relaxation be permitted in security measures attendant on the President of the United States or Members of his Cabinet.

Although the Army of Northern Virginia surrendered two days ago, numerous embittered, reactionary agents—Pro-slavery Confederate officers, and certain civilians of both the North and South—are known to be agitating great danger to the Union Government.

Specifically: a War Department secret agent has reported that a plan has been uncovered to seize President Lincoln on the night of January 18 from the Ford Theater in Washington. He was to be bound, gagged, and whisked south to Richmond.

The President, however, canceled his theater plans.

Specifically: A daring plot by the Confederate Secret Service operative Thomas Nelson Conrad to abduct the President on his way with his family to a cottage on the grounds of the Soldiers' Home was thwarted by the appearance of a Union cavalry guard.

Specifically: The smashing in New York City by Union Intelligence Agents of a Rebel ring of enemy officers—Robert Cobb Kennedy, John Headley, Robert Martin—that planned the notorious conflagration intended to burn down much of New York City. Now, it can be reported that at a secret trial, the traitorous band of arsonists confessed after interrogation that its motive was retaliation for General Philip Sheridan's scorched-earth policy in the Shenandoah Valley.

Before their executions, various of these criminals boasted that their fellows would continue the underground struggle to, as one dying traitor put it, "reverse the Yankee efforts to end slavery, encourage racial mixing, and destroy the Southern way of life."

Recipients of this Bulletin are ordered to maintain a maximum state of alert and to take all necessary measures to protect the President of the United States, its Citizens and Property.

Signed: Maj. Gen. Anthony Akers

"Sergeant, we should be at the President's side." Jesse's eyes had taken on their hard gunmetal glint.

"I, too, would wish to be with the President, sir, but be easy in your mind, Mr. Lincoln's personal bodyguards are highly competent men, John Parker in particular, and besides, half the United States Army is in Washington now, celebrating there as we are here. In due time we'll get appropriate recognition for our efforts in breaking what very well one day might be called the *Inept Arsonist Bunch of Hooligans*. Even they, if not for your work, Colonel, *could* have burned down the City, though."

"True, Nicke, but that should be 'our' work." Jesse tossed the end of his cigar into the fire and strode toward the door, his mission of the moment a strong need to find Lorena. "After you light the gas lamp you may go. Be on duty outside the dining room at eight."

CHAPTER 11

The novelty of the new gaslighting in the Longworth mansion enthralled Lorena. It was smokeless and much cleaner burning than oil lamps. It fell, soft as candlelight, on her face as, with concentrated inquisitiveness she studied her reflection in the full-length cheval glass. Her room was termed her *boudoir* rather than an infirmary, now that she was quite well, but for her memory, and even that was improving, releasing odd bits of remembrance with increasing regularity. The most recent had been a mind's-eye image of a grove of apple trees on a mountainside, changing with the seasons—flowering with sweet-smelling blossoms in the cool of spring, weighted with little green globes of fruit dripping with summer rain, and, toward fall, clusters of ripened apples of wonderful large size and high-red color. She felt the crunch of her bite, tasted the crisp sweetness, even felt the juice running down her chin. She had been in that orchard, pleased and proud of its success, and not alone, but who was there with her she could not summon up.

"Who are you?" she asked of the pretty girl gazing out of the mirror with large hazel eyes in a perfectly oval face. The girl looked back at her quizzically and offered as an answer a verse of poetry, which Lorena spoke aloud:

> *My mother says I must not pass*
> *Too near that glass;*
> *She is afraid that I will see*

> *A little witch that looks like me,*
> *With a red, red mouth to whisper low*
> *The very thing I should not know!*

There was more to the poem but though the rest of the rhyme did not come to her just then, she realized that 'the very thing' it spoke of had already been whispered in her ear, and demonstrated astonishingly, by Jesse Sparhawk. Where *was* he? she wondered in a bit of a pique, after she'd been yearning for him the whole day long? He *had* to come back soon. The dinner hour was fast approaching and she had never known him to arrive late for a good time or an important occasion during the whirlwind week they had just passed together.

They had attended gatherings of Jesse's friends and cohorts who spanned the social spectrum of New York's denizens. For an excursion into the rough nether regions of New York, to fit the scene and not to attract attention, as if that were possible, Lorena, at Jesse's suggestion, did not wear one of her stylish new day outfits but a ready-made, blue velveteen suit with glass buttons. With dangling paste earrings and long ringlets and wisps of golden curls about her face, she looked the perfect image of a shop or factory girl—a beautiful one—right down to her red laced boots. He also wore scruffy mufti.

Their first stop was a visit to the studio of an esteemed portraitist, Orlando Johnson, who, as his contribution to the effort, sketched possible suspects described to him by Jesse and his operatives. Johnson was a man of average height with a muscular, beefy build. His full, round face was almost cherubic beneath curling sandy hair and he had none of the arty quirks of appearance or manner Lorena had half expected. The two hit it off at once. Entranced, Orlando insisted on both painting her portrait and giving her drawing lessons, as soon as time permitted.

"Lorena will perhaps be able to draw what she cannot find in her thoughts to describe," Orlando speculated. "And I? I have never had a model with a smile so bright or hair so golden, or eyes so warm and shining. She is a beam of sunlight and I must capture her glow on canvas."

"Of the many suggestions offered to further my recuperation, yours, Mr. Johnson, is the one which, so far, I find most appealing," Lorena said, smiling. She clasped her hands beneath her chin like a happy child, caressed a paintbrush and inhaled the smells of turpentine and oils, which hung in the air. "I can hardly wait to begin," she added.

Glancing from one to the other of his companions, Jesse was loath, to his amazement, to leave his prized beauty for hours on end with a man so obviously taken with her. Jealousy was a new, ignoble sensation for him. He rebuked himself at once for doubting his friend or his lady and, before hurrying Lorena from the studio, accepted Orlando's offer, with her enthusiastic approval.

"Perhaps we will begin early next week!" Orlando called as the door closed after them.

The next destination was a French bistro close by, the Restaurant de Grand Vatel, a flight above Pine Street near the site of an old French church, the Eglise du St. Esprit. A heavy, aged woman with loose, wild gray hair sat in a rocking chair at the top of the stairs and glowered at them with hostility as they ascended, while two disgruntled parrots, one perched to either side of her, their feathered topknots standing in protest, screeched loudly in garbled, raucous French.

"*Tranquille! Tranquille!*" the old woman shrieked at the agitated birds, her rapid rocking chair thumping on the wooden floor. When her colorful, beady-eyed pets quieted, she demanded suspiciously, "What is your business here, *monsieur?* I do not know your face." The small establishment was crowded with young men, many in unusual military attire, accompanied by women dressed not unlike Lorena. The room, which had hummed pleasantly with chatter, laughter, and the clink of glasses, went silent. The diners all turned and stared, as hostile as the old woman to the newcomers until a man in the full colorful garb of a French Zouave officer stood and beckoned to Jesse with outspread arms and a bellowing laugh that did not at all match his pixyish face, with its small features and waxed moustache.

"*Mais oui*. You are lunching with Alain, *mademoiselle, monsieur*? You should have said so at once!" The old woman actually smiled, showing a few yellowed teeth, and then screeched again at the parrots when they broke into strident voice once more at the approach of the officer, *Capitain* Alain LeFevre.

Like most French speakers in the Union Army, he was from the Continent, not Canada, and had come to the United States as commander of a French military drill team, the Zouaves, fighting on the Union side. Known for their bravery and also for their uniforms of baggy red pants, white leggings, short jackets trimmed in red, and either a tasseled red fez or a turban, they were an interesting lot. Among LeFevre's men were also some French Canadians, none of whom, in the Frenchman's grand opinion, spoke any language decently. He deplored their mangled New World French, but this deficit made them excellent spies who could slip back and forth undetected into Montreal. There they monitored Confederate plotters and some of the hundreds of deserters from both Confederate and Union armies said to be on "French leave" north of the border.

After *sotto voce* business was done between Jesse and Alain, all the tables in the establishment were pushed together for a substantial peasant meal.

"This is my last *cassoulet* of the season. The weather now turns too warm for such hearty fare," grumbled the old parrot woman who served the meal herself. It was enjoyed with much wine and toasting. Candlelight lent a glow to long stemmed glasses that she never left empty, through much of the afternoon. The leave-taking of Lorena and Jesse was long and dramatic with much both-cheeks kissing in the French way.

"*Mademoiselle*, one thing more I must tell you," insisted Alain holding Lorena's hand as she inclined toward the exit. "This fine bistro, it is named for the great Vatel, chef to Louis

XIV. He was a man of such passion that upon the occasion when he was failed by his fishmonger—no fish were brought for a royal dinner—Vatel fell upon his carving sword and made an end of it then and there for the sake of honor. Unfortunately, he spoiled the pudding to boot. Ah, but my point is this: Jesse Sparhawk, like Vatel, is a man who would risk his life if need be, but never his honor."

"I don't doubt it, Captain," Lorena answered as she kissed the air beside his cheek and fled after Jesse who had made it to the door. Even after the long goodbye was done, two young women, enamored by the Colonel's dark, sleek good looks, his gallant manners, and especially by his whispering, flirtatious eyes, followed the departing couple halfway down the stairs. Lorena turned to face them with a honeyed, though not-sweet smile that sent the girls back to Vatel, their escorts, and the complaining parrots.

Lorena and Jesse passed through narrow, winding tenement-lined streets teeming with people rushing home or to the taverns and pubs at the end of a workday.

Lamplighters moved from post to post like fireflies in the neighborhood where gaslight had not yet arrived. There was a carnival feeling about that part of the city with cart men shouting at their nags and at each other, ragpickers moving slowly, bent under the mountainous burdens on their backs, cindermen with sooty faces leering at streetwalkers waiting in doorways for the evening's business to begin.

Jesse stepped into the shadow of an unoccupied stoop, drew Lorena to him and kissed her deeply. He watched her cheeks grow warm and rosy, felt the sweet acquiescent eagerness of her response. His mouth sought hers again and she moved to him. Her breath came faster and she moaned softly as his arm encircled her waist, then his hand found the rounded softness of her breasts before it began to glide down her back. The unbroken, voracious kiss went on and on, neither one able to break away as their bodies surged together. Lorena fingered the hard tensed muscled of Jesse's back when her arms encircled him beneath his jacket. His hands slid beneath her skirt and petticoat to rove the soft smooth skin of her hip and the firm full swell of her haunch. When he leaned back against the wall and lifted her to him, Lorena's long legs enfolded his hips, her hand caressing his face, her body ready and pliant when he went into her, the rigid swell of him surging and strong. Rippling shivers passed through her body to his and at once became a long, profound shared spasm of release.

"Something just . . . came over me," Jesse said, his voice low and smoky.

"Over me, too," Lorena answered in hushed delight, shaking back the yellow flame of her long hair that had become undone. They rearranged their clothes and, slightly dazed with pleasure and surprise, went on their way, holding hands and grinning at each other from time to time.

"Ho, Colonel! I hardly knew you, dressed as you are like a stevedore," a thick whiskey voice growled as Jesse and Lorena passed beneath a streetlight. "I'll dice you for the blond, aye?"

"This one's all mine, Q.," Jesse replied with a wolfish, possessive grin while the undercover police shadow looked Lorena up and down.

"Pardon, Miss Reed," Q. said quickly in his natural voice, pulling off his cap. "I didn't recognize you, neither, because of that dress, I suppose. Suits you, though."

"Doesn't it?" Jesse asked.

They stopped for a 'quick one,' with Q. at Flood's Bar. Though women were not welcome there, an exception would be made for Lorena if she and her escorts would sit in a dim curtained-off space at the rear of the pub.

"Keeping real busy, Colonel," Q. replied to a question from Jesse about the state of the city. "Now that it's all but sure, real sure, the Union'll soon win this war, there's more Confederate sympathizers and secret agents than ever, passing through New York on their way to safe haven in Canada. We keep our eyes on 'em. The ones we know, leastways. Oh and here's a spot of local good news. You know Bud and Lara at Forrest Spring

House at South Ferry. Someone, they don't have a clue who, has paid their debt *and* bought 'em that tavern to boot!"

"Do tell?" asked Jesse with mild interest.

"So they're out of that back alley shanty shack and looking at a fine future. How wonderful!" Lorena gushed, taking a sip of water. "They have a secret benefactor! Give them our best, please, Q., if you see them before we do. Oh, and Q.? Before we take our leave of you now, please tell me one thing more. Why on earth is this part of Flood's Bar called the Velvet Room?" Q. pounded a fist down on the table startling everyone, including a skinny cat sleeping beneath, which streaked away complaining.

"Hear that? Solid oak," said Q., "but it feels soft as velvet to the swillbelly bottlesuckers who come in here later, to finish the night and wait for morning. They get a bowl full of alky for a nickel, or all they can down straight from the bottle without taking a breath. Even if the swill's thinned with prune juice and hotted up with cayenne, it puts them under for what's left of the night and that's all they're lookin' for."

That evening, Jesse and Lorena attended the opera, joining the "twinnies" as their adoring mother called them. Robert was in extravagant, blue-velvet evening regalia. Rachel, his lovely but strange sister wore her usual dove gray but in deference to a formal event, it was gray silk. They were settled in their box at the Academy of Music when their guests arrived. The entering couple, fashionably tardy, caused a stir. All eyes and opera glasses were raised first to Jesse who was darkly handsome in civilian evening dress, showing white silk and linen against freshly tanned skin. Just before the lights dimmed and the curtain rose, attention shifted to Lorena, an elegant, perhaps even an aristocratic, beauty, it was being said, new to the city's social scene. A perceivable stir passed through the hall. "Who" it was asked, "was the bejeweled, glittering blond swathed in a light, spring white-fox wrap, which her admired, well-known escort swept from her shoulders, as if undraping a work of art?"

Over the next days, the Colonel and his lady drove in his open, lightweight, white brougham along the new Central Park Drive. Jesse handled Jupiter himself as they passed other carriages—landaus, Victorias, four-in-hands—on promenade, most commanded by coachmen in brass-buttoned jackets and curly-brimmed hats. Many of the larger vehicles were decorated with elaborate paintings of the Swiss Alps, of American Indians, or storm-tossed, full-rigged ships on raging seas.

"That one's big as a ship," Lorena jested, returning the nod of a lady who was practically falling out of her coach to stare with curiosity at the Colonel's companion.

"Do you mean Mrs. Caldwell or her carriage?" Jesse jested, eliciting a stare of mock disapproval from Lorena.

At other times she wore her new riding suit, and did well after a few lessons, sitting sidesaddle, her well-mannered mount prancing beside Jesse's high stepper on the park's bridle path.

They walked the Ladies' Mile together.

They coached out to Jesse's summerhouse at a place designated Ninety-sixth Street on the city's grid, but was just bucolic countryside.

They went to Long Island to watch the trotting matches.

They rejoiced with the rest of the city on the day Lee surrendered to Grant and tonight, three days later, they would attend Doc Ben's celebration dinner.

Lorena getting ready, wrinkled her nose at the 'little witch' in the glass and turned her full attention to her toilette. She vigorously brushed her golden hair, parted it in the middle and, with the expert help of the ladies' maid Ethel Hope, gathered it smoothly into a bun at the nape of her neck. In conformity with respectable Northern style, there was no hint of bangs, or of the working girl's curls and ringlets. The effect was one of simplicity, modesty, and calm.

Ethel set out the evening's attire. Lorena's own bespoke wardrobe had been delivered from the courtier that very day, and she was delighted with its tasteful restraint and the perfection in Ann Overton's every stitch. The elegance, Lorena was sure, surpassed anything she had worn before or perhaps had even seen.

There were six layers of clothing to put on, usual for fashionable women in New York City, with each layer serving a useful purpose and adding to the overall demure effect. Ethel handed Lorena a pair of crotchless drawers, for convenience, the maid said with a wink. A slow flush rose from Lorena's throat to her face.

"I do beg your pardon, Miss Reed. I did not mean to discomfit you. You and the Colonel have been obvious in your affection. Everyone in the city knows he is captivated by you, that he is your prince and that you are his . . . well, his Cinderella. There is much conjecture about whether the glass slipper will fit. But I have been most discreet about your . . . activities. Is that the right word?" Lorena nodded. "I have often overheard Mrs. Longworth and Mrs. Wharton discuss . . . well, you and the Colonel."

"Mrs. Wharton? What does *she* say?" Lorena asked with alert curiosity.

"That your 'friendship' with Colonel Sparhawk will not last. He visits with her every day, she said, to talk and enjoy a game of hearts, as he always has, and, though he is distant, she is convinced that he will come back to her. He could not possibly be satisfied with a child—you. So says Mrs. Wharton. And dear, scatty Mrs. L. who thinks the best of everyone, expresses her certainty that the Colonel is too honorable a man to lead you astray, as she puts it. Of course, I hold my face straight as I serve their tea and do not give anything away though once I was annoyed so with that Wharton, the secret of your betrothal nearly burst from my lips."

"Every day? He visits Mrs. Wharton every day?" Lorena, astounded, fixed on the precise portion of Ethel's account, which struck her most deeply.

"It means nothing. Anyone who has seen you and the Colonel together is aware of that. They share business ventures, your colonel and Wharty. We servants, who find her haughty, call her 'Wharty' for short, amongst ourselves. Today, her sister is arriving for a visit, I overheard her say to Mrs. Doc. They will both be at dinner this evening. I do hope they are not two of a kind, Maud Wharton and Estelle Partier."

"What more do you know about them, Ethel?" asked Lorena, who was dabbing mild essence of gardenia in strategic corners of her anatomy, a change from the ubiquitous scent of lavender that pervaded New York society social gatherings.

"Only backstairs gossip, Miss, but that's the best kind! One sister, Haughty Maud Wharty, wed an English viscount. The other married a Frenchman, a merchant banker. Neither marriage went well, rumor has it. The banker was ruined by bad investments in South America and the English nobleman preferred the company of his dogs to that of his wife."

"One sister is well off and the other not. Any offspring?"

"That I do not know, but now, Miss Lorena, we should finish dressing you before your officer arrives to escort you down."

"My escort and I talked, a few days ago, of being married after supper, but we've not found the time," Lorena mused. She stood and regarded herself in the glass as she stepped into the 'convenient' drawers of fine soft cambric, which stopped, just above her knees.

"Mrs. Overton has given you the new bold length," Ethel smiled. "Good. Most ladies still wear the garment reaching down at least to mid-calf." A chemise was slipped on next, a one-piece, unfitted float, soft as swan's down and rather like a nightgown, Lorena decided but without a high neck or long sleeves. "This of course is to keep your tender skin from being pinched by the corset, which you don next." Lorena held the corset in front of her while Ethel began to lace up the back.

It's not to be drawn too tight," the maid said pulling quite firmly, however. "The Doctor doesn't approve of strangling young ladies. He is right in tune with the suffragettes there, isn't he, Miss? Doc Ben's called a progressive man."

"Suffragettes?" The word and its meaning were vaguely familiar to Lorena. "Ah, suffragettes! I recall something about them," she said. "Votes for women and . . . bloomers! Amelia Bloomer gave lectures wearing full trousers, tight at the ankle, under a short skirt."

"Yes, Miss. I don't know if she was at that notorious Women's Meeting in Seneca some years back, but she's part of that agitating set of talkers and scribblers."

"Seneca. The poet?" Lorena wrinkled her brow, aware of an important thought teasing just at the tip of her mind. Try as she might she could not grasp it. Doc would have said it wasn't time yet for her to know whatever it was. Then Ethel's voice distracted her.

"Oh, I wouldn't know about poets. There's a town named that, up near the Finger Lakes. There's camps for Rebel war prisoners on the lakes, and a lot of lady reformers who think corsets silly."

"I think they think more than that, Ethel," Lorena answered, still preoccupied.

"The corset is meant to make a smooth line from chest to waist and hide any unsightly rolls of fat. But that is not your concern, Miss," added Ethel. "You are so slim you do not have to put on a corset early in the day and keep tightening it as evening approaches. Now Mrs. Longworth, older and fuller of figure, begins to complain of it after the midday meal, but she soldiers on."

"I don't find corsets uncomfortable and certainly not silly, but that may be because I have never worn one before this evening," Lorena answered, watching in the glass as Ethel threaded and tugged the laces behind her. "I do have reservations about the hoop cage that fashionable women must wear."

Ethel had selected a dome-shaped hoop that was just right, Lorena soon realized. Its flexible steel rings were malleable enough for easy maneuvering and it stopped ten inches from the ground, also a bit daring, Ethel explained, thinking but not saying—she was one who knew when to hold her tongue—that this lady herself was more than just a bit daring. And of course, the length had been chosen for Miss Reed by Ann Overton, who was never gainsaid in Molly Longworth's house.

Lorena capered before the mirror rocking from side to side and laughing as her cage swung like a bell, until Ethel dropped first one, then another petticoat over her head. They were white linenette, delicately embroidered with pink silk and bordered with fine, narrow bobbin lace edging.

"Those will keep the hoop ridges from showing through your silk evening dress," Ethel explained. "Look," she said with admiration when she had removed the tissue wrapping to reveal a gown, stunning even on the dressmaker's dummy, the color of the faintest yellow rose. Silk ribbon ruching encircled the skirt; beaded passementerie of a deeper pink covered the bodice. With delight, Lorena slipped on white silk stockings and pink kid slippers. There were kid gloves to match the slippers and a reticule of the same beading as the bodice. There was a ribbon to band her slender throat and fresh tiny rosebuds, grown in the glass house by Hamson, for her hair.

"Will you put on the gown now, Miss?" Ethel beamed just as a lively knock sounded at the bedroom door. Lorena slipped on a wrapper and Ethel admitted the visitor. The Colonel had arrived. He was standing straight as an arrow, yet lithe and relaxed and looking, Lorena thought, even for Jesse Sparhawk, uncommonly handsome, particularly when he flashed his smile. It revealed esteem and approval, and more than a hint of sensuous inclination even as they heard the sounds of expectant pleasure in the voices floating up into Lorena's window as the carriages of the first guests were beginning to arrive below.

CHAPTER 12

At the sight of Lorena, wasp-waisted in her laced-edged corset and adrift in petticoats, what had been Jesse's more or less constant inclination of late—to have her—became his immediate intent. And she knew it. She looked, perplexed, and from him to Ethel as a pink wave of color suffused her face.

"You may go now, Ethel. You're needed in the cloak room downstairs," said Jesse, sauntering into the room, his eyes never wavering from Lorena's face. Her eyes were animated, certainly with anticipation of the evening ahead but, even more he knew, by her need of him. The radiation of their shared passion as they moved toward each other was almost palpable.

I'll help Miss Reed with her gown, sir, the back hooks and eyelets and silk cord lacing before I . . ."

"No, *I'll* help Miss Reed with her gown, thanks," Jesse replied nonchalantly, shooing Ethel out the door and locking it behind her. He took a deep breath before he turned to face Lorena again.

"You're ready for more than dinner," he said. "Your eyes tell it all."

"Perhaps that's because your shoulders are . . . most admirably broad," she smiled, admiring the golden eagle insignia on the boards.

"Think so?" His voice had that hot smoky edge Lorena knew well by now.

"Yes. I do. Your waist is pleasingly narrow. That sash, the gold trim, the Federal blue of the coat, they suit you. I mean, the dark blue, the white collar, they intensify your eyes. Of course, you do as much credit to the uniform as it does to you."

"Think so?" he said again, when they met at the center of the room, stopping a few inches apart, their delighted eyes exchanging impatient signals.

"How much time is required to undo your fourteen buttons?" she asked touching each one as she counted them.

"It depends on circumstance and urgency. If you'd care to test your dexterousness, please do so."

"Oh, all right," she replied coquettishly, first placing her hands at his waist. When she stepped back smiling, she had relieved him of his sash and sword, unsheathed it and raised it before her. The brass hilt reflected the gaslight as she brought the flat of the plated blade for an instant to her lips, an astoundingly provocative act. One Jesse would never forget. "And *now* for the buttons," she said laughing softly, working nimbly.

"Ah, this is an urgent circumstance, indeed. That was record time," he rumbled as she helped him slip the frock coat from his shoulders. With care, she hung it on a chair back beside her gown, which waited on the dressmaker's form.

His arm went about her and he drew her upper body to his, holding her hard against him, once again feeling the warmth and malleable lush density of her breasts—the cleavage at least, pushed high, by the corset. He pressed his ardent mouth to hers almost harshly and sucked on her lower lip.

"The hoop," he whispered. "The hoop must go."

"Just the hoop?" she queried.

"It's all we've time to meddle with." He went down on one knee and reached beneath her layers of frothy petticoats to undo the cage at her waist before he lifted her out of it, leaving the belled hindrance to stand on its own as he kissed her again. This time they met full length, pressing thigh-to-thigh, and he kissed her silken, creamy shoulder. She inclined to him and threw her head back when he kissed her throat, and her hair came undone, tumbling to her waist. He stroked the curve of her belly and the smooth contours of her hips, set her

whole body shuddering when his fingers made precise use of
the convenient feature of the lace-trimmed drawers. "You are
a magnificent instrument to be played gloriously," he said.

"May I show you now how to play an instrument?" she
bantered, and her soft but sure hand moved over the swell of
his close-fitting breeches. Their need of each other became
so pressing, their impatience so acute, that this time he helped
her to undo his fastenings. Lorena never did bother to count
the precise number of buttons on the front of the Union Cavalry officers' uniform trousers.

"We didn't muss your collar tie at all," she noted as she
helped him on with his jacket with less alacrity than she had
relieved him of it. She did up the fourteen buttons and shone
away any smudge of her finger marks from each one with a
soft handkerchief. Then he helped her to rearrange her pretty
petticoats over the hoop cage. She brushed her golden hair
and he couldn't resist stroking it, lush and soft as satin velvet,
before she refashioned it into a coil at the nape of her neck.
In that moment of easy, almost domestic, intimacy he set his
lips to her shoulder and he gloried in the subtle aroma of her
new fragrance.

"Essence of gardenia," he said with approval as her graceful arms emerged from beneath the gown he held for her. At
that instant, Lorena brought to Jesse's mind the most divine
of swimmers, the goddess Aphrodite, rising perfect from the
sea. She smoothed the beaded bodice and settled the billow-
ing skirt at her slender waist.

"Jesse?" Lorena began brimming with love and confidence,
"do you recall some days ago, actually, that we contemplated
being married after supper?" He observed her, tenderly, draw
on a long kid glove and with care work her fingers into place.

"We've kept a hectic schedule," he laughed, bringing her
ungloved hand to his lips, "but when this evening's done, before the guests disperse, we'll be celebrating more than the
Union's win. There'll be a number of ministers and judges,

even the Mayor of New York, at the festivities, any one of whom would be flattered to do me the honor of making you my wife." He spoke with resounding certainty. At that sparkling moment in time, he had not a doubt in the world that Lorena was the only woman for him and that what he said was true beyond question or doubt. When their eyes met in the mirror, she spoke the words of the poem, which had come to her earlier:

> *My mother says I must not pass*
> *Too near that glass;*
> *She is afraid that I will see*
> *A little witch that looks like me,*
> *With a red, red mouth to whisper low*
> *The very thing I should not know!*

"I haven't been able to get those lines out of my mind," Lorena explained, "since they came into my head earlier. You've already whispered to me precisely what the poem says I should not know, haven't you, Jesse?"

"I've more than whispered to you, my little witch-wife," he said with a hard one-sided smile. "The poet you quote is Sarah Piatt, a Kentuckian. Some of her work disturbs the more 'genteel' readers of *Harper's Weekly.* I find her remarkable. There's more to that poem,

> *Alack for all your mother's care!*
> *A bird of the air,*
> *A wistful wind, or (I suppose*
> *Sent by some hapless boy) a rose,*
> *With breath too sweet, will whisper low*
> *The very thing you should not know!*

"I'm lucky, Lorena, that I'm your whisperer."

"It couldn't have been otherwise. It had to be you, Jesse. I could not have heard whispered nuances or even shouts of love from any another," she answered solemnly. With intense concentration, she drew on her second glove.

When they were both reassembled—he had done up the back hooks of her dress and she had given an unneeded polish to his gleaming boots—a smiling young lady of great beauty, took the arm of *her* Colonel—a dashing cavalry officer of a newly victorious army.

Ethel, among many others below, watched their descent and most, though not all, the onlookers (Mrs. Wharton and her sister Mrs. Partier the sole exceptions) thought them the most glowing and perfect of couples. No one seeing them at the start of that joyful, matchless evening could have begun to guess that before long, Jesse and Lorena would both be remembering, with longing and regret, their brief time of shared trust and certitude of love. It would have seemed beyond possibility to either Jesse or Lorena that he would soon be left with only a residue of cool, disenchanted anger, and she with a ferocious need for the settling of scores with him.

The dining room table, large enough to seat several dozen, was covered with a starched cloth, bright white in the light of silver candelabras at the table ends and of the gas-lamp chandelier suspended above the table from the top of the grand, spacious high-ceiled room. Placed beside each of the candelabras were copies of the dinner's menu, elegantly handwritten in ink on porcelain slates.

Each geometrically precise place setting consisted of a gold-edged Derby dinner plate on which had been laid a large napkin, folded square with a place card displayed on the top of each.

To the left of the plates were three sterling-silver forks of assorted sizes and, to the right, three knives, a soupspoon and a dessertspoon. There were four variously shaped glasses of Alsatian hand-blown crystal—sherry, champagne, burgundy, and cognac—placed at the right of each setting. In the exact center of the table was a low, long, elegant arrangement of

sunshine-yellow roses, an early-blooming American species
but not so early that the just-opening buds could have come
from any outdoor locale in April, but only from the Longworth's own glasshouse, tended by Hamson. "Named for a
New York banker, a Mr. Harison, spelled with one 'r' oddly.
This rose just showed up, maybe thirty years ago, on his Manhattan farm," the gardener had told Lorena on one of her
regular visits to his domain. "It's a hybrid of Rosa spinosis-
sima and somethin' else. Don't know what else, Miss,"
Hamson had concluded withdrawing into silence, leaving her
wondering about him, as she usually did, this reticent ar-
borist-of-few-words who was also the highly articulate spy
she had seen at Jesse's. For the celebratory feast, Hamson,
fulfilling duties as horticulturalist, had supplied a quantity of
Harison's Yellow roses to adorn the center of the sumptuous
table along its entire length.

    Jesse and Lorena entered the large, well-lit antechamber of
the dining room as the other ladies and gentlemen began filing in to dinner. The young couple had arrived too late for
pre-dinner drinks and hors d'oeuvres and Jesse regretted
missing a good swallow of Doc Ben's fine twenty-five-year-
old bourbon. However, the pair was just in time to avoid a
serious *faux pax*. As they disengaged their arms, a white-
gloved footman offered Jesse a silver tray, on which there was
just one remaining envelope where there had, minutes before,
been twelve. On the vellum card inside was inscribed the
name of the woman he was to escort into dinner, Caroline
Louise Tree, a celebrated star of the New York stage, he knew.
The exotic, dazzling creature returned his smile and captured
nearly his full attention, though from the corner of his eye
Jesse took the measure of a cavalry officer a few years his senior and of higher rank, who offered his arm to Lorena. She
graciously accepted this courtly proffer, smiling up cordially
at her own dinner escort as if no one else existed. It did not
escape her notice, however, that Caroline Louise Tree was
slender and beautiful.

    The actress flaunted flaming red hair, which hung down

her back in two thick, red braids. This diverged from the acceptable vogue of the day and was especially noticeable on a celebrity of such fame. But as a star who lit up a room as well as she did a stage, she was granted fashion license by the polite members of society, at least by those few who welcomed her into their homes, and Caroline Tree had often gazed across a dinner table at an important gentleman of stature by whom she had been pursued.

While watching the actress perform, many a man had fantasized slipping up behind her, entwining those braids and, by various methods of *legerdemain*, having his way with her. But no one took Miss Tree by surprise. When she did engage in one of her frequent, often blatant, sexual dalliances, she did so by choice, often with an eye to a man's wealth and her own future comfort.

Jesse would have preferred sitting beside Lorena but protocol precluded his escorting her, his special 'friend,' to the formal table. If he had to have another woman on his arm, he was pleased it was Caroline Tree, the companion selected for him by their hostess, Molly Longworth. This outgoing, famously clever beauty with a gift for the theater and a flare for flirtation was reputed to be a diverting conversationalist and Jesse intended to fully enjoy her company at dinner.

Miss Tree was also delighted with Molly's handiwork. The actress was enamored of Jesse Sparhawk's gallantry, good looks, and uniform, at first sight. Even before, she had been aware of his touted appreciation of feminine grace, charm, and wit, qualities he himself was known to possess in masculine measure. His reported lack of disdain for women of her less-than-respectable reputation made them, in Caroline's opinion, an ideal if supposedly impermanent pair. However, she had all evening, quite long enough for her to affect the longevity of their association. She'd entangled men with a mere glance. With this one, she had four or five courses and a glut of champagne abetting her efforts.

Guiding her through the pleasantly buzzing room to her to place at the table, Jesse appreciated the attention they—mostly

she—were receiving. He was not much pleased, though, to find
Mrs. Wharton seated immediately to his left or to be introduced
to her sister, placed opposite. Of course, there was not the
slightest suggestion of his true feelings in his manner toward either and after whispering a *bon mot* in Caroline's ear, which
made her laugh, he searched the room for Lorena.

Before taking her own escort's arm, she had hung back a
bit to ask Rachel about the ebullient and beautiful creature at
Jesse's side.

"There will be one gentleman too few at the table—
Brother is called away—as if my twinny had any *serious*
enterprise to be called away by, but for a new tailor or a new
tart." Lorena wished she could tell Rachel of Robert's bravery and service to the Union but she bit her tongue and
instead complimented Rachel's gown. It was sedate but elegant, a color close to the girl's habitual gray but with a lighter,
pearly glow in the gorgeously layered silk.

"Mother's matchmaking for me again. I did not wish to
cast a pall over her evening by ignoring her wishes totally.
I've dressed and deigned to attend, but as I say, Robert's gone,
making the table one man light. Consequently, I shall be able
to sit beside you, Lorena, and supply any tidbits of fact, or
even gossip," Rachel said, "which you might require to help
you make sense of this extravaganza of New York's upper
echelons here to recognize our victory and, I do hope, the
peace and, of course, your birthday."

"The actress is said to be woman of strong will, born to
money, then impoverished at a young age when her father
suddenly lost his fortune and passed over," Rachel whispered
to Lorena as soon as they were seated. "Caroline later acquired her own fortune acting on stages all through America
and Europe."

"Ah," Lorena nodded, darting a glance across the table and
to her right. To her unpleasant surprise, she discovered Jesse
bracketed by not one, but two, possibly predatory females to

whom he was dispensing his charm—Miss Tree and none other than Mrs. Wharton. Lorena at once turned her full attention to her own escort, noting with admiration his striking profile with its strong jaw and Roman nose.

"Sir, your epaulets announce you to be a Major and a cavalryman. If it's not forward of me, may I ask of your organization and war-time postings?"

"Major Aldrich Chapin, Seventh Cavalry, Army of Tennessee, at your service, ma'am. And it is not at all forward of you to ask. I take it as a sign of most admirable curiosity, a delight to find in someone so young and, if I might say so and not myself be considered forward, so very attractive. I fought under General William Tecumseh Sherman."

"Suh," Lorena began, surprising herself with the sudden emergence of a faint drawl, "you speak the General's name with pride, perhaps even awe. Is he such a great man?"

"Next to Grant himself, the greatest of this war. I rode with him, I am proud to say, north from Savannah through South Carolina, where we made the Rebels pay dearly for this dire war. When we burned Columbia to the ground, General Sherman said we were reaping the whirlwind."

"Yes, but what sort of *man* is he? I read a piece by James Gordon Bennett, printed in the *New York Herald,* who compared him to Julius Caesar. That is Mr. Bennett, is it not, sitting down near the end of the table?"

"Yes, and also I see Horace Greeley, fickle Greeley, as he is called, for his vacillation in support of Mr. Lincoln. Greeley gained influence as founder of the *New York Tribune*, one of the first penny daily newspapers. In addition to the daily *Tribune*, Greeley does a weekly edition that reaches a million readers throughout the states and our territories. The man writes capriciously, sometimes for pacifism and at other times bellicose with war fever. 'Sign anything, ratify anything, pay anything. There never was a good war or a bad peace' he once said in print, no less. The detestable man and his papers will use any ploy to outdo other publications with the up-to-the-minute war news. President Lincoln wrote to the man, after a critical editorial, 'in deference to an old friend, whose heart I have always supposed to be right, I intend no modification of my oft-expressed *personal* wish that all men everywhere could be free.' The president added that having Greeley's support would be 'as helpful as an army of one hundred thousand men.' Politics I say, and pure bosh!" exclaimed the major, adding, "Not that I mean to criticize Mr. Lincoln, for he is shrewd enough to know Greeley has immense influence on opinion in the United States and our Western Territories.

"As to your question, young lady, I know Bennett also and I must say that my Roman history is not that strong, so I will not comment on that journalist's appraisal of William T. Sherman, except to say that the general considers his so-called brutal march through South Carolina the greatest of his military feats. He has written, 'The simple fact that a man's home has been visited by the enemy makes a soldier in Lee's or Johnston's army very, very anxious to get home.' In my opinion," said the Major, "the Rebels became most familiar with the successful foraging tactics of the Federal 'bummers' living off the land. That is what our army came to be called in South Carolina."

"And in North Carolina?" Lorena asked, with a deep unease she herself could not fathom.

"North Carolina was one of the last States that passed the ordinance of secession, General Sherman reminded his officers, and he said, 'From the commencement of the war there has been in this State a strong Union party. It should not be assumed that the inhabitants are enemies of our government, and it is to be hoped that every effort will be made to prevent wanton destruction of property, or any unkind treatment of its citizens.' "

"And his appearance, sir. How would you describe that?" Lorena asked.

"General Sherman is certainly not imperious, Miss Reed. Indeed, he differs from most men by being plainer. He dresses plainly, talks plainly, fights plainly. As to his physical bearing, he is a slight, wiry man with wild and wiry red hair. He has pale, almost colorless eyes. One thinks of an eagle." Major Chapin, none too quietly, began to sing, ostensibly to Lorena, though others looked their way.

> *Our camp fires shone bright on the mountains*
> *That frowned on the river below*
> *When a rider came out of the darkness*
> *That hung over river and tree*
> *And shouted,*
> *"Boys, be up and be ready!*
> *For Sherman will march to the sea!"*

"Beg your pardons, folks," Chapin told the entire, now-silent, table. "It just came over me."

There were protests of, "No pardon required, Major," and, "Hear, hear!" And, "A toast to William Tecumseh." Emotional voices bounced across the table and echoed around the room until the lilting, rich, famed alto of Carolina Tree soared, singing the last verse of "When Sherman Marched Down to the Sea."

> *Oh, proud was our Army that morning*
> *That stood where the pine darkly towers,*
> *When Sherman said, "Boys you are weary,*
> *But today fair Savannah is ours.*
> *Then sang we a song for our Chieftain*
> *That echoed o'er river and lea*
> *And the stars in our banner shone brighter*
> *When Sherman marched down to the sea.*

After the cheering, clapping, toasts, and the general joyous uproar subsided and calm again descended over the Longworth dinner party, guests once again turned their attention to talk with their immediate neighbors.

"Under her father's will she was named ward of the Cavalry Commander Philip Sheridan," Rachel told Lorena, who regarded her friend with incomprehension." Caroline Tree, my dear!" said Rachel. "That is who I was telling you of before she broke into full-throated song. Jesse, by the way, later in the war served under Sheridan."

"Oh, I know that. Go on about her."

"Under her Uncle Phil's tutelage, Caroline developed into a superb horsewoman."

"Jesse admires that ability in a woman," interjected Lorena. "He's told me so when he was giving me instruction in it." Rachel nodded and hardly paused for breath before she went on relating the history of Miss Tree.

"In her teens, she entered into a most advantageous arranged marriage with a man educated at Phillips Exeter Academy, Dartmouth College, and Harvard Law School. Like Mr. Lincoln, he was a railroad lawyer, and like Abe he made money, but unlike Abe, Mr. Tree made a great deal of it. In any case, the marriage didn't last long. Want to know why?" Lorena now nodded almost wearily. She had never before heard Rachel talk so much, so long and with such animation. "Just after her return from the honeymoon, Caroline was forced to invite her spinster sister-in-law to live with her. She, the sister-in-law, was a woman of very rigid and high moral standards, more aptly, a snobbish prude, as a matter of fact. In the sensational divorce trial that dissolved the union, the evidence was provided by the sister-in-law that Caroline is . . ." Rachel looked about, leaned closer to Lorena and whispered, "*a nymphomaniac.*" Coincidentally, just then a momentary silence hung over the table—'angels passing' it was said of such silences—and this made it possible for the man to Rachel's left, her father's friend, Dr. Talbot, to hear her. The buzz of random table talk started again before he corrected her.

"That, Rachel, is a medical term more often used in error to describe a woman of promiscuous practice than one suffering a malady." Rachel, who rarely mentioned or even allowed herself to think of sensual matters, was mortified at being overheard.

"I've been told," Rachel spoke fast, in a barely audible voice, her eyes lowered, "that respectable women don't have certain urges. Well-brought-up young ladies must be shielded from anything which might stimulate them in that way or be subjected to surgical treatment to cure an overly-passionate nature."

"Nonsense!" Talbot responded in an indignant roar. "There are doctors who recommend such measures, but it's nonsense!" The doctor cleared his throat as if to begin a lecture on the subject. To Lorena, Rachel's interest in the Shaker life made a bit more sense and to relieve her repressed friend's painful discomfort of the moment, she formally introduced Dr. André Talbot of the Columbia College of Physicians and Surgeons, whom she had met on several occasions, to Major Chapin.

"Dr. Talbot is an authority in the new science of psychology. He has been considering my condition, Major," she added.

"My dear Miss Reed, I am saddened to hear that you have a condition. May I make so bold, as you've mentioned it yourself, as to inquire its nature?"

"It's nothing to do with decorum, sir," she answered making light of the last topic under discussion. "I am suffering from traumatic amnesia. I hardly remember who I am or what has happened in my life during the last few years. You see, I was struck down in an accident recently."

"I'm hardly a psychographic expert, Miss Reed," Dr. Talbot protested modestly. "Our science, Major, is still in its infancy although much good work is now taking place at the Harvard Medical School by a group of brilliant mind researchers. I am in correspondence with the young Dr. William James at Harvard. I am looking forward to a reply from him soon concerning Miss Reed's problem and the best way to treat it. As you know, doctors don't always agree, as in this case."

"Doc Ben says I am getting better and though I am most indebted to him, I do so hope that Dr. Talbot can convince him that his method—telling the patient all known facts directly—would be the best course."

"Miss Reed, I find it difficult to accept that such a charming, quick-witted woman as yourself could be troubled with a condition of the mind," said Major Chapin with warmth and concern. "I have witnessed what appeared to be a tragic instance of a troubled mind run wild, a mind belonging to a very prominent person. It is a situation I would not speak of if the event had not been observed by so many and widely reported."

"Please do go on, Major Chapin," Lorena said. "Sadly, I might gain some insight from the misfortunes of another."

"Yes, do," added the Doctor.

"I've had the honor, helped along by my uncle's strong association with Senator Sherman, the General's brother, to be assigned to the General's Staff, as you know Miss Reed," said the Major.

"Your uncle is?" asked Dr. Talbot.

"Secretary of War, Edmund Stanton, sir." Several other guests, on hearing that name, paused in their own chatter to listen as the Major went on. "Just last month, when General Grant ordered his generals and their aides from his armies north to City Point for a Council of War, I was included. We knew it to be an historic occasion, especially as General Grant had also invited the President and Mrs. Lincoln, reckoning the President would welcome a chance to escape the hubbub of Washington."

"You were speaking, Major, of a medical condition, I believe," Doctor Talbot interjected.

"Yes, I'm getting to that. Mrs. Lincoln and Mrs. Grant were seated prominently on a parade field to see a division of the Army of the James, under the command of General Ord, pass in review. The President rode with them. Mrs. Lincoln expressed great distress at seeing a slender woman, sitting tall and strong, on a large stallion, riding beside the President himself. 'I thought women were forbidden at the front,' said Mrs. Lincoln with fury. 'And why is she with *my* husband?' It was explained to her, though she seemed not to hear a word, that the striking horsewoman was actually riding beside her own husband, General Ord. The lady had been given special permission to be at the front, and had a singular privilege to accompany her husband. Mrs. Lincoln became livid, considering the woman's presence an affront to her position as First Lady."

"It is said there is no fury like a woman scorned or who feels herself to be, and that jealousy is a green-eyed monster," Lorena said pensively, once again glancing toward Jesse. He appeared to be enjoying himself thoroughly and his dinner companions were enthralled. Her attention turned to the Major again, who went on with his narration.

"Here's an odd coincidence. Mrs. Lincoln discovered that it had been my uncle, Mr. Stanton, whom she detests, who had petitioned on behalf of Mrs. Ord and that made her behavior even worse. When Mrs. Ord rode up to pay her respects to the President's wife, Mrs. Lincoln first screamed incoherently, then called the general's lady a 'slut' and a 'whore'." There were gasps and exclamations from listeners nearby.

"Oh, dear heaven!" exclaimed Rachel bringing her hand to her mouth. "How pathetic. How heartrending! What then?"

"Then Mrs. Lincoln swooned. She had to be carried away. It was very sad and troubling to all who witnessed the episode, I would think especially to the President, though he said not a word, not then or at any other time that I'm aware of."

"Major, on the basis of your account, which I do not doubt," said Dr. Talbot, "it would appear that Mrs. Lincoln is a very troubled woman, perhaps on her way to full-blown madness. I hope she gets swift treatment and fervently pray no further calamities, such as the recent death of her young son, Willie, beset her." Dr. Talbot looked about and decided it was time to dispel the solemn aura which Mrs. Lincoln's tragic tale had brought to the faces about him.

"Aha! And now, for pleasant matters! This is a festive event," the doctor smiled, inspecting the bowl of soup just set before him. "Young ladies, this soup is delicious. Yes," he said, sipping again as if to confirm a suspicion, "I believe it's sorrel soup."

"*Soupe Geminy*," Lorena informed him in a perfect imitation of Madame Montespan's accent. "And you must try the champagne, it's *Veuve Cliquot* eighteen-sixty."

"Is there anything you do not know, Lorena Reed?" asked Doc Ben, at the head of the table, with delighted admiration. "Is there anything she doesn't know, André?" he asked his colleague.

"Who she is. *That* is all." Both doctors fixed proud eyes on their patient as if somehow her accomplishments were all due to them. "*Veuve Cliquot* 1860? Who told you, Lorena?"

"Doctors, I cannot tell a lie. That information is written right there on the menu," she laughed. The attractive sound caught Jesse's attention. He winked and smiled and raised his glass to her. Her heart skipped. She smiled at him, too, telling herself she was being nearly as batty as Mrs. Lincoln, to have mistrusted Jesse Sparhawk for even so much as the twinkling of an eye.

CHAPTER 13

Mrs. Longworth presided at her end of the table, blond, pink-faced, and robust in a blue satin moiré gown that fell just slightly off her fleshy shoulders. She wore a snug choker of pearls about her full neck with more strands of varying lengths riding over her ample bosom, eventually to reach her waist. She was crowned with small, fruit-shaped golden pins and feathers.

As hostess, Molly was the last at that festive table to be served and when she raised a fork in one diamond-laden plump hand to delicately carry a morsel of the entrée to her lips, so then did the rest of the company begin. No matter how devotedly engaged in conversation the guests had been, they all knew of Doc Ben's enthusiasm for French cuisine and expected the repast set before them to be the best available in a city known for the best food in America. One of the great, long-to-be remembered pleasures of that memorable evening would be partaking of a splendid French Dinner.

Dr. Talbot, a gourmet as was his friend, Ben, tasted slowly, swallowed, breathed deeply and said, "The veal and artichoke hearts . . . delightful as expected!"

Lorena said, "I will be sure to tell Madame Montespan who, of course, will be pleased though not surprised, that her *Rôti de Veau à la Parisienne avec Fonds d'Artichauts à la Barigoule* met with your approval, Doctor." Pleased with her playful performance in perfect French, she looked to the other side of the table to gauge Jesse's response to the food and flushed with pleasure to find him concentrating on her. When he was certain that he had caught her eye, he smiled broadly, nodded once and touched the third finger of his left hand. Her heart rose and with joy, she nodded.

The exchange did not escape the attention of Dr. Talbot, who correctly gauged the situation. He raised his glass of burgundy and said to Lorena, "Best wishes, my dear. And congratulations! When is the ceremony to take place? I hope that by then you will have recalled . . ."

"Thank you, Doctor, but the event is to occur this very evening, after the cream puffs, but before the brandy. It's a secret until then."

"Good heavens! Not between *Profiteroles au Chocolat* and the V.V.S.O.P. Cognac!" Tolbert exclaimed. Lorena nodded with a charmingly happy little smile as she observed Jesse who had turned his attention to something Mrs. Longworth was saying.

"Jesse, my dear, so many hearts will be broken tonight as New York's most desirable bachelor leaves the courting game."

"It isn't a sport, Molly," Jesse laughed.

"Not for you perhaps. For me, matchmaking is the best of all games! And I do so well at it, except where my own children are concerned. Well, Colonel you are quite sure about this step you're taking, I hope." Jesse nodded. "You know I have always harbored a secret wish that you and Rachel . . ." Molly sighed.

"A not-so-secret wish, Molly. All of New York knows what you had up your sleeve. I love Rachel of course, as I would a sister. And I am *sure* about Lorena so, now, please go on describing your plan." Molly pouted. With full lips in a large round face, she did it better than any woman Jesse had ever seen try. "You know, dear Molly, that I put this important event in your capable hands because you arc the most talented, formidable hostess in the city," said Jesse. Molly swallowed a sip of wine, then smiled, mollified, and with enthusiasm presented her scheme.

"There will be a footman stationed between the chairs of every two guests and at my signal there will be a virtual bombardment of champagne corks! You then will go to your young lady's side and ask our good friend, Judge Bodner, to preside." Molly and Jesse looked at a man seated at the precise center of the long gleaming table, where he was expounding between mouthfuls of veal and potato balls in butter. A small, venerable, distinguished-looking old man with a fringe of white hair and wild white eyebrows, he was making what appeared to be an inarguable statement.

"There must and *will* be reconciliation between North and South after these bloody years of war. Mr. Lincoln has said so to General Grant and many others. With our President's wisdom to guide us we will heal the nation."

"We in this great city have much to do, Judge Bodner, by way of reunion and reconstruction," said New York's Mayor Gunther. "Not only dockworkers, streetsweepers, all the lower classes, but many others—wealthy businessmen and most of our politicians—opposed the war and would have let the South go its own way. Some even advocated that New York City, like the South, secede. Not a few at this table advocated something to be called the Republic of New York."

"Mayor, you know New York City's primacy seemed back then to be founded upon the commercial ties between the North and the South," apologized Doc Ben for some of his friends. "To our shame, New Yorkers were all too well aware of who planted, picked, and hauled the cotton—slaves—and they yet opposed the Abolitionist cause."

"Now Ben, we all know," said the Mayor, "that you never were one to support a nefarious and immoral trade."

"The business of America could well have left this city to go through a Confederate New Orleans!" insisted a former mayor of New York, Fernando Wood, growing red in the face.

"But of course, once *we* captured the ports of Memphis, Vicksburg, and New Orleans," interjected a man seated to the left of Caroline Tree, "we got cotton cheaper than before. Trade on the stock market was as good as it had ever been. Gold prices plunged and soared, and many a fortune was made."

"Listen here, Dabney, some of those fortunes were made

by you, sir, " another guest said belligerently. "I resent your use of the collective *we*. You were a Johnny-come-lately to the righteous cause."

"This is a Democrat city, Van Ness," answered Dabney, "but after the election of Lincoln we at once joined with Republicans to save the Union and, if necessary, to destroy the Confederacy."

"Gentlemen, *please* do not fight the war again at my dinner table," Molly implored, suffering a sudden attack of heat vapors that brought her fan into play.

"Dixieland must and will be rebuilt, restored. We must reach out to our Southern brethren and share our wealth," pronounced the Judge with conviction, "share the goods of our prosperous industry and . . ." The Judge, moved by his own generosity and several glasses of wine, choked up with emotion. "Miss Tree," he managed to say, "please do serenade us once more, this time with a song of the south."

Miss Tree had taken a sudden obvious interest in the merchant banker, Charles Dabney of the New York banking house, Duncan, Sherman & Company. "Sir, you are just the person I require to help me to comprehend all this talk of the 'gold standard.' I just do not understand." Caroline continued purring close to Dabney's ear, "Why not the bean standard or some such? A commodity is a commodity, is it not?" Dabney beamed with pleasure under Caroline's focused attention.

"A very insightful, even a brilliant economic observation, Miss Tree!"

"*Caroline* will do."

"Caroline, I'll not answer so sophisticated a question in the midst of dinner and merriment. Perhaps," he said looking at her knowingly, "you will honor me with a more private audience very soon? Now, I'd rather learn of your acting triumphs and your future plans. It's not often that one gets to chat with a great star such as you, if indeed there is any other with whom to make a comparison."

"Mr. Dabney . . ."

"Charles. I insist."

"I am used to fulsome flattery, copious outpourings of it, and even to knowledgeable admiration of my voice, but never have I been praised as insightful and brilliant about matters of high finance by one who knows whereof he speaks. I have had little opportunity to talk to well-informed persons. Wise men in exalted positions think that because I am an actress *and* a woman, I don't posses sufficient brains to comprehend such matters. Thank you so much, Charles." She looked straight into the man's faintly bloodshot eyes with profound earnestness.

"I . . . uh, my comment was meant not as flattery but as sincere admiration. Do go on, Caroline."

"Lord knows my story has been broadcast far and wide, but I know little more of you than I've heard just now. You are a successful man of great wealth and power, a merchant banker said to be a very private if not secretive person. Do please tell me *all* about yourself, Charlie."

"*Caroline*," he sighed. "Dear Caroline, I . . ."

"Caroline! Miss Caroline Louisa Tree!" boomed the judge's best bench voice. "I am not a man to be ignored. I am waiting, we all are waiting, for a Reb song from one of the great voices of this or indeed of any, day." Caroline slowly turned toward the stern-faced judge and languidly smiled.

"And I am not a woman to be interrupted, but on this occasion, if you name your tune, Judge Bodner, I will perform it for you at no charge. Usually, sir, I sing for legal tender, you know." Bodner was speechless, but not for long.

"'Old Unreconstructed.' Do you know that one, Miss Tree?" he asked in a modulated tone. She did.

> *I rode with old Jeb Stuart*
> *And his band of Southern horse,*
> *And there never was no Yankees*
> *Who could meet us force to force.*

After Caroline had rendered every verse and acknowledged the applause, but before she resumed her seat she whispered to Jesse, her hand on his shoulder, "I suspect you, Colonel, are spoken for so I do hope you will not think me lacking in social niceties if I concentrate my attention on another."

"Enough of that, you two," Dabney protested with more than a hint of rivalry. He had determined he had best not wait any longer to recapture Miss Tree's full attention from Jesse Sparhawk, infamous for his winning ways with pretty women. Jesse amiably gave Caroline her privacy to attend where she wished, though he much preferred her easy charm at the art of the tête-à-tête to Maud Wharton's, the only choice left him until he could claim Lorena. Before commencing to tell Maud about his imminent marriage, he tried to engage her dour-looking sister, across the table. Estelle Partier, who had yet to utter a word to anyone, was eating efficiently with concentration until her plate was spotless, as if Jack Sprat and his fat-favoring wife had 'licked the platter clean.'

"Miss Tree . . . Caroline, I mean," he heard Dabney say to the actress, "I suspect when you described me as *secretive* you might have truly thought *sinister*. And to dispel any such possibility, I'll tell you of myself."

"Please do, Charlie, and remember I am also interested in . . . What did you call it? High finance?"

"In the way of Homer and all true storytellers, I will start at the beginning. My life as a New York City merchant banker began five years ago when I became an international trader. I financed both the sellers of cotton, that is the Southern plantation owners, and the buyers, fabric manufacturers in England. I made a profit from both."

"Yes?" Caroline encouraged, already feeling her eyelids getting heavy. She opened a fan that had been dangling, folded at her wrist, to show its elaborate decoration of bright painted flowers on silk and a bucolic scene of well-attired young people cavorting in a garden. Fluttering the fan energetically she was somewhat revived by its little breeze, but Jesse was fed up with Dabney's oft' told tale.

"Mrs. Partier," he ventured, "have we met before? I feel I know you."

"I think not, Colonel Sparhawk," the woman opposite him replied.

"It must be Estelle's resemblance to me," Maud Wharton suggested, "which makes her seem familiar. She *is* my sister. And on the subject of familiarity, will I be entertaining you later, Jesse? This is an historic occasion and it has been a while since you've stayed a night with me, or even until tea time."

"I've other plans, Maud. I have news." He glanced down the table at Lorena. Mrs. Wharton's eyes followed his.

"Your news will keep. Rather tell me, Colonel, what of your innocent, pretty little plaything, the Reed girl, dressed tonight like a Dresden doll?"

"What of her, Maud?" Jesse asked with a cool smile on its way to turning icy.

"Or Cinderella," said Estelle, who had been openly eavesdropping.

"What makes you say that, Estelle?" Jesse asked with squinted eyes. "Do you know something of her?"

"Now the war's over, what future is there for your little girl lost?" Mrs. Wharton interjected, scowling at Estelle. Maud's arch manner so annoyed Jesse that he spoke more abruptly than he might otherwise have done on a delicate subject.

"Her future and mine are settled. We'll be man and wife." He looked at the great clock against the far wall, "in under an hour." The natural hauteur of Maud Wharton's expression, the greenness of her narrow cat's eyes, and the paleness of her skin all intensified. She sat very still.

"It's of no moment to me who you take to wife," she said. "A child bride will be able to give you heirs, which I could not, even if I were free to wed again."

"And of course, you are not." Jesse rested his hand upon hers on the table. "Free."

"As you know, with solely physical passion, pleasure is all there is and that short-lived. She will soon bore you as others have. You and I have worked well together, Jesse. We share a cause, a mission. We've a bond. When you tire of *her*, come back to me. I do not expect to have to wait long."

"Maud," Jesse said with iced venom in his lowered voice, "do not attempt to hold your breath as you wait." Her eyes sparked with outrage when he smiled and brought her hand to his lips.

"Will you kiss me off so lightly, sir?" she hissed, also smiling as she rose to set her lips on his.

"The way a woman makes use of her fan indicates a good bit about her social grace," Rachel told Lorena. "A lady's skill with a fan is rather like to a man's use of a sword."

"Unfortunately, I haven't a fan or a sword," Lorena complained as she watched the charade being played by Maud Wharton and Jesse Sparhawk.

"Oh, dear!" Rachel sighed. "Lorena, I'm certain things are not as they appear between those two. And you must be eased to see that Miss Tree at last has turned her attentions to another man."

"I was afraid for my own fortune . . ." Dabney droned. Caroline's fan fluttered. "The men of wealth and power in this City . . ." The actress looked for relief to Jesse. Maybe the Colonel *was* available after all, she fretted to herself. ". . . found new ways to meet the needs of war—food in airtight cans shipped by rail, uniforms precut and sewn to 'standard sizes.' We bankers provided the capital and accumulated, what I consider much deserved, fortunes."

Caroline, barely hearing a word he said, studied her companion in scrupulous detail. She appraised his well-groomed looks and expensive accoutrements. His suit was of lightweight, tightly-woven, dark-blue wool and worn with a silver gray, four-in-hand cravat. His hands, without a single callous, had long tapering fingers. On the pinkie finger of the left one was a conservatively-sized, black onyx stone set in antique silver. His perfectly arranged light hair would do any theatrical dresser proud. With it all, he was young, short of thirty, she estimated. Of late, her conquests, men who had taken longer than Charles had to amass enough wealth to interest her, tended to be of advanced years. His robust youth weighed well in his favor. He just might do, Caroline decided.

Charles Dabney knew he was being studied and paused for a sip of wine. He would take his good time before resuming his story to allow the lady to note his good looks, better, in his own opinion than those of Sparhawk, no matter what most women said. When he cleared his throat, she had to prevent herself from moaning aloud and bit her tongue to let him lecture on.

"And so we celebrate here tonight," Dabny began again, "the surrender at Appomattox. You will see dramatic changes in this city and throughout much of the nation: New machinery in new factories, new people replacing those who have fallen on the battlefields. You will be amazed at the thousands who will come to these shores. A veritable immigration of the masses. Finally, there will be greatly enlarged markets and, therefore, even greater wealth than this city and country and I have ever yet experienced."

"Amen!" sighed Caroline. "By the way, the theater will be dark Monday. It would be a good time to pay me a call, if you'd care to."

She had made her decision about Charles Dabney. Boring as he was at dinner, he was a man interested in women. He was used to the very best of everything and she fit the bill: beautiful, accomplished, clever, talented and famous. Caroline knew so herself and she knew he would agree.

"Say no more. I will collect you at your home. We will dine at Delmonico's." Just then Charles felt Caroline's hand slide alongside the inside of his thigh and rub it meaningfully. He looked into the actress' face, which was smiling beatifically and in all innocence.

The dinner plates and glasses were cleared, the table brushed free of crumbs and the dessert served. A rare sauterne, moments earlier delivered to the Longworth house and not listed on the menu, was poured and poured again to satisfy the desire of each guest. When the hostess observed that all at the table had had enough of the chocolate-sauced cream puffs, she placed her dessert knife and fork on her own empty plate. At this signal, a virtual army of footmen set a champagne flute before each guest and Dr. Longworth rose to stand at his place. When expectant quiet had spread around the table he lifted a glass of sauterne.

"Ladies and gentlemen, a toast to the President of the United States! May Mr. Lincoln bring a joyful reconciliation and prosperity to our entire nation, north and south, in peace as he has brought it a just victory in war."

The toast was greeted by every man at the table getting to his feet and by everyone raising and clinking glasses. Shouts of "Hear, hear!" rippled up and down the table.

When all had sat down, Colonel Sparhawk arose as if to propose a toast of his own. Instead he walked about the table to stand behind Lorena. As dozens of corks popped, all at once, from frosty bottles and bubbles rose in glasses filled with pale golden champagne, Jesse said, "I would now add to the joy of this occasion by asking you all to join with me in wishing Miss Lorena Reed a happy birthday. In addition, I have the great good fortune and pleasure to announce that she has most graciously agreed to be my wife. Judge Bodner, sir, will you do the honors, now?"

Jesse's words were greeted by all the gentlemen, once again, rising to their feet and lifting their glasses. They offered joy to Lorena and then in unison called out, "Hip, hip, hooray!" for Jesse. There was a great flicking of fans and gasps, sighs, and smiles from the seated ladies as the groom drew his bride, glowing with happiness, to her feet. Dr. Longworth couldn't contain himself and rushed over to the couple to pound Jesse on the back, shake his hand, then kiss Lorena first on one cheek, then the other, then finally on her brow. Rachel was near tears which, Lorena assumed, were tears of joy for her.

The pandemonium subsided and was followed by a happy

buzz of conviviality and delighted laughter as the Longworth mansion's majordomo unceromoniously burst into the room and handed a folded sheet of paper to the Doctor. Silence settled as the diners observed the growing seriousness of their host's countenance.

The Doctor, showing none of the joy and pleasure he had earlier, paled and appeared visibly shaken.

"I have in my hand a telegraph message of the gravest import. Please prepare yourselves for the worst possible news." After a hesitation, he was finally able to speak.

"At ten o'clock this evening, President Lincoln was mortally wounded when he was shot, at close range, in the back of his head, by a Southern sympathizer. The President is not expected to survive the night."

CHAPTER 14

The tracks of the Hudson River Line hugged the base of rising hills and outcroppings of rocks, and ran some of the way along man-made embankments. There were boats on the river all along the way—ferries, rafts, canoes, and barges being moved by tugs. On the banks of the river, small houses and grand summer villas were tucked into the hills and small cities and villages were set into a landscape that changed with every river bend as the soaring cliffs of the Palisades gave way to the successive ridges of the Catskill range.

On an exceptionally warm spring day, Lorena and Rachel, sitting side by side, shielded their eyes from the glare of sunlight off the river. Smoke and soot from the engine came drifting back through the open windows of the cars where the few fashionably dressed women aboard—tight-laced, buttoned, and bonneted—vigorously waved their fans between visits to the cooler at the end of the car for glasses of iced tea. Gentlemen accompanying them pulled at starched collars and mopped dripping brows.

The quiet, simply attired pair of pretty young women in cotton day dresses attracted some curious attention. Rachel was in a frock of her characteristic dark gray color. Lorena's outfit was a deep maroon red showing a white cotton collar and a small red ribbon tie at her throat. Both wore spoon-shaped bonnets, which shaded their faces, and fine hair nets to keep wind-ravaged strands in place. The wind, the noise and rattle of the train, and regular hooting of the engine made conversation difficult and each girl was lost in her own thoughts. Lorena kept returning in her mind to the last time she had seen Jesse, at Doc's dinner, which had changed from a scene of celebration to one of confusion and despair with the arrival of the ghastly telegram about Mr. Lincoln.

She had been standing beside Jesse, about to become his wife forever. The little judge, Horace Bodner, was scurrying toward them looking for all the world, Lorena had thought, like a delightful, elated elf. At the same time Jesse, with his most winning boyish smile and eyes glowing dark forget-me-not blue, reached into his tunic jacket and withdrew a flat velvet box. When he snapped it open the words 'Tiffany & Co.' Lorena saw, were embossed on the inner lid and, below, shining like the Milky Way against dark satin, were a hundred small sparkling diamonds covering a chain of large gold links. A square-cut emerald pendant on the chain glowed against the satin and beside it nested a ring on which another emerald, surrounded by baguette diamonds, shimmered. Doc was reading a telegraph message to the table-at-large, which, Lorena assumed, was one of joy at war's end from an absent friend, or perhaps Robert. She paid Doc scant attention as Jesse set the jeweled chain about her throat. As he began fastening the clasp at her nape Lorena felt a tremor shake him. It was a tremor not of love, as she first supposed, but of rage as she saw when she turned to look into his narrowed, icy eyes which had gone gunmetal gray and hard as bullets. He was looking at her as if he did not even see her, and then looked away at Maud Wharton.

"Maud!" he called out, turning his back on Lorena. "We must go! Now!" Even as he stalked in the woman's direction, Mrs. Wharton was beckoning to her sister, gathering up her things and smiling crookedly with what Lorena took to be smug pleasure at the interruption the nuptials. The click and clatter of dress boots sounded on wood and marble floors as members of the military ran from the room and from the house, to return to their posts. The soft weeping of women was audible, and the curses of some men, the moans of others. The name "Abraham Lincoln" was everywhere being whispered with reverence and someone had said, "There can be no conciliation now, only retribution! The whole Confederate government from Jeff Davis down plotted this! Hang 'em all." Another added somberly, "These promise to be bloody times." Only then, after a passage of time that felt like many slow hours gone, but was barely sixty seconds since Jesse had raced off and Doc had slumped in his chair, did Lorena accept the truth of the telegram. She ran to the window in time to see Jesse handing Maud into a carriage. Estelle Partier, awaiting her turn to step up, looked back over her shoulder and her eyes met Lorena's.

"Hester Potts," Lorena gasped to Dr. Talbot beside her. "That woman is Hester Potts!" she called loudly through the open window to Jesse as confusing memories came flooding back to her. Jesse's gift, the glittering golden and diamond chain, left unfastened, fell then from Lorena's bosom to the floor. Ethel Hope, snuffling and red eyed, came to pick it up. The emerald ring, Lorena's unused wedding ring, was still in the velvet box which she had let slip through her fingers. The smaller jewel rolled away out of sight. No one, least of all Lorena herself, saw it lodge beneath a sideboard cluttered with half-empty bottles of champagne and an uncut wedding cake. What she did see in a flash of remembrance was herself kneeling at the bedside of an injured young soldier, holding his hand and replying to the question of a sad-eyed minister standing over them. "Do you take this man, Lorena Reed . . . ?"

"Ah do, with all mah heart," she had said then, and whispered aloud now. Only Dr. Talbot was close enough to Lorena to hear the sweet mountain drawl with which she had spoken those fateful words.

"As disturbing a shock to mind and heart such as the dreadful news from which we are all now reeling may affect the brain as surely as a blow to the head. Lorena, hearing the return of your southern inflection of speech allows me to think

your memory has returned, more or less. Before very much
more time passes, I predict you'll know yourself again and recall your past."

"Perhaps ah'll summon up a whole lot more about me than
ah wish to, Dr. Talbot," she answered thoughtfully, turning to
the window. "I know now the thief who made off with my savings was Maud Wharton's sister. What the woman's true and
actual connection is to Jesse, I haven't a hint. And doctor? I do
believe I am already wed."

"What suggests that to you, my dear child?" asked Talbot
with professional neutrality.

"I have a picture in my mind and I hear the sound of myself
saying 'ah do'." Lorena clasped her hands beneath her chin and
closed her eyes.

"It happens, on occasion, with amnesiacs and others suffering problems of the mind that just at first they cannot
distinguish between actual memory of a real event and a dream
or fantasy. I am convinced that no matter what you evoke, you
will handle it with honesty and valor. I know you well enough
to believe in your innate goodness and courage, my dear."

"Ah do wish I had reason to believe in myself as you believe
in me, Doctor. But my heart now urges me in one direction and
my common sense in another. However, this is not the time for
us to think of ourselves but of Mr. Lincoln and the future peace.
And of poor Mrs. Lincoln for whom this ghastly loss may well
be, as you suggested earlier, the misfortune that destroys her altogether. She will not know to whom to turn or who she may
possibly trust."

Outside on Fifth Avenue, Lorena's eyes searched the throng
of soldiers and ordinary citizens running every which way.
Jesse and his companions were gone. More than anything else
at that moment she needed to know where and why, and what
the future could hold for her *and* him—together, or apart.

Lorena waited four days and virtually sleepless nights for
some word or sign. She never left the Longworth mansion ex-

cept to pace the garden for fear of missing Jesse if he came seeking her or sent her a messenger—Hamson, Nicke, Q., most likely Robert. None appeared. Molly and Ben worried about their son in silence while Rachel criticized her self-interested twin for abandoning his family at such a tragic time. Again, Lorena kept the secret that Robert had risked his life during the war, and might still be doing so.

All during those days and sleepless nights Lorena waited with Rachel at her side. Sometimes they walked arm in arm around the fountain where Jesse and Lorena had often dawdled so happily. At other times, after tea or supper, Rachel read aloud, from the comforting *Book of Common Prayer* and from the distressing *Herald Tribune*.

Rachel quoted items from the newspaper:

> *We give the dispatches in the order in which they reached us. The sudden shock of this calamity is appalling, frightfully startling. The head of thirty millions of people has been hurried into eternity. Six former rebel generals accompanied General Grant on the funeral train.*

Then, Rachel read from the *Book of Common Prayer*:

> *There was a war in heaven. Michael and his angels fought against the dragon, and the dragon fought and his angels; and prevailed not . . . and the great dragon was cast out, that old serpent, called the devil and Satan.*

"Evil will not prevail, Lorena. If the actor Booth is indeed the assassin, he will suffer the consequences. 'For man walketh in a vain shadow, and disquieteths himself in vain.'"

And then Rachel quoted again from the *Tribune*: "'I carefully wrote my dispatch, though with trembling and nervous fingers. I was afterward surprised that I had succeeded in approximating so closely to all the facts in those dark transactions.' That is reported by a Mr. Gobright for something calling itself the Associated Press."

"It's a news bureau, 'working to the pulse of the telegraph,' it is said. *The Tribune* and papers all over the country have published many of the man's dispatches. Jesse mentioned him to me," Lorena explained. "He was disposed to do what is fair and right, and was the government's chosen newsman, the first to get official information about the progress of the war."

Rachel continued the items:

> *Lincoln lying in state.*
> *Preparations for the Funeral Train of Lincoln . . . retrace his inaugural route back to Illinois. His horse Old Bob, draped in black, will follow after him riderless in Washington procession.*
> *Governor Curtin of Pa. offers a $10,000 reward for the capture of Booth.*

"Here is something else of interest," said Rachel.

"William Herndon, the President's former law partner, writes that Mr. Lincoln should be remembered as a *human* and hence as an imperfect—a very imperfect man."

During those awful days, Rachel fended off Lorena's callers, even members of the household, who sought her company until finally, early on the fourth anxious day without any word from Jesse, Lorena insisted and Rachel concurred, that it was time to visit Washington Square. At several street corners as they hurried along the avenue from the Longworth's, sad street singers rendered new sad songs: *Rest Spirit, Rest, Old Abe's Body,* and *We'll Sing to Abe Our Song!*

The Wharton and Sparhawk townhouses were shuttered, locked, and abandoned. Lorena was able to enter Jesse's house from the mews behind it and found all trace of the secret spy quarters obliterated.

"Rachel, I think Maud and Jesse have run off together to escape."

"Oh, my dear deluded friend! Escape what?"

"Justice. It is possible that they were double agents working together and that his interest in me was merely one more ploy in the plot against Mr. Lincoln."

"Jesse Sparhawk? You must now be quite mad in addition to suffering amnesia. We must return home to put you under Father's care again, at once."

"No, Rachel. I'm recalling many things now about myself and about Jesse, how those two exchanged whispers and glances during Doc's dinner, how he called upon her every day, even after he and I swore our love. You saw how he spirited her and her sister from your father's house when the news came. And of course, he has kin in Carolina and might have harbored secret secesh sympathy all along." Rachel shook her head doubtfully, deeply worried about Lorena, but a seed of doubt had been planted.

"Don't you love him anymore?" she almost asked, loving him herself and about to say so. "What will you do?" she asked instead.

"I will love Jesse forever, but that is of no matter now, I think. I will get to the truth of all this and settle the score. First, I must go to the military hospital in Seneca. I must leave here at once before Doc, or anyone, attempts to stop me."

Rachel, thinking her friend was either in real danger or somewhat unbalanced, could not allow Lorena to travel alone and so after a brief stop at the Longworth mansion to pick up a few things, among them Lorena's old carpetbag, they headed for the Hudson River Railroad depot. A few hours later, they sat rocking side by side, both thinking about the same man.

Lorena relived all the times he had kissed her awake, again and again in the night as the ebb and flow of passion moved him; how she had done the same, letting him know she wanted him, with her body moving against his and her hand bringing him to life before his eyes flicked open. How he then would thoroughly fondle her with those dark blue eyes, offering his inviting lecherous low laugh just before he began to skillfully touch her body, moving his hand between her thighs and then questing into her. *Stop this at once, Lorena,* she commanded herself, not for the first time. She took a shamefaced peek at Rachel who appeared to be drowsing.

Actually, she too was silently lecturing herself. *'It is quite impossible to put a stop to love, except in the very first stages.'* Stendahl had written that so long ago. *Your love for Jesse Sparhawk is well beyond that. And his for you? It has never existed except in a brotherly way.* A firm believer in the 'only one true love in a lifetime' theory, Rachel had withdrawn, as soon as she came of marriageable age, from the New York social world. She concentrated all her zeal on her good works—planning events for the Ladies' Aid, visiting immigrants and war orphans, knitting for soldiers at the front, wrapping bandages. She had even gone to Washington City for a time, to nurse the wounded. She had done much good in the world for many, though not for herself. She could not, of course, labor all twenty-four hours of a day. No matter when she stopped to rest, no matter how tired she was, Jesse appeared in her thoughts, and a great longing came into her heart.

She glanced at Lorena daydreaming beside her and felt sadder than ever. The concerned and open person who had become her dearest friend was in love with the only love of *her* life. No matter what Lorena said now—that Jesse had never loved her and she would not have him if she could—Rachel didn't believe it. And even if Jesse had really abandoned Lorena, that didn't mean he would ever fall in love with Rachel Longworth. Rachel's best, perhaps only, choice once this mystery of Jesse was unraveled, was to join a Shaker commune and immerse herself in the contemplative, celibate life. She and Lorena planned to stop one night at a Shaker village on their route north. Rachel sighed aloud.

" 'Weeping may endure for the night but joy cometh in the morning.' You pair of misses are looking disheartened and low," said a voice behind them and both women turned to see a ruddy old man's face. The eyes, under snowy plumed brows were sad but bright. "They'll soon be bringin' Mr. Lincoln along these very tracks, taking him to Albany. He's to travel a winding way home to Illinois so's we can all pay respect. He himself, I do believe, would agree that joy must come if not this morning, on one soon.

"Well, and where are you young things heading, may I inquire? I am Bradford Leathers, Captain Leathers. Oh, not an army captain, misses. I sail on this river, ferries now, river sloops once, loaded with bricks and butter. The sloops are gone nowadays. We on the river were heroes of sorts all during the war. Now, with peace more or less upon us, there'll be the high season soon at Saratoga, folks taking the healthful mineral waters, watching thoroughbred racing and the boat clubs launching their racing shells on the lake."

"When I was a girl, traveling with my parents to Saratoga, I remember the sloops on the river, Captain Leathers," said Rachel. "They were beautiful vessels. I did not care all that much for Saratoga in summer. Ladies changed their outfits five or six times a day and searched for husbands. The sloops and the horses were the true beauties." Rachel smiled, relieved to be distracted from her own thoughts. So was Lorena.

"I'll say!" answered the old man. "They—the sloops— were a real lovely sight, a hundred feet long and flyin' five thousand feet of sail. Nothin' compares to swingin' a seventy-foot boom doin' a Hudson River jibe.

"Look there. Them's ice houses along the shore. They cut it from the river and lakes all winter and then ice-hauling barges take it down to the city all summer. We're comin' up on West Point now," Leathers pointed. "Most of the best generals, North and South, was educated there. They'll be of one army, united again. Joy in the morning. Where are you pair headin'? I talked on so, I never did give you a chance to say."

"To visit the Shakers a bit farther up river," answered Lorena, "and then we'll be traveling more northerly and west some."

"That scribbler, Greeley, writes about going west."

"'Do not lounge in the cities!' Mr. Greeley wrote," said Rachel. "'There is room and health in the country, away from the crowds of idlers and imbeciles. Go west, before you are fitted for no life but that of the factory.' That's exactly what he wrote," quoted Rachel from memory. "He showed me a draft of an article he intends soon to publish."

"I do agree with his advice," Lorena said thoughtfully. "West may be the way to begin again." She had come from generations of westering stock. She would visit at Seneca according to plan and learn all she could about the husband she might or might not have. She would go to the mountains of home, then, if all was well, just keep on going, following the sunset. She would do her damndest to forget about Jesse Sparhawk. And facing him down, getting even with him? If ever they met again, which was most unlikely if she put miles between them, who could predict what she, or he, might do? It was best to try to avoid even the possibility. A new life on the plains would be a challenge and would, over time, help her put Jesse Sparhawk out of her heart and mind for good. She did not believe that would happen, not ever, but it was worth a try. "Rachel, I've just had the most splendid notion," she announced. "So please do not commit yourself too quickly to the Shaker life!" Rachel was so relieved to see Lorena animated once more, smiling and bubbling with plans, she gave her promise without the slightest hesitation.

"When you first arrived here at Seneca, Lorena, you were a knowledgeable young woman, and possessed a delicate musical sensibility. Have you told Rachel how often you played the dulcimer, so prized by a Rebel prisoner who had sheltered the wooden instrument through many a battle? Rachel, your friend soothed the heart of many a bereft and lonely man with old mountain melodies, even if they were played on rusty strings."

Elsie Frost, a middle-aged, fair woman smiled and lit up the room where she faced Lorena and Rachel across a small desk in a paper-piled office at Seneca Post Hospital. The cap and a pinned apron she wore over a much-repaired dress of homespun teased at Lorena's memory as Elsie went on. "Anything new to you, if it engaged your attention, you learned instantly. Do you recall all the books I gave you to read? The

Art of Dancing, which included hints on etiquette, and the sheet music to play, was the first volume you read. How you loved to play the mazurkas and gallops, especially! And how you cheered us all so, and our patients, with your piano performances. From the set of the Ladies' Family Library, I believe you committed to memory Mrs. Child's entire *American Frugal Housewife* and half of her *Mother's Book*."

"I've had some dislocations of memory, Miss Frost, one of the reasons Rachel and I have come here," said Lorena. "Will you tell me please what brought me to Seneca, how long I remained here?"

"I'm not surprised to hear you've submerged some of the events which befell you here, Lorena. Much is being made of late of personality symptomatology of "*idées fixes*" as some French physicians have termed it, a splitting off of painful thoughts and submerging them. Some of the men here share your difficulty. It's most prevalent among Confederate prisoners held at the camps along the Finger Lakes, but no one is immune."

"Lorena suffered a blow on the head, Miss Frost," Rachel explained. "In an accident."

"An accident? Did it involve Miss Potts, the woman with whom you left to go south?" Miss Frost's expression was one of worried concern when she leaned forward to rest her elbow on the desk after moving several files aside.

"What are you able to tell us of Hester Potts who is really Estelle Partier, a flimflammer, the sister of a New York resident?"

"Sister of Maud Wharton. Yes, I know," Miss Frost nodded taking Lorena and Rachel offguard. "Potts or Partier or whatever, like you Lorena and so many others, was searching the prisoner of war encampments for her young nephew. The boy, fighting for the South, had been missing since early in the war."

"Her nephew's name?"

"Arthur Randall Wharton, heir to a title and fortune from his noble, elderly English father.

"Wharton's son! He was a Rebel while his mother supported the Union."

"Now, Lorena, things are not always what they seem. Maud may really have been a secret supporter of the Confederacy as you think, but . . ."

"That makes Jesse either a traitor or a fool, and if there's one thing we both know the Colonel is not, it's a fool," Lorena said to Rachel.

"I think you had best tell me what this is all about." Miss Frost leaned back in her chair, waiting.

With an economy of words, Rachel brought her up to date on Lorena's adventures since her friend left Seneca, right to the interrupted wedding and the fact that 'Miss Potts' was not who she purported to be.

"A wedding?" Miss Frost gasped, appearing agitated. "Lorena Reed, marriage is *not* a pastime to be entered into lightly or often. You had best hear me out at once.

"You had been sent a message. A discharged patient offered to try to get it to you and obviously, he succeeded. You came to care for a wounded young man named Clint Reed, who was on the mend until he contracted the scrofula. He was dying when you arrived. You never left his side. You granted his last wish—to be wed to you so that he could pass on content."

"Poor Clint!" Lorena whispered. "Clint Reed was kin, my cousin twice removed, my friend. He loved me from childhood. It's of no account now that I didn't share his love. I'm his widow just the same, it seems." There was an uncomfortable silence before Miss Frost spoke again.

"That is not quite a certainty. You had fallen asleep, Lorena, for the first time in days, on the empty bed beside his and when you awoke he had disappeared. Clint Reed may not have been as close to death as it appeared to the doctors."

"But even so, he would have had to get help leaving here, would he not?" asked Rachel.

"In times such as these, in places like this, there *are* no certainties. I'm sorry Lorena."

"I very nearly did commit bigamy by marrying Jesse," Lorena said in disbelief. "I must go to the valley as quickly as I can, to see if Clint managed to get home somehow or if anyone there has learned his fate."

"That is exactly what you said when you left here before. This time, Lorena, better luck and all God's speed," Miss Frost said with a firm nod.

"But what of Jesse?" asked Rachel. "Do you believe in your heart he left you at the altar to combine his fate with Maud Wharton's?"

"It no longer matters what I feel in *my* heart. His is deceitful. He had made his own bed so let him lie in it with Maud. He has always thought his destiny was in his own hands, but should Jesse Sparhawk and I ever meet again, his fate will be in mine."

"Have a care, Lorena," Rachel said softly. "I think you misjudge him. Even if you find yourself wed to another man, will you give Jesse a chance to explain?"

"That remains to be seen," Lorena replied succinctly, turning away to hide her true feelings, which she knew her friend would easily read in her eyes.

CHAPTER 15

After leaving the Longworths that fateful evening with Maud and Estelle, Jesse sat opposite them in the speeding carriage in complete silence. When they reached their house in Washington Square, Colonel Sparhawk delivered the spies into the custody of alerted army officers, who placed them under house arrest.

"What is going on? Help! Help! Murder and mayhem is afoot! Unhand me you idiot boy!" Estelle squawked as she was hustled inside. On the threshold of her house, Maud Wharton, unprotesting, turned to Jesse with a cold bitter smile.

"How long have you known?" she asked him.

"From the very start, Maud," he answered. A muscle jumped along his clenched jaw. His eyes blazed. "Your information was discarded. What you learned from me was false. All your deceit has gone for naught."

"Not quite all."

"*Mr. Lincoln?* You knew of the plot against him?" Jesse clenched his fists at his sides.

"From its very inception, Colonel. You see, I never quite trusted you either, particularly as the tide of Federal victory swept south." Maud's laugh was wicked. "I did honestly take delight in your private attentions though—until that girl interfered. Pity she showed up." Maud turned away and allowed herself to be led, a prisoner, into her own home. Jesse sprinted across the Square toward his own house.

* * *

When the basement telegraph in the hidden command post went silent, Robert Longworth began decoding the encrypted message of dots and dashes he'd taken down. Six minutes later he said, "Colonel, this just came in from the War Office in Washington. It is marked *Most Secret and for Immediate Action*."

Jesse's assignment from General Akers was clear. He and his fellow agents were to proceed to Washington with all haste, there to receive further instructions in the urgent matter of catching the assassination conspirators—dead or alive. Others would interrogate Wharton and Partier. Now, his own duty called and he would respond as ordered. He had to get some word to Lorena without revealing even a hint of his highly classified orders. Separation from her now, for even a short while, would be hurtful for them both. Their marriage ceremony had been shattered and the solution to the mystery surrounding her, delayed. Thoughts of her were never far from his mind. Who was she *really*, this young woman of singular beauty who had trusted him with her future, her very life? She, who instantly smoldered with longing for him at the touch of his hand, she, who burst into passion at the brush of his lips. But she was more than a delightfully sensual woman. Her quick intelligence and nimbleness of mind, particularly her unaccountable learning, for a backwoods-bred girl, never failed to captivate him. Jesse knew that, for the first time in his life, he was deeply, totally smitten. He wanted her hard and his mind filled with images—of himself lifting up her dress and slipping it over her cascading hair, of her standing, waiting, in her thin clinging chemise. She always had helped him slowly tease it off until she was standing nude and splendid while he fondled her visually, thoroughly with his eyes before he put his tongue to her nipples and felt them stand, felt her arms go around him, and her legs tightly encompass his thighs.

The door opened and ended Jesse's reverie. Corporal Hamson hesitated to enter, and Jesse, not for the first time, thought

Take A Trip Into A Timeless World of Passion and Adventure with Kensington Choice Historical Romances! —Absolutely FREE!

Enjoy the passion and adventure of another time with Kensington Choice Historical Romances. They are the finest novels of their kind, written by today's best-selling romance authors. Each Kensington Choice Historical Romance transports you to distant lands in a bygone age. Experience the adventure and share the delight as proud men and spirited women discover the wonder and passion of true love.

Get 4 FREE Books!

We created our convenient Home Subscription Service so you'll be sure to have the hottest new romances delivered each month right to your doorstep—usually before they are available in book stores. Just to show you how convenient the Zebra Home Subscription Service is, we would like to send you 4 FREE Kensington Choice Historical Romances. The books are worth up to $24.96, but you only pay $1.99 for shipping and handling. There's no obligation to buy additional books—ever!

Save Up To 30% With Home Delivery!

Accept your FREE books and each month we'll deliver 4 brand new titles as soon as they are published. They'll be yours to examine FREE for 10 days. Then if you decide to keep the books, you'll pay the preferred subscriber's price (up to 30% off the cover price!), plus shipping and handling. Remember, you are under no obligation to buy any of these books at any time! If you are not delighted with them, simply return them and owe nothing. But if you enjoy Kensington Choice Historical Romances as much as we think you will, pay the special preferred subscriber rate and save over $8.00 off the cover price!

this man of middle height, graying hair and gray eyes to be the perfect spy, an unnoticeable person. He was also gardener, blacksmith, stableman, armorer.

"Good morning, sir," Harmon said in a strong voice, very unlike the one he used working at the Longworths.' "What is it *now*, sir?"

"Morning, Luke. What it is *now*, as you so inelegantly put it, is that I want you to call upon your armorer's expertise. I am confident you have kept it up."

Stiffening straight, almost to the tip of his toes, and throwing out his barrel chest, the corporal, the proud possessor of many skills essential to war, said with the feisty tone of a self-confident, noncommissioned officer, "Colonel, I am clean, reasonably sober, and ready for duty, that is, ready for duty if I know what it is. Unlike some in this service, I cannot read minds. *Sir!*"

"Yes, yes, Luke, but it won't do to get huffy. We are all still in shock over last night's terrible murder. Our mission is to catch and, if necessary, kill those who assassinated the President and tried to kill Secretary Stanton. We leave in four hours. The unit, men and horses, will embark on the Hoboken ferry, and then board the train to Washington. What can you arm us with?"

"For what you are describing you'll need a more powerful pistol than the Smith and Wesson Model Two you've been using. You'll need something with more killing power and longer range than a thirty-two caliber rim-fire. It just so happens that we are in luck, if luck it is, that finally gets us what we long wanted and deserved."

"You were saying, Corporal."

"Yes, sir, I was saying that you'll remember last year when we ordered a shipment of Remington New Model Navy revolvers, the ones converted from thirty-six-caliber percussion to thirty-eight-caliber metallic cartridges. Well, the Federal Armory finally was able to fulfill the order. They are ready for action, rubbed free of grease, re-oiled, polished and targeted-in."

"Good. And what rifles or shotguns?"

"There is still nothing better than the Spencer. I know you prefer the carbine model, all cavalrymen seem to, but I suggest that other than you and Sergeant Nicke, the rest of us carry the Spencer rifle. The last Armory shipment also included three Blakeslee Quickloaders. The Quickloader boxes we received *now* hold thirteen tubes each. Since each tube holds seven cartridges, we have firepower of ninety-one shots for each box or for our three Quickloaders alone—more than several hundred rounds. We can stop a small army."

"Yes, yes, Corporal, I learned my multiplication tables when I was in knee breeches and I learned them very well. How else do you think I could have managed at West Point? By the way, the correct firepower calculation for the boxes is two hundred and seventy-three rounds. But that aside, I am very pleased to be armed with such power and I commend you for your preparation and good work.

"One other thing, I expect the horses to be ready, first for the railroad trip and then for hard riding, if necessary, when we go south."

In a cavernous office of the nearly finished War Department building, in the shadow of the nearly finished Capitol dome, General Akers said, "Colonel Sparhawk, I am pleased you got here so soon. Now, by order of Secretary Stanton, you and two of your best men are to ride to Fredericksburg where you will take command of the Federal forces there—those now in hot pursuit of the assassin, the actor John Wilkes Booth. Here is a package of photographs so that you will be certain to identify the man, or do you by chance know him?"

"Yes, sir. I saw him perform almost two years ago in the play *Marble Heart*, at the Ford Theatre, in fact."

"Ah, yes. Good. And, to brief you fully, here is a file jacket highlighting Booth's leadership of the plot. He is a very bad man, Colonel, sure to become one of the great villains of history. You are charged with capturing or killing him with all possible haste. The country is in an uproar, demanding blood. Therefore, I will not detain you longer. Just remember that the Secretary and I, not to mention the entire Grand Army of the Republic, know you to do your duty, which will be to exact the full force of retributive justice."

In the light of a kerosene lantern, Jesse read quickly, committing the relevant information to memory.

Military Intelligence Profile
John Wilkes Booth
Assassin
April 14, 1865
[Compiled from Earlier Reports]

The subject is the ninth of ten children. His siblings are not known to be Secessionists. His father was Junius, also a famous *and* eccentric actor. The family along with its *slaves* lived on a farm near Bel Air, Maryland. As a member of a Shakespearian company, John Wilkes made his debut at seventeen and then went on to considerable fame performing throughout the United States and most famously in Washington's Ford Theatre.

[**N.B.** Agents should pay particular attention to actors, actresses, and places in the thespian world for information that might lead to the apprehension of the Assassin.]

The subject has a long history of radical nativism, having been politically active since 1850 when the War Department first opened a file on him. He joined the Know-Nothing party, which opposed immigration, especially of the Irish. Since then he has come to the Department's attention as a virulent supporter of slavery. As an agent of various militant slavery organizations, he helped capture John Brown after the raid on Harper's Ferry in Virginia. He was an eyewitness to the martyr's execution. And since then he has been known, by certain branches of the Federal government, to be a Confederate agent and to have met frequently with other agents in the United States and Canada, especially with Jacob Thompson and Clement Clay, in Montreal.

[**N.B.** Therefore, Federal forces should not hesitate to un-ceasingly harass and interrogate Southern sympathizers who have had any known contact with the Assassin. Nor should Federal Secret Service agents ever again fail to be fully dili-gent in reporting to the Secretary of War all activities of suspected enemy agents.]

A careful study of all reports concerning the assassination shows John Wilkes Booth to be a maniacal, evil-tempered killer with a belief in his own historical destiny. He has been known to compare himself to Brutus and after shooting the President in the head, from a distance of only four feet, jumped to the stage shouting, '*Sic semper tyrannis*!' Then, minutes later, with a knife's handle he viciously struck the skull of a small black groom who was holding the horse that the Assassin rode to his escape.

[**N.B.** Federal forces pursuing Booth and his party can ex-pect to be met with cruel and wanton acts committed by desperate men void of all decent principle.]

Agent Thomas Lewellyn of our Service soon after picked up the trail of an injured Booth, who on leaving the city was joined by another conspirator, David Herold. During the night, they reached the Bryantown, Maryland, home of Dr. Samuel Mudd, a known Southern sympathizer and suspected spy. The traitor set Booth's broken leg and sent the two fugitives farther south before Agent Lewellyn could arrive. He did arrest the doctor, who is now incarcerated in the Arsenal Penitentiary.

April 16, 1865

Booth and Herold were briefly sighted at Rich Hill, Mary-land. Contact was lost.

April 22, 1865

Under questioning, a fisherman, one Joshua Reynolds (no known political sympathies), said that another fisherman, a cousin of his by the name of Willie Jett told him that Booth paid him, Jett, to sail with the fugitives across the Rappahannock River to Port Conway, Virginia.

Federal troops were swarming along the south bank of the river, so many men, in fact, that Jesse realized they were getting in each other's way. The army was good for frontal assault and even broad flank movements but for tight pursuit and quick capture, Jesse far favored a crack cavalry troop. Turning to a somewhat bemused infantry officer, Jesse ordered, "Lieutenant, take a detail of soldiers—two platoons—back over the river to the other side. Comb the banks and every structure on it for five miles up and down. Booth is wily. He might have decided to cut back."

No sooner had the Lieutenant ridden off than Jesse spotted Corporal Hamson bearing down on him. If the occasion were not so serious, the sight might have drawn a smile of delight. The usually subtle and nondescript man was hunkered down close to his horse, galloping with the grace of a charging Cheyenne. Whatever news he was bearing, Jesse believed it would be important. Luke Hamson was known never to waste energy, of neither man nor horse.

"Sergeant Nicke's duty, sir. I am to report that he is riding on to Port Royal. He states that he expects to corner Booth and Herold there." Jesse replied calmly, but with all the authority of a battle-hardened, full Colonel. "Corporal, tell me what happened, but first get off that horse before it collapses."

"Colonel, in Bowling Green we got a tip that Willie Jett, the fisherman who carried Booth, was holed up in the hotel. We roused him and when he seemed vague and unresponsive, at a sign from Sergeant Nicke, I hit him in his belly—not so hard as to hurt him bad or render him unconscious but to get his attention, which we got."

"Then the sergeant demanded, 'Where are the two men you brought across the river?'"

"'You mean, the assassinators?' Jett replied."

"The Sergeant then asked, 'Yes. But how do you know that?' "

"To which, Jett said, 'They made no attempt to hide their identity. Herold boldly declared to me that the pair of them are the assassinators of the President and that the man with him, John Wilkes Booth, actually shot Lincoln.'

"Lastly, sir, Jett told us that the two men were going to the home of a Mr. Garrett, on the road to Port Royal. That is all, sir."

Upon questioning, all Richard Garrett reported was that the two men had gone to the woods—a response that did not satisfy Sergeant Nicke, who turned to Corporal Hamson and ordered him to fetch a lariat rope. Then, in an icy tone, he said, "Old man, I am going to hang you high, from the top of that locust tree until your tongue hangs out and finally twists up."

The threat was too much for the youngest of Garrett's sons, who said, "Don't hurt him. He's old and scared. The men are in the barn."

Dusk had fallen and the moon was still low in the eastern sky on the evening of April 25th when Jesse dismounted and crawled to within fifty yards of the slightly ajar barn door. Having commandeered a megaphone from a cavalry bugler, he shouted, "I am Colonel Jesse Sparhawk of the Seventh Cavalry acting under the direct authority of the Secretary of War. I order you to surrender. Drop your weapons—all of them, knives and guns—and come forth with hands clasped together and held high over your heads. If you obey this lawful command, I guarantee your safety under the rules of war."

A shot rang out and a bullet stirred up the soft dirt not three yards from Jesse's head.

"Let's charge the bastards and kill them," shouted the bugler.

"Silence!" commanded Jesse. "Hold your positions and await orders."

Jesse, flanked on either side by Sergeant Nicke and Corporal Hamson, spelled out his plan. "I want bonfires, one every ten yards all around the perimeter. Set half the men to cutting and gathering wood so that the fires are at full blaze all night. The rest of the men are to stand guard between the fires. I don't want our prey to slip through, although I doubt they'll try, what with one lame and the other, no doubt, scared near out of his wits."

Through the night, the men worked and watched and warmed themselves at the roaring fires. The circle of flame, visible for miles around, attracted the farmers of the countryside, most of them newly freed slaves, who waited with rapt attention for what they hoped would be the bloody death of the assassins. It was as if the watchers, both civilian and military, were expecting a dawn execution. Jesse remained in the saddle, his carbine loaded, circling the barn outside the ring of fire. As he passed the soldiers, he said simply, "Wait and watch."

At dawn on Wednesday, April 26th, the sky was clear, the wind brisk from the northeast. Jesse, still mounted, once again raised the megaphone and called out, "If you don't come out, the barn will be set ablaze."

A voice from within, a deep well-modulated theatrical voice, responded, "Give us five more minutes."

After a short time, the voice was heard again, "If you withdraw one hundred yards from the barn, I will come out and fight you, Colonel—gentleman-to-gentleman."

Hardly containing his outrage, Jesse roared back, "You deserve to have your head blown off and I can do it. I can hit a quail's egg at fifty feet. I don't have to get within four feet, as you did when you shot the President. You're a cowardly murderer and deserve no honor. You will either surrender or burn." Then he gave a quiet order. In a response of pent-up fury and frustration both the soldiers and the newly freedmen rained hundreds of pine boughs against the sides of the barn.

Sergeant Nicke had already lighted a torch when Booth's

theatrical voice declaimed, "Well, soldiers, prepare a casket for me." Then quickly after, he said, "Wait! There's a damned coward here who wants to come out."

David Herold stepped from the barn into the hands of Corporal Hamson.

Sergeant Nicke touched torch to pine boughs. As flames rushed to engulf the barn door, John Wilkes Booth, carrying a carbine, stepped forth. A shot rang out. He fell and was pulled from the flames. Looking at Jesse, he said, "Tell Mother, I die for my country."

Jesse, a hard man who had seen much of war and dying, looked at the bleeding figure with no sympathy and when the assassin pleaded, "Kill me, kill me!" Jesse turned to the assembled solders and said, "Holster your weapons. This man is my prisoner and if he lives, he'll go to Washington for a fair trial and a just execution."

Within a few hours, the assassin was dead.

In a suite in Washington's Willard Hotel, an aged white waiter, on a Secret Service retainer, poured two, four-ounce glasses brimful. "Colonel, I managed by hook or by crook, and I won't say which, to procure—and I choose the word carefully—a half-dozen bottles of the tastiest bourbon in Kentucky. Do you know what it is?"

"Busheba Fristoe, you old coot," answered Jesse kindly, "I've been sipping Elijah since I was knee high."

"I know it's whiskey but I never heard of Elijah," interjected Robert Longworth, who had joined Jesse for breakfast the morning after the hunt for Booth had ended.

"Elijah," said Busheba, "is a blend of whiskey from northeastern Kentucky, which was named bourbon after one of 'em French King Louises because of his aid in the American Revolution. The 'Elijah' part comes from the name of a Baptist minister, the Reverend Elijah Craig, who was the first distiller of the whiskey."

"And an abolitionist, Colonel," said Robert.

"Before we get into the politics, what about breakfast? What do you have? I haven't eaten a grand meal since I left New York, which seems like a long while ago. Oh, Rob, as soon as we've finished I must get to the telegraph office. I'm concerned for our people at home. Lorena and the rest must be anxious wondering what's become of us.

"Now, Mr. Fristoe, the menu if you please."

"What we have, sir, is a feast in the southern manner. After you've satisfied yourself with blueberries and sweet cream, there is boiled smoked tongue and scrambled eggs. By then you'll be ready to enjoy a mess of ricebirds, which are seldom to be had nowadays and are great delicacy in my opinion. With appetites like you two fellows have, I can well expect you'll each eat a half dozen. That may seem like a lot but you'll notice they are very tiny, even if plump. I roasted them myself, after wrapping them in vine leaves and then basting them in butter. I'll serve them in a bed of hot crusty mashed potatoes."

After Busheba went off to his pantry, Jesse said to Robert, "There, young man, goes a treasure of a man; he not only can cook and talk but also has supplied us with a trove of information. It's amazing what he has been able to gather throughout this long war. Because he's so old, some patrons of the hotel think of him as dotty and of no account. Actually he has probably been worth more than a battery of artillery. In fact, I'm going to recommend to Stanton that he give the old man a commendation and a big bonus."

"Colonel, why don't you make your decision about bonuses and such after you've tried eating those little birds he talks about—head and bones and all."

"I have, friend. Ricebirds, really meadowlarks, feed in flocks in the Carolina rice fields. They were killed thousand upon thousand and sold, skewered a dozen to the spit. Now, they're more rare, a delicacy. Remember, I am something of a Southerner. I hope to ride down to Albemarle before long to show Lorena what is left, or what may be made of, my father's plantation."

There was coffee after the meal—very strong and very

black—and for Robert's sweet tooth, sugared *brioches* while for Jesse, another double Elijah and a fine Havana cigar. The mood of contentment was shattered by Fristoe's abrupt shuffling and unsteady entrance, waving a telegraph message above his shiny bald head. Jesse read it and looked up at Robert with consternation.

"It's from your father. Doctor and Mrs. Longworth are distraught. Lorena and Rachel have gone missing."

"Foul play?" demanded Robert leaping to his feet and upsetting his chair.

"I must telegraph Doc at once, for more detailed information," Jesse answered, already half across the room on his way to the door.

CHAPTER 16

As two riders passed over from southern Virginia to North Carolina, it poured as it had for three days and three nights— warm and wet in the daytime and very cool and wet at night—as a coastal rain came blowing from the sea and on across the Piedmont. In the mist of dawn, with their slickers flattened by the wind and their field hats drawn tight to their skulls, the pair of slight figures sitting high on their mounts, followed by a lariated mule, splashed slowly but determinedly to the crest of a hill and stopped. The horses stamped and the mule nuzzled in the muddy earth for spring crocuses and wild tulips.

A forty-five caliber revolver was hanging from a leather gun belt and holster at the narrow waist of the lead rider, while slung over the shoulder of the second was the newest of advanced carbines, a Winchester repeater. Both guns were conspicuously displayed so that any hidden observers waiting in ambush on what appeared a quiet trail could not fail to notice them. These were desperate, bloody times. The last battles of the war were still being fought in parts of the South and anarchy prevailed in much of western North Carolina.

The riders, aware of the strong likelihood of lurking danger, sat still and silently for a time, slowly rotating in their saddles to peer into the mist and to watch the sunrise. Undramatic, curtained by clouds, the dawn merely penetrated the sky's several shades of gray and cast shadows on the ground without really brightening the forest bordering the trail. This was both a hindrance and an advantage to the travelers. The dimness would make it harder for them to spot potential assailants but it would also be harder for would-be molesters to detect the ages or even the sex of the riders who were completely covered from head to toe by rugged high boots, leather-chap pants, dark India rubber ponchos, and brimmed slouch hats concealing their faces.

The lead rider gracefully dismounted, stood a bit unsteadily before taking several determined steps to the edge of the trail, then stooped and picked a daffodil. Turning, she smiled and raised the flower in pleasure.

Lorena Reed and Rachel Longworth had arrived in the Blue Ridge Mountains.

"Do you ride in peace?" asked a low, firm voice.

"We're peaceful if you are, but where do you hide?" Lorena answered, her hand on her open holster.

"Ah, I do detect a female voice. I been watching and wondering, but couldn't hardly tell whether you were boys or girls or maybe even wisps of the woods."

"These horses carry no wisps, but actual women," said Lorena. "And well armed."

"One thing is sure as sap in spring, you're young women— and one of you, the talkin' one, is from these parts."

"What is your name and why don't you show yourself?" Lorena coldly asked removing her pistol from her gunbelt and cocking it. A very thin, tall, slightly bent man with a full mane of graying dark hair and a thick beard stepped from the overhang of a locust tree after extending a large calloused hand to clear away the brier screen that half concealed him and had partially obstructed his scrutinizing stare.

Wrapped around his shirtless bony shoulders, from which dangled a loose pair of braces, was a heavy, tattered blanket woven long ago by some forgotten Cherokee squaw. A gun, an Enfield musket, was held in the crook of his left arm. His head was bare and he had little other clothing than a pair of

faded, torn sky-blue kersey trousers, obviously of Federal
Army issue, held up by a Confederate belt of painted canvas
with a U.S. oval buckle. The soles of his leather brogan boots
flapped as he came closer to Lorena.

"I have not been to the war nor have I scavenged battle
grounds, if that's what you're thinkin'. I was given these odd
bits of soldierly clothing by prisoners and deserters escaping
through here, getting rid of identifying garments. I had me a
plain pair of overalls I traded off for these britches and a bottle." His intense expression was one of curiosity mingled with
the ferocious caution of a mountain man not used to visitors,
women in particular. "That Yankee was the last human individual to lay eyes on me. I am not much for strangers."

Lorena saw in his rough, frowning visage twinkling eyes
much like her father's and in spite of the woodsman's appearance, she felt a rush of tenderness toward him and a sense
of safety in his presence. Rachel, who did not share these
feelings and had yet to utter a word, stared back at the man
with suspicious eyes as round as blueberries.

"We are all strangers in a strange land, sir," Lorena offered
and the fellow nodded.

"My name is Ezra Jack Adams," he said in the soft, lyrical
cadence of the mountains, which still echoed the Scots Highlands of his ancestors. "I am called Long Jack on account of
my tallness. I have not heard from my son, Little Jack, since
he left for the fighting. Neither him nor me can read nor write
but I had hoped he would send me a spoken word. You
haven't got a message for me, do you?"

"I so wish we did but, no, sir," Lorena answered.

"Don't go looking so sad. Ain't your fault. Well, Long Jack
greets you both just the same and proposes that you join him
for a taste of breakfast, what there is of it."

"We smelled the smoke of your fire. Are you burning
maple wood?" asked Rachel finally breaking her silence and
some of her reserve.

"Hickory. What's your names?"

"I am Rachel Longworth, late of New York City. My friend is Lorena Reed."

"Lorena Sue Reed of Reed Mountain Laurel. I have been long gone from home. Do you have news of goings on in the valley, sir?"

"Some, and I know your people, at least those who remain. Before we get to talkin', first come to my fire to warm and rest yourselves. From the look of you, you been travellin' some." Lorena slid off her mount and got to the fire in a flash. When she tipped her head, water ran from her hat brim and hissed in the flames.

"Jonah's luck, dripping in the fire," Long Jack mumbled. He reached up to grab a fistful of pine needles, which he tossed in the fire, then spit twice. "That's the antidote. You'll be fine now."

Thank you, Mr. Jack," said Rachel almost warmly, dismounting and stretching her arms toward the clearing heavens. "This is certainly our good luck day, meeting you."

"At sunup nature was bountiful to my gun to the extent of two spring-fattened rabbits. As a start, they will ease our hunger some. Sorry to say, I have no coffee to offer. I doubt there is any in these mountains, hasn't been for two years. I have no biscuit neither, but I have fresh-killed bear meat."

"Bear meat?" Rachel repeated skeptically.

"Yup. I killed that bear so dead he never waked up."

"Oh," said Rachel politely. "Be that as it may, Mr. Long Jack, our mule carries coffee beans *and* a grinder. Also a generous quantity of hard tack. And for the coffee there's whiskey for a touch of flavor."

"I do not intend to gainsay a city lady, ma'am, but this is *my* lucky day. You two take care of the fire and coffee and I'll tend the rabbits, unless *you'd* like to skin and gut 'em." Long Jack grinned, showing a lot of pink gum and few teeth.

"I could skin the rabbits," said Lorena. "I've done it before, but my brothers usually took charge of their own catch."

"I've never seen a dead rabbit, except cooked and in a sauce, on a plate," added Rachel.

"Can't skin a rabbit! Now, how could that come to be?" Long Jack asked as he took the rabbit's head in his right hand, holding its body firmly at its chest in his left hand, and twisting. "You have to know, or likely starve. I'll teach you. See, it is the same twist for a rabbit as for a chicken or a squirrel." The snapping neck made a crunching sound. "Who did your killing, your skinning, and gutting, young lady?"

Trying to disguise a tone of embarrassment at her lack of practical skills, Rachel said, "The cook did, and she would rarely let me watch. In fact, she was reluctant to even let me into her kitchen."

"I heard things are different up north as they are surely different in the cotton lands south of here, chiefly on the big plantations. There's cooks there, like where you hail from. They're slave women, or were, reported to rustle up glorious food, but around here everybody tends to their own self. Otherwise, we'd go hungry, which sometimes happens nevertheless. The mountains are a hard place, made harder in these last years by outsiders coming through and people killing each other, stealing, running off most of our animals. I used to have me hens, a goat, and a big-bellied sow once. No more."

While Lorena set a can of water on the fire to boil and spooned in about three handfuls of ground beans, Jack, a little way off with Rachel who was timidly looking over his shoulder, grabbed the ends of the rabbit's front and back legs and stretched.

"He's kind of stiffening up. That's the best way to loosen the innards and the skin, too. Now, you take a hold of the front legs, hold them in front of you. A little lady such as yourself must shake for all your worth."

"But why on earth must I?" Rachel sounded on the verge of tears or rebellion or both, Lorena thought as she went to join her friend.

"You must shake the critter so's the innards drop down inside." Using just thumb and forefinger the mountain man tugged at the rabbit and pulled the entire skin to the tail. There was a sucking sound. Rachel backed away, even though there was very little blood on the denuded rabbit carcass. The meat was crimson, almost black, where the shotgun pellets had spread through it. With the rabbit's belly turned up Long Jack stabbed the tip of his knife into the soft flesh at the chest and slit downwards. There was an intense foul stench as the hunter cleared out the offal before he plunged the carcass into a bucket of water. The air became wholesome again when he hurled the guts away into the woods. "There!" said Jack with satisfaction, handing his neat result to Lorena and starting on the second rabbit.

Soon, wrapped in bear fat and speared through on an ancient rifle barrel, breakfast hissed and crackled over the fire as Long Jack said, "You asked about the folks in Laurel Reed Valley. Some have fared better than others, though no one has come through this war good."

"Does my mother live?" interrupted Lorena.

"Yes, last I heard. Your father has gone, killed. One of your brothers, the young one, is with her. Another is missing."

"Frankie is still with Mama. I am relieved for that and Daddy's at peace. I know that for I had a letter from Little Brother. I lost that letter somehow. It told more but I can't recall what." Lorena sighed. "But you hinted at other sadness besides."

"The Reed family, as all the others in the valley, and indeed all through these mountains, are a hurting people, still determined and proud, but bad hurt. I remember when your forbears and kith and kin was flourishing. I will not forget to my last day your old granny, Lorena. I heard her say to her sons oncet, 'If you got to die, die like a damned dog with your teeth in the other's throat.'"

"That's my old granny," Lorena nodded. "What of your forebears, Jack?"

"I was brought here as a very young boy by my father who had been a farmer in Scotland. He came indentured, but once free of debt, he brought us to the mountains where the people was righteous and the land free for the taking—that is after the Cherokee were driven off. And good land it is too, with its high, cool weather but yet with a long growing time, being south. It rains heavy in the spring and summer we know well, turns dry in the fall, just fine for apples, which some say to be the best of the whole country. Peaches, another fruit of the high country, are the best anywhere known, I am told, when they are rightly cultivated and harvested accordingly. It takes the hands of many people, both young and old, who can work safe, pickin' in the valley orchards. And there's a need of folks to trade the fruit in the down-land market. There's been no safe travel and no markets to travel to. Most all, too many of the people are gone, leastwise all of the men."

"Not *all* the men," said Rachel.

"Most all, anyway. Last winter, by count, there were seven home places in the valley being run by women doing the best they are able with trampled fields and no livestock. At the start of the Rebellion, six of those farms had working men, fathers and sons. Sure, they were wild and foot-loose but they hunted and fished, even when they were liquored up, and fed their families.

"Young people are gone now. There's only four out of near a hundred fifty souls in these parts who have not yet marked forty years. It's that way all over the Blue Ridge, preacher said on Sunday."

Rachel, who long had impressed Lorna with her detailed knowledge of the war's progress and her keen curiosity about the workings of the world, began to question the old man intensely, not through suspicion but from an evident desire to understand the people of the mountains, so different from anyone she had ever known in the teeming streets and great mansions of New York City. As they sucked the last bits of rabbit meat from bones, then gulped coffee—Long Jack with great reverence and relish—Rachel asked if there had been any considerable battles in the areas as there had been at Bull Run, Fort Donelson, Shiloh, Antietam, Gettysburg. She knew the numbers of casualties—Confederates and Federals—lost at these and at other sites. She knew the names of the Yankee gunboats on the Mississippi.

"Is it casualties of battle, Jack, that accounts for the absence here of men?" she inquired. "There were hostilities at Averasboro and at Bentonville in North Carolina."

"You know a lot, don't you, and you ask a lot questions," Jack said with faintly suspicious narrowed eyes and caution of the mountaineer.

"I'm a doctor's daughter brought up to question and to speculate in the scientific manner. My knowledge of the specifics and sad casualty numbers of the War I largely acquired from my brother Robert—gleaned from just about everywhere. He always knew facts so quickly; he must have had access to a telegraph machine though I do not know where. Did he ever mention that to you Lorena?" Lorena shrugged noncommittally, lapsing into her own thoughts about Jesse. Despite her anger, hurt, and determination to get over him, she missed him more than she should, in fact, terribly.

"Up here in the mountains," she barely heard Long Jack say to Rachel, "the terrain is too steep and rugged for a vast pitched battle."

"If one of the generals possessed the brilliance of Hannibal, and had elephants, as he did to do the climbing and to carry supplies."

"I never met Hannibal. There's much you are informed of that I am not but then you can't skin a rabbit. It seems folks learn what they have a need to know. As for elephants? That is an uncanny thought, Miss Rachel!" Long Jack quipped, laughed and slapped his knee, hoping to lighten the tone of the chat. He was finding these young women, each a very attractive female in a refined way, to be most intense and unfathomable. Not unexpected, he reckoned. The one, the doc's girl, was a citified Northerner. The other even if she was raised up hereabouts was the child of an interloper; a bookish woman brought to the hollow by Reed. Some of that lowland refinement must have rubbed off on this girlchild, Lorena, even if Hazel Reed had done her best to become indistinguishable from the backwoods women who were her neighbors. Proud, self-willed, church-going folk, all the

Reeds, all us southern highlanders, thought Jack. This Lorena was self-assured like her daddy and likely had a touch of his recklessness, too. She just rode into the lawless wilderness with pistol at her hip but no man at her side.

Jack observed his guests shed their outer garments in deference to the rising heat of mid-morning. That done, the Reed girl meandered off. "Have a care you don't get turned around and lost in that there woods!" he called after her before he turned his attention back to the doctor's daughter.

"There was very little battling hereabouts. Rather Madison County right from the beginning of the war was a lure to deserters, Union and Confederate, to bushwhackers and such. For a time it got kind of crowded around here."

Lorena, leaning back against a tree, closed her eyes, lifted her face to the sun, remembering first the faint scent of lime and soaped leather, which often clung to Jesse. She felt his hands on her body and let wave after wave of languorous sweetness seep through her. She saw the light in his flinty gray eyes and the pulse at the base of his throat when she had stretched out on the bed, waiting. His nostrils flared slightly when he had whispered that her hair was a flaxen storm. He traced the lace inset of her satin bed gown from one breast to the other, his slow endless caress making her feel nearly transparent under his eyes. And her hand went instinctively to the hard swell beneath his belt. He stretched his length beside her, and with care and mastery, he set his hands and his hard controlled body to animate her slender form, turning her to pure light and heat with his dilatory fingertips and lingering hands. She was incredibly responsive, he had often told her, seemed to burst into flame when he found the enfolded secret point at the core of her undulating body. With a gasp, a formless cry she had raised her hands to grip the bedstead above her and parted her legs inviting his invasion with every gesture of her articulate body.

CHAPTER 17

Jesse stood ruminating at the open window of his darkened room at the Willard Hotel. Only the recurring flare of the tip of his cigar revealed to Hamson, who was casually standing watch in the street below, that the Colonel was wide awake at three in morning, restless and cogitating. Hamson had learned from experience to interpret the implications of Jesse's way with a cigar. When he drew slow and easy, sipping, as he said, he was a contented man. The more quickly the colonel's Havana burned down, and the brighter it glowed, the grimmer was Sparhawk's mood.

Jesse was mulling over the news he had gotten two days earlier from New York. It had not been to his liking, and he was impatient for more details, eager to ride out of Washington as soon as he got them.

There had been another communication for Jesse just coming in when he and Robert arrived at the telegraph office with Doc's message in hand. It was from Ryan Q. Runion.

Wharton and Partier escaped STOP Army officers standing picket duped by devious spies STOP New York City shadows and coppers superior guards—Incarceration in Tombs Prison best—Too late now—My men in pursuit STOP Sketches being posted from NY to Chicago. Q.

"Colonel, do you think the spies' escape has something to do with the disappearance of Lorena and Rachel?" Robert had worried, pacing the telegraph office as the two men awaited further information from Doc. When it arrived, Jesse read the communication eagerly, then answered Robert's question, crumpling the sheet of paper in his clenched fist.

"Apparently not," Jesse snarled. "There was a note for me from Lorena. She left behind all her fine things and an IOU for the clothes on her back. There was a one-line postscript; 'I am no Cinderella for a false prince.' I can't reckon what the devil got into her but I can guess where she and Rachel have gone. To Seneca Falls."

"And once Lorena finds what she's after there—what then?" Robert questioned, carefully picking a piece of lint from the sleeve of his new custom-made Federal blue jacket. Their mission was no longer secret and he was proud to be in uniform.

"No matter what she learns, or doesn't, she'll get from Seneca Falls to her mountain home. She could run into serious trouble on the way, but my guess is she'll tough it out and make it through to Reed Valley. We'll be heading more or less in the same direction after more Reb schemers. That's our official mission, but, now, I also have two personal scores to settle up there in the Reed Valley—one with Lorena and the other with Yellow Cat Pete."

"I do hope Rachel doesn't decide to stay on at one of those Shaker settlements up that way, when Lorena heads home." Rob frowned. "It would break my mother's heart. She's set on grandchildren."

"You must give her some. But I can't believe Rachel is a young woman to live the single life. Should she think she is, the Shakers won't allow her to join them until she's twenty-one."

"Ah, I do agree!" Rob smiled. "The burden of providing my parents with the next generation of Longworths does not yet rest solely upon me, not if I help my sister find a husband. That's a relief. Thanks Jesse.

"Oh, and Jess, tell me another thing—who the devil is Yellow Cat Pete?"

"You'll hear his fiendish tale all in good time. Now I'll telegraph Q. I require him, or one of his protégé shadows, to go to Seneca Falls Infirmary. I need to know when the girls were there and every detail of what transpired.

Two days later Jesse was still in Washington, full of restless energy, pacing his room in the small hours, waiting for Q.'s report from Seneca and thinking of Lorena Reed incessantly. His erstwhile Cinderella had cast him off as a false prince, and damn it, he *would* hear the reason why from her own exquisite lips. It was a virtually unique experience for him, being unceremoniously rejected by any woman, and never by one with whom he had actually fallen in love.

Going over in his mind the many ways they had been together, Jesse could not believe Lorena had simply walked away. He vividly recalled how he had gathered her to him and felt her heart fluttering against his, like a little bird taking wing. Then again he remembered those occasions when his vital need had compelled him to peel off one be-ribboned stocking and ignore the other, to loosen a sash, slip a button loop, dispose impeding bits of silk before rushing her to bed.

There had been gracious evenings as well when they enjoyed each other in unhurried luxury, when he carefully took the pins and jewels her from hair, when he little-by-little, freed her from her gown and delighted in her lovely form slowly emerging—slender arms, smooth shoulders, white breasts, rounded hips. Standing behind her, watching their images in a mirror, he delighted in the expressions of wonder and passion that flitted like butterflies over her oval face. Her widening eyes would be alight with a merry joy in the moment and with the anticipation of pleasures to come.

There were occasions when she offered an almost shy smile and a submissive tilt of her head. His dark hair contrasted with her golden mane when he kissed her throat, then her shoulders. Her revealed skin was silken, soft and pale, and her fine breasts were a lovely sight reflected in the glass.

She would move about him, take the jacket from his shoulders, lead him to a chair and kneel to pull off his boots.

Frequently she set her sensuous full lips on his, yet managed to elude his grasp, which would have entrapped her and put an end to their playfulness before she was quite ready to surrender. She would continue, with concentration, the sensuous task of undressing him, then trace a soft hand over the knotted muscles of his chest and stomach, move about him exclaiming softly at his perfection.

In their brief time together there had been countless idyllic moments, some playful, others dreamy and slow, more often voracious and passionate as they perfected practiced pleasures and made breathtaking discoveries. And afterward, when they were in bed together half awake, she would stretch and curl against him, set her lips to his shoulder before he heard the steady breaths that came with deeper sleep.

"I won't stand for it!" Jesse roared.

Hamson, still on duty on the street below heard the shout and watched the red arc of the cigar the colonel flung away sail over his head to extinguish in the dust of the road.

"He really is in high dudgeon tonight," Luke Hamson said to himself. "Colonel Sparhawk's got his dander up and his gorge too. He's roiled, riled and fit to be tied, and I'm real pleased to be down here on guard duty and not up there." He began to whistle, under his breath, the tune *Black Eyed Susie*, pivoted when he came to the end of the walkway, and then sang a line or two. "*All I want in this creation/ A pretty little wife on a big plantation.*" Unable to recall any more of the words, Hamson went on whistling in the dark.

The telegram from Q. so impatiently awaited by Jesse came with the first streak of dawn.

Misses Reed and Longworth here and gone STOP Unable to question head nurse they spoke with STOP Elsie Frost delirious with fever STOP By chance rested myself near a Confederate grave with stone STOP Most Rebels passing-over up north buried unmarked for all eternity STOP This one marked Arthur Randall Whar-

ton STOP Superintendent of Graves reports Hester
Potts signed paid recipt END

"Coincidence?" Rob asked Jesse after perusing the telegram.
"No," Jesse answered calm and cold. " 'Hester Potts,' who
I strongly suspect is Estelle Partier, went to Seneca to find her
nephew, Maud Wharton's son. It seems she did. Later, the
woman made off with Lorena's purse, tried to arrange her
kidnapping then her murder. We must know the reason why,
now that the spy sisters are free. Lorena and Rachel may be
in danger in more ways than one. We need to find them—
fast! Rob, as you know, I have the greatest admiration for
independent, headstrong modern women who know their own
minds and take charge of their own destinies. Be that as it
may, and aware as I am that the queen of hearts is a desperate
card to play *and* whether she likes it or not, I'm going to meddle with Lorena's destiny in the tried and true old-fashioned
way. I'm going to ride to the rescue of my damsel in distress.
Let's get moving on the double. Blast it all, I wish I knew
exactly where Lorena was and what she was up to right now."

"Tell me please, Jack," she asked in a low voice, staring
into the mountain man's fire, "all the truth that may be told,
all of what happened at home in my valley." Long Jack looked
away into the woods, up at the sky, down at the ground, then
into the fire.
"If I don't stop talking and start frying we'll all three be getting right hungry," he said putting a small chunk of bear blubber
in an heavy iron skillet already well heated by the glowing red
coals of the fire. When the blubber began smoking, he spilled
it off and replaced it with two pieces of thickly salted meat from
the bear's rump, each piece the size of his spread open hand and
as thick as his thumb. After a while he turned the steaks over.
Lorena realized her question about Reed Valley was a dis-
quieting one the man did not want to answer. She would have
to be patient with Long Jack, up to a point. She said, "I

watched you salt the meat, Jack. Has the salt been restored to these hills?"

"No, but since it wouldn't come to the mountains, the mountains, so to speak, had to go to the salt."

"How?" she asked.

"The want of it got so bad that about a year ago I decided I had to do something. Salt is good for taste, sure, but more important we need it to preserve meat for the hunger months. I heard that in the North people sometimes use ice for the same purpose. Here we might get us a good chill but it ain't never cold enough to cut thick ice. So some of us slashed hickory saplings, about the thickness of a man's arm and we bound 'em together in stacks, loaded 'em on wagons and took 'em to the salt works in Virginia. We traded. The Confederates need them saplings to make hoops for the barrels to ship supplies to their army. I didn't like aiding or abetting my enemy, nor did I like to leave the mountains, but for salt, I had to and I done so. Too bad I don't have butter, but a good slug of that whiskey you mentioned would give this old bear some real flavor. I got me a jug of real hot sauce, too. I put it down twice a year. Make it mostly from ground-up fiery peppers, wild onions, and sassafras root."

Lorena managed to catch Rachel's eyes, which had been riveted as much by curiosity as by the craving for the sizzling bear steaks. Lorena said, "Maybe we should take notes for Madame Montespan."

"And who might that be?" Jack asked with a hint of wariness.

"The cook at home, the one I mentioned before. She's from Paris, France, and once was the chef in a famous café there," explained Rachel.

"I haven't never been to Paris, France, but I heard of it," Jack nodded. "I would take me a taste of your Madame Montespan's rabbit stew if I could but I wouldn't want to go far for it," he said as he placed the bear steaks on his guests' field-ration, tin-plate contraptions that had been issued to soldiers of the Union army. Though he had never had any use for one himself, Jack knew they were traded widely in the mountains at the going rate of one squirrel skin for one tin plate.

Lorena poured whiskey. All three gnawed and drank. Long Jack took up the root of a vegetable asking, "Want a chunk?" to which Rachel said, "I don't have any idea what that vegetable may be." Lorena, though, knew.

"It grows wild around here. That's ginseng. The root is of great use and value."

"What's it used for? Why is it so sought after and so profitable a commodity?" asked Rachel.

"I'm a bone setter and healer of some modest repute hereabouts. I can tell you in the precise words of the peddler who sells a number of roots and medicines through these hills about sang. Some call him the medicine man. What he recites about 'sang' as we folk up here call it and know our own selves, after the root is brewed into a sipping tipple, goes like this, to the best of my recollection:

Its virtues are that it gives uncommon warmth to the blood, and frisks the spirits beyond any other cordial. It cheers the heart even of a man that has a bad wife, and it makes him look down with great composure on the crosses of the world. It promotes insensible perspiration, dissolves all phlegmatic and viscous humors that are apt to obstruct the narrow channels of the nerves.

Pausing to catch his breath and, looking fixedly ahead of him as if reading from a page, Long Jack, like many illiterates with nearly perfect memory, continued:

It helps the memory and quickly ends all dullness. 'Tis friendly to the lungs, it comforts the stomach and strengthens the bowels, preventing all colicks and fluxes. In short, it will make a man live a great while. And very well while he does live. And what is more, it will make old age amiable by rendering it lively, cheerful, and good-humored.

Jack looked proudly and shyly at Lorena then at Rachel, smiling at both with modest self-satisfaction at his performance.

"Well done. Thank you Jack, but I'll decline, just at the moment," said Lorena.

"As will I," said Rachel, thinking Long Jack an unusual, knowledgeable darling of a man, one who her father would find interesting. She might also, if he were a decade younger. Since she had forfeited, for the time being at least, Shaker celibacy, Rachel had taken to worrying that she might never find another man to equal Jesse Sparhawk, who she realized yet once again, was lost to her forever.

Jack, Lorena, and Rachel had sat for a good while sipping hot coffee. Lorena said to Rachel, "We are now not far from my home at Reed Laurel, so I must once again press Long Jack for the details of the evil done there. I need to know what to expect."

"Young lady, I told you once there wasn't much killing around here but what there was mostly occurred in Reed Laurel, and it was grisly."

"What exactly happened, Long Jack?" Rachel asked.

"Nobody on this green earth can tell the veritable cause for the killings, which were seen by many around here who had secretly trailed the forced march. It ended not far from Marshall in the death of men too old for the army, and of two boys too young, who were rounded up in Reed Valley and herded along the road to Knoxville. Over in Tennessee. It is known for true fact that at the first dawn after the group was marched off thirteen of the prisoners—by then, two had escaped in the night—were told to halt. Five was ordered to kneel near a small creek. The Confederate soldiers who had took 'em, shot 'em dead. Then they forced five more prisoners to their knees and shot them dead, and then the remaining three."

"What dishonorable loathsome men killed these defenseless people?" asked Rachel who was indignant and pained.

"Soldiers of the 64th North Carolina Regiment supposed

to have turned loyal to the Union by then, under the command of a Lieutenant Colonel J. A. Keith."

"Why would a Southern officer commit such a crime, even one who had turned his back on his own side to swear fealty to his enemy?"

"I think he lied about his loyalty to the Union. Keith was vindictive, a born killer, and when he committed these crimes still a Reb officer at heart, a rogue officer who did this on his own. In war, those who think their own cause just above all others, may behave like animals, like wolves on the chase."

"But wolves kill out of hunger," Lorena said sadly. "These rogues killed only in vengeance."

"Those soldiers under Keith, who had been bad harassed and picked off by mountain guerrilla crackshoots, were feeling mean and cold on that early January day. A defenseless lot of little boys and old fellows were easy victims to men lusting for a cruel retribution. I heard tell Keith had a expression on his face like he was burnin' snakes in a rock pile—that's how much he despised his victims. He and his troop became nothing more than savage blood-hungry bullies, hunting their own kind, something I never heard tell about wild animals, not even wolves, as you just said. You pair of pretty females had best cover up to appear like boys again and take great care as you go on up the mountain. There's still lawlessness and transgression. Nothin's the same as it was when you went away, Lorena." She stood, wiped her hands on her britches.

"We've come safe this far, Jack. We'll be wary and we *will* make it the rest of the way home just fine." Her determination was so strong, Jack tended to agree with her, but at the back of his mind, worry remained.

"I'll go with you myself, if you'll have me," he offered.

"That would leave your home place and supplies vulnerable to outlaws, thieves, and squatters. Thank you Jack, but no thank you." Lorena stood up on tiptoe and managed to set a kiss on his scraggly chin. He blushed scarlet and took a step backward nearly falling over a log. Rachel restrained her urge to hug the long skinny figure of a man for fear of making him even more ill at ease.

"We will never forget you, Long Jack," said Rachel. "Perhaps we'll meet again one sunny day." He grinned, nodded, shrugged, and shuffled his feet.

"I ain't plannin' to be goin' nowheres," he said. "You know where to find me if you have a need to. Now Misses, I'll put forward one strategy: Rest yourselves here a while and leave at dusk. You'll be less likely to run into trouble then and you can be guided by the stars. Mountain folks like me and you, Lorena, are born knowin' how to navigate on this earth by following the glowing heavens."

"Celestial navigation. I have been taught that skill, city girl that I am," nodded Rachel. "And I certainly could use a bit of a nap." She stretched and looked about for a comfortable spot to curl up. Conversation gave way to suppressed yawns and, even, a quiet burp or two. Soon, silence and stillness settled over the encampment, the only sounds the cropping of horses nibbling grass and the deep even breaths of the sleeping girls.

At high noon, the sun's rays penetrated the early spring leaves. The fire had all but died out, the last dregs of the coffee grown cold. At the edge of the campsite, Long Jack was tapping the frying pan against the trunk of a tree to rid it of fat when, stealthy and without a sound, two men stepped out of the woods. One leveled a shotgun at Long Jack's chest and signaled silence. Rachel, who had awakened a few minutes earlier, was leaning back against a tree, eyes closed, getting her bearings. Lorena sat on her slicker a few feet away cross-legged, Indian style, with a light leather jacket over her shoulders, taking mental stock of their supplies. Cool and unmoving, she looked up and studied both strangers, each in turn. Clearly, these were not the sort of people one would have met at Dr. Longworth's dinners nor were they to be counted among the proud hardworking folk of the mountain hollows and settlements. These men were scruffy outlanders, bushwhackers, thieves, or worse, she had no doubt. One continued covering Long Jack when the other stepped over to the drowsy, oblivious Rachel and kicked her wide-awake as he snatched up the Winchester, which she had leaned against a tree stump.

"You'll sure do for what I got in mind. But first get up and let's get a look at you and your friend there, not that it matters to us if you're pretty or you ain't," he said glancing over at Lorena and then, with a knowing lecherous grin, at his partner. Of the two intruders, he was the shorter and older. He was pasty-faced and red-eyed. He had a stained mustache so crooked Lorena wondered if he had shaved in the dark and without a mirror. A rope belt had slid below his overhanging belly and a hunter's knife protruded from the belt.

Still, Lorena did not move.

"I said, 'up'," he repeated, "on your feet, you backwoods fillies." Still, Lorena neither spoke nor moved, just looked the man in the eye. "You're bringing to mind some kind of eerie cat, with them steady eyes. You ain't a hant are you? I heard tell there's witches up in these hills." The man looked again at his partner, uneasily now, as if for orders or reassurance.

At that instant Lorena made her move. She, too, turned to look at the younger, taller man, who still had his shotgun on Jack. She began to rise in a smooth glide, flicking the jacket from her shoulders already firing the Colt forty-five caliber revolver before she was on her feet. Her first shot missed but so startled the outlaw that he never even saw Long Jack's blade before it penetrated the base of his throat to sever his jugular. Lorena fired again, fast, at the other man, and then once more, both shots hitting him just above the rope belt. Still standing, he touched his belly tentatively, concentrating hard. His waist and then the crotch of his rough-spun trousers reddened. His began to tremble, fell to his knees, and then pitched over on his side, rolling back and forth. His lips were the deep purple color of crushed pokeweed berries. As he writhed about on the ground, he seemed, surprisingly, to become stronger. He managed to get up, first to his knees and then to his feet. He stood, wobbling, before he took a step toward Lorena. He rocked back on his heels, and then stag-

gered forward. Lorena fired again, at his head, and again he
fell, this time almost at her boot tips. He lay there with a death
rattle in his throat, his tremors slower and weaker until he
opened his mouth. A stream of blood gushed out. He lay still.
Lorena reached down and put her fingers to the throat of the
fallen man. There was no pulse.

Long Jack's eyes were wide with amazement and remnants
of the fear they had all felt when faced with imminent death.

Rachel, who had remained immobile as a statue until then,
looked at the two fallen men and then, with puzzlement that
gradually turned to admiration, at Lorena. She got to her feet,
retrieved her carbine and said to her friend, "I'll get the animals ready to travel. I think we had best move on after all
the gunfire."

Long Jack took Lorena's hands in his, an unusual gesture
for so reserved a backwoodsman. "You would have made
your father proud. I knew him some. He, too, was very brave.
You've a ways to ride yet, to reach Marshall town and your
people. I have no doubt, after what I just saw you do, that you
and Rachel will be able to take care of yourselves. I'll hide
the bodies. These men are Kirklands, part of an evil-bad, cowardly clan from a homestead over to the Little Tennessee
River. They been preying on both sides during the War of
the Rebellion, specially on outlying farms and the lonely
women running them. Their kin will come looking for 'em,
so keep a real sharp eye and ear peeled specially for Yellow
Cat Pete, the most vicious Kirkland of them all."

CHAPTER 18

A week after Lorena and Long Jack had taken care of the bushwhacking, predatory Kirklands, Jesse and three other riders—Hamson, Longworth, and Nicke—were approaching the town of Marshall, in Madison County. Like the trail Lorena and Rachel followed, the road was perilous to travel. Thievery and violence were commonplace and retribution for wartime treachery to settle grievances was rampant. Jesse and his hard-riding troop had been warned that men were being shot outright for as little as a pair of boots and for as much as a small fortune in greenbacks. Others, lacking anything worth taking, were dragged to the nearest tree and strung up.

As the riders, cantering single file, approached a bend in the road, shots rang out. The four men leaned low in the saddle and their battle hardened mounts never shied, but charged on along the road, all but the lead animal. The black gelding, having been hit, reared and then crashed, his rider thrown forward to the ground. The fallen horse writhed in the dust while Corporal Luke Hamson, who had fallen clear, crouched behind the animal and rapidly fired his pistol at the assailants appearing from the trees on both sides of the road. The wildly-cursing, fearful-looking undisciplined highwaymen, who just moments before had been lying in wait, intent on robbery and murder, thought they had felled at least one victim whose companions had bolted for safety around the next turn. They were wrong. Jesse and the others, who had reined in their horses, swung about and came galloping back in the direction from which they had come to perform a classic light-cavalry charge, soon cutting down the enemy one by one.

Dismounting and calling out to Hamson, the riders cautiously approached the fallen men. Two were dead and the third fading rapidly. When a pistol was kicked out of reach of the dying man, he looked up in terror at a Union officer.

"You! I thought you was done for, Yankee," he choked in anguish. "Sparhawk, help me." Jesse did not move, just gazed down with icy rage and contempt at the whining man at his feet. Sergeant Nicke was standing close by. Perceptive as he was of Jesse's feelings, he was awed by the intensity of anger and contempt he saw in the Colonel's hard face.

"Is he a Reb, sir?" Nicke asked.

"Not as good as an honorable Reb, worse than the foulest traitor. This man is a doublecrosser. He made a deal, on a gentleman's handshake, to lead me and two others—young Union volunteers of the First Regiment, Rhode Island Detached Militia—through the mountains to freedom. We had been captured at Bull Run and then escaped while being transported to Andersonville. Then this bastard reneged, set us up, sold us out. He hanged those young men with his own hands after the others had their fun tormenting them. His name is Yellow Cat Pete Kirkland and he's just gone to hell."

"You've done what you've set out to do, sir," said the Sergeant, with respect, before he went off to shoot the fallen horse and start digging a grave for the dead bushwhackers. He had gotten about three feet deep when he first saw the dog. The handsome field spaniel, a parti-colored black and tan, crept to the side of one of the dead men and was whining pathetically. Corbett Nicke was not a sentimental man but he did love and respect a noble well-made canine. This one, whoever or whatever his master had been, appeared to be exactly that. Not able to keep a dog of his own since he had joined the army, Nicke got a rope, secured the dog to a tree, talked to it, petted it, hand fed it a pieces of salted beef from his kit and poured water for the animal into his own tin plate. "I don't what they called you before," said Nicke, scratching the spaniel's ears, "but you're 'My Dog' now. I'll be right back. I got to check on the Colonel."

Still seething and as tense as a tightrope, Jesse watched the body at his feet being dragged off by Hamson. And then, fists clenched, he relived in his heart and mind how his fate and that of Yellow Cat Pete Kirkland had intertwined.

In the fall of 1863, Jesse and two junior officers, young lieutenants, captured in northern Georgia, escaped. By day they hid in woods and underbrush and in the cabins of welcoming field hands. These slaves fed them from the meager food available and passed them along to others on the next plantation for help. On their flight back toward Union lines, the three Yankees traveled only by night. As they approached the North Carolina border there were fewer and fewer black faces. Some whites were willing to help, not those who lived in the large rich townhouses but those who lived in the small isolated country cabins. It was among these hill people, many of whom were Union sympathizers or Confederate deserters, that a guide could be found, they hoped, to take them over the all but impassable trails through the dense mountain woods north to safety. They had to be extremely careful in trusting such a person, because a mistake that would reveal them to the enemy could cost them their lives.

Near Hendersonville, they were spotted and chased by Confederate guerillas, but managed to elude capture, and hide in a thicket of laurel bushes. They wandered the woods for several days, cold and near starvation. They came upon an isolated cabbage patch at the edge of woods. As they began gathering as many of the heads as they could, a party of young women came upon them.

Jesse smiled and talked low, as if gentling a horse and, like the spy he was, even on that mission, he subtlety and circuitously felt them out for their political allegiance.

"Don't be frightened. Upon my honor as an officer and gentleman, we won't hurt you," Jesse said. Aware of the usual effect of his smile on ladies, he used it then. Even starved and shabby as he was it began to work its magic.

"Who are you?" the bolder of them inquired, a bird-like wisp with the angular cheekbones and taffy colored hair of the mountain clans.

"Soldiers, ma'am." Jesse embellished his remnant of a Carolina drawl. That, like his smile and reserved manner, also proved useful.

"What kind of soldiers?" the girl asked, edging closer.

"Confederate soldiers, ma'am."

"Hadn't you ought to be engaged in better business than stealin' cabbage?" the girl giggled.

"What better business might that be?" Jesse winked.

"Helpin' us pick huckleberries. Better than fightin'."

"Why, I believe you *are* a Yankee," Jesse said, "trying to deter us from rejoining our Southern brothers in arms. Will you tell me your name, pretty lady?"

"No, I ain't a Yankee, but I'm no sesech, neither. I believe in tendin' to my own business and lettin' other people alone. My name is Clara. These here are Olivia and Elsa May, my sisters." Jesse tipped an imaginary hat to them all.

"Would you have Yankees overrun the South, steal our slaves and rob us of our property?" he asked in a calm, impartial tone.

"We never had us even one slave. We don't want none, neither," Clara bristled. "It's you Johnny Rebs got us into this and you ain't yet won your war of rebellion nor will you quit this fightin' and killin' y'all fetched on this war. You forced men into the army to do battle for Jeff Davis, men and boys from these parts who did not want to go 'cause this ain't our fight. You have got the whole country in such a plight that there's nothing goin' on but men huntin' and killin' one another and huntin' and killin', all the time. I do not know. But maybe if them darn Yankees would hurry on and get here, all this'll end. It couldn't get worse, of that I do not conjecture." The two sisters, obviously frightened, tugged at Clara's dress and Olivia whispered loud enough for Jesse to hear.

"Have a care what you say, Clara! Them strangers could be vigilantes comin' after Paw." All three girls appeared worried and fell silent and edged back from the men. Jesse was persuaded of their indifference to the Southern cause, if not of their warm allegiance to the Union. He needed to put them at their ease and ask for their help before they bolted and with purpose or by accident revealed the hiding place of strangers in their woods.

"I've an admission to make, ma'am and young ladies," Jesse said in a very serious tone. "My two companions and I *are* Union Officers, escaped prisoners of war. We've been in hiding for days eating berries and roots and heading north by the stars, when we could see them, at night." The young women, hardly more than girls, took him at his word. The two younger officers came forward to better show themselves and the sisters smiled shyly, all but Clara. She grinned.

"I'd like to hear one of them boys talk Yankee," she teased. "We won't tell on you to the Rebs," she said. "Right now, there's nobody on our place, but deaf Granddaddy. Paw gone off to get fish and Maw walked to the Kirkland's place, five miles as the crow flies, over this hill. Kirklands always got some provisions—flour, salt, and such. They are sellin' a few supplies, chargin' dear, lettin' our maw and other folks run a tab 'til the war's done and we can plant on our land again and pay them back. Today Maw took 'em some cabbages from this little patch we got hid up here. We'll fix you all up some slaw and a mite of whatever else we got that won't be missed. You can hide in the barn while we find you a guide."

The girls fed and sheltered the men for three days. On the last night, late, when Clara brought the news she had found them an escort, she knelt down in the barn straw beside Jesse and slipped beneath the quilt she had provided him. Theirs was the intense union of recently met strangers in time of war sharing only one certainty in their precarious lives. They soon were about to part almost surely forever. They were generous and passionate lovers that night until, toward morning, Clara reluctantly crept away.

At first cockcrow, she returned with Yellow Cat Pete Kirkland, the man who had agreed to guide the Yankees over the mountain ridge to East Tennessee.

From the first, Jesse was leery of the bleary-eyed, half-inebriated rustic, but there was no choice. They had to move on. The three Union officers and the taciturn mountain man set out. Before the sun was noon-high, as if they had left a trail of breadcrumbs after them for their enemies to follow, the group was overtaken and trapped by a band of Southern Irregulars. The 'guide' fell flat on the ground, passed out apparently from drink. Jesse and the others fought until their ammunition was gone and their situation became hopeless. As prearranged in case of trouble, each man crawled off in a different direction into the forest. When Jesse stopped to look back, he saw Yellow Cat Pete, steady on his feet, taking money and parleying with a Rebel soldier. Valiant Colonel Jesse Sparhawk could do no more than watch as his two companions were mercilessly slaughtered.

Jesse, betrayed, demeaned by helplessness, blaming himself for the debacle, made good his own escape, vowing one day to return the valley to hunt down and kill the cowardly conspirator who had sold them out—Yellow Cat Pete Kirkland.

Now, he had done it. Jesse had carried out his oath of vengeance. As Robert and Luke, the burying party, helped Hamson plant the body of Yellow Cat Pete, one incentive for Jesse's journey south was satisfied.

Now, he had to find Lorena to fulfill another sort of vow, one of love. A man used to working his will and keeping his word, he had little doubt he would succeed at winning her back. He had to. She was always in his mind and in his dreams. He would, staring into every campfire, see her there, a dancing golden vision of unadorned beauty. He heard her laugh on the breeze, saw the light of her eyes in flickering leaves and remembered how the sun had set her hair aflame with golden color. He remembered, too, in vivid detail how she concentrated with the intensity of a child while arranging flowers from the greenhouse, how she tasted kissing him in the garden, how her hazel-brown eyes teased or caressed him. Her smile glimmered in her delicate, beautiful face, her throaty voice purred with love when she was ready for him, her body a column of ivory perfection as she came into his arms. But where was she now? Why had she left him without serious explanation? He had to know. And he would.

For two days, Lorena and Rachel rode south and west from Long Jack's camp, both ever alert to danger. At night, they made no campfire. They ate hardtack and beef jerky from the new tin cans that fed the Union Army. Before dawn they rose and rode by fading moonlight. Rising in great rows of emerald green and sapphire blue, the grand peaks with great trees reaching the sky seemed to roll away like towering waves to the far horizon. They rode beside creeks cresting with white water torrents of melting mountaintop snow. Remnants of summer weeds and wildflowers—goldenrod and Queen Anne's Lace—were scattered among new, fiddle head ferns, trillium and lady's slipper, other wildflowers, blooming profusely on the floor of the forest. Lorena revealed to Rachel the half-hidden, tight little green rosettes of buttercups about to erupt into bloom, and fork moss, untouched by winter.

As they rode, they often stopped in pure wonder. To Lorena, the beauty was familiar; to Rachel it was a revelation. Once, while checking the trail and nearby clumps of bushes within the forest groves, searching for signs of marauders who might be lying ahead in ambush, Lorena sensed a presence. She sat perfectly still and motioned Rachel to do the same. They waited until, on a branch, high above them they saw a hawk. Lorena was sure she could feel the stare of its fierce, orange-red eyes, fiery eyes which, she remembered, held no sign of warmth, or of soul, not even of cruelty or heartlessness, only a determination to hunt and to kill and to feed. She shuttered within, and saw Jesse's face, in her mind's eye, angry and determined.

The goshawk was perched on the limb of a beech tree where its coloring blended with the gray of the bark. Seeming to lose interest in the humans below, the great bird's head moved back and forth. Occasionally, and very slowly, it changed its position to stare in another direction. While the bird peered about in slow rotation, Lorena and Rachel watched and waited. The leaves of the forest floor still matted down and caked from the recently melted snow, softly stirred and the head and then the body of a field mouse appeared. Lorena saw the goshawk's neck, until then sunk into its shoulders, extend to its full length. The bird's body leaned forward and its wings cocked. The dive was startling, even if anticipated. It occurred instantaneously and in complete silence until the lethal-looking, inch-long talons clamped deeper and deeper into the screaming, then squeaking, then finally silent victim.

Lorena and Rachel, followed by the pack mule, moved on. Only the wind high in the dark fir trees and the calls of migrating birds disturbed the quiet of the forest.

Later, as the trail opened and looked out on a valley deep below with endless sky above, the two riders stopped again to admire a bird soaring, scouting, wheeling higher and higher in larger and larger circles. Perhaps it was the same goshawk.

They rode down the mountainside along a stream that rushed over a waterfall and emptied into a pristine mountain lake so clear that pebbles and stones sparkled and glistened at its bottom.

The sun was setting, the wind had died and the air still held a measure of warmth. They dismounted and like spirited schoolgirls began peeling off their clothes. Lorena would bathe first while Rachel stood guard. After removing soap and towels from the mule pack, Lorena set to work with the dampened soap before plunging into the icy lake. A sharp scream, that seemed to go on forever and ever, echoed off the mountain walls. Almost as soon the echoes stopped, Lorena was back on shore wrapping the towels around her. "Well, so much for secrecy. The whole world knows we're here now," she said, her teeth chattering.

Rachel could not stop laughing, no matter how she tried to stifle her peals of merriment or how unladylike she sounded.

Her toilette was more subdued as she tiptoed in and out of the water daintily splashing handfuls over her body until she was covered with goose bumps and also shivering. "We should have something to eat," she announced as the sun disappeared into the trees.

"I'm hungry and cold," Lorena answered. "Let's chance a small fire under those boulders, for warmth and cooking, especially for brewing us some coffee. We need a few creature comforts about now. I'll prepare. You stand guard and shoot anything that comes within range that has two legs."

"Amen," said Rachel wrapping a blanket over her shoulders and taking up the Winchester.

After supper, as the moon rose, they sat very close to the fire's last embers. They had decided it would be best to let it die out in the darkness. They heard the nocturnal animals of the hills go down to the water's edge to drink and snuffle about. They listened to the hooting of a screech owl and the piercing scream of a wild cat making a kill. It was a normal, starry night in the Appalachian wilderness.

Later, still in darkness, Lorena was dimly conscious of the distant call of a loon. Fox after eggs, she thought as she rolled onto her side. She curled for warmth drawing her knees up, her thighs moving sensuously one against the other. Memories of Jesse invaded her dreamy half sleep and she became aware of her nipples firming. Sighing softly she came more fully awake, her needy body aroused by memory. The first kiss had been a revelation. She must have invited it. Jesse directed it. His breathing had quickened as he drew her to him. She had felt, with momentary surprise followed by pleasure, the silky foreign pressure of his tongue in her mouth.

She had been so eager, even proud, to offer herself to Jesse the first time. She had wanted him badly but innocent that she was, she had not known what to do after the first sweet piercing kiss. He had shown her, had taken her to bed; spread her undone hair luxuriously over the deep pillows. Her lips, he told her, moist and parted, were glistening in candlelight. She had kissed him deep and long, sucking on his lower lip. His hands

moved over the skin of her breasts and down along her ribs until
he was tracing the smooth flesh of her belly, the inner curves of
her thighs. He explored and invaded the moist channel between
them and she parted graceful legs to invite him truly inside her.
Then as he entered her velvety softness and as it parted for him,
she felt the strong, hard pressure. She had gasped as he took
possession of her, had clasped his shoulders and felt his hips
swiveling, his body piercing hers as they moved together, looking into each other's eyes when they rode the peak of passion
together, their matched desire and lust and yearning vented at
last in a long sweet hot shudder of release.

Later, when they were exploring each other, she discovered
how it delighted him to find her in bed, unaware of him he
supposed, lying nude on her belly and feigning sleep, her
smooth, round buttocks jutting up invitingly from her tiny
waist. But he had also delighted in leisurely discovery, slow
provocation. Between kisses he would take the pins from her
hair with precision and displace layer upon layer of silk and
lace as if unfolding the petals of a rose, he had said, to slowly
reveal her body to his eyes in, as he had whispered, all her
glowing perfection.

Lying alone in the moonlight on the shore of a mountain
lake, Lorena trembled with memory and yearning until sleep
engulfed her again.

Lorena awoke, heated by dreams, to the crackling of a
good fire. When she looked to the place where Rachel had
slept, she saw the empty bedding. In a moment of anxiety,
Lorena looked about until she saw her companion at the edge
of the lake fishing with a branch as a pole and heaven only
knew what for bait, hook, and line. She constantly amazes
me, Lorena marveled, and when she saw Rachel's pole dip
and her friend pull up the line, a squirming, wiggling fish of
good, frying-pan size, she asked herself where a city girl had
learned to fish so skillfully.

"The answer to your question," explained Rachel when
Lorena had posed it aloud "is that I learned to fish, seriously,
on Lake Candlelight, in Connecticut. My father has a com-

fortable cabin there to which he invited only a very few others. I was one of the lucky few. Father escapes to the cabin when he's not too busy with patients and the weather is right—warm enough for comfort or cold enough to freeze water for ice fishing. He taught me to catch, clean, and cook up a batch of fish over a campfire and the taste is like nothing else I ever enjoyed."

"Better than any of Madame Montespan's masterpieces of culinary art?" Lorena asked.

"Yes. I'm not precisely certain why. Perhaps it is the freshness of the catch or the smell of wood smoke that infuses the flesh or the clear air of outdoors changing the chemistry of taste. Most of all it was having my father all to myself, I really think and just two of us able to work together at an elemental human task—catching and preparing our own food." She paused. "We never hunted, but one day I may be able to teach *him* something—how skin a rabbit," She laughed, then her expression became serious. "Doc must be sick with worry about me. And you, too, Lorena. It was unkind to leave home as I did but I didn't want anyone to interfere with my becoming a Shaker. As soon as we're out of the wilderness, I intend to post a letter home saying we two have gone west to start over."

"I think we'll do right well at surviving in a raw new land, we two," Lorena smiled. "I can shoot straight and you can fish quick. What've you got there?"

"Small ones. They don't put up much of a fight so it isn't much fun hooking them, but there are a great many already hatched so early in spring, and ours isn't a sporting venture. We need to eat. I've never seen fish as colorful as these in our lake. We get mostly bass, speckled silver crappies, and such."

"You've gotten us some speckled trout. They call them brook char up north in the streams of New England. And fun to catch or not, they sure are good eating," said Lorena, who was happy to be watching Rachel arrange the fish in the pan, which she kept shaking over the fire, frying up the batch, a couple of minutes on each side. They had two each.

"Well, how do you like them?" Rachel asked looking quizzically and a bit anxiously at Lorena.

Lorena, not wanting to give offense said, "They're quite good."

"Only fair, I thought. They're going to be better," commented Rachel happily. She had gradually been lowering her usual guard and was becoming open and very much at ease speaking her mind to Lorena. "The first set wasn't done perfectly. The next batch will get four minutes a side." She did exactly that. Both girls relished their breakfast and finished it off chatting over steaming mugs of coffee.

"You know, I love him," Rachel said with no preamble.

"Yes," replied Lorena knowing precisely of whom Rachel spoke.

"It started as a school-girl crush on my father's handsome and charming friend. He flirted with me when I was a child as a young uncle might. But as soon as my childhood ended so did his attentions to me, attentions of *that* sort. He is a sensible, thoroughly honorable man. I'll always love him. I wanted you to know."

"Thank you for telling me. It's better for us to be open about Jesse," Lorena answered, refilling their coffee mugs. "You were so guarded Rachel, so brittle and serious when you and I were introduced. You shook my hand. You didn't even try to smile."

"Yes. That was my way with everyone then. I should not have behaved so with you flat on your back in bed, lost, not knowing who you were or where. Recalling my unkindness makes me cringe!" Rachel rested her forehead on her drawn up knees, letting her loose and curling red hair fall to cover her face.

"I don't hold it against you, Rachel," Lorena smiled. "I never did. I was not a lady, you surmised, because my hands were work-hardened. You *were* right but oh, how unhappy you looked and dour in your little brown dress with your glorious red hair pulled so tight into a bun it must have been paining you. I remember thinking so at the time."

"And then Robert offered to teach you to play shuttlecock!" Rachel laughed, flinging back her hair. "What an odd lot we were—still are, really—my *bon vivant* brother with his waxed mustaches and perfectly fitted coats, me plain dressed, Mother grand as a queen and big as a boat, all of us so absorbed in ourselves. Not Jesse, though. He was thinking of you and what you would need to get well. Then, he fell in love with you. That truly put an end to my lingering hopes."

"Dear Rachel, you and I are in the same boat now, in love with the same man who neither of us will ever have."

"You could if you only would, wed Jesse and have him forever. You've misjudged him, I'm certain."

Lorena wore a pensive frown before she abruptly stood, shook her head, and tossed away the last of the coffee in her mug.

"No matter how we feel, we *will* get over him. Jesse Sparhawk is not the only bull in the pen," she stated, adamant. "Time to go."

Almost reluctantly, because the lakeshore was so isolated and idyllic that life's demands seemed far away, they broke camp. They covered over their fire and campsite to hide any signs they had ever been there, and set off for Marshall, with luck just hours away, Lorena reckoned. Her emotions were roiled with anticipation of being in her home place and seeing her loved kin after being so long gone. There was apprehension, too, after Long Jack's tale, of what awaited her there.

Lorena was also awash in longing for Jesse Sparhawk. Their paths must not cross again. It was the only way she would be able to resist him at all. She would get in and out of Reed Valley right quick, stay just long enough to give comfort where she could, give her mamma the mule and a hand with planting, then head on west as planned. His mission of revenge would, eventually, bring him to Reed Valley. She must be long gone before he got within a mile of her she insisted even as her heart protested and broke inside her.

CHAPTER 19

Jesse and the others regrouped on the main road to Marshall, after settling the score with Yellow Cat Pete. Sergeant Nicke, Corporal Hamson, as well as Colonel Sparhawk had expressed their admiration to Robert Longworth for his calm under hostile conditions. Rachel's twin brother had fired his first and perhaps his last shot in the War of the Rebellion. He had all along risked his life as an outstanding undercover agent, pretending to be an irresolute mamma's boy. Now he had shown himself to be a first-rate, bold marksman. He had fought with unflinching bravery, and had been responsible for striking down the murdering thief named Mashburn.

The four riders, in somewhat faded Union Army regalia, followed the road running along the swiftly flowing French Broad River. In the shadow of the mountain jutting up from the water's edge, they entered the town of Marshall, which consisted of just nine houses, three stores, a cobbler's shop, a blacksmith's establishment and two uninviting small hotels, one in need of paint and the other of a new roof. The courthouse of the Madison county seat and its adjacent two-cell jail added to the forlorn appearance of the place.

The travelers had been hopeful of better accommodations, a first-rate hotel that would promise hot baths, good food and drink, soft beds, and female company. Looking about, they swallowed their frustration, except Robert Longworth who grumbled under his breath about getting his uniform brushed. As they sat their mounts discussing which of the two available lodging houses to choose, they saw as if in a vision, two slim, graceful young women step from the cobbler's shop. They wore wide-brimmed woven straw bonnets and artfully patched colorful work dresses of homespun that stopped just above their shapely ankles. Both were barefoot.

"Lorena Reed!" Jesse roared. "I'd know your form and figure and that stride, anywhere!" Lorena, flabbergasted at the sound of his voice, clutched Rachel's arm, and tried to compose herself before she turned and glared as coldly as she was able. She spoke not a word of welcome nor did she display a gesture of greeting, but merely lifted what she hoped were uncaring eyes. There were shifting lights in Jesse's eye—angry sparks, and barely hidden flashes of longing—when he pressed his booted heels against the flanks of his horse and the animal leaped off at a full-out gallop, racing down the almost-deserted dusty center of the only street of Marshall.

"Keep your distance, deceiver!" Lorena commanded regally as horse and rider bore down on her. Jesse's laugh was menacing as he leaned from his saddle without reigning in at all and scooped her up. The horse, a strong cavalry chestnut, never missed a step but galloped on with two riders, one somewhat precariously dangling and struggling, up the road and out of town. They raced along French Broad River and their pace did not slacken at all until, descending a slope, Jesse spotted a small strip of beach at the water's edge. He slowed the horse and released Lorena abruptly but with controlled calculation. She slid to ground, startled but, as he had carefully maneuvered, unhurt. He cantered on, circled back to pull the stallion to a stop and scowled down at Lorena. She stood with her hands on her hips, bare feet set wide, meeting his angry eyes with a provocative look of her own.

"*What* did you call me, Miss Reed?" His tone was incredulous and daunting.

"Deceiver," was Lorena's one word reply. The huge horse danced a step closer to her. She did not flinch.

"*Why* would you call me that or even *think* it?" Jesse demanded. Lorena was becoming unnerved. She had to crane her neck to look up at the tall, imposing figure of Colonel Jesse Sparhawk, the man more intimidating atop a large horse than he would have been looming over her with his feet on the ground.

As a bullfighter in a ring would taunt his dangerous adversary, Lorena casually turned her back and walked several steps away from the threat of an unpredictable, powerful mounted man. Her ploy to get him on a more equal ground footing was successful. Jesse dismounted with a swift tiger's grace and swung her about to face him. Lorena still had to look up to meet his glare, but not as far up.

"You and your mistress and her sister bolted the scene and disappeared together. You deserted me at the very moment, the very moment . . ."

"We were to be married?" Jesse asked. Lorena nodded.

"I realize now it was for the best you left me, you and your fellow spies!" she said, her words ringing false in her own ears even as she spoke them. Her amber-flecked, hazel eyes were glinting with an expression meant to show implacable wrath as she gazed steadily at Jesse with what she hoped was disdain. She was riveted in place by the proximity of his lithe body and handsome severe face, where a nerve jumped along his right cheek. Her every nerve responded, evoking memories of both the wild and the sweet moments they had spent together. Her love and need of him unfurled and sprang up like wild flowers in spring sun. Might she have misjudged him? No! She inwardly exclaimed though she had serious difficulty maintaining the scornful pitch of her voice and her look of disdain.

"Fellow spies?" he roared, incredulous and indignant as a series of emotions flickered over his face—confusion, indignation, pained tenderness, then more fury until the mask of his face hardened to hide his emotions. His fists were clenched at his sides and tremors of rage shook him.

"How could you think that of me?" he demanded and the ice-cold tenor of his voice almost disarmed her completely.

"I know you went to call on Maud Wharton every afternoon, even after we were together," replied Lorena with forced pride, as if what she had just said put her undeniably in the right. "When you left the house, Warbird, I waited days for some word from you and got none. Finally, I went to Washington Square and found you and that Wharton woman gone. I was devastated. However, I'm over you now. Shall we let it go at that?"

"Let it go at that?" He barked a hard laugh. "How could you just walk away from me?" he gritted slamming his right fist into left palm.

"You did. From me. How could *you*?" she countered. She leaned back against a tree to steady herself.

"I was on a *mission*, a secret mission for the United States Government, the most important one I'd ever been charged to carry out. As soon as my work allowed, I tried to contact you. *You* had left. Did I so misjudge the strength of your affection for me?"

"No, not at the time, but now? I was not exactly myself, you may recall. I was your Cinderella. The prince, you, found me and made me royal. I could not ask, or even dream, of wanting more. At first. But then, you helped me discover who I really am. Jesse, I was raised up plain to be honest and truthful and to keep my word once I a made a vow."

"Do you mean to say you are not who I thought you were, Lorena, not the free-spirited woman I fell in love with, the one who trusted her own impulse and intuition? I loved her— you." He waited. "Do you believe me?"

"I'm still that girl, too, but different as well. There's more to me than you or I supposed. I cannot be your Cinderella. I need to choose my own way." She lifted one shoulder in a dismissive shrug, reluctant to grant that he might be speaking the truth. Have a care, she warned herself. He's a smooth one, this Jesse Sparhawk, a true spy at heart.

"What of Maud Wharton?" Lorena asked in a subdued voice.

"She, too, was a *mission,* never more than that to me. It was my job to stay close to her."

"How close?"

"As close as need be to win her trust. I don't think I fully succeeded at doing that, but while we were playing out a cat-and-mouse spy scenario, never quite sure who was the feline, who the rodent, Maud and I engaged in another most human diversion. There was never any confusion in our battle of the sexes about who was tomcat, who the canary." Jesse spun on his heel and walked a few steps away. "I was a free man; she was a sophisticated, adept woman of the world. It was mutually gratifying."

"Our connection, yours and mine, Jesse could also be characterized as 'mutually gratifying.' Did you ever love Maud at all, even a little?"

"Not for a minute. I put Mrs. Wharton and her sister under arrest that fateful night in New York, house arrest. They escaped, got away." Lorena set a finger to Jesse's lips to stop his words.

"Don't say any more, please," she asked, abashed and perturbed. Jesse would not be silenced.

"Lorena, from the first moment I saw you, you twinkled and glimmered with a luminescence like sunshine. You brightened my gloom. You lit my darkest day and I put my heart in your hands," he said. "I told you then you saved my life, rescued me from myself, that you were the one I'd been waiting for always."

She took a side step to get out of the heat of his glare but he moved with her and loomed before her again like a wall. She moved the other way. He stopped her again. He set his hands on her shoulders and drew her hard against him before his mouth came down on hers, brutally possessive. With monumental strength of will she held rigid, arms at her sides, mouth closed, eyes wide. Her every instinct was prompting her to part her lips and melt against him, to merge her softness with his commanding body. She needed to fold her arms about him, to trace the long muscles of his back with her finger tips, to see him in the flesh as she so vividly did in her mind's eye—strong neck and shoulders, the angular lines of his hips, the swell of his flanks as his rigid strength probed her deeper and deeper. When he finally released her, her racing heart was pounding in her chest and Lorena choked back a gasp that was very nearly a sob. She moved away from him to stride toward the river and he came after her, taking care then, to keep a distance between them.

"You love me," he said in a low, smoky, confident voice. "You're not as unfeeling as you pretend to be. Admit it."

"Our marriage would have been a disaster," she managed to say.

"Perhaps. Particularly if you distrust me as you profess to. Let's give it a try anyway. I'll prove you're wrong." She was beginning to falter, he knew.

"But what if . . . ?" Lorena started to say, looking at him over her shoulder.

"Forget 'what if.' There's no time for dallying. There's too much living to do. Love conquers all, or so I thought. Perhaps I was wrong," he said in a heart shattering lost-little-boy tone.

"You *are* wrong," Lorena went silent when he offered her his crooked half smile and when he shrugged and tipped his hat, about to turn away, she hurled herself at him, into his arms, taking him by total surprise and nearly bowling him over. Lorena melted with reckless desperation into his urgent embrace, her mouth wide, his slanting across hers, hungrily while his hands slid beneath her dress, moved up to her waist, found the soft, warm, ready places of her body. He went down on his knees to set his teeth to the tips of her breasts, which stood against the soft, damp circles he had made on her soft dress. She too sank to her knees, her arms enfolding his neck, after she had flung his hat away.

"I accept all blame because . . ."

"Be quiet," he whispered. "I don't care why. There'll be a preacher not far down the road."

They clung hard and close, relief and desire coursing through them so urgently Jesse could not be bothered with the row of hooks and eyes down her bodice. With a tug he easily tore them open, pressed Lorena down. It was the sound of rending fabric as the dress hooks tore away which stopped Lorena cold.

"Stop!" she exclaimed, both her hands on Jesse's chest pushing him away. "I must tell you. I *must* give you some explanation."

"Oh, blast! I don't care," he laughed lifting the top of his body from hers with an easy push up. "You already left me one IOU and a cryptic complaint—about Cinderella and a 'false prince.' We've settled the false prince problem. Out with whatever is on your mind this time but you'd better be damn terse. My patience is wearing thin."

"I think—I know, rather—I love you."

"And?"

"I need to clarify."

"Nothing. Love is all we need. It justifies anything, everything."

"Even if I have a husband?" Lorena asked sliding out from under Jesse and moving beyond his reach.

"You *are* married!" he exploded. "But I was the first man—you were a virgin, blast it! Who the hell is he?"

"Clint Reed maybe, if he's still alive. I'm sorry, Jesse. I want this as you do, but I have to know before." She waited. He stood.

"Before we see the parson?" he asked.

"Before anything. If Clint Reed survived his injury and the measles in that Seneca infirmary, I've already betrayed him. With you. I will not do it again. Where are you going, Jesse? Are you leaving?"

"I cannot possibly stay," he roared striding toward his horse. Her heart plummeted.

"Cannot stay, or will not?" she asked. When he glanced back at her, she was sitting cross-legged on the ground, her yellow hair aflame in the light of the setting sun. There was the suggestion of a pout on her lovely lips. Beautiful. He did not care a fig if she had a dozen husbands. He would make her his, whatever it took.

"Have your pick of 'cannot' or 'will not'," he grumbled. "Whichever, I don't think I can be trusted alone with you."

"Oh, blast it all, Jesse!" she called after him. "Are you going to help me settle this once and for all, or not?"

"I'll wire that excellent New York City detective, our good friend Ryan Q. Runion, to investigate the whereabouts of Clint Reed. You and I have much to talk over before I leave Marshall, Lorena, but with a chaperon in attendance."

"Talk over?" she asked, wishing he would never leave, but supposing it would be for the best.

"You're in danger, for one thing, and not just from me. Hester Potts, who has already tried to kill you, is Maud Wharton's sister, Estelle Partier. They most likely are still intending to do you in. Any idea why?" Lorena shook her head.

"All I can think is it's something to do with events at Seneca. That, of course, is where I made the acquaintance of Hester Potts. That's also where I was wed to Clint. It was his deathbed wish. And then, he disappeared."

"Seneca is also the final resting place of Arthur Randall Wharton, Maud's son, who had been a Rebel volunteer and prisoner up north. Estelle Partier, in her guise as Potts, had the grave marker placed.

"What you have to do with the wicked sisters, Lorena, I don't know. I'll find out, though. They were last spotted in Chicago. I'm heading west after them. Before I go, I'll see to it you're safe here with a military guard."

"West? But I'm going west!" Lorena protested. "It's all been decided."

"Don't you think the West is big enough for both of us, Miss Reed?" Jesse teased and grinned. "Once again it just so happens, I'm going your way."

"You said those exact words to me the day we met. The direction then was south," she said. He stopped in his tracks and looked hard at her, a plan forming in his mind.

"Why don't we travel together?" he asked. "That way I can keep an eye on you myself and also take the opportunity to woo you again, slowly and properly this time, so we can really get to know each other. That way, maybe you'll learn to trust me for certain. Things happened so fast between us, too fast for you maybe, the first time. What do you think?" His plan would work! He would never let her out of his sight, Jesse promised himself, never be far away from her. Whenever she lifted her eyes, she would see him. If she stretched out her hand, she would touch him. That way, he could have her wanting him every minute of every day until she willingly came to his bed. He could take it as long as she could. Longer if need be.

As if reading his mind Lorena said tentatively, "If we do go west together, it must be as friends only. I likely am another man's wife, don't forget."

"I'm willing to take the chance that you're not. Lorena, you were meant for me alone," he grinned. "We'll get to the bottom of this—together. Come on. I'll give you a ride home."

"Thank you kindly, sir," Lorena said returning the smile. "I'll introduce you to Mamma. She's going west, too."

"The perfect chaperone," Jesse said, lacing his hands to give Lorena a lift into the saddle. He adjusted the stirrups for her, his hand caressing up the length of her leg, his eyes continuing the climb to the curve of her breasts.

"Mamma?" Lorena mused, wondering about her mother and the man Seek. "A chaperone? I think you'd best come meet her right quick, to see if she's willing to take on the job." Jesse, smiling to himself, just took hold of the bridle to lead the horse back toward town. He did not think riding double with Lorena would be wise just at the moment. The trip west was going to be interesting, to say the least.

"On the way into town please tell me how it came to pass that the Reeds, some of them at least, decided to leave these green hills of home to go West."

"It's a long story, Jesse."

"I'm in no great hurry. Are you?"

"I'll begin the story back on the morning Rachel and I broke camp at the lake."

CHAPTER 20

This is what happened to the two friends following their supper of fish, their heart-to-heart talk and a refreshing night's sleep under the stars.

After rinsing their tins, Lorena and Rachel had collected the horses and the mule as they drank at the lake's edge. Each animal was fed a generous ration of oats before the mule was packed and the horses saddled. Lorena knew that she and Rachel had an easy ride to their destination.

They moved out under the dome of a clear, brilliant sky.

They passed through a lowland meadow carpeted with wildflowers, acres of groundsel and saxifrage and yellow gentian. There was new thin-leaf goldenrod just beginning to show and varied small blooms spreading before them like a multi-colored quilt. The meadow diffused into a blue haze until they came to shrubs and then trees as they rode up the mountainside. A drizzle of rain began and then there was a shower even as the sun continued to shine. They rode in wonder toward a rainbow.

"Whoa-a, whoa-a, whoa-woo," came the shouts reverberating through the valley as, in the distance, a strapping young boy ran down the narrow trail toward the two riders.

Lorena shouted back, "Whoa-a, whoa-a, whoa-woo, Frankie!"

By the time the boy had reached them, the two women had dismounted. Rachel held the horses while Lorena embraced her youngest brother and smothered him, as much as she could, in a great bear hug and in a flood of kisses. He stood awkwardly, returned Lorena's hug hastily, then broke away, embarrassed. Frankie was a shy boy just approaching manhood and uneasy in the presence of a pretty stranger not many years older then himself.

After he had been introduced to Rachel and had reported their mother to be fine and anxiously awaiting their arrival, Lorena asked, "But how does she know, how did you know we were coming?" Frank looked over his shoulder at the man who had come down the mountain with him but now hung back to let the long-separated sister and brother greet each other without restraint.

"Ma'am, I knew you'd reach us today. I told your mother and brother."

"You, did? How did *you* know Mr.—?" asked Lorena, clearly taken aback.

"Sequoyahson is his name, but we call him Seek," said Frankie. "He's my friend and my mother's friend. He helps us working the patch."

"A friend of our mother's is a friend of mine," said Lorena. Her smile was friendly and sincere, if puzzled, as she extended her hand. The man was tall and solidly made, an Indian, probably a Cherokee, of calm, majestic bearing, with an aquiline profile and long black hair. He was dressed in the attire of the local woodsman—leathers and homespun—but for a wide bead bracelet on his left wrist. Lorena took notice of it when he clasped her hand.

"You *are* Cherokee, sir," Rachel said as she dismounted and came forward to extend her hand also. "I have read that after The Removal Act was implemented by the Army, members of your tribe no longer reside east of the Mississippi, that four thousand of your people perished on the way west." she said. "My name is Rachel Longworth. I am privileged to make your acquaintance, sir."

"The Removal, which lives in endless memory, took place more than thirty ago, ma'am. Back in that time, some of our people were able to hide in these remote mountains of North

Carolina. Some agreed to exchange Cherokee nationality for United States citizenship later. Others returned from 'the trail of tears,' so called because they cried for these mountains, our true home. Now our numbers, though small, are enough to help us know what transpires for many miles around. We are simple people. We pass on news in age-old ways. In the matter of your progress, runners brought news."

"I know from your speech that you are not simple, Mr. Sequoyahson. I am not surprised in the least. I know of some of the great accomplishments of your tribe."

"Perhaps, Miss Longworth, you have heard of my father, Sequoyah?" Rachel shook her head 'no,' never taking her round blue eyes from the man. She found him splendidly stately and appealingly virile. She shocked herself with that thought and retreated into silence. Lorena, sensing her friend's unease, came to the rescue.

"Indeed, I know of Sequoyah," she said. "Everybody from Georgia to Virginia, who has been to school at all, knows of Sequoyah. I have always been fascinated by what he was able to do. In a small way, I, like your father, Seek, seem to have a gift for languages.

"Frankie," she said drawing her shy brother into the talk, "will you please tell Rachel about Sequoyah." The boy looked at Rachel in same way she had been gazing at Seek.

Rachel blushed. So did he.

"Sequoyah was also called George Guess. He made the Cherokee alphabet. It was their first writing. When they wrote, they could keep their own government records. They had a newspaper, too, for a time; Sequoya's 'talking leaves' it was called by some. With the eighty-five figures Sequoya made, they can write the sounds of their own tongue." Frank looked to Seek for approval. He got it in the form of a slow nod.

"Thank you, Frank," said Rachel. To her further chagrin, she was finding this clear-featured, good-looking boy, young as he was, appealing, though not in the same way exactly, as she did Seek. She was becoming more puzzled and curious than uncomfortable about herself.

"Young women, I've been told of your bravery back up on the trail when you were with Long Jack," Seek said after a momentary pause in the conversation. "You survived the bushwhackers. Impressive."

"We killed them. A terrible thing to do, but we had to," answered Rachel.

"Don't be troubled. Those men were some of the Kirkland brothers—Tom 'Bushwhacker' Kirkland and John 'Turkey-Trot' Kirkland. They lived between Yellow Creek and the Little Tennessee in Graham County. They raided all through the war, up here in these mountains. They didn't take sides. They were their most brutal on the lonely farms, attacking women left alone, trying to keep their families alive until their men could return. The Kirklands were evil and ruthless. Few in the mountains will miss them and many would like to have killed them. Everybody will celebrate what you have done.

"There is other news about the Kirklands. One of their kinsman, 'Yellow Cat Pete' Kirkland, was killed two days ago on Isaac Carringer's creek, about a half mile from its mouth. Shot in a gunfight with Yankee soldiers he tried to ambush. Two other thieves, Mashburn and Hamilton were sent to their Maker in that same fight. The three had just ambushed a young Indian boy near Robbinsville where some of our people reside under Junaluska, a Cherokee chief. He sent a runner to me."

"Is there is a Cherokee chief left in this part of the South?" Rachel asked.

"Yes. Junaluska is a true chief. A very old, old man now. In his youth, he saved the life of the General Andrew Jackson in a battle with the Creek tribe. Even so, when Jackson was the top white chief, he had Junaluska later removed with all the other Cherokee people. Junaluska walked home from the west. A lesser chief, his old friend, a white Colonel called William Thomas, went to the Chief's Assembly of North Carolina. They gave the old Cherokee citizenship and 337 acres of land for his long ago loyalty and bravery. Junaluska was a great fighter. He admires great fighters. He admires the soldiers who fought Kirkland and the others for their bravery and with great skill. The soldiers rode their horses with a skill nearly equal to the Cherokee. They shoot straight.

"The Yankees were riding up from Asheville on the road to Marshall on the other side of the mountain. The leader was called Sparhawk. Colonel Sparhawk."

Seek saw a change in Lorena's face. Her cheeks grew pale under her tanned skin, which was a pale berry brown, and she seemed unsteady even on her feet. It was hard for him to always understand white women, even his woman, Hazel, a big, fine female. And now her beautiful daughter, this Lorena Reed, who had stood up to killers many a man would fear to face, had become weak before his eyes. It amazed and puzzled him how such women could be strong, then change so quickly. Usually it was something about love. 'Inscrutable,' was the word for white women, he thought.

When the cabin came in sight, neat and snug with a curl of smoke rising from the stone chimney, Lorena touched her horse's flank with her boot heel and covered the distance between herself and home in a gallop. She slid from the saddle before her mount had come to a stop, took the porch steps in a bound and hurled herself through the open door.

Inside, all was quiet, but for the crackle of a small fire. And deserted.

"Mamma?" she called. "I'm home!"

Silence. Lorena looked about. All was just as she remembered. With the shutters open, the afternoon sun poured into every part of the main room. The jelly cabinet was near the door, a spinning wheel occupied one corner and a quilting frame another. On the frame, was a cotton quilt half done, and Lorena traced its pattern of sunbursts done in reds and pinks and shades of green. A hoe and a rake, cheese baskets and gathering baskets hung on pegs from the heavy beam that spanned the room. There were the long benches at the old oak table. The surface had been smoothed and worn by the touch of many hands over time. It had served three generations of Reeds, at least. A kettle, hanging on a

crane over the flames, was steaming. The old tin coffeepot
sat on the hearth to keep warm. Looking down on it all from
the mantel was Lorena's old sock doll with a button nose
and a few strands of yellow wool for hair. "Lizzie!" Lorena
laughed. "Wheres' Mamma?"

"Right here is where I am," said a warm, loving voice and
then Hazel and Lorena were both laughing and hugging as if
they never would stop.

Suddenly, the room was full and soon the group gathered
at the table.

"There's still not much to choose from in way of supplies,
but I managed to bake you-all a corn bread to eat with your
chickory coffee," Hazel said, looking from face to face.
Frank, Seek, the little red-haired girl from up north, Rachel,
and Old Granny, tiny and gnarled, sucking her corncob pipe,
and joining in the laughter though she was nearly stone deaf.
Best of all, there was her dear and only daughter, Lorena.

"Bubbles in your cup? Someone is going to be kissing you
before long, Lorena," the old woman pronounced. Lorena,
who was not planning on kissing anyone for a good long
while, smiled warily at the prediction.

"We got chicks hatching in the chimney cupboard," said
Frankie, who had been quiet for a time. "Seek says it's best to
keep them safe from foxes and such. We ain't seen an egg for
a long time, until Seek brought us the hens and rooster."

"On Mayday, eat the very last egg ever laid by a old hen,"
shouted Granny, "you'll give your man a son nine months
after!"

"I will try to remember that, Granny Reed," hollered
Lorena, laughing.

"You, with red hair, you still single, too, like your friend?"
Rachel nodded and flushed. "Drat," said Granny, "both of
you-all is nineteen if you're a day and gettin' on to spinster-
hood. Here's how to get you a husband 'fore it's too late.
Name one of your bedposts for a man, hug it every night, and
he'll be the one you wed!"

There was more talk and jest and chatter, each person at the table holding on to the joy of homecoming and reunion as long as possible, before thoughts and words inevitably turned to the faces missing from the circle, from the hills and hollows and from the surrounding towns and hamlets. A hush fell. Seek and Frank left to see to the animals. The four women were left alone, Granny snoring in her rocking chair near the hearth.

"Mrs. Reed," Rachel began tucking her legs beneath her, "I am struck by your appearance. Are you a native of this valley or an 'outlander' as I have already heard folks called even if they're from over the next ridge."

Hazel was unlike most mountain women with wiry thin bodies and straight pale hair. She also lacked their angular facial features and high cheekbones. Hazel Lenore Reed, the young matriarch of the Laurel Hollow Reed clan, was a full-figured woman with a handsome round face and a head of curly dark hair. Rachel was surprised at Hazel's outgoing style and her mannerly grace that suggested lowland society rather than mountain isolation.

"Mamma was raised as a true lady of the Southland," Lorena explained, "not on one of the great plantations of the coastal plains established by the British crown, but in a very comfortable setting. Her father, my grandfather, had commercial interests in Savannah and kept a fine town house there. Her mother was one of the city's most prominent society ladies." Rachel nodded.

"That explains in a way, Lorena, how you so naturally and quickly became part of our metropolitan family and conquered New York society," she said. Hazel looked uneasily from one to the other of the girls. She realized then that her daughter was a very different young woman from the one who had left home almost two years before. And of course, the same.

"The home I grew up in was a lovely one," Hazel agreed. "We weren't *very* rich like the Oglethorpes but we were well enough off to have a housekeeper, a butler, a cook, a children's nanny, two lady's maids, a gardener, and a coachman.

That would be Samuel. The staff were all literate, refined, devoted folks, all of them well-trained house slaves."

"I see," said Rachel. "We were strong Abolitionists at home."

"Mamma became an Abolitionist as she grew up. We
helped many a runaway on the road to freedom," explained
Lorena. "Mamma's nanny Ethel, taught her to read and write
before she was five years old and later she was sent to Miss
Weaver's finishing school."

"About then, a courtly musician from Vienna, who had
been a pupil of Mozart, moved to Savannah. Three times a
week he came to our house in the afternoons to give me
lessons on the pianoforte and voice lessons as well, although
my singing was not so exceptional as my piano playing.
When I was fifteen, I performed Beethoven's *Hammerklavier*
sonata and Gottschalk's, *The Dying Poet* at a debut recital at
the Savannah Music Academy. It was well received," Hazel
said with self-conscious modesty. "After a dinner party at our
house, there was always a musicale in the drawing room. The
musicians were friends of our family." Hazel smiled with a
soft, distant look in her eyes.

"Mother could have become a renowned professional like
the German concert pianist, Clara Schumann. Are you sorry
you didn't take that road, mamma?" Lorena wondered.

"I would not change one choice I made even if it were possible to start all over again. Lorena has heard all this history
many times before, Rachel," Hazel said, as if not wanting to
bore her newly citified child with repetition.

"I could listen over and over forever to stories of your girl-
hood. Hearing them again and again makes me feel safe and
happy. They also help me better understand . . . myself. Besides, you always add something new. Tell Rachel about you
and my father, now, please."

"Oh, yes, do go on," Rachel encouraged.

Assured that she had an interested audience, Hazel continued.

"Not six months after my debut and cotillion, I attended an
Anglican church lecture and social. A minister from London

spoke on the evils of slavery, which was a frequent subject of debate in the more sophisticated circles of Georgia society. The talk was followed by a supper and singing.

"Perhaps you'll think me hopelessly romantic if I tell you that during that evening I lost my heart for the first and last time." Both girls sat forward in their chairs.

"This is my favorite part," sighed Lorena. "My father." Hazel nodded.

"He was there, young and quiet, soft spoken, yet not at all shy. He was a strong presence in that room, handsome, rough-hewn, interested in everything, just a country boy a long way from home having the time of his life studying out the Savannah swells, the so-called quality." Hazel clapped her hands and laughed with delight at the memory.

"And he could *sing*! *Jeannie with the Light Brown Hair* was his first offering. He had a manly but sweet, bell-clear tenor voice I had never heard the like of. No one spoke or even moved. I could not take my eyes off him.

"His eyes found mine and then his gaze roamed over me from head to toe with no attempt to hide his, ah, well public appreciation. I fell in love right then and there. I had never felt anything like it with the beaus who had begun to come courting. I shimmered with delight and anticipation, he told me later. You have no idea."

"I have an idea, Mother," Lorena stated, and Hazel made a mental note to return to the subject a bit later.

"You and your daughter are very much alike in more ways than one," Rachel noted.

"Yes? Let me finish my love story and then you girls must tell me yours. I sat down at the piano. He soon joined me. We sang duets all evening. The next afternoon he came to call on me. My parents were civil, but when he had gone, they forbade me to see him ever again. He was without important family, wealth or status. In short, he was not a gentleman and therefore no fit suitor for a young *lady* like me.

"Three nights later we ran off. He took me home to his

mountains. Within a year your brother was born, Lorena. It was glorious.

"And then one night two years ago, masked men surprised him in the barn and while some of them kept me and Frankie covered with shotguns so that we couldn't help him, they bound him up and dragged him away. I can still see it. Later they found him far to the south, and brought him home to lie with his kin out yonder."

When mother and daughter were alone—Rachel had tactfully excused herself—Lorena felt free to ask about the presence on the patch of Sequoyahson.

"All the men were gone, the animals stolen. I worried last year about this time whether we would make it, Frankie me, if we'd be able to put up enough wood for the winter or salvage any corn from the trampled field. We trapped some game but we couldn't hunt and draw attention to ourselves out here, all alone. That's when Seek appeared. He had been in Oklahoma with the Western Cherokees because his own people, the Southern Cherokees nation, favored the Rebellion. He didn't but he missed the mountains too much to stay away. He's a good, strong man. He's taken care of us."

Lorena said, "I am so glad that he did. I worried."

"I was alone for so long, you know."

"I know, mother, and you are still a young woman."

"You bet I am. Forty, but I think I could get by for thirty-five," she answered in a jocular tone, "but be that as it may, let's have another cup of tea, daughter. I hope real coffee will be had in the hollow again soon." Over the rim of her cup, Hazel looked at her daughter, who had become a woman since they last had met.

"Tell me, Lorena, about you? Do you have a love?"

"Mother, I've been wed. I don't know whether or not I still am now. It was never—we never were together."

"Do I know the man?"

"Yes, Mother. It's Clint Reed."

"Oh my! First, your brother went north to fight, then you went north looking for your brother, then daddy was taken, and now you found Clint. Well, I would not have ventured to guess that you'd ever accept Clint, no matter how many times he asked you to be his wife. He's been doing that since you were all of fourteen and you've always turned him down."

"I was about to leave that Federal Infirmary at Seneca when I couldn't find brother. But there were many other boys there, from North and South, who needed care and company. I stayed on, and one day it was Clint on the stretcher. They thought he was a Reb, from his way of talking. He was badly wounded. I saved him from the prisoners' field hospital where there would have been no chance for him. In the Infirmary tended by Yankee doctors with decent medicines, there was a shred of hope. Then one day, that hope was gone. Death had placed its hand upon him. He asked would I marry him so he could pass happy. I did. Right after, I came down with ague and fever. Soon's ah could stand I went to see Clint. He was gone, mamma." Lorena covered her face with her hands.

"Passed?" asked Hazel, taking Lorena's hands in hers and peering into her daughter's eyes.

"No one knows for a certainty. He had just disappeared from that hospital. There was no record of a burial and none of his papers or personal things, what few there were, were found. I would have been looking for him, trying to solve the mystery, until this very day, but I got a letter from Frankie saying how bad it was here at home. Has any word come here to the valley about Clint Reed?" Hazel shook her head 'no.'

"His poor mamma," she said.

"He might be alive somewhere or not able to talk," Lorena said. "I intend to find him, or learn for sure what befell him."

"There's more isn't there?" Hazel asked. "Another man."

"The answer is 'yes'."

"He's not married *too*, I hope."

"No, not that."

"What, then?"

Lorena told the story of Jesse Sparhawk. She spoke precisely and calmly, with such a detached demeanor, it seemed to Hazel that Lorena was speaking of someone else, not of

herself, as if she were narrating another girl's tale of lost love
and a broken heart. When Lorena came to the end, that last
magical day and night in New York City, the Celebration Dinner and her near marriage, on the very day Mr. Lincoln was
shot, Hazel was visibly upset.

"Rachel was right, Lorena. You, falling into this sweeping
love so hard, so fast? You *are* very much like your mother."

"I am so glad about that," Lorena smiled wistfully. "I didn't
understand what was happening to me, if it was right. From
the first moment to the last, I was all a-tremble whenever he
was near me, if he touched my hand, or looked into my eyes.
Even now, I'm astounded to be needing him so. Surprised at
the strength of it." Lorena closed her eyes for an instant as a
surge of yearning sadness swept through her. "Oh, don't *look*
so sad, Mother, or I shall cry myself," she said when she
looked up. "I've made up my mind." Lorena stood up and
grasped the edge of the table. "It's *over,* really over, now that
I've been able to talk about it with you."

Hazel went to the bucket for a cool cloth and patted her
eyes with it. "It's so strange, isn't it, love? Well," she brightened, breathing in the fresh mountain scent of the spring
evening, "one always has, I'm sure, a special feeling for the
man who was the first, but that doesn't mean there can't be
another."

"Mamma, I've another thing to tell. Now the war's over,
Rachel and I have decided to go west. We've both lost at love
and we both want to find a new way, a different way. We will
leave the past, the East—these hills and the cities of the
Coast—behind. With Seek here to look after you and help on
the patch you don't need me. I'll sure miss you and Frankie
though."

"No, you won't miss us. I won't give you any chance to,"
said Hazel. "We, the three of us, Seek, Frankie and me, are
going west with you!" Lorena shouted a jubilant laugh.

"Stir with your knife, there'll be strife, "Granny suddenly
started up, wide awake. Rachel and Lorena exchanged
glances.

"I hesitate to transplant her now. Granny has spent her entire life here in the valley," Hazel worried. "I don't suppose she's ever been farther than Marshall."

"She's got lots of kin—daughters, granddaughters, great-granddaughters—to care for her. I need *you.*"

"But, I'm the one she always wanted beside her," Hazel sighed.

"Think carefully, Mother," Lorena said, standing. "I must go to town now, soon's I take a bath in the creek. Rachel and I must have our boots repaired before we head west. The cobbler in town may be the last one we see for a long long time."

"I made you a new dress," Hazel called after Lorena, "and your old one's here, too. You and Rachel can go to Marshall looking like a fine pair of young ladies!"

And they did. And, that's where Jesse Sparhawk found them.

CHAPTER 21

Under a horned moon, hours past the time everyone at the Reed cabin was asleep, Jesse brought Lorena home. They had met the others in Marshall and eaten a meal together in town. Then they had, despite Jesse's earlier reluctance to chance such close physical contact, ridden double up the mountain. Lorna fell asleep against Jesse's chest with his arms bracketing her, keeping her steady in the saddle. She wore his military tunic about her shoulders and it dropped when he lifted her down from the tall horse. She slid into his arms, her own entwining his neck, her mouth nuzzling for his. He turned his face to one side and her lips found only the hollow at the base of his throat. She came more fully awake and looked up at him.

"Your eyes are polished by moonlight," he said almost roughly, needing her, not moving to show it. Her hands remained on his shoulders. She did not step away or speak but her expression told it all. "In the forge of my dreams I could not have fashioned a more beautiful woman than you, Lorena. I'll sleep in the barn."

"Oh," she said. Still, she did not move. Jesse enjoyed a moment of her charming self-betrayal—a rush of color to her smooth cheeks, a widening of her eyes, tempting pursed mouth the precise shade of rose petals. He knew what she wanted and, at the same time did not want, or said she would not have.

"Lorena, do you know the Code of the West?" he asked.

"Is it similar to the Chivalric Code?" Her voice was a whisper. "I understand about honor, valor, a knight's loyalty to God, king and to the mistress of his heart, the lady he had sworn to love. Chastely. She usually was another man's wife, or a virgin maid, and her knight was never to lay hand upon her person or touch her lips with his."

"Chivalry was a medieval arrangement. The Code of the West is more practical. It's the Golden Rule, and then some. 'Do unto others as you would be done by, feed the stranger and ask him no questions, help your neighbor at barn-building.' As for women, where they are scarce, as in the New West, most men don't ask too many questions."

"Same as for the stranger?" Lorena asked. He nodded.

"And most men don't care overmuch about a woman's past. What's needed is a hardworking partner who'll give him babies. No one can afford to waste much time. Where settlers are building a future in the wilderness, there is no time to waste."

"When are we leaving, heading west?" she asked. Jesse was bemused by the question. Did it mean she might modify her prohibition and come into his arms when they had quitted the East or was it a hint that she would have him now? Resolutely, he reminded himself that before he'd take her again, no matter how much he lusted for her elegant jewel of a body, there was something he craved even more—her total, unconditional love, body, heart and soul, and her husband be damned.

"We'll leave as soon as we can, a week or so, I conjecture. It will take us that long to get ready. Also, I'm waiting for a telegraph. From Q., about Clint Reed, I hope."

Hazel was awakened by voices and was now watching the young couple from her window. Lorena's Yankee colonel was a well-made handsome man, she saw. He looked strong and resilient unlike the decorative boys she had once known in Savannah. To escape such superficial refinement she had run off with a down-to-earth country boy. Hazel was suffused by a poignant memory of her own first love. Since those long-ago days of her young womanhood, she had learned much about life. She knew now that some men took pride in being

lovers. Along with excessive good manners and elegant
clothes, they prized their gentlemanly finesse in pleasing a
woman. Lorena's father had done so naturally, instinctively.
Thinking Seek, in the bed behind her, was sleeping soundly,
she sighed aloud. Seek wasn't artful but he had bountiful
strength and when he thrust into her there was no mistaking
it. Her passion rose higher and higher and when they reached
their peak it was something primordial. Every time.

Seek, though, was not asleep. He had heard the approach
of Jesse's horse before Hazel had even stirred. Whether it was
inborn or trained into him, Seek's dreams were easily invaded
by any unusual sound or faint echo out of place. Now, unmoving, he watched Hazel as she observed Lorena and he
read the depth and intensity of the woman's passionate emotion. It was now curling her shoulders and drawing little sighs
from her mouth. He was ready for her.

Somewhat to his own puzzlement, Seek loved Hazel exceptionally. She had asked him to go west with her, to leave
his valley again. He had said he would think about it. He did
not need to. He'd follow the woman anywhere. That had been
a disconcerting realization for Seek, who valued his freedom
and independence, but he owned up to his feelings. Tomorrow, he would tell Hazel who was still deep in thought.

She was remembering how she had once come upon a
party of young Indians, in a glen. She had seen braves draw
their loincloths aside like curtains, and girls lift their skirts,
simple as that, so she did not take it amiss, the first time she
and Sequoyahson came together, that he had raised her skirt
to her waist and never quite bothered to remove his britches.
Simple as that. Now she was sure, even though he had
seemed to hedge her invitation, she would have her own powerful brave to make love to her, as they set off on the journey
west. Hazel sighed again, more deeply. The rooster, who had
no hen house, was nested with his mates in a tree. He was
also awakened and protested with a long shrill crow.

"What, is it mornin'?'" Seek asked in a sham sleepy voice.

"Never you mind," said Hazel, turning from the window,

lifting her chemise. "That damn rooster has been off time since the day he got here." She slid back into bed, pleased that Seek had finally given up his blankets on the floor to spend his nights beside her. Below, Jesse and Lorena murmured on but Hazel was soon oblivious to anything but Seek.

"Come on now, be of good humor," Jesse whispered to encourage Lorena as her spirits appeared to flag. "Think of it this way: I'm your chivalrous knight. You're another man's wife, at least for the moment. Nevertheless, solemnity doesn't suit you.

"May I have this dance, Madam?" he asked grinning and ceremoniously bowing at the waist. She nodded and a smile began to tug at her full lips.

"It isn't right that a lovely flower such as you should cling to the wall." He placed a hand at her waist and kept the other at his side. With her hands on his shoulders, they waltzed, barely touching, her hair flowing on the breeze, her lilting laugh floating between them until, quite breathless, she pulled away and perched on a porch step.

"Short but sweet, our waltz. Thank you kindly, ma'am," Jesse said. "On further thought, I'd best sleep in town at the hotel tonight. We'll be here after first light for a meeting. We'll plan our way west together." Lorena nodded.

"At least we know," she answered, "exactly where we're heading—to your land in Iowa. That's more than some folks understand when they set out for the west."

Earlier, they had discussed Jesse's land and some of the plans for it over a meal at the hotel while the accommodating young waitress hovered about attentively, listening to every word Jesse and then the others spoke.

Before the war, when Jesse was at the West Point Military Academy, he had come into a sizeable inheritance from an uncle on his paternal side. Jesse, being a prudent young man, who had wealth of his own and had no need of cash, took the advice of the Academy economics professor to invest in land.

Sight unseen he had purchased six-thousand virgin acres at the conjunction of the Missouri and Big Sioux Rivers in the western state of Iowa. When Jesse returned to active duty with the Secret Service in New York City, after escaping as a prisoner of war, he continued to follow the professor's advice—develop the land, which, it was envisaged, would one day be a thriving agricultural community. To that end, Jesse recruited settlers, several families of related immigrant Germans living in New York City. Many of the men working at menial jobs had been members of skilled labor guilds in the old country—clockmakers, carriagemakers, cabinetmakers, and the like. Others had been small farmers whose depleted ground was unproductive or, more often, hired help on other men's land.

Jesse went from family to family in the area of the city known as Yorkville, where many of German heritage had settled. He had no trouble persuading the men, their wives, and their older children who, he knew would be valuable workers, to leave the crowded tenements for the spacious fields of Iowa. Most appealing was his promise to provide every family with a plot of land and supplies to build a home of their own. During these sessions, it was the older children who translated for Jesse, who knew little German, and the older immigrants who spoke hardly any English.

In the spring of 1864 as the war was winding down, the first group of immigrant families arrived in Sioux City. Within months, they reported with enthusiasm to their Yorkville friends and relatives, about the verdant new land and ample rain, and others followed west.

Jesse had been given a letter written from Iowa by a daughter of one of the families. The letter, in nearly flawless English, was to a classmate back in the east urging her to leave the "dirty, smoky" city for the "clean, sweet-scented country." She concluded her letter with a passage that Jesse, pleased and touched by it, recited word for word to the company gathered:

Your parents will surely want to know what I saw the other day. My father and I went a short way along the river from our camp into the countryside. There, he set to with the shovel he carried and began to dig. "Watch this," he said to me as the black dirt began to rise in a mound and the hole got deeper and deeper. He did not stop until the shovel rang on something hard and father had to struggle to dig deeper. When he did, his shovel came up with clay, not top soil.

'This shovel,' my father said, 'is four-and-a-half feet long. That is how deep the topsoil is here on Colonel Sparhawk's land. That means to me this plain in Iowa is the Promised Land. It will never wear out from cultivation. Great farms will flourish here. There will be rich communities with big houses, orchards, gardens, such as the ones others and I worked on in the old country. But here we will own the big houses and some of this land.'

My father grabbed my hands and in joy he jigged me around. Although my mother says that my father is given to exaggerations we do believe that in this matter of farming in Iowa he is right.

After Jesse finished his recitation, Robert Longworth said, "And where there are prosperous farmers many of civilization's amenities will follow."

"So, you will go with us, Brother?" Rachel asked.

"If I do not, I will always long for the way untaken, for all the might have beens," he answered.

"As would I had I remained with the Shakers," she smiled happily, overjoyed to be with her brother again.

"I'll telegraph father and mother of your safety, Rachel, and say you're going west to search for a husband."

"Oh dear, Rob, don't get Mother's hopes up," Rachel lightly cautioned. "I doubt I'll ever wed."

"Somehow I find that hard to believe," Rob replied. "In any event, I shall extend to our parents Jesse's gracious invitation to migrate to the new settlement. There'll be plenty of need for a physician, and perhaps Mother will fill her time bringing culture to the Iowa frontier—music, art, theater, and such."

"You don't really suppose *our* mother would ever leave New York for the Wild West?" Rachel giggled.

"She might," laughed Rob, "if she could bring her own *couturier.* Well, Sergeant, what are your goals for this excursion?" he asked turning to Corbett Nicke.

"Me and My Dog are comin' along to watch the Colonel's back and see what develops," nodded Nicke, leaning to scratch the ears of the spaniel asleep at his feet. "How about you, Hamson?" Nicke asked in turn.

"Well, I've been reading a scientific book, *The Manual for the Profitable Cultivation of Bees in the New World.* I am sure that the propagation of bees and the harvesting of their honey will be a highly profitable venture for me—for us all—in Iowa."

"Luke's a practical man," said Jesse. "He's convinced me of the efficacy of his scheme. A telegram went off to Boston to a bee breeder of note known by Luke to have in his apiary several Italian queen bees. We made a very good offer."

"Why Italian bees?" Lorena asked. She had been uncharacteristically subdued during the lively dinner. Seated next to Jesse she took care they did not touch even so much as elbows. She stole a sidelong glance at him now and then but never found him looking in her direction. Hamson, who had from the first a special feeling for Miss Reed, was keen to answer her question.

"The first colonizers of North America brought European black bees with them. They're a panicky lot, and belligerent. When they sting, it isn't pleasant, I tell you from personal experience. Now, the Italian bee is smaller, a faster breeder, of better disposition and beautiful to boot. Bright yellow in some of its parts, black-striped and golden elsewhere, altogether a lovely sight to behold and a pleasure to work with! We should have an answer first thing tomorrow," smiled Luke as the waitress served more of everything to everyone.

It was a festive meal and happy reunion. It went on long and late until finally, all the guests but Luke Hamson had gone their separate ways. Puffing one of Jesse's cigars, he moved into the next room to a barstool.

The grandly named Marshall Arms Hotel lived up to the first impression it had made. It was indeed shabby, but to Luke's eye, it had one redeeming feature: the young waitress who seemed to him, master gardener that he was, a peach just ready for plucking. Now, as he sat happily musing about Italian queen bees that would make his fortune, smiling to himself at the prospect of raising bees as they had never been raised before, thinking of their mating and multiplication, it seemed to him that, perhaps, the time had come to consider his own role in the biological scheme of things. He had been reading in Darwin's great book. In addition, he had heard rumors of a theory of reproduction being developed by an Austrian botanist named Mendel. In short, Luke told himself, it was time for him to become a father.

As these things are wont to happen, whether by design or sheer accident he did not know which, in the middle of his reveries, Luke became powerfully aware of the presence of the waitress clearing the table. She had told him her name was Haley. It even occurred to him that the girl had been taking every opportunity to cross his path and to ask if she could be of service. He inspected her plump, supple body, observed the easy way she moved, appreciated how playful were her green eyes shining in candlelight.

When Haley's glance met Luke's in the mirror above the bar, she caught him looking at her as only a man in heat can look at a woman. Haley had always been a bit of a flirt but nothing of a fool. She was already eighteen and not spoken for. She had by then rolled around in the hay and the woods and fields with a number of boys and she had learned ways to attract and to gratify them. However, none had remained in Marshall. Some went for soldiers, others to hide up in the forest and a few, catchpenny drifters, had headed on west. About the only man paying her court, if you could call it that, was the owner of the hotel, her boss, Jim Smith. When Jim wasn't tending bar, he was trying to put his hands up her skirt. Haley was sick and tired of slapping him away and she was becoming increasingly worried she might pick up a knife and push it into him. She smiled at the thought of Fat Jim bleeding like a stuck pig.

Luke saw her smile in the mirror. He moved two bar stools closer to her and nodded affably. He was not exactly what might be called a ladies' man. He knew that, but he also knew that he possessed the sort of common sense strengths and abilities that appealed to some women—nonpretentious ones.

What Haley saw reflected in the mirror was a man of middle age and middle height with faded yellow graying hair and quiet gray eyes. In a crowd, he might have been close to invisible, but alone at her bar he surely did stand out. The question was, did she want to give herself to this Yankee who was not handsome, not even very young, but surely eager and strong and able-seeming. She had heard dreadful things about Yankees, that they were as full of fire and brimstone as the devil himself. They had sly crooked ways of loving and leaving. That wouldn't be worst thing to befall her, Haley reasoned, or the first time it had happened to her. Something in the look of him was right. He conveyed dependability, Yankee or not.

Haley could not have helped overhearing the plans of these Northerners. They were going to a splendid place where you had to walk carefully so as not to crush wild strawberries. The woods were crowded with deer and the sky with plum pigeons. They were heading to a country where the water flowed in wide streams filled with jumping fish and ran through fields of tall grasses and high corn to cascade in a sparkling waterfall into large lakes blossoming with lilies. Even if all of it was not quite as perfect as they said, anything had to be better than Marshall. She could go along and see for herself if she played her hand well. When Luke stood and came toward her, Haley turned and "accidentally" backed into his advancing midsection.

* * *

In Marshall there was no railroad station, only a water
tower where the powerful, mountain-climbing locomotives
replenished their boilers. At the foot of the tower was a telegraph office, hardly more than a shack. Jesse and Robert kept
the operator busy sending off instructions to the Germans
telling them to hurry their work in constructing the hotel that
Jesse wanted completed in time for the arrival of his party.
There was also a steady stream of messages east to Q., still on
the job of tracing down Clint Reed. And orders for materials
and supplies to be shipped by rail from Chicago and up the
Mississippi from New Orleans.

While these preparations were going on in Marshall, Hazel
and Sequoyahson on the patch tried to sell off what equip-
ment and furniture they could, but no one in the hollow had
money to spend and when the time came, they walked away
with only the family Bible and a rooster and two hens in a
basket.

Five days after that dinner, the Sparhawk Settlers, for that
is how they came to be known, gathered in Marshall before
entraining. The last two to join the group were Luke and
Haley. They had spent the previous night and the three pre-
ceding it in Luke's bed, two sensual, famished lovers joyfully
gorging their appetites.

On the morning of their last day in Marshall, the couple descended the stairs hand-in-hand. Haley leaned over the bar
and said to her employer in a saucy tone, "Fat Jim. I quit.
We're going west." Fat Jim, washing the floor, struggled up
from his knees, paused for a moment of contemplation and
after looking at Luke opened his cash box and plunked down
a week's wages for Haley in gold coins.

"Good luck to you both. I wish I could go, too, but this
place, somebody's got to run it." Then with rare generosity,
he poured out three large shots of whiskey, raised his and offered a toast, "To a good trip and a real big future."

On the way out of the hotel, for what she knew would be

the last time, Haley whispered, "I guess Fat Jim isn't so bad after all, even if he can't keep his hands to himself." The irony did not escape her as she felt Luke's hands moving down her rump in a most delightful way.

The Sparhawk Settlers gathered alongside the railroad tracks while the huge locomotive took on water. As they waited, basking in the warm sunlight, a horse-drawn wagon drew up. Painted on its side in large, gilt letters were the words PHOTOGRAPHIC VAN and in smaller letters the legend *Record Your Likeness for All Posterity*. A young man, not much more than twenty, surveyed the waiting group. When he saw its obvious leader, the man said, "Colonel Sparhawk, I presume. I am Tim O'Sullivan, and with your permission I have come to join you on your way west."

"O'Sullivan? The photographer? I know of you. I was with the Army of the Potomac when President Lincoln visited and you, I think, were, photographing him. You were with Matthew Brady, weren't you?"

"No sir, not at that time. I had apprenticed with Brady in New York City, but by '62, in October I believe, when I photographed the President I was associated with Mr. Alexander Gardner. In any case, I am now on my own, although I do have a government contract to survey the frontier and to take photographs of what I think may be of interest in the development of the West."

"You are very welcome to join us. The more the merrier, as the saying goes. As to what is of interest, I hope you will find much in western Iowa where we are bound."

"Record Your Likeness for All Posterity," Lorena read aloud. "Tim, set up your camera. The locomotive's boiler isn't full yet and if you hurry, posterity will be pleased."

That's how it came to be that, months later, one of the most celebrated of Timothy O'Sullivan's group portraits was published the *New York Tribune*.

It was a wet plate photograph taken in brilliant sunlight. Not a soul was permitted to stir for five seconds. Each person's likeness was captured by O'Sullivan's lens with a clarity that was almost three-dimensional—all nine of them: Sequoyahson and Hazel, he, statuesque and dignified with his hand on her shoulder, she with a smile of contentment; Robert and Rachel, every bit the sister and brother; Corbett Nicke, intense and serious with his spaniel, My Dog, beside him, on command facing toward the camera; Jesse and Lorena, two very handsome people, not looking exactly joyous; Luke Hamson and Haley Austin, her arm through his, smiling—very much in love.

Tim emerged from the hood that covered his head and the back of the camera. Just as he was about to speak, to say, "Just one more," the locomotive blasted its whistle and then blasted it again. The trainman shouted "All aboard." As they were scrambling up, Lorena insisted on paying Tim for his work. She handed him a dollar from her purse, the last one she had in the world.

At the Marshall Arms Hotel, Jim heard the hissing and tooting of the massive locomotive. As he always did when a train left town, he went out to the porch to watch the engine slowly lumber into motion and the trailing clanking cars in its wake gather speed to leave Marshall deserted and quiet again. As he was about to turn back to his work, he saw two women, each struggling with a heavy carpetbag, make their laborious way toward him. Both were tall and both looked padded as if dressed in several layers of clothing beneath dark knit cloaks, which they paused to remove and carry.

"Mornin' ladies. Hot as Hades, ain't it?" Jim said pleasantly when they reached the hotel porch steps. He saw sweat dropping from their brows to make dark stains on the bosoms of their dresses. One woman was dour, with a long uninviting face. The other, though, was a green-eyed beauty, not young but well configured. Jim was interested.

"Help you?" he asked, almost leering at the pretty one. She looked up at him with the most lethal glance he had ever seen.

"Take the bags, lout," she ordered, haughty and cold. "You should have come across this excuse of a street rather than watch us struggle."

"I don't carry bags, ma'am. I am the owner of this establishment. Besides, I got me a bum leg." Jim took a few stiff steps in a circle.

"Never mind," said the other woman. "Have you a room? I require a bath." Jim nodded.

"I got a few rooms. Not fixed up. Chambermaid quit on me this morning. You'll have to clean for yourselves," he said. "And cook. How long you plannin' on favoring me with your company?"

"That depends," snarled Maud Wharton beginning to peel off the top layer of her clothing. "We come in search of the Reed family. Can you inform us of their whereabouts?"

"The hills are alive with 'em, ma'am. Which Reeds in particular are you seekin'?"

"Actually, we're here to see only one—Lorena." Estelle Partier wiped her brow with the back of her hand. "We couldn't pack all our things. We are wearing several dresses one over the other. We are anxious to change into something more comfortable. May we register, sir?"

"If it's Lorena you two are seekin', you're out of luck. She just left Marshall headed west. She and the others got on the very train you ladies must have got off of."

"When is the next train due to pass through this ditch of a town?" Maud demanded.

"Uh, let's see." Jim scratched his head. "Next train is due in five, maybe six days." There was a shriek from the pretty one furious and loud enough to make his hair stand on end. "And it's goin' east. You pair better step inside now," he frowned, "unless you'd rather go on down to the other hotel," he added hopefully. His suggestion was declined and he rolled his eyes heavenward in anticipation of the week ahead.

CHAPTER 22

Flora Dudley's Deluxe Rooming House on Fourth Street in the young town of Sioux City, Iowa, provided adequate accommodations for the Sparhawk Settlers. They arrived in June at the river town on the Missouri after a long railroad journey. It had terminated in Iowa City where the Chicago and Rock Island Railroad's tracks came to an end. Then they had covered the last miles by stagecoach and horseback. It had been an exciting but frustrating expedition. Lorena and Jesse were never far apart and never alone together.

For days and nights as the train rumbled along, no matter how she tried to avoid him, Lorena was always running into him, at meal times in the dining car, at tea in the afternoon, over cards in the lounge in the evenings. The engineer blasted his whistle as they approached a town or city to bring residents running to see the iron horse. Passengers stretched their legs, new ones joined the group, and others left. The engineer also blasted his whistle at water tower stops in the wilderness, just for the fun of it, Lorena thought. It was a hot spring surging into summer. The train windows were always open, and cinders from the engine's stack blew into the passenger cars day and night.

Jesse went into every telegraph office along the route to keep in contact with Q. The policeman reported on the wicked sisters' extended stay in Marshall, but they had left town, and their trail was lost again after they skipped out one night leaving most of their clothing and their unsettled bill in arrears. There had been reported sightings of Clint Reed, a tall gaunt mountain man in one guise or another—drunk, thief, psychic, preacher, beggar, in uniform, and in rags—but all proved false, Jesse informed Lorena.

The estranged couple spoke, almost always politely but with a distance and reserve that made them yearn for their former, impulsive sensual friendship. Occasionally they couldn't help but express their true feelings.

One night, Jesse stepped out onto the deck of the caboose and found Lorena there. His first response was to back away. He didn't.

"I remember, Lorena," he whispered in her ear, standing close behind her, "exactly how you look when you're flushed and glowing with heat. I know you remember the touch of my hand on your beautiful breasts." His arms on either side of her imprisoned her against the railing and his breath was warm at the nape of her neck. Over the noise of the train, she had not heard his approaching footsteps. She started, flinched and tried to turn on him. Instead, her head fell back against his shoulder.

"Stop!" she demanded, furious with him and with herself. He released her.

"If you're ever in my arms again, I'll never let you go," he growled. "You won't be able to leave me. I doubt if you, or I, will be able to hold out much longer."

"You, sir, are arrogant and overconfident. I could spend every day and night with you and never succumb." Tight lipped, Lorena rushed away from him, summoning all her adamant stubborn strength to resist.

At St. Louis, a long telegraph message from Q. was waiting for Jesse. On the platform as the train took on water, fuel and passengers, he read it aloud to Lorena.

Army Nurse Frost the good friend of Miss Reed passed over STOP Buried among soldiers with salute fired over grave STOP Here are the full contents of note

found among her papers STOP My Dearest Lorena **I**
*am going on West to live as a hermit in the wilds STOP
I fear I am no man no more since I got shot and no fit
husband STOP Forget we was ever wed STOP Forget
me STOP Clint Reed*

Jesse patiently waited for Lorena's reaction.

"Poor dear Miss Frost," she said turning away until she was
able to speak. "I don't believe that message was ever penned
by Clint," she said.

"Why?" Jesse asked.

"He could neither read nor write," she answered. "He *could*
make his mark. Did he?" she asked. Jesse sighed deeply.

"Someone could have set down his words for him as he
spoke, but I'll wire Q. now with your question. We'll pick up
the answer when we reach the next station stop. Our train is
about ready to pull out."

A few hours later, walking in opposite directions, Lorena
and Jesse inadvertently confronted one another in an aisle of
the passenger car. Each tried to step aside. Both moved in the
same direction. They tried again with the same result and
Lorena began to laugh.

"I'm glad you can see the humor in all this," Jesse grumbled. A lurch of the train sent her into his arms. When she
looked up, he found her wide eyes were shining and read
the small secret smile lurking about her velvet lips. Her veneer of self-control was transparently thin. He saw
acquiescence in her stare. "Turn and walk away from me,"
he said into her ear. She did not move an inch but kept leaning into him, seeing him in her imagination as she often
had in reality, unclothed, tall and slender with long muscles flexing, ready for her.

"I'm sorry, but I cannot walk away," she said softly. "I need
you now. Follow me?" He placed his hands at her small waist
and set her aside into an empty seat.

"If we give way just yet," he leaned to whisper before he
strode off, "you'll likely be angry and blame me."

"No, I would blame me," she sighed, but by then he was gone.

When, finally, they rode into Sioux City early one evening, Lorena retired as quickly as she could to a commodious bedroom, one all to herself. It was the first real privacy she had had in weeks. Tired as she was, she was not quite sure that she was ready for sleep.

Smiling to herself and beginning to yawn, she stripped off her travel clothes, washed her face in the basin of water on the bureau and slipped into a nightdress . . . Virtually unclad and indecisive, she stood stock still in the center of a room, her every instinct prompting her to go down the hall to Jesse, to be with him again. Even though she was alone, Lorena felt her cheeks burning at her thoughts, so contrary were they to her resolution to keep her vows to be a faithful, morally proper wife.

"I haven't broken my promise to myself—not yet," she said aloud as she dropped onto the bed, pulling the mosquito netting closed with such angry vigor she almost brought it down around her.

She reclined and sighed. She tossed and turned. She rolled from her back to her left side. She shifted to her right side. She sat up, furiously pulled off her nightdress and flung it across the room. *That* seemed to help. Exhausted, at last, she finally drifted into a deep, dream-filled sleep. Not for long.

"Jesse!" Lorena whispered awakening slightly but still caught in a web of sweet dreams of him. Her eyelids fluttered, though they didn't quite open, as the muted tapping at her door persisted, becoming part of her sleep's fantasies at first. Disoriented, she whispered, "Come in," so softly no one could possibly have heard her. But Jesse did.

"Oh, stay, *please*. You mustn't go so soon," Lorena said drowsily. Becoming vaguely aware of him in the doorway, she thought he was leaving her with all her senses fretted and aroused, and her heart suffused with his dream-conjured presence.

"Must you really leave me alone?" she protested, answering his unvoiced reply, which only she, in her reverie, had heard. "Won't you kiss me just once more? I *want* you to." She stretched languidly toward the phantom Jesse with whom she had been passionately entwined just before the real one had set his bare foot through the doorway.

The tangible, actual Jesse, not realizing what an agreeably muddled dream state Lorena was in, stood motionless, his expression bemused, regarding her in taut silence. She, with a soft whimper of disappointment and a pronounced pout, began to drift into deep sleep again, drawing a light cover up to her chin and curling inward in a solitary self-caress. Irresistibly drawn, wanting to relieve her distress and his own, Jesse crossed to the bed and slowly parted the mosquito netting. The diaphanous cloth, through which he had been gazing at Lorena, made her once again seem as ethereal and enchanting as a fairy-tale princess. Just like the first time they had come together.

For the half-asleep Lorena, the gauze barrier heightened the aura of unreality, making Jesse appear elusive and immaterial. The angular lines of his handsome face were, to her disappointment, oddly blurred, and the graceful hard body she once again ached for seemed far away, beyond her impassioned, despairing reach. Her sense of loss and longing were so acute, Lorena's delectable dream began to turn into an outlandish nightmare. She struggled to come more fully awake, roused by a fear that the object of her desire was drifting away, leaving her bereft and lonely.

All that covered Lorena's nakedness was a worn soft linen sheet that revealingly followed the curves of her splendid body beneath. Still more groggy than alert, she seemed to feel the sheet move, as if on its own, to expose her shoulders. Befuddled by the odd occurrence, she faintly murmured her misgiving, but made no attempt to secure it. It lingered a moment, then slipped lower with faltering, caressing slowness. Little by little, Lorena's sumptuous breasts were undraped, first the upper swells, then the pronounced cleft between

them. When the delicate pink, conspicuously bright tips were
wholly displayed, she very clearly heard the flesh-and-blood
Jesse suck in a sibilant breath.

"As I remember them. The most beautiful," he whispered
with the profound appreciation of a lover returning to his
greatest prize.

Lorena, at last jolted wide-awake by his low voice, was
scandalized by the brazen pose and tantalizing position in
which she discovered herself. And yet, already voluptuously
aroused by her own wanton, heated dreams, her fleshly desires were now further heightened by Jesse's predatory stare.
Her first clear thought was to protect what little remained of
her decency as a woman who had sworn herself to virtue. But
she wasn't quite quick enough. Before she could secure a
hold on the sheet, it slid down once more, the top edge coming to rest just below her hips, exposing her well-defined
waist and the creamy skin of her flat stomach. If she moved
again, even the least bit, she would lose the last vestige of
modesty.

"Jesse, I took a vow," she said with more force than she
thought she could summon.

"I wouldn't compel you to do a thing against your own
will," he said in a tight voice, his expression melting with desire, his eyes ablaze with longing need. "I'd never want to do
that, force you, but . . ." Purposefully, deliberately, he moved
toward Lorena again, then hesitated, staring down at the beau-
teous sight of her near-naked body.

As he towered over her shirtless, with tousled dark hair
falling over his brow, he seemed almost menacing. Lorena
clenched her eyes tight, and then opened them almost at once,
unable to resist looking. Afraid and aquiver, she wanted his
touch, yet didn't want it. He inclined his fine body to her,
muttering a faint oath under his breath, extended a hand toward the silky curve of her hip, and very gently took hold of
the sheet. Then he drew it up to cover Lorena's bosom, tucking the material so securely about her, it perfectly delineated
and revealed her opulent body. One knee resting on the edge

of the bed, he leaned and cautiously kissed her lips, then drew back a few steps.

"As an officer and a gentleman I would not force myself on you, and you did say *no*, which is a woman's right." Then his lips went down to hers and his tongue penetrated her willing mouth. When at last he withdrew, he said, "You did say you wanted a kiss, and as an officer and gentleman I thus oblige you."

He stood back, stared fiercely at her and said, "Lorena, you try a man. I advise you not to try this one too hard."

He left, quietly opening the door and just as quietly closing it. Slamming doors was not Colonel Sparhawk's style.

Next day, the travelers reached their final destination—the site of the new settlement of Sheridan, Iowa. The hotel Jesse had ordered built stood tall among simple log houses and temporary 'soddies' of wet prairie earth hardened by the sun. Already, a work shed at the far end of the settlement was home to a Bavarian carriage works, a Berlin sign painter and a fancy mill work carpenter from Westphalia. Each pioneer arrived with his or her own mission and hopes for the future. The Europeans had emigrated for land and safe haven. The particular aspiration which Lorena, Jesse, and the others who came west with them shared was to begin anew, after the war, where unravaged rivers flowed free of blood. A quirk of fate had led them to Iowa, the state that had been the source of virtually all the lead-shot used by both sides in the War of Rebellion.

Jesse cantered along the Little Sioux River to Red Hat Creek where he crossed over a covered bridge, hoof sounds echoing in the shadowed space. Pausing, he surveyed his purchase, which extended as far as he could see. He was pleased with the gently undulating land's incline downward. The heavy Iowa rains would leach deep into the subsoil and gradually drain into the river. He dismounted to scoop up a handful of the earth, letting it sift through his fingers.

"Black gold, Colonel," Corbett Nicke called out as he reined in his horse.

"Good morning, Sergeant. Isn't this the most beautiful spread of farmland you have ever set eyes on? I know you can tell a good thing when you see it."

"Yes, sir. That soil you were caressing is full of natural fertilizer—phosphates of lime."

"On my father's plantation, where I spent time as a youth, the only fertilizer we had was dung from the barns and stables," Jesse replied.

"Colonel, not even the fertile Shenandoah Valley farms that I worked all my life, until the war set me free, could compare to the demesne you have here."

"Sergeant, you use an interesting word and it speaks to a point I wish to make. This purchase of mine is not going to be my 'demesne.' My father had a domain. The plantation I spoke of was his manor and he its lord. The people who lived on it and worked it were his tenants and slaves. That's not my way."

"Colonel, are you considering a *commune*?"

"No, no, not here. This is the United States of America, land of the free and since the War that means everybody is free. Freedom means private property, a homestead for those able to work one, or a shop maybe or some sort of factory for those of that mind."

"But you bought the land. You own it."

"I wasn't going to announce my long-term plans just yet, but now that the subject has come up, here is my proposal: I bought six thousand acres at two dollars an acre."

"That's a great price sir. Excuse me for interrupting you, Colonel, but at twelve thousand for all this," Nicke gestured at the horizon, "you've done exceptionally well. Your purchase might be called a steal, by some."

"Sergeant, it wasn't a matter of thievery but of timing. The reason all this land came at so advantageous a price was due the Iowa grasshopper scourge some years ago. I am told that when the pests came, the skies darkened, the limbs of trees broke off under their weight. Trains running east of us were unable to get traction on the rails slippery with the crushed insects. The swarms devoured everything in their way within minutes—crops in the fields, the leaves on the trees, even curtains and sheets in houses. Earlier settlers had a choice of staying and starving or heading off to California. They went. A few that did remain were finally frightened off by the tornados."

"Colonel, if I may interrupt again, the Department of Agriculture has new poisonous mixtures of bran to kill off the insects."

"Yes, and the danger from tornados may be somewhat lessened by windbreaks. With that in mind, I had hundreds of rows of trees planted when I bought here five years ago. Orchards also.

"But, as I was saying, this is my vision: If Sheridan City is to thrive, it's going to need people—good people. I hope you will agree to be one, and to help me run things To induce you to settle here and to seek your fortune by farming the land, I offer to sell you now one hundred prime acres of your own choosing at two dollars an acre."

"But, that's what you paid, Colonel. There's no profit for you in such an offering." Nicke looked askance.

"Stop interrupting and listen, man. I will see you one hundred acres and contract with you for four hundred more, which will be yours for eight thousand dollars after you have farmed them for five years. I'll provide the development capital. In the interim, we'll split the net profit. Do you agree that this would make for a fair deal?"

"I certainly do sir, more than fair. I'd be a damn fool not to take you up on it, but before we shake on the deal I think you might want to reconsider, especially after I tell you what I've heard. A fellow not three miles from here has already made a fortune in corn—it grows real high and yields many ears per plant. He gets more bushels per acre than I've ever heard tell of. He says he's going to become the king of something he calls the Corn Belt. He says it's the rich earth and plentiful rain makes it happen."

"Does this king of yours have anything else to say, Nicke?" Jesse smiled, pulled a stem of tall prairie grass and set it between his teeth. "Sweet," he nodded.

"The man who would be king here says he wouldn't sell for even fourteen dollars an acre."

"Good. I must get to know this fellow, discuss his farming methods, but right now, I want your answer Sergeant. I gave you a price and I am sticking by it. Do you accept?"

"I do, sir. Thank you, sir. It's a done transaction, Colonel," Nicke said extending his hand. Jesse shook it vigorously, showing a broad grin.

"There is just one more thing. It's a deal only if you solemnly promise, now that we are in business together, to never again address me as sir or colonel, but only as Jesse. I'll call you by your given name also, Corbett."

"Yes sir, Jesse," Nicke said with a smart military salute. To show he could enter into the new spirit of things he said, "But only if you make that *Corby*."

"Corby, we'll drink on it. Let's head home."

Lorena, Rachel, and Haley stood on a stone pathway leading to the wraparound porch of a grand, spanking new three-story structure.

"Tilt it more to the left, Luke!" Lorena called, shading her eyes with a hand and looking up. Luke did as instructed, then climbed down to join his friends in admiring the elegantly painted sign he had set in place above a pair of wide double doors.

UNION HOTEL
SHERIDAN, IOWA

"Good job, Luke," said Jesse after a swift appraisal.

"No, no, Colonel. Don't praise me. One of the German

settlers made it and another painted it. I never could have filigreed those corners like that. Only a master carpenter could do such elaborate work. And as for those deep rich oil paint colors, they are not from my palette. I couldn't have done that, either. I'm a gardener and a beekeeper. That sign was decorated at Wertz's Carriage Works."

"I've been over to the carriage works, Luke," Lorena said. "It's a very impressive factory."

"Yes, ma'am," answered Hamson. Another one of the Colonel's fine ideas." Lorena noted the admiration in Luke's voice.

"Yes, he has so many, doesn't he?" she asked glancing up at Jesse. She half-hoped he was having ideas about her, but the look in his eyes brought to mind the cold stare of goshawk back in the Blue Ridge, just before it swooped down on its prey. That seemed such a long time ago now.

In response to Lorena's comment, Jesse had an all but overpowering desire to possess her, if not on the spot, then soon in one of the hotel bedrooms above. His restraint was made the more difficult by her almost imploring, needy expression. He was strongly tempted to scoop her up and carry her off. Instead, he changed the subject.

"Luke, tells us about your passion," he asked. Luke shyly turned to Haley.

"Oh, look at the man!" she exclaimed, unblushing as always. "He lights up like a sunrise whenever he glances my way. Luke, I don't think the Colonel meant you to talk about *me*."

"I want to hear all about your other passion," Jesse laughed, "Bees."

"That's a subject close to my heart all right—second only to Haley, here." The couple exchanged fond looks again. Luke was having thoughts like Jesse's, about the comfort and privacy of the upstairs bedrooms. Unlike Jesse, the only thing stopping *him* from following through was the thought of lunch. There would be time after lunch, all the time he and Haley would need.

"The settlers have done well again," Luke said. "The carpenter and his helpers worked to my high standard, building frames for twenty hives. The queen bees are healthy, settling in well. The drones are busy and soon there'll be more bees and plenty of honey." Lorena's attention wandered as Luke talked on describing many details of the apiary. She dwelled on one fact, that the queen bee's only purpose in the world was to reproduce more bees. And her own primary drive, Loren mused, though not her only one, was the same. No drones for her however. She wanted Jesse.

"Bees are romantic critters," Luke was saying, capturing Lorena's attention again. "Each type of bee—queen, workers, nurses, and so on—seems to have only one job, like breeding or working all the time, but I think like humans, they have moods that vary. When we all got here last week, the fruit flowers were in blossom. The bees were very happy. I just know it. They were smiling I'd swear, and certainly they hummed with contentment."

"Oh, Luke," Haley teased. "You must be harebrained! Bees smiling!"

"I know where of I speak, miss," he smiled at her. "If the queen dies all the bees get so quiet and torpid, I'm convinced they must be dejected. They don't do anything until a new queen, hatched in another hive joins them."

Hazel and Sequoyahson had come along during Luke's recital and had until then stood quietly, listening.

"Before the white man got here, my people had never harvested honey from the bee tree," Seek said. "Honey was unknown to us. Possibly that was because bees could sting. I know my people had observed bears taking honey being stung. The squaws and children, even the braves stayed away from the hives. When they finally tasted honey, it reminded them of the white man's liquor and with just a taste of honey on their lips, they would act as if they were drunk.

"A honey tree is one thing, Luke, but your twenty hives are something else all together. How much honey you countin' on?"

"A lot, Seek. The white clover pollen and nectar has been so abundant that the bees in our strongest hives are filling a forty-pound crock every four days."

"What are you going to do with it all?" asked Hazel.

"In the fall,' Jesse answered, "we'll package it up and send it down river to market. Let us hope the Hamson Honey Company makes Luke's fortune."

"Hallelujah!" shouted Haley.

"As for you young lady, I have a plan that I believe you will approve of. With Luke's advice and plenty of help from the younger German settlers, you can keep a vegetable garden that will supply the entire settlement. You'll get ample land and turn a pretty profit. I'll have the seed bed plowed and prepared. This season you still have time for carrots and tomatoes, late season cabbages, maybe. Next spring, besides carrots and tomatoes you'll be able to grow herbs and spices, kale, lettuce, onions, potatoes. I've brought some seeds and cuttings."

"Sounds good to me," nodded Haley happily, "and it certainly beats working at The Marshall Arms Hotel back home."

"Fifty years ago, people in North America ate no tomatoes," Hamson mused. "The plant and its fruit were thought to be part of the deadly nightshade family. Not so. That was proved false by a fellow in New Jersey who staged a tomato-eating display. He ate a whole bushel of them on the courthouse steps of his town, drew people from miles about who came to watch him die. His own doctor stood by waiting for him to double over and froth at the mouth. He didn't. Now we put them up, make preserves and catsup," Luke added still thinking about lunch, and after. "They got to be simmered three hours or more, not a minute less, to be preserved."

Then, he pointed out a batch of wild roses and said, "It's the same strain I grew for the dinner table at Doc's. It's the early blooming Harison's rose." That led him to another thought, "It's told that settlers, who passed through here before, brought cuttings of this rose rooted in potatoes. The women nursed them and shared their own water with the plants and took new cuttings when they went on west."

"How lovely for us all, isn't it?" Lorena smiled. "Thank you, Luke, for the delightful anecdote. "I'll go off to gather some now, for tonight's table."

CHAPTER 23

"Corbett Nicke, Madame, at your service."

"Ah, Monsieur Nicke! Don't be so formal with me. I have seen you many times at Dr. Longworth's mansion. The cook has eyes, even if she is seldom seen. I even remember your favorite dish, which I sent up several times when you were with the Colonel in his quarters. Yes, sautéed chicken livers."

"And delightful they were, Madame the Cook, even if I don't know difference between your French *sorty* and my way—frying in lard," Nicke said. He was pleased at the memory of a savory flavor and intrigued that the woman standing before him not only remembered him but also seemed coquettishly interested. Her charming accent was an additional attraction. In Sioux City, he had come with a wagon to meet her at the stagecoach stop of the Butterfield Overland Mail. He claimed a canvas postbag tagged *Sparhawk Settlers near Sioux City* that he put into the wagon bed beside supplies for the hotel, Madame's sizeable straw trunk and several smaller pieces of luggage.

"Someday perhaps I will personally show you how to *sorty*, as you say. One of my reasons for traveling here is to bring European *finesse* to the Great American West."

"Good thinking," said Nicke, not any too comfortable with the word *finesse*. He kept that to himself and nodded. Now that he took the time to really study Madame, he was captivated by her pretty oval face and bright dark eyes. A dainty little woman, her posture was ramrod straight and the top of her head came no higher than his shoulder, but she held it high. She had exactly the type of small but solid, full bosomed form he most admired in a female.

In New York, Nicke had heard a little gossip about Madame Montespan who, although still young, was a widow. It was said that her husband had been a dashing, handsome fellow; a highly praised Parisian pastry chef and that, true to the reputation of the French, the pair of culinary connoisseurs had been an ardent couple. It was the debonair Monsieur Montespan's passion, not as much for women, which was considerable, as for cards that did him in. Montespan had been no gentleman, actually little better than a scoundrel who had met his fate in a knife fight after a *saucier* accused him of cheating at whist. Paris was scandalized. Madame Montespan, bereft, fled to America where Dr. Longworth had offered her employment.

Madame's bright eyes really were rather flirtatious, Nicke decided, looking into them. His interest in the lady intensified when she spoke in her delightfully accented but perfect English.

"As so many others are doing now at war's end I've come to the west, wandered 'into the unbroken wild, far from Schools and Churches,' as Mr. Greeley wrote in his book. I want to be a true American. Never mind that *Madame* title. Here in this great democracy, all people seem always on a first name basis. Sergeant, I am Simone!"

"Howdy do, as they say in Iowa. Pleased to make your acquaintance on a first name basis. And you must call me Corby. First the Colonel and me got relaxed and now you and me, too." He grinned at her. "I read Greeley's book, too, from cover to cover. Did you find it of interest, as I did?"

"Oh indeed. There, you see. We have something in common—*An Overland Journey.* I do not always concur with Horace Greeley's views but he is informative.

"Oh, and Corby, where appropriate as in matters of commerce and my profession, I am still Madame Simone Montespan. Unless of course my status and name should change," she said. The implication of her words was not lost on Nicke. This woman was looking for a husband, he decided. He grinned more broadly.

"Greeley also said the two most important developments for the good of the west would be extended railroad tracks and a large rise in the number of intelligent, capable, virtuous women." The woman he was scrutinizing fit the bill. She smiled up at him.

"Corby," she began, "I am rather stiff from the long inactivity aboard the train and battered by the jolting of the stagecoach. Would it be possible to walk about and see Sioux City before going on the rest of the way to Sheridan?" Corby was very happy to oblige, although he knew Sioux City certainly was no New York and, from all he had heard, no Paris either. The streets here were paved with a paste of mud and animal dung.

What *was* impressive was its energy—the bustle of people, many of whom stopping on the way further west and many others selling them the supplies and outfits needed to get there. The sounds of hammers hitting nails mixed with the shouts of workmen—teamsters driving wagons piled high with lumber sent up river from St. Louis, and bricks locally made, of drovers herding lowing cattle and squealing pigs up the main street to the slaughterhouse, a business which added to the general reek and riot of the place. It was exciting, this new America even if raw, noisy, and often rank. Simone was pleased to see a school building, post office, and a church. When the bell began to peal from the belfry, Corbett Nicke looked as proud as if he were ringing it himself.

"A steamboat, the *Kate Kearny*, snagged and sank at the river bend just south of here. All that was retrieved was its bell. It was put on a tripod at the schoolhouse. Later the folks moved the thing to the church and there mounted it in the belfry."

"Mr. Greeley was wrong about there not being schools and churches, wasn't he?" said Simone. "But something here is *not* acceptable. I like the simplicity and equality I find, as I have already said, but one aspect of the western adventure is puzzling and displeasing to me, a woman who has been a chef in New York and Paris."

"Displeasing?" asked Corby with genuine concern. "What might that be? I'll see to it."

"At the American lunch we shared, I did not understand the manner in which these people were consuming their cuisine, if one may call it that. Jammed together, the customers managed to consume an entire meal in fewer than fifteen minutes. As soon as a diner put down knife and fork, he or she was expected to make way for others hovering but a step or two behind the chairs. So impolite."

"Everybody was treated the same and everybody seemed jovial enough," Corby commented in a puzzled tone. "Most of them were working people keen to get back on the job."

"To me," answered Simone, "it is not a gracious way to dine no matter how many heads of cattle and pigs are waiting in pens and along the streets. 'I fear this cattle ranching . . . is destined to half-barbarize many thousands of the next generation.'"

"You're repeating Greeley again, Simone," Corby said, with a hint of impatience. "When the box cars get here, there's no time to be wasted. They got to be turned around. The cows have to be loaded. If the men didn't hop to it, your favorite author would accuse them of 'sloth, selfishness, and cupidity.' Besides the rush, were you at all pleased with the food in that eatery?"

"My beefsteak was barely acceptable only because I was able to get the meat *sanglant*—bloody, but all about us people were gnawing on overcooked slabs of meat that looked like shoe leather covered with tomato sauce." She clucked her tongue in disapproval.

"That's catsup, Simone," Corby informed her. "A popular condiment out here." She pinched her nose between her thumb and forefinger.

"As for the rest of the fare, it was barely edible, unsauced, lacking in seasoning, and soggy. This rushed indifference to 'grub' will change if I have anything to say about it! Well now, Corby, shall we be on our way? I wish very much to see my friends again and to get about starting up my own dining place—Simone's Palace—in the Colonel's elegant hotel."

"Call him Jesse, Simone. I do," said Corby, offering her his arm.

Corby, as even *he* had began to think of himself after so long being *Sergeant* in his own mind, could not help but notice that Simone was sitting so close to him on the wagon bench that her womanly leg was pressing against his. He found that instantly exciting. When they clattered over a covered bridge, he took advantage of the momentary darkening and placed his hand lightly on Simone's firm, ample thigh. When she shifted even closer, he was emboldened to slide his touch between her legs. This bolder action did not meet with success. She gently but firmly moved his away.

"Patience, Corby. *Finesse* is in order. You Americans should not make love the way you eat—grabbing what you want with no attention to nuance and enjoyment. In France, we take our time with our pleasures. I find eating and other activities, all the more gratifying that way." Simone was being a bit disingenuous. Quite to the contrary of what she had said, when it came to sex, though never food, she had often been sated by a hasty brief encounter.

As a very young woman, Simone had come to understand that her sexual appetite was as intense as her need for food. She arrived in America to work for the Longworths free of the bonds of marriage, still youthful, but no innocent. As an attractive widow and something of a celebrity chef, she was found to be very appealing by men who assisted her in her kitchen, by the waiters who served the doctor's guests, often some of the guests themselves who sought her out to compliment her cooking skills and discovered some of her other talents.

Madam Montespan also socialized with others of her profession, most of them men, who created excellent food in grand mansions of the city and in the famous restaurants of New York. She had freely yet discreetly engaged in a number of gratifying relationships and, unattached as she was, saw no harm done, not even when she relinquished all propriety and restraint. A few of her lovers had been strikingly handsome, though that was not her highest priority. One, perhaps two, had been outstanding lovers and pleased her more than many a pretty face had been able to do.

One man, one incident stood out in memory. The event, one of stunning recklessness, had followed her professional visit to the kitchen at the deservedly famous Luchow's Restaurant. There, after meeting the owners, who were impressed by her reputation and tried to hire her away from the Longworths, she was presented, after the dinner rush, to the head chef. A young fair-haired, piratical-looking Italian he had a mustache that seemed a half-foot long and a ponytail that reached to his waist. So great was his talent and notoriety as a chef, that his eccentricities of style and behavior were tolerated.

The attraction between Lorenzo Del Bene, who had a most handsome countenance, and feisty Simone Montespan, was instant, mutual, and electrically charged. An assignation was arranged. Five minutes later under a brightly shining moon, Simone waited beneath a linden tree near Luchow's kitchen door. Without hearing a sound behind her, she felt her skirts being lifted. Her practice in the summer was to wear no lingerie beneath her petticoats and Del Bene, bending her forward, entered her unimpeded. It had been a brief, excruciatingly pleasurable union. No words were exchanged and no demands made by either party. All in all, the fleeting, never-to-be repeated encounter had been a tutorial in lovemaking for Simone, who was inclined to linger at her pleasures and savor them. Swift gratification could be exhilarating and sweet. Minutes after it began, the joining was over. Lorenzo offered Simone an appreciative bow and a click of his heels. She left him nothing more than her satisfied smile.

But those were bygone days. Now, rather than indulge her bubbling Gaelic lust, she was determined to restrain herself with this man, Corby. She knew much of the game of love, knew that she must not give hers away, nor seem too easy a conquest for this upright, uncomplicated American. He's was not an outrageous, good-looking Latin chef, but neither was

Sheridan, Iowa, New York City. Corbett Nicke would fit perfectly into her current plan. Always a good judge of men, Simone believed this one would make a fine husband just right for her new life in the Great West.

She had liked being married and she was eager to enjoy wedded bliss and a warm bed again. This time she wanted children. The offspring of the appealing man beside her, whether girls or boys, were likely to be strong and tall and as hard-working as their father was reputed to be. With her own good looks, nimble mind, and ambition as part of the blend, it should be a fruitful successful match. She had no doubt of Corby's virility. His loyalty, of nearly equal importance to her in a husband and father of her children, had been highly praised by Jesse Sparhawk.

Simone shifted away from Corby on the wagon bench. He stiffened somewhat and took up the reins in both hands again.

And that was the way things would be with them Simone determined. She would give the man little *soupçons* of tenderness that were aptly restrained. That was her plan for only as long as necessary to lead Corby to the altar. She suspected it would not take long at all. For the remainder of the ride, they chatted pleasantly, catching up.

CHAPTER 24

"I have not had a smidgen of chocolate since the train pulled out of Chicago," Simone announced as the wagon rolled along on its way to Sheridan.

"We'll see you get some. The Colonel—Jesse, that is— orders up anything that's wanted. He makes pretty frequent trips to Iowa City where the tracks and the telegraph end. He's gotten all kinds of stuff, even bees."

As Corby clucked at the horse to encourage it up an incline, Simone said, "The last place the hotels had room bells and baths was at Leavenworth, in Kansas."

"Jesse's guaranteed that already," was Corby's reply. "He's just waiting on materials."

"And the Longworth twins? How are they faring?"

"Right well. Rachel wants to give singing lessons soon as there is someone who wants 'em. Rob still hasn't settled on anything of his own. He's just Jesse's friend, and he does a little land speculating. Yes, I know, Simone," Corby laughed as she opened her mouth, "I know exactly what Greeley had to say about that activity: 'the infernal spirit of land speculation is the only business in which a man can embark with no other capital than an easy conscience.' Robert Longworth does not lack either capital or conscience. He lacks only someone to love, in my humble estimation, which reminds me of the mountain man from the wilds of North Carolina, Daniel Boone, who said that all a man requires for a good life is a good gun, a good horse, and a good wife." Now Simone was silent, as Corby talked on.

"Lorena's ma is on the place with a friend, an Indian. Hamson's in the honey trade. And he has got himself a real sweet lady friend."

"*Très bien.* Good for Hamson," said Simone with a tilt of her head. "And the young bride and groom? How are they faring?" Corby didn't say anything, just fussed with the reins, shifted his shoulders.

"Jesse's been real busy buying mares for breeding stock, looking for the worthy stallion, learning the lay of the land. He's going to build a mill where our creek falls into the lake.

"Lorena, she's been sketching constantly, pictures for a book of fables and nature stories she's writing. She's been studying out all kinds of weeds and wildflowers, doing flower painting and the like. Bugs. 'Insect pests' she calls some of them. She does bee studies."

"Aha! Birds and bees perhaps? Progeny is in the offing, I suspect." A long silence from Corby followed Simone's exclamation. "She is not yet *enceinte*? *Bon,* okay. It can take time." Again, silence from Corby.

"Lorena and Jesse were married as soon as possible, were they not?" There was no response from Corby. "No! They were not! But why not? Tell me all. At once!" Simone was clearly upset.

Corby did tell her what she wanted to know. The tale of Lorena, her lost husband, and Jesse occupied the travelers' time during the rest of the ride.

Where the river broadened into a lake, wide and long, stretching almost as far as Simone could see, stood the hotel. As the wagon moved toward it, Simone made out a wide covered porch that ran all the way around the building. It stood three stories high, as imposing a structure as any she had seen since passing through St. Louis, the city where the great rivers met—the Mississippi and Missouri—before each went its way. She knew of nothing in Europe like these immense, noble rivers. She had, of course, seen grander hotels on the

Continent, but this one was impressive enough in its plains setting, reflected in the lake on whose shores it was built. The Union Hotel would provide a fitting stage for the superb restaurant she had been planning since she left the East.

The exterior clapboard of the Union Hotel was painted a soft white with the shutters and doors a pale yellow. She thought its appearance very clean, even classic in its lines. There, on the verandah, as they drew closer, Simone and Corby were able to see the waiting welcoming party.

With elaborate courtesy, Corby handed her down and she was not unaware that he kept his manly but gentle grip on her hand several moments longer than necessary.

"Madame Montespan, I'm so delighted to see you again!" smiled Lorena. "I bid you welcome to Sheridan and to the Union Hotel."

"Thank you so much, Mademoiselle Reed. I heard, sadly, that you and your Colonel are not yet wed. But nonetheless you are looking more lovely than ever. Is it the climate? And you, Colonel," she mildly flirted, turning to Jesse, "I have rarely known any other man so handsome in all of America. Just one other perhaps," she teased with a fast glance at Corby.

"You flatter me, madame," Jesse laughed. "And I must tell you how pleased I am to see you and how fine and full of energy you seem, ready and eager to start your project— Simone's Palace Restaurant."

"Enough of this effete drawing room banter. We're on the Iowa plains now. We must be simpler, more American," Lorena said.

"It is my thought exactly! And to that end I would like to tell you both the same thing I told Corby here. Now that I am in Sheridan I am not Madame Montespan but *simply* Simone."

"You must be tired after your weeks of travel, Simone," Lorena smiled aware of the exchange of private glances between Simone and Corbet. "I'd venture to guess you'd enjoy a good hot bath. Let me show you to your room, number five, one of our prettiest, with an endless view to the west."

Late that same night, actually in the small hours of the next morning, Lorena stepped through the French doors of her room, which opened onto the verandah. Soft lace curtains followed her to flutter under a bright sky. She stood still, embroidered in moonlight, as the sky swung low overhead heavy with stars, then she floated to a rocking chair to sit still, not wanting to make a sound. Without looking, she felt Jesse's body close by.

"I'll go in now," Lorena said. "It's late. Past midnight."

"And send me off alone, again?" Jesse hoarsely asked in a half whisper.

"You promised!" she said accusingly, longingly.

"But I want you now." His voice took on an all too familiar smoky, rough edge. "And you want me. I *feel* it." Her chair rocked on its own when she sprang from it. He caught her hand.

"Oh this is madness, Jesse. In good conscience you must let me go."

He kissed her hand, and then released it. "Love that isn't madness isn't love, a poet once wrote. I won't try to tempt you tonight. Tomorrow's another day." He half smiled. When she, disconcerted, fled, he determined to press what he knew was his advantage.

In the still darkness of every night that followed, Jesse gave Lorena a lovely small object, which he left on her nightstand: a rare wildflower, a bluebird feather, a basket of fresh laid eggs, a kitten in a box. Every morning she relented a little more as she imagined him soundlessly standing over her while she lay curled in sleep. He was a frustrated voyeur but he was playing fair and keeping his promise. If he only knew, she thought ruefully, that all he had to do was reach out and touch to have all he wanted. I could be in his arms now, she admitted, angrily throwing off the bedclothes.

One morning, Lorena's eyes opened on a fine bridle of beautifully worked Spanish leather and a note in Jesse's clear, strong script, "The glass slipper may not fit. This will."

At breakfast, they exchanged secret smiles before turning their attention to the sideboard laden with stomach-filling food and pretty delicacies. There were eggs, scrambled and

devilled, grits, muffins, beefsteaks, bacon, goose liver paste
that Simone called *pâté* slathered on toasted, sourdough bread
rounds. Also little fruit pies—tartlets to Simone—and soft-
ened butter, heavy rich cream, slivered crab apples in clover
honey, coffee and tea. When they had both eaten their fill,
wordlessly, Lorena followed Jesse to the stable. The strong
sweet odors there were instantly intoxicating and when her
eyes had adjusted to the dimness she saw, in the first of six
stalls, a finely bred and beautiful mare that took her breath
away. The animal danced on delicate hoofs with her long neck
arched and long tail held high.

"She is perfect as a sculpture in black marble, in onyx,"
Lorena said in a low voice.

"She's yours," replied Jesse. "Take her for a run." Lorena
did. Riding astride, she cantered the horse across a meadow
and when, unexpectedly, a bramble barrier loomed ahead, the
strong black mare rose as if on wings, neatly tucked up her
legs and took the jump easily. Lorena's hair spread like a
golden cloud behind them.

When Jesse reached them, the mare was pawing the
ground, ready to be off again. Lorena, was lying in the midst
of the field of blue-eyed grass, laughing aloud with delight,
her head thrown back, lips shining, and sunlight dancing in
her eyes.

"You belong here on the plains with me and no other place
on earth," he said. The ache of his need was so strong he
groaned aloud. Lorena briefly met his imploring stare, and
then turned away.

"We must talk, Lorena, about the future."

"Of our enterprise here at Sheridan?

"No. Of us." Jesse was unwilling to release her eyes. She
could not turn away.

"No, I will not talk of that. We may not have a future together," she managed to say.

"We are both here now! I want you and I need you to help
me with this grand experiment of Sheridan. I need heirs to
carry on my, our work."

"Go and have them," she replied with a catch in her voice, finally breaking his stare.

"I want children only with you," he insisted. "Soon." She looked straight at him again.

"They'll be bastards."

"Perhaps, unless I find Clint. But you will not be a bigamist. Whatever our babies are, do you really think I care? Do you?" was Jesse's reply. Lorena sat up, unable to answer because she thought to herself that there wasn't any answer but no, I do not care one whit so long as I'm with you. And so, she realized he had won! She knew it, but she wouldn't say so, not yet, perhaps never. What he was proposing wasn't upright and proper. It was not the way she had envisioned her fate, but fate it seemed was pushing her toward him.

Lorena arose, hesitated, and then ran as fast as she could across the meadow until Jesse, coming after, easily overtook her, lassoed her with arms about her waist and drew her back against him. She turned in his arms, eager to be claimed by his stare, to meet his dark blue marauding eyes. They sank down together where they stood into tall prairie grass. He pressed into her and her legs enfolded his narrow hips. He was an easy rider not about to be unseated by the impassioned, vigorous maneuvers of his golden-maned mount.

"We'll say our own vows, make our own promises, get on with life—mutually," Jesse insisted when they rested together." There was a rasp in his voice Lorena loved. "Tonight, tomorrow, now? Let's promise."

"I promise, Jesse, to love you forever, but I'll not be in your arms again, or in anyone's until I know about Clint," she whispered, clinging to him, her hands playing over his wide shoulders. He grinned down at her and shrugged, stroking her cheek, claiming her mouth.

"I'll try to keep my distance. We'll both try, but I cannot offer guarantees," he said between tastes of her lips.

Nor can I, Lorena thought, but did not say.

Later that evening there were only four in the dining salon of the hotel—Simone and Corby, Lorena and Jesse. All the others were off about their business. A light supper of lake trout, mashed potatoes (which Simone found lumpy), wild nasturtium salad, and freshly baked bread was served by one of the settlers' wives. Several bottles of very cold Moselle wine were generously shared. The mirrors around the walls of the room reflected light from candles and the prairie sky that was still glowing beyond open French doors, a quarter of an hour after sunset. The diners were enjoying the serenity of the summer evening as they quietly exchanged reminiscences.

Simone, relaxed and gregarious, had just finished describing the wonders of her railroad trip when she sat up straighter than usual and clasped her hands beneath her chin.

"Ah, I have almost forgotten a most amazing coincidence!" she exclaimed. "It happened when the train arrived in Iowa City, while the passengers were waiting to disembark. You know, of course, Colonel, Jesse," she amended, "the person of whom I will speak, the woman with whom you were in association, shall I say?" Jesse nodded, showing no emotion though he was already alert to the significance of what would follow. "She, that Maud Wharton, was there at the train station. That woman, who had always sparkled with so much jewelry set off by her pale skin, Mrs. Wharton of the intense green eyes, was dressed simply as a missionary and poor as a church mouse in black homespun and a plain bonnet. Even so, she was striking. She stood out in the crowd and appeared haughty as ever, cold, with her usual expression, as if she had smelled something bad. In these cattle towns, she actually might have," Simone laughed. "Well, and with her was a dour-looking shabby companion, the same woman I had seen when I looked in on Doctor Longworth's Celebration Dinner that turned out to be no celebration, as we all, of course, know." Simone shook her head sadly, then brightened and went on describing the coincidence. "Well, when I tried to greet them, both women ignored me—first the one then the other. They hurried from the train station without speaking, but I'm certain Mrs. Wharton at least, knew me."

Lorena looked to Jesse and she was not surprised to see

that his eyes had the fierce glint they took on at the first sign of danger. The subsequent silence was broken by Nicke.

"The hunters are closing in on their prey, the sisters might be supposing. But, it's the other way around. The moths are circling closer to the flame."

"Corby, please do not speak in metaphors. Just what do you mean?" Simone asked.

"I mean, you bring information the Colonel has been eager to get."

"Have you been expecting Mrs. Wharton here at Sheridan?"

"In a manner of speaking, yes," Jesse answered grimly. "Simone, you've just provided information of two escaped Confederate spies. Maud Wharton was a double agent working for the Confederacy and a likely conspirator in the assassination of President Lincoln."

"We had her under surveillance from the moment she stepped off a boat from Liverpool in New York harbor," Corby explained. "We suspect she is now intent on murder. The other woman, her sister, has already attempted to do away with Lorena but we don't know why!"

"*Mon dieu*! Wharton and her sister, murderers?" Simone said softly, the color draining from her face.

"The sister is Estelle Partier, known also by the assumed name of Hester Potts. Don't fret, Simone," said Lorena sympathetically patting the Frenchwoman's hand. "I'm on my guard and, also, I have my champions watching out for me. If the wicked women did follow you, which I think likely, that's all to the good. We'll get them before they do me." Lorena let her smile embrace Corby before it settled on Jesse.

"Wharton and her sister are widows," Nicke explained. "Lord Wharton, Fifth Earl of something British, passed on a few months ago. So did his only heir, a son he had with Wharton. We learned from Q. that Arthur Randall Wharton, the poor lad, was a Rebel volunteer. He never lived to become Sixth Earl."

"Now that you are fully informed, Simone," Jesse said, "I

ask you to be alert to any dubious news or sightings. Corby Nicke and I, and other members of the Secret Service whether still officially on duty or not, are charged with capturing those women, dead or alive. We are especially concerned to safeguard Lorena. She is safe here at Sheridan. I'll do my best to see that those women are safe nowhere."

Conversation soon turned to lighter subjects and future plans. More wine was poured and time flew by. The diners finally, reluctantly, bid each other goodnight after one in the morning.

CHAPTER 25

From their separate rooms each looked out alone at the full moon in a sky filled with stars. The heavens hovered, glinting low. It was a night for love. Simone was kept awake by the roaring din of cicadas and crickets in the wilds of Iowa. She was restless. Tempted to throw caution to the winds and go to Corby, who was just down the corridor, she held firm to her original plan—wedding bells, *then* fun. She wished this time out to be married in a conventional, traditional way to an altogether regular American man. If she had read him rightly, Corby would appreciate her all he more for waiting.

Corby, burning and bothered, had no doubt Simone was the woman for him and he wanted her, now. Rather than go and make demands on the pretty widow, he reckoned he would propose to her first thing in the morning. If she agreed, which he happily expected she would, they could be man and wife before sundown after a speedy visit to a minister up in Sioux City. Mollified by thoughts of his elegant, talented, modest prospective bride, Corby dropped off to sleep, My Dog curled beside him. His last thought that night was how the spaniel would get on with an added bedmate.

The next morning was already hot at dawn in early August. The first rays of the sun shot across the flatland. It penetrated the trees in the young apple orchard, and the wild plums which dotted the fields. Jesse was at his window. He was sit-

ting on the sill leaning back against one side of the frame, a
booted foot propped on the opposite side. A pile of short cigar
stubs had accumulated on the dark hearth nearby where he
had been flicking them for hours. A gas lamp that had burned
all night was dimmed by the dawn before it spluttered out.

An hour later, Hazel and Seek, walking hand in hand out
onto the prairie, looked back at the Union Arms. They saw
Lorena standing in the French doors, about to walk out. Three
rooms away Jesse stood at his window, rapidly puffing up a
cloud of smoke with his cigar.

"Those two are thinking the same thought," said Seek quietly. Hazel sighed.

"Where are you heading so early, Miss Reed?" Jesse called
in a stage whisper, not wanting to awaken the others. Lorena
paused, slowly turned and looked up at him. She was bare-
headed and barefoot wearing a short, ankle-length skirt and a
boy-styled collarless shirt. "I'm going to paint while the
morning dew is still clinging to the prairie flowers," she whispered in return.

"You're not supposed to be wandering about the countryside alone. May I accompany you?" Jesse asked. And then,
"No chaperone? No need, I promise." He raked back his tousled dark hair and grinned appealingly. "You, too, must give
your word to be restrained, if you're able," he teased. "Well?"

"You have my assurances, sir, that I will not molest you. I
gave in once, but that doesn't give you the right to infer I lack
self-control altogether," she answered, with a flicker of a smile.
"Now, if we don't go at once there won't be any dew left on the
daisies." She turned and marched off, Jesse close behind her.

"I have to be back before the sun is noon high. I'm expecting the bricklayer and his sons, from Sioux City. Now
that the barn foundation is in place, they'll be starting work
on our house, all right, *my* house" Jesse corrected himself
when Lorena sighed with what she meant to sound like exasperation, but seemed to Jesse more like regret. Lorena set
up a small easel where the edge of the meadow met a stand of
hickory woods. Upon it, she set the stretched canvas she had

been carrying beneath her arm, wrapped in cloth. Only a few feet away, Jesse sat and leaned against a tree in the shade. He watched her take a palette and several paint pots from her box as well as a sketchbook and pieces of charcoal.

"This only requires a bit more work before I'll consider it done," Lorena explained, uncovering the canvas, revealing a subtle riot of rich colors. "I prefer doing botanical paintings in a natural setting rather than collecting samples to take away."

"That's a vibrant and perfect picture of those grasses," Jesse said. "The colors are softly amazing."

"The plant is most interesting in early morning with the sun lighting the dangling seeds. Looks like wheat," said Lorena, concentrating intently on a touch of green. "It's called Northern Sea Oats—*Chasmanthium latifolium*. I don't know why it's called that so far from the sea and it's not truly a prairie grass, either, but I see a lot of it at woodland edges, under walnut trees and hickories, areas that flood in spring. It likes the damp, apparently."

Jesse came to look over Lorena's shoulder as she worked. "May I page through your sketch pad?" he asked. Lorena passed it to him, and said, "It was in the bottom of the old carpetbag I was carrying when you found me. Remember?"

"Could I ever forget?" he replied.

"The lady's maid at the Longworths' brought it to me. Doc hoped its contents would help me regain my memory. Some of the sketches are years old," explained Lorena. Jesse hunkered down on his heels beside her and began turning pages. There were charcoal sketches, studies, and a few detailed shaded drawings. There were likenesses of Hazel and a fine looking man, Lorena's father, Jesse decided, and of Frankie as a youngster rather than the adolescent he had now become. A group of women quilting or sewing was depicted by just a few suggestive lines that managed to convey both energy and intimacy. There were dense trees, a log cabin, a stream between outcropping banks, and then the subjects changed. There was a page of studies from varying angles of a nurse's headdress, and a detailed picture of a man's narrow, sickly face with sunken cheeks and pained staring eyes. Toward the end of the sketchbook were a few New York City house fronts, wide streets, and masts at the harbor. Then Jesse found his own image.

"You flatter me, you know," he commented. "Is the ailing soldier in your sketchbook Clint Reed?"

"Yes. Jesse, I've nearly decided on something and this is as good a time as any to tell you. As soon as the harvest is in, preserves put up, root cellar stocked, I should be . . . moving on." He was thunderstruck but hid his feelings.

"Why?" he asked coolly. "If you're troubled about fairy tales and princes and vapid damsels, don't be. There are no Cinderellas on the prairie, Lorena. There's land to plant, livestock to foster, children to rear, hard work, deprivation, and with it all there are the vagaries of nature threatening all that's accomplished. A man needs a woman at his side not as an ornament to whisper sweet nothings in her ear but as a helpmeet."

"You are dearer to me, Jesse, I can say, than anyone has been or will be but, you were not entirely mistaken earlier, asking about self-restraint." Lorena set aside her paintbrush. "And also . . ."

"Also, there's Clint Reed," he half smiled. "Now's as good a time as any for me to tell *you* something also. Corby brought a telegraph message from Iowa City, along with Madame. Your husband did not mark his X on the note he left for you. We're no closer to knowing his fate than we ever were. But if he didn't compose this message to you, have you any idea who would, or why?"

"I have an idea that the 'why' of it is to discourage me from trying to find my husband."

"I agree. You'd have made a good secret agent. Well, you'll be here until harvest you say? Thanks for that," Jesse said. "Time to go." Lorena said nothing, just packed up her things. He took up the paint box and strode off. She waited until he was almost out of sight. He turned and waved her forward.

"I am not leaving you out here alone, blast it!" he shouted. "Not while bloody Maud Wharton's on your trail!"

Jesse and Lorena reached the Union Hotel just in time to wish a pleasant expedition to Hazel, Seek, and the Longworth twins as they were setting out on an adventure.

"Molly, your dear mamma, would not *believe* her two city children were off to wander about this wild countryside!" called Simone, wiping her hands on her apron. "When you come back I'll prepare a *ragôut* of tripe!"

The foursome had planned a trip of several days' duration to explore the geography to the south of the Union Hotel. Under Sequoyahson's direction, three mules were loaded with provisions and gear and the adventurers mounted fine saddle horses from the Sheridan Stable.

The horses picked their way through the same hickory and walnut woodlands at the edge of which Lorena and Jesse had stopped earlier. After some time of slow going the party emerged from the forest, which bordered the Little Sioux River, and took up an easy canter along a trail made years earlier by the wheels of prairie schooners heading farther west toward California gold. Along the way, whispering grass grew as high as a horse's shoulder. From time to time, without warning, a wild turkey or some prairie chickens would explode out of the grass and blossoming wildflowers, flushed by My Dog. Corby Nicke had suggested they borrow his willing spaniel. Corby and Simone were off on a journey of their own to Sioux City, Corby had told Seek. What Nicke did not say was that the lady had agreed to become his wife. Simone preferred not to spend her wedding night with her new husband *and* My Dog.

"We're going to call him Our Dog," Seek had jested, in a rare moment of levity.

The riders continued mostly in silence, awed by the beauty of their surroundings.

"Rachel, look at that!" Robert exclaimed when a flock of mallards flew overhead in V formation. Rachel looked, smiled, and remembered the gliding hawk high over the Blue Ridge.

They made camp, rather, two camps, brother and sister in

one and the two mature lovers, deep in their passion and on a honeymoon of sorts, in the other.

Robert took a small military tent from the supplies loaded on the packhorse while Rachel, keeping an eye on him, unloaded other necessities.

"Don't worry, Brother," she laughed. "Lorena and I did this many times while traveling in the mountains."

Laboriously, Rob assembled the military-issue shelter according to the instructions issued by the Army. When he had finished, he spread several blankets and canvas covers, also standard for soldiers in the field, then stood back to admire his work. As a city-bred boy, he was proud of himself though he had needed the occasional hints that Rachel provided.

"Good job, Rob," she said with a grin and a nod.

"I could never have done it without you," he grinned back. "It's so good to be with you again, Rachel."

They made a pot of coffee and dined luxuriously from a basket packed by Simone. They had hardly finished a second cup of coffee when a strong wind came up without warning and began to blow dried weeds and dust along the ground. The embers of the campfire scattered wildly over the tall grass igniting dozens of fires. The sky went black, lightning flashed over the prairie, and the heavens roared with thunder. The howling of unseen coyotes could be heard between thunderclaps. My Dog, responding to the wild calls, threw back his head and joined the chorus.

"This animal is really brave!" shouted Rob.

"Or dumb as a box of rocks. He's no match for a coyote!" called Rachel chasing down a linen cloth tugged away by the wind. Then the rain came, hard and straight down, mixed with hailstones. The grass fires were extinguished.

"One of the German boys, who was among the first in Sheridan, warned me that the weather is often unpredictable and rigorous in Iowa," Rachel said when they had struggled into the tent and stretched out under ponchos with My Dog between them. The tent billowed and shook in the wind.

"It certainly is noisy weather! I hope the stakes hold," bellowed Rob. "But, Rachel, let's not worry. We may get wet, but we won't drown. We've moved too far off the river. Let's try to get some sleep. Sequoyahson will have us up before dawn, I am certain."

"Rob, I must tell you something," shouted Rachel using her two hands as a megaphone. "I find Seek a most attractive man, even if too old for me."

"That's a match that would cause Mother's hair to stand on end!" Rob roared with laughter at the image in his mind's eye. "Be that as it may, Sister, Hazel's got him. You must find your own man! A good one is not easy to come by, I know."

"I did find one, but he didn't pay any attention to me."

"Remember the law of attraction. There were no sparks between you. For another thing, I think Jesse looked upon you more as a young sister than a prospective wife. I think he sensed you would be tediously devoted to him. Some men can't abide that."

"Will I ever find somebody else?" she worried.

"Be realistic, Rachel. You are young and very pretty and bright and refined and there are a great many more men here in the West than there are women."

"But I am looking for someone very special. Here's my list of the qualities I require in a husband." Rachel took a slip of paper from a pocket of her dress and passed it to her brother. Rob had some difficulty lighting a lantern. It burned just long enough for him to scan the Rachel's much-folded inventory.

1. Strong mind and a comfortable house
2. Capacity for tender feelings
3. Musical competence
4. Sense of humor

"Don't you think they are the essential points for me—plus a certain youthful vigor, which I take for granted in any man I regard?"

"Rachel, don't make what you want too hard to find or you

might be searching forever. Now, please go to sleep. We'll talk about it in the morning."

Rachel was quiet for a long while. The rain let up some, but was still falling gently on the tent.

"Robert, that German lad told me the mercury often goes below the zero mark in Iowa in the wintertime and rises to over a hundred in the summer. He said besides rains and floods that wash the lands away, droughts and insects have often killed off a whole season's crops. Do you really think we'll thrive here?" There was no answer. Rob was already asleep with My Dog curled up at his feet.

"Seek, what is this place? Where are we?" Hazel had asked when the storm started.

"It's a traveler's shelter, thrown together years ago by folks like us on a night like this. We're lucky to have come upon it. It's stood up to worse conditions than this. Better than being in a tent like Robert and Rachel, hoping the wind doesn't blow it away." The low, rough log shelter quickly became a private sanctum of sensuality and intimate comfort. Sequoyahson had stretched out regally, relaxed near the fire to watch Hazel. He leaned on one elbow, and his straight hair, falling forward over his brow, was coal black in the firelight. Hazel knew how much Seek wanted her comfort, how hungry he was to feel her in his arms. She knew, too, how quickly and completely she could please him with her full, rounded, eager body. It was like distracting a child with fantasy confections of sweets beyond dreams. When he stood and stepped to her, they were nearly of a height. She had to reach up only a little to brush her lips to his, tentatively, testing his mood. When they had first chanced upon one another, Sequoyahson had been detached, spoke little and smiled never. He had since changed. Now he laughed aloud with pleased anticipation when Hazel unfastened her fine auburn hair and shook it loose to tumble about her shoulders and down her back.

"May I?" she asked when he began to unfasten his britches.

Without waiting for his answer she relieved him of his soft leather vest. Her quick hands moved again like fluttering birds, loosening his belt and buttons, touching him, stroking and fondling with calculating, tactile intent and purpose until the subtle tremors she felt beneath her sensitive fingers built to flares of writhing energy, and Sequoyahson stood naked and hard, emanating a crude, raw power that made her moan with longing.

"You always know what it is I require, before I know it my-self," Sequoyahson whispered coarsely, catching Hazel in his arms. He slipped her simple camp dress over her head and was once again delighted to see the solid, ample, nurturing body it had hidden. He brought his grasping mouth to her hard breast tips, each in turn. Her arms closed around his strong neck, and her head fell back as she arched her body to him before she twisted away. She stepped slowly to the blanket spread in the center of the shelter. Sequoyahson, leer-ing happily, watched her muscles work beneath an amplitude of firm flesh. There was so much *more* of her unclothed. Not looking directly at him, knowing what she'd see—rampant, risen power, his half-glazed, greedy eyes, and heaving chest—Hazel teased him by sitting on the blanket, her knees together and her arms folded across her breasts. She smiled to hear a lusting laugh rumble from his deep chest. He lunged on top of her so that her arms came free, her back went down and her legs opened. Both were laughing wildly, until he kissed her and furiously drove deep into her welcoming depths. Their rhythmically surging bodies were swept by the engulfing fury of their passion. With guttural moans and sighs, they shuddered and rolled in satiating pleasure. Hazel, lost to the world, felt the entire universe throbbing in her wildly beating blood.

At the end of their second day on the trail, the four adven-turers arrived in the substantial town of Wolf, home to nearly five hundred residents who had built two schools and four churches. There was a train station, a grocery and dry goods store, a smithy, several saloons. Stuck up in the window of the newspaper office was a directory of men looking for wives headed:

YOUNG FELLOWS OF WOLF, PEN SKETCHES FOR THE GIRLS

Howard Holt—would make a grand husband for some maiden. He is young, tolerable good-looking, kind and rich. Who will have him?

James Regenberger—a quiet fellow inclined to be a little bashful, but he likes calico as well as any of the other boys. Just too good to live so lonely.

Mike Hoxley—A rustler. He is handsome, and the girls call him "darling." He is always happy and gives everybody a good word. His tongue runs like clock-work and he can out-talk a stump.

When her friends entered the news office seeking information, Rachel remained outside diligently studying the sketches and reading the descriptions of available boys. One "has a good head for business, and is bound to accumulate wealth before he gets baldheaded." Another was listed as "a confirmed bachelor but, we think a good loving girl could get him to the altar with chloroform and fix him all right." There were also a capital story teller worthy of a good girl, a boy worth a wagon-load of ordinary fellows, "and the girls all know it, but as yet have failed to make an impression upon his heart," and more. Rachel was encouraged. On the way back to Sheridan she intended to inquire further about Wallace Wells, said to be a capital storyteller and a sensible man who earned lots of money.

Two miles beyond Wolf, the foursome came to the English Settlement. There some years before, a middle-aged nobleman had bought a huge tract of land, which he had divided into smaller "estates." He was selling them off to his countrymen, mostly second sons of British nobility, whose older brothers would inherit titles and wealth. Rather than insist on the clergy or the army, titled fathers provided the initial capital to get younger progeny started as country gentlemen, and continued to forward remittances as necessary, to keep their sons going. The founder of the enterprise, was the self-styled King of Corn, who was expected back soon from England where he had been raising more capital to buy more land to sell to more young English gentlemen.

The visitors were warmly welcomed, the citizens of Wolf taking great pleasure in seeing new faces. Hazel and Rachel quickly drew about them a number of farmers—English gentlemen all. A few unmarried, nubile girls showed some interest in Robert Longworth and everyone was eager to talk with Sequoyahson, an educated Native American Indian.

As good luck would have it, the foursome had arrived late on a Saturday afternoon, and after the warm welcome, Seek and Robert were handed printed invitations that read:

COTILLION PARTY
Yourself and Ladies are cordially invited
to a Cotillion Party
at
Blair's Hall, Saturday Evening, August 30
Music by Commander Cody's Band of Denison
PER ORDER COMMITTEE OF ARRANGEMENTS

After they had been shown to their accommodations and allowed to freshen up and rest briefly, black coats were found for Rob and Seek and suitable dresses for the women who had brought only trail clothes with them.

The dancing lasted for three hours with very few breaks for the musicians or dancers. The music was not of the sort heard in England or in the eastern cities, but what it lacked in sophistication it made up for in the high spirits of fiddle-playing and banjo-strumming. Everyone was encouraged to participate in every dance with couples frequently exchanging partners. In an early round, Rachel found herself in the arms of a young man who introduced himself simply as Sir Arthur

Randall. He was handsome, elegantly attired for a prairie gathering, and admirably self-possessed. Rachel found herself quite taken with the fair-haired Englishman, with his aristocratic profile and dark shining eyes. He was obviously captivated by Rachel. As the couple danced on, always managing to get back together quickly, she grew more enthralled with each turn until she was bubbling with delight.

At last, the music stopped and the revelers withdrew for a midnight feast of oysters—raw oysters, fried oysters, and oyster stew—with loaves of still-warm sourdough bread drenched in melted butter. Sir Arthur told her the oysters, packed in barrels of ice, had been shipped by rail from the Chesapeake Bay.

With the party ending, and the guests taking leave of each other, Rachel had to speak up and make her feelings known.

"Sir Arthur, we'll be leaving at sunup. I've had such a good time that even though there's a two-day ride separating us, I very much hope to see you again."

"Miss Longworth, you will. As soon as the harvest ends I will come calling on you in Sheridan. I'm not a 'hop-over' I wish you to know. That term is applied to blokes whose fathers pay a fee to us, to allow their sons to visit here a short while. I'm in America for good."

"Sir Arthur . . ."

"Please! My very good friends call me Archie."

"As Archie, then, and hopefully soon to become your very good friend, I invite you to our First Annual Harvest Festival in Sheridan on the first day of October."

"I accept. And, if you'll permit me to say so, I will miss you every moment until then."

CHAPTER 26

September 4th was hot. The air, heavy with the scents of late summer, was thrumming with the sounds of insects. The day's primary work was to get on with painting the big new barn. Most of the Sparhawk Settlers, including the German families—Dunkels, Haberstrobs, Stoetzers, Wentzes, Wertzes, Guengerichs—and their numerous offspring, had been hard at the job for days. There was a core crew and other workers came and went as their own chores permitted. They started at sunrise and stopped only when the light was gone in the evening. The job had to be completed in the fall, well before the ravages of the Iowa winter set in.

It had taken the small community most of summer, after the red brick foundation was made, to raise the timber-framed structure. At Jesse's direction, the massive barn was set into the side of a low hill so that both levels, the upper intended for vast storage, the lower for livestock, could be entered at ground level. Chutes in the top floor would allow feeding bins below to be easily filled. There was ample space above for tons of hay, corn, oats, and wheat and for twenty horses and as many head of cattle below.

Lorena and Jesse, joined by Frankie Reed, worked as one painting team among several.

The first-rate cabinetmaker, Freddie Foshardt, had orders waiting in his shop for many fine pieces of furniture, not a few of them for Jesse's rising house. The items had been designed and drawn in detail by Lorena. Jesse trusted her judgment and style and had given her free rein to furnish his home before, as it was rumored, she left the settlement for points farther west.

Jesse, like everyone else waited while the cabinetmaker taught less skilled men to make straight cuts and plane boards during the barn raising. Freddie had seen to all the joints himself to be certain they were tight, and he himself set the hinges supplied by the carriage maker, Peter Allmann. The hundreds of nails the structure required were mostly factory made, though the blacksmith, Ralph Dunkel, hand-forged ten dozen copper-coated nails himself for use in the great barn doors.

At late morning on the hot September day when the barn painting was nearing completion, Lorena was anchoring a tall ladder as Jesse, high up, painted the barn's peak. Frankie served as all-round helper. He carried buckets of oxblood and whey mixed with lard, the best formula for painting barns. He also saw to cleaning brushes and delivering them as needed.

When Jesse came down to grab a full bucket, no one else was near. Lorena innocently traced a finger along his tanned jawbone. With a swell of innate tenderness she couldn't suppress, she took his hand to her parted lips.

"Your hands are getting stained and rough. It's unfitting for such an elegant officer and gentleman. You'd best let me see to them." Her gesture of innocent intimacy captivated him.

"My hands have been calloused before. They're soldier's hands and fighter's hands." He paused, watching her. "And lover's hands, right? Don't blush so. I can hear you thinking, Lorena. I can even read your dreams."

She turned from him. "We'd best get to painting," she said in a throaty voice. Jesse was back on the roof a few minutes later when Hazel appeared at the worksite with food and lemonade prepared by Simone Nicke, as the chef, wedded, had recently become. Hazel, unnoticed, had witnessed the by-play between Lorena and Jesse. The brief, stilted exchange between the young people added to her growing maternal concern about her daughter's future. She took Lorena aside.

"I couldn't help but observe you just before. Must you be

quite so cool and distant with Jesse?" she asked. "I know your principles. I taught them to you. They are honorable and upright, but there are times and situations in this life which call out for lenience, for a change of course of the sort I've navigated with Seek."

"I don't judge you amiss," Lorena made haste to say emphatically. "I wish you both all possible pleasure and happiness, but I have a husband, Mamma. You do not."

"Clint might never be heard of again. If he does turn up, the bonds of your marriage to him would not hold. I *know* you were not in love with the boy, no matter how much he wished you to be. You and Clint were not together as man and wife. Don't lose Jesse now you've found him. Any fool is able to see how you love him."

"I don't deny that," Lorena protested.

"And Jesse surely loves you."

"I don't question that, either. Please don't scold me as if I were a child."

"Remember, miss," Hazel went on undeterred, arms folded across her chest, "Jesse is a proud man with a man's desires."

"I know, Mother, better than you might think. I wavered in my resolve one time. I gave in to Jesse and to myself. I gave and took pleasure, then felt wretched later, for compromising my word." Lorena was agitated and fell into her mountain drawl.

"When I was up there in that city with no recollection of who I was, they said, 'follow your own instincts and you cain't go wrong.' I did that. I just went on and fell in love without so much as a fare-thee-well and maybe I done wrong. I'm not sure that *was* myself I was hearing. Now, Mamma, I am trying to grasp what is right for *me*. Jesse says marry up with him and don't fret. Jesse says 'love conquers all' but I'm not certain." Lorena was briskly pacing between the corner of the barn and the edge of the tall grass. Hazel, listening patiently, paced at her side.

"What about the law of the land? I'd be disregarding it," Lorena went on, throwing up her hands. "In truth I'd be flouting it were I to marry now, knowing another man might come along to claim me as his lawful wedded wife. I can't marry, at least not until I know something about Clint. Well, fine, says Jesse, just stay on here and be his common-law wife. I don't know that I could live that way, raising up babies and telling them untruths, feeling deceptive." Hazel stood still, which caused Lorena to do the same.

"There are different kinds of law, Lorena—man-made court law and the law of love," Hazel said firmly. "After your father was killed, even before my set year of mourning ended, I longed to be in love just one more time again. In some small, secret place in my soul, I never stopped hoping for that.

"You know, Lorena, I've always been a romantic. I think those 'instincts' you followed come straight from me. I couldn't believe I would never again feel as I did when I first saw your daddy. That's true for most folks; no matter how resigned they seem to a lonely loveless life." Hazel paused to reflect a moment and then decided to go on. "Now, hear me out, Daughter.

"Seek transformed me. He roused my passion. He let me love again. Course it's not the same as the first time, but it's real love. *Not* everyone gets a second chance. Some don't even get a first. Don't drive Jesse away by refusing him. Denial will tarnish even the brightest jewel of love."

"What are you two lovely ladies lollygagging about?" called Jesse. He had been following their actions with interest from his high vantage place and he was sure a serious mother-daughter dialogue had taken place. Knowing Hazel as he now did, he expected she was pleading his case. Shirtless, hands set at his hips, feet placed wide on the roof peak, Jesse could see to the boundaries of the settlement and beyond. He shifted his gaze back to what he most wanted to look at— Lorena. And he didn't merely want to look. She, in turn, was staring up at him, holding her straw sun hat in place with one hand. He could not read her expression and she was not about to say that, to her own chagrin, she was appreciating his masculine perfection.

At that same moment, all attention abruptly turned toward

the sound of a shrill whistle. Luke Hamson, who was splitting logs into rails for fencing, had spotted Hazel and her jug of lemonade. He set down his axe and, with his fingers at the corners of his mouth, blew two piercing notes to let the workers know what he had seen. Children encircled him as if by magic and their elders came running from all directions, several scrambling down ladders leaning against the barn. Jesse, wiping his brow with the back of a hand, sought Lorena. She held out to him a tall, sweating glass, which had been cooled in the hotel's ice cellar.

"Wait," he said when she began to turn away. "Just what I needed. Thank you, Lorena," he smiled and gulped down the lemonade without taking his lips from the glass. "I need something else, but I doubt you'll give it to me as you did the long cool drink. Perhaps I will take what I crave."

"Jesse!" she managed to say, just that one word, no more, as she anticipated his kiss, yearned for it, willed him in her heart to crush her to him right there in front of everybody. His dark blue eyes were sultry and he produced his smile that was all charm and seductive invitation. She stood, unable to move, feeling like a soft little animal caught in a lion's stare. When he leaned to brush her lips with his, they felt firm and cold and tasted of lemonade. Anger flared in her eyes when he let her move away and the angle of his body, the gesture of his hand told her it had not been easy for him to do.

"I may not be able to wait forever," he said softly so that only she could hear.

Later, after the air was cooler and the paint party had quit for the day, Luke went to join Haley in her garden. On the way, he watched his large, furry bees humming in the sunny air as they fed on clusters of white clover blossoms. The bees hovered, he thought, like fish in a somnolent pond, wings treading air like gossamer fins in water. He had already collected copious honey and made note to himself to allow swarms in spring. He thought of the biblical injunction to "be fruitful and multiply."

"By this time next year we could well have double the

number of bees to pollinate your fruits and flowers," he said when he came upon Haley tending her rose bushes. He surprised her happy at her work.

"Double? Really? Are you sending for more queens?" she asked handing him a fragrant rose.

"A beekeeper takes over a swarm by hanging a welcome sign for 'em. That would be an empty hive or frame for them."

"Will they swarm soon?" she asked. "Have you got a new hive ready for them?"

Luke recited,

> *A swarm in May is worth a load of hay.*
> *A swarm in June is worth a silver spoon.*
> *A swarm in July isn't worth a fly.*

"Too late now, to be of any use. No honey would come of it. A spring swarm is what we want."

"Do the bees know that?" she asked.

"Usually. If life gets tight in the hive and overcrowded, which happens when the weather warms it, then they swarm. The warmer the winter, the earlier it happens. Its a real beautiful thing to watch, just like you, Haley, my love. You'll see—there'll be thousands of 'em workers and drones—a great swirling dark cloud. They take the old queen with 'em, leave a new queen behind ready to hatch. That's all after the scouts have done their dance to find a new home."

"You look real happy, just thinking about it!" Haley laughed.

"Haley, you're looking pretty pleased, yourself."

"I couldn't be more so. I have you and I have my vegetables *and* these gorgeous red roses."

"Know how the rose got its red color?" Luke asked, and did not wait for an answer. "When the goddess Aphrodite rushed to the defense of her lover Adonis, she pricked her foot on the thorn of a rose, staining the white flower with her blood, and creating the red rose. And now here you are with your red roses reminding me and all the world of love."

He threw his arms around her and pulled her to him. As she

snuggled into him very tightly and as she raised her face, she managed to say, "But Luke, it was only last night—no, just early this morning." He kissed her and she remembered vividly how delightful their lovemaking had been. Always was.

"There can never be too much of a good thing," he whispered softly, "I want *you* now. *Now*," he breathed, lifting her off her feet and carrying her into the shadowed depths of the tool shed. Standing, pressing her back against a wall, he lifted her dress, his hands delving beneath it, probing and exploring before settling on her hips, steadying her. Her fingers, made deft by urgency, undid his trousers buttons to free him before her arms enfolded his neck. Eyes closed, she felt him prod and thrust and then delve full into the sweltering human heat of her desire, penetrating and lunging, his breath a rasp in her ear, deafening her to all else, even her smothered cries as her teeth left an imprint on his bare shoulder.

A short time later as they were walking along the garden path examining the nearly ripened rows of vegetables, he said, "Haley, you'll be a very good mother."

"But first I have to be pregnant."

"The way we're going, I have no doubt you will be very soon."

"A love child."

"No darling, a child of love; if you'll have me, I'll be your husband. Haley, will you marry me?"

"Oh Luke, of course I will. You are my love, my one and only real true love."

At just about the same time that Luke and Haley were planning their future, Jesse and Lorena were riding through row after row of tall plants heavy with ripened corn. With them was the bridegroom, Madame the Chef's new husband, Corbett Nicke.

Beyond the cornfield, they saw a glittering sea of golden wheat, planted in the early spring as soon as the ground was dry and ploughed. In an adjacent field, there were seedlings of recently planted winter wheat and rye.

Corby took off his deep-brimmed dark hat. He extracted a few kernels of wheat from the husk and crushed them in his heavy, calloused hand. Then he split a single kernel between his teeth to see if it was dry enough to store.

"It's ready," he pronounced. " 'Put ye in the sickle for the harvest is ripe,' so saith the prophet Joel. First thing in the morning we'll start bringing it all in. Even with the newfangled monster of a machine we got, we'll be needing every one of the new settlers you recruited, Lorena."

"She did a good job, sending that advertisement to Greeley for his New York paper," Jesse agreed. "It took me by surprise and helped us to solve a real problem—getting more workers. I hope that most of those who responded will be permanent settlers in Sheridan. We need all the hands we can get to work the land, tend the cattle and horses, and staff the hotel."

> To the West. Land of the Free.
> Emigrants to the West.
> Join the Renowned Colonel Jesse Sparhawk
> And His Sparhawk Settlers at
> Sheridan, Iowa. Affordable Land. Generous Terms.
> Workers, Farmers, Craftsmen ONLY.
> NO clerks, lawyers, professors wanted.

They had come in groups of two or three families, many originally from Scandinavia, Ireland, and Germany by way of New York harbor. Once every week someone from Sheridan met the train at Iowa City. The most promising men and women were signed on. A few, tempted by recruiters at the terminus of the railroad went on farther west by wagon, also an option for Lorena, when it came time to leave Sheridan and Jesse once the harvest was over.

It began the very next morning. The dawn serenity was broken by the appearance of a great, complicated machine pulled to the fields by a team of six Belgian draft horses.

"It's a new one, delivered just in time from Cyrus McCormick's company in Chicago," Jesse said.

"I've seen one of these machines before, up in the north of New York, but never this close," said Lorena.

"There have been mechanical reapers on wheat farms since the eighteen-thirties. It seems that each year a bigger, better, faster one comes along. This model has a self-rake, hand binder, and twine binder."

The apparatus was driven first by Jesse, then by the others in turn, and it lumbered and clanked on and on through the day in ever-narrowing circles. The work progressed. The reaper startled birds out of tall grain. It left in its wake dark swarms of gnats, grasshoppers, and crickets, and it drove field mice deeper into the shrinking stand of yellow grain.

Many watched as the combine threshed and winnowed and beat the grain from the husks, then blew off the chaff—chaff that hung in the still air and filtered into their clothes to scratch and grate against the skin. Everyone in Sheridan worked, many following after the machine to gather up what was missed or spilled.

In her heavy linen dress and big hat, Lorena and the others similarly attired for protection, felt the blaze of the sun as fire-fierce. Perspiration trickled tickling between her breasts and soaked her back. When it flooded her eyes, she wiped them with her cuff, pulled her hat a fraction lower and persisted, laboring and learning, as she always did. Jesse seemed to be everywhere, supervising, helping. His face, like Lorena's, was tanned and flushed.

"I'm proud of you," Jesse told her during a noon pause. "You were meant to be a farmer's wife."

"If we get the whole crop in before the rains come again, we'll all be proud of each other."

CHAPTER 27

The approach of fall found Sheridan bustling with activity. The culmination of intense work, applied to rich opportunities, resulted in abundance.

Train cars laden with corn from the settlement rolled to the cattle-fattening pens of Kansas City. Bulging sacks of wheat piled up on the dirt floor of Corby's stream-powered mill until no room remained, and then the granary filled, too. The produce of Rachel's garden overwhelmed her and even with the aid of all the women and every child over five, she was hard pressed to get all her vegetables picked before they over-ripened.

There were enough apples from mature trees on the property to make cider and apple butter. Jesse had ordered a huge kettle of finest copper and the cabinetmaker Freddie had produced an ash-wood stirrer. These would be used for nothing but preparing apple butter, a two-day endeavor and a good excuse for some socializing. Lorena delightedly took the project in charge.

"How many bushels have we?" she asked Jesse when he navigated a flatbed wagon into the kitchen yard close to a small, temporary hand-worked cider mill. Three little boys, tow-headed brothers of about eight, ten, and twelve, Lorena estimated, jumped from the wagon bench and began unloading the fruit-filled baskets.

"There are twenty bushels," Jesse answered. "These aren't quite as large as those we used for yesterday's cider, but I bet you're going to end up with almost twenty gallons of apple butter. Hey there, Ralph," he called to one of the boys, "toss me one, please!" The youngster obliged with a smooth overhand pitch. Jesse snatched the apple out of the air, took a crunching big bite and handed it over to Lorena. She, too, tasted and they stood side by side chewing and passing the apple back and forth until they were down to the core.

"These are pretty juicy," Lorena commented. "I bet we'll get more than a gallon of butter a bushel from these. I think we're going to end up with nearer to thirty gallons."

"How near to thirty?" Jesse asked her, putting up his hand to indicate to the boys he was ready for another apple. Again, he and Lorena shared it and munched thoughtfully.

"I'm saying thirty right on the head," she replied through a mouthful of fruit, wiping juice from her chin with the hem of her apron.

"You're on," he grinned and shrugged. "What will you give me, Lorena, if I win?" She instantly recognized the look in his eyes.

"Not what you're already asking for. Think of something else that would pleasure you," she said, darting off as a group of older, taller children arrived to help her press apples.

Jesse came by several times during the course of the day, to watch the work and count the resulting jugs of cider as they were lined up. He and Lorena exchanged challenging, happy glances.

"Have you decided what you're going to give me when I win?" he teased her.

"*If* you win, which you won't, I'll give you a smile," she answered. "Will that do?"

"Well, for starters maybe. But you're of a naturally happy temperament. You give me a fair number of those as it is. I'll think of something singular to ask you for."

"Don't worry yourself over it. You are not going to win," she smiled, sweetly smug.

By sundown the apple crushing-and-pressing was done. The shining copper kettle sat ready on an iron tripod over piled wood ready to set afire. A thick shaven greenwood pole ten feet long was passed through the kettle's handles for balance. At either end, the pole rested on forked props.

"What time is the party beginning?" Jesse inquired catching up with Lorena as she neared the kitchen door. Her apron was stained with apple juice and her chin, which she dabbed at, was smeared with it. She appeared rather tired, but content.

"I must fill that kettle and start the fire not one minute later than five tomorrow morning. Rob and Rachel will help me with that part. The cider will take all day to boil down by half so we can expect folks to arrive right after supper, just before dark."

"I put by a bushel of the biggest, finest apples," Jesse told her, "for us all to peel and cut and add to the kettle while we're visiting and stirring and drinking cider."

"Simone and Haley will bake up plenty of doughnuts to have with the cider. Well Jesse, what are you going to give me when I win our wager?" Her crooked little half smile, tired as she was, glowed. It pleased him.

"You *are* the confident one," he said reaching for her hand. She let him take it. It was very sticky. He didn't mind at all. When they were standing at the door, Jesse brought Lorena's sweet hand to his lips and tasted every finger.

"Apron strings undone? That's a clear sign your lover has been thinking of you," said Jesse coming upon Lorena the next evening, and undoing the sash of her starched apron. It was very white against her soft yellow dress. Her sleeves were rolled to the elbow; her hair was coiled at her nape as she industriously directed the ongoing work that had begun for her at four in the morning. Jesse saw no hint of fatigue in her face. Her eyes were sparkling with pleasure as she gave directions or bantered with visitors. Some had arrived from as far away as Sioux City to join in the apple butter gala, and would spend the night at the Union Hotel.

In the group around the kettle, there were mostly Sparhawk

Settlers, young and old, some with babies sleeping on their shoulders. Many had been stopping by all day to add wood to the fire, check the cauldron of cider as it bubbled down. Several women remained with Lorena to peel and quarter the last remaining bushels of the best fine-grained apples. By early evening when only half the liquid remained, a small, happy crowd had collected in the kitchen yard of the Union Hotel. It was time to add the quartered pieces of fresh fruit to the kettle and for the mixing to begin. Jesse took the first turn himself.

The careful, slow stirring would go on without a break for hours until the contents of the kettle had become so thick it would no longer drip from a spoon. Until close to midnight, folks would work in turn. The two-foot ash wood mixer had a long handle, nearly six feet, which helped workers keep some distance from the fire. Incessant stirring kept the kettle-bottom from scorching and tainting the brew. When, finally, it became too thick to drip from a spoon, the cider had become apple butter. The fire was extinguished. With large ladles, Simone and Corby filled warmed stoneware crocks with apple butter. Settler women had brought their own crocks and glass bottles to be filled.

"I win our bet, Warbird!" Lorena said gleefully when she found Jesse leaning casually against a tree, watching the festivities wind down.

"Come to claim your prize, have you? May I make a suggestion?" he asked. Lorena's eyes narrowed and she took a step away from him. "No, not what you're thinking," he said as he laughed and locked his hands behind his head. "Allow me to escort you on a week of late fall shooting excursions. Rachel tells me you're a fine shot. There's plenty of good game and some fine country close by that you've not explored. You'll be safe with me."

"Safe with you?" she asked teasingly. "Safe from Maud Wharton, of course, but I can think of other risks."

"Frankie will be our chaperone. He's already agreed."

"Frankie?" Now it was Lorena's turn to laugh.

"You can trust me," Jesse said with mock wounded inno-

cence. "I've been amazingly restrained I think, given our circumstance." Lorena agreed to consider his offer, but her
decision had already been made. She would try him, hold him
to his promise and enjoy herself thoroughly.

"Tomorrow, after the butter is cold and I've tied paper tight
over the crocks, I'll give you my answer," she said, yawning
daintily behind her hand. Jesse heard her chirp of laughter
as she turned away and knew her answer would be "yes."

The chores of the harvest and preparations for winter progressed apace. Simone, as chief cook, supervised the laying
up of foodstuffs. She watched over the storing of grains—
wheat, barley, oats, and rye—in bins and cribs in the barn and
in stacks that were raised off the ground away from rats and
mice. Cats were put on guard. In the cavernous cellar of the
hotel, Madame Simone *Nicke* as she often reminded the others, saw to it that eggs, cheese, and butter were put into the
cold room. Her group of kitchen workers that at one time or
another included everyone in Sheridan never had an idle moment. Some worked at brining cucumbers and pickling
onions and shallots. Some saw to drying fruits that were hung
in nets in the cellar rafters. Many large containers of preserves were filled and sealed. Some of the recent arrivals
from Sweden who brought with them generations of experience at preserving food for long dark winters were assigned
to the smoke house. There, using their unique seasonings and
skill, they preserved fish and slab bacon over slow-burning
hickory wood. Soon there would be pheasants and wild
turkeys to dress and smoke, and deer meat, too—venison as
Simone Nicke insisted on calling it.

Soap was made from a mixture of wood-ash lye and melted
lard poured into square boxes to harden. Candles, more eco-
nomical than oil lamps, were made from melted beef tallow,
which burned very quickly unless mixed with the beeswax that
Luke supplied. Strings, dipped many times in the melting pot,

became coated to the thickness of candles and then hung to dry. Cream was skimmed from milk and churned into butter.

Three log cabins with clapboard roofs were put up near town for late arriving newcomers to use until they could build houses in spring. Jesse, the settlers knew, would reward their industry and long hours with a proportionate share of the harvest and game.

Soon after the apple butter party, Jesse took Lorena and Frank hunting. It was more a holiday from the grinding work of the farm than a task. Their purpose was to supply the tables of Sheridan. Young birds just coming into plump, fall maturity were prized not only by Simone but by gourmands everywhere and the cook insisted on shipping a barrelful to Doc Longworth in New York.

The hunters carried open bore, twelve-gauge shotguns that threw a wide pattern of shot to hit the birds neatly at under thirty yards. Counting downed game each day made for spirited competition. Usually Jesse, often Lorena, occasionally Frank took the lead. Effective hunting required a lightning-fast response to a fast-moving target at a short range.

The party followed My Dog along the river through large stands of alder, birch, and poplar thickets. All three appreciated the ways of a good pointer as they focused their attention on My Dog moving cautiously and slowly through the heavy cover. When he picked up a scent, he slammed hard on point so that one of the gunners could flush the prey into the air.

As the days of the hunt passed Jesse, Lorena, and Frank became a close threesome. They could share silence with comfort and each became adept at anticipating the actions of the others. The weather was mild but held an intimation of late afternoon chill. The foliage was beginning to turn with the onset of autumn.

On the last day of the week's sorties, Frank, laden with bulging bags of birds, hurried home to receive the acclaim of Simone and Rachel. Lorena and Jesse rode alone together, delaying the end of their shared venture. When Sheridan came in sight, Jesse reached out to set a hand on Lorena's shoulder.

"Don't spoil it now," she said earnestly. "It's been such a *good* time, shooting together and being friends."

"I've thought of a verse for you, for us, one of Ben Johnson's:

> *Follow a shadow, it still flies you;*
> *Seem to fly it, it will pursue:*
> *So court a mistress, she denies you;*
> *Let her alone, she will court you.*

"I won't press it. I'm going to wait, 'friend,' for you to woo me. I know it will happen—soon."

"I truly wish I was as certain of that, 'friend,' as you are." Lorena lightly touched her heels to the black mare's flanks and set off on a canter toward home.

Sir Arthur arrived in Sheridan on October 1, 1865.

Rachel had been in a dither for weeks wondering if Archie would keep his word. He did, and when he dismounted in front of the Union Hotel, she rushed to the verandah to greet him. She paused for breath to compose herself before she burst through the door. They looked at each other tentatively, the tall fair-haired young man and the calico-clad blue-eyed girl, who twisted her apron nervously.

"Miss Longworth," Archie said, "Here I am. These are for you." Bounding onto the verandah, he gave Rachel a pair of iron candle molds shaped like evergreens. She took one in each hand and nearly struck him on the head when she raised up and stepped into his embrace.

Rachel had already made her very serious interest in Archie known to the others at the Union Hotel. Some, aware of her past behavior, were skeptical, Simone most of all. Rachel, all of eighteen, had long proclaimed herself an intransigent old maid with a broken heart. But even the cook accepted without doubt that Rachel was in love when the girl came down for supper that evening. Her red hair, parted in the center, was done in coiled braids that framed her face. She wore a simple pink silk dress.

It showed off her fine figure to advantage and was so elegant in detail it might have come straight from Paris, France. Actually, the garment, designed by the couturier Ann Overton, had just come by post from New York. Molly Longworth, with a mother's intuition for the decisive moment, had had the wardrobe shipped to Sheridan just in time.

Rachel, animated and eager, formally introduced her guest to Jesse and Lorena before they sat down to supper.

"May I present Sir Arthur Randall," she said beaming and then quickly, "And Archie, may I present Colonel Jesse Sparhawk and Miss Lorena Reed."

"Excuse me, Rachel, but I believe it would be better in America from now on to be introduced by my name without title. My full name is Arthur Randall Wharton." There was a stunning silence in the room. "If I've given offense in any way, please accept my deepest apologies," said Archie, puzzled. "Colonel, I heard much about your service and bravery on behalf of the Union during the War. If the circumstance of my having served in the Confederacy at Gettysburg disturbs you, please be aware that after that battle I never fought again. I reconsidered my position, and realized I could not serve either the so-called Lords of the Lash—slave owners—nor the Lords of the Loom, northern factory owners. After, I passed a year interned in Seneca Falls. When I was freed in a prisoner exchange, I knew it was time for me to head west."

Lorena gasped, and then asked as calmly as she could manage, "Are you the son of Maud Wharton?"

When the reply was *yes*, Jesse, reverting to his role of spy chaser, was at once on his guard and posed several questions. Although it was not exactly a classic interrogation, it came uncomfortably close to one. To Archie's credit, as a gentleman, he responded calmly, fully answering every query, until Jesse was satisfied with his truthfulness and honor.

"If you know my mother at all well, as I take it you all do," Archie frowned, "you must be aware that she was not a model of parental love and loyalty."

"Archie, your mother and aunt, Estelle Partier, are wanted

to stand trial for their role in Mr. Lincoln's murder. And that's not all. They are plotting to control your fortune by declaring you deceased. You *are* the Sixth Baron Wharton of Sussex, and your life, as well as Lorena's, is in grave danger."

"Has my old dad passed on?" asked Archie. "I have gotten no wind of that. I dare say, the merchant, Jason Stillwell, the chap known as the King of Corn, will return from England with the news. May the old earl rest peacefully. We were not close."

"Archie, I made the acquaintance of your aunt at Seneca!" Lorena exclaimed. "She was searching Yankee prisoner camps for her young nephew—you."

"Clearly, she did not find him," said Rachel with a shudder. "But, Archie dear, the woman found someone and she set your name on his stone. Obviously, you are not buried in Seneca. Who could it be under you name?"

"We may never know the answer to your question, Rachel. Let's not dwell on sadness now," Lorena said and smiled cheerfully. "This is a celebration, Our First Annual Harvest Festival! It's time for us to join the others. There's to be dancing right after supper!"

The men shuffled about impatiently as the fiddlers tuned. When the first reel began, partners were quickly chosen, and Jesse Sparhawk, as dashing and handsome in civilian attire as he was in the full regalia of a cavalry colonel, led a beautiful Lorena out first. The spirited couple of Archie and Rachel closely followed them. Archie, seen by many of the Sparhawk Settlers for the first time, was deemed an elegant swain if there ever was one. Also, for the first time his partner, whom everyone knew, was so radiantly happy she was pronounced a great beauty. She and Lorena were the belles of the ball.

Children simmering with excitement, and old people, smiling, surrounded the dancers, and ribbons and petticoats swirled to the tempo of the music, which went on into the night under a full harvest moon.

When the last dance ended Jesse called for attention, and then said, "Friends and neighbors, as this extraordinary night ends an important announcement is to be made by our new friend, Archie. May I present Lord Randall, the Sixth Baron Wharton."

"Simply put," said Archie, "in the way of the West, I have asked the lovely woman on my arm, Rachel Longworth, to be my wife and she has agreed. We expect to be married here in Sheridan at the Christmastide."

Among the cheering settlers of Sheridan was the fireworks maker from Hamburg, and while the sixth baron and his future bride were still deep in their betrothal kiss, the night sky burst into multiple colors and filled with thunderous sound.

CHAPTER 28

"Good grief, Maud! Are those rockets I see exploding!" Estelle Partier asked her sister. "In all different colors. The noise is frightful. It hurts my ears."

"Pyrotechnics, fireworks. They're celebrating at the Union Hotel. I always find such displays annoying and gauche," Maud Wharton replied. "I cannot wait to get out of here, once we've taken care of Arthur and his new friends."

"Maud, isn't it going to be more difficult now that Arthur is betrothed?"

"No, not really, Estelle. All it will mean is an extra bullet for our great coup—four in all: one for the lord, one for his lady-to-be, one for Lorena, to shut her up, and one for Sparhawk. We wouldn't want him to come chasing us afterward," Maud said.

"Must he be killed too—after all that he meant to you? You did have a great appetite for his attention, did you not, Maudy?"

"Regrettably so, Estelle, and still have. I never trusted him, but even so, perhaps more so, you have no idea how exciting he could be. He was in a perpetual state of lust when he was in my presence, and he certainly roused me as no other man ever had before. But there will be another, of that I am certain. I'm still young enough," Maud said.

"And still very beautiful, Maudy."

"Estelle, if you call me 'Maudy' again I shall order a bullet for you, too. I detest being addressed as 'Maudy' and you know that." Maud gave her sister a withering green-eyed look and Estelle withered.

"Sorry. I forgot . . . really I did," answered Estelle. The plainer of the two, she fawned over her prettier, stronger if not wickeder, ill-tempered sister. Together they witnessed the last of the fireworks standing far back from the edge of the crowd, hidden in a wooded grove where they went on speaking with pleased anticipation of the sinister deed they had planned.

"Jesse will be the only one of them I'll have even the slightest regrets about," said Maud. "I'll certainly be jolly to see the end of that Reed girl. She's more of a Dresden doll than a warm-blooded woman."

"And dishonest to boot, pretending to have lost her memory," Estelle scoffed. "I do look forward to seeing you jolly again, Maud. It has been far too long you've griped and grumbled. Why, I cannot recall how you look with a smile on your lovely face." At that, Maud again glared at her sister to see if Estelle was being critical. Estelle looked back blankly and was given the benefit of the doubt.

"What are your feelings for Arthur?" she asked.

"None. You know I never loved him; indeed, I hardly knew him, he spent so much time at Eton. He was an ill-conceived child, sired by a boor."

"Your husband was dull, I agree, but he was a very rich nobleman."

"I'll get none of those riches if we don't get rid of Arthur now, as you were supposed to have done at Seneca." Maud sent a chilling look to Estelle.

"I did the best I could, Maud," Estelle whined. "If we had gone east on a ship set for England instead of west to do away with the Reed girl, we could have claimed Arthur's fortune by now. He'd have been none the wiser for months, if not years. Now we must eliminate him, too."

"Keep a civil tongue and do not presume upon my good nature with second guesses. And I'll remind you it is not 'we' who will claim Arthur's fortune. It is I!"

"Not if he lives long enough to take a wife."

"That boy has been nothing but trouble from his first day! His birth almost killed me and prevented any other. His lordship wanted a second son but when he learned he'd not get one from me, he wrote me off and out. Arthur would get it all. The Earl cared only about his lands and parks and his yapping dogs. He was always out on the hunt, but I certainly did not mind. There were many young gentlemen in that part of England to keep me diverted."

"Yes, yes," said Estelle impatiently. "But, what of Rachel Longworth? If the Sixth Earl does make her his Baroness, she will be the sole heir to the entire Wharton estate. Unless, that is, he or even his father, have other stipulations in their wills."

"Arthur's Last Will and Testament specifies me his only beneficiary. I'll see to that by writing it myself."

"Just as you forged the note from Clint Reed to his wife—actually his widow? It is Lorena Reed's own fault she must be done away with. Why she insists upon searching for the man is beyond me!"

"How could I have forged anything, Estelle, for a man who could not even write?" Maud asked, taking affront.

"Be that as it may," answered Estelle, "I suggest you start work on Arthur's bogus bequeaths almost immediately. The meeting in Nebraska with our hired gun is but a few days away. The earl's demise will follow soon after."

A rainbow decorated the misty, dawn sky as a lone rider dismounted and entered a nondescript inn on the road to Dakota City. It was just over the Iowa border in still war-troubled Nebraska. He joined two women, who appeared to be nurses, stiffly waiting. The proprietor suggested breakfast. The rider declined but accepted a cup of coffee.

"Captain Andrew Maguire, Confederate Cavalry, *Retired*, you might say," the dust-covered rider announced and waited for some sign of recognition from the women of his little joke. He met with only hard stares from both.

"Have you done your research, sir?" asked Maud, not

amused. Maguire's manner changed. He became wary look-ing, pushed his deep brimmed hat to the back of his head and tilted his chair to rest on two legs.

"The woman—girl rather—rides every day at dawn and at dusk, never alone, sometimes with another pretty girl about her age—a Rachel Longworth. These women are often ac-companied by Colonel Sparhawk and a titled English gentleman—a Sir Arthur, visiting from Wolf. Are you Maud Wharton?" Maud ignored Maguire's question.

"Can you do what I need done? When?" Maud asked. She was the more attractive of the two women and spoke in an im-patient and imperious tone as if dealing with a servant. She had an aristocratic English accent, but though she was strik-ing, perhaps beautiful to some, to the captain she was arrogance itself. Miz Wharton, as the Captain decided she must be, didn't have the charming manners he expected of a lady—English or Southern for that matter. In any case, he re-sented being condescended to.

"Madam, I have ridden with John Singleton Mosby him-self, and now I have orders from Cole Younger to perform a certain task for you. Cole says you were part of the Confed-erate Secret Service. He told me no more, and I didn't ask him any questions, or will I question you, except to ask, 'Do you have the money agreed upon?'"

"My arrangement was with Quantrill, not Younger," Maud said, drawing to her full height, bringing to Maguire's thoughts an uncurling rattler.

"Quantrill is dead. It's Younger who is now in charge." Maud didn't answer as she reflected on the one time she had met Charley Quantrill and Cole Younger.

She remembered Quantrill was a blond Apollo. He had had very blue, soft and winning eyes. He was handsome but not boyish, rather time hardened, no doubt by the cruelty of war. It had been savagely fought on the plains and still had not really ended in Nebraska. Quantrill had possessed cunning, skill, nerve, and daring, but now she learned he had gotten himself killed despite his talents. When she had met with the man, the war had ended. He had already become an outlaw with a price on his head, leading a gang of bandits and killers. He was the perfect man to do the job she wanted done. As part of his payment, she had planned to reward Quantrill with more than money. She had been intrigued by the idea that he was fond of "fast" women, and she looked forward to showing him what an English lady could do.

Her meeting with the guerrillas had taken place in the home of a strong Confederate sympathizer. After Maud and Quantrill had concluded their business arrangement, Quantrill proposed a toast:

"Here's to Abolitionist Abe. We'll use his bones in Hell as a gridiron for frying Yankees!" Maud had been impressed that any man could hate so much as Charley Quantrill. It was with a rare hint of sentiment that she posed a question to Captain Maguire.

"Did it end badly for him?"

"He was shot down by Federals in a blazing sheet of fire. Two of his men, who had returned to try and save him, were killed with him." Captain Maguire spoke coldly.

"And Cole Younger?" Maud asked. She remembered a huge man with a good-humored face, said to be as murderous as his cronies. She hoped that was so. "He's in charge now?"

"That's what I said. Do you want to keep the deal or not?" Maguire asked, not bothering to conceal his harsh edginess. With no sign of emotion, Maud Wharton placed a leather pouch upon the table, and then spilled out its contents of gold coins. The man gathered up the money and rose to his feet. The other woman, long-faced and hard looking, spoke for the first time.

"You *must* murder all four of the riders you saw. I hope you will have enough men. The colonel is dangerous."

"You are a bloody pair, " Captain Maguire snarled. "I have been a soldier. I don't take murder lightly. I've seen men and women too, shot down in Kansas. I have known hatred incarnate and heard the howling of kin. My own kin are hungry back home in Alabama, my buildings burned, so I will do the job but it will cost you more. You contracted for one shooting but whether I like it or not, the murderer can leave no witness. The others with the girl would have been done for, in any case. Now that you've added them to your list, I want more gold to do the deed. As an officer and gentleman, I'll be tainted forever. So will you pair and the blood will be on *our* hands—mine and yours. Colonel Sparhawk is widely known and highly reputed. But I will have enough men to take care of the colonel, a British lord, and two helpless girls."

"If you don't mind telling me, where and when do you expect to act?" Maud asked.

"As a matter of fact, I do mind. You'll be duly informed in time enough to do your part. I expect you to be in Sioux City, awaiting instructions."

A rowboat moved slowly on the mirror-like surface of Lake Sheridan with the setting sun slanting across the distant Union Hotel and the hills beyond. Distinct contrasts of light and shadow and the vast scale of the scene was reminiscent of an Albert Bierstadt painting. The renowned artist from Dusseldorf visited German friends in Iowa and then had gone on west to Yosemite to paint the wilds of America.

Lorena, awed yet again by the vista, felt small under the wide sky, yet protected by Jesse.

He rowed. When she wasn't dreamily studying the horizon, Lorena watched the rippling muscles in his arms.

"Frankie, come on up here next to me," she summoned her brother. "I'm going to ask Jesse to tell us about Cedar Lake Place, where he grew up."

"That's in North Carolina, on the coast. I've never been that-a-way," Frank said as he slid forward from the boat's stern where he had been trawling for whitefish. "I heard tell of the big plantations and slaves. Were you born with the silver spoon Jesse? Did you have slaves?"

"Yes to the first question," Jesse replied. "No, to the second. My father kept slaves."

"Frank, as you well know Jesse wasn't a Secessionist," said Lorena. "His mother took him north because she was an Abolitionist."

"And a Suffragette," added Jesse. "As I told Lorena when we first met back on Manhattan Island, my mother was descended from Roger Williams—the fiery freethinker who was banished from Plymouth Colony for his views. Among other things, Williams believed all men were created equal. My mother was very proud of her ancestor's memory," Jesse said as the rowboat drifted. "She told me the story of how he was rescued from the snow in the wilderness by Indians and then bought his land from them, fair and square, in what is now Rhode Island. When Roger had success at farming, other free thinkers joined him at the settlement he founded and called the Providence Plantation."

"You're doing the same as Roger Williams, Jesse," Frank said with admiration, "making a new settlement in a far place."

"My mother was named for Roger's wife, Mary. My Mary was born two hundred years after her forbears but she inherited old Roger's strong temperament and attitudes. She could not abide slavery. She left Father and took me north."

"He stayed at Cedar Lake Place," Frank said. "Why didn't he go after you and Mary?"

"They were both too strong willed to compromise. Besides, my father's own history and fortune were invested at Cedar Lake. Before I was born," Jesse continued, shifting the oars to keep the boat from drifting ashore, "he managed by various deals and purchases and an inheritance to take control of the Cedar Lake Place. He turned it into the biggest plantation in North Carolina, one-hundred-thousand acres around Cedar Lake, which by the way is about three times the size of this lake, but the fishing isn't as good, if I do say so. About two hundred people, most of them slaves, farmed the land. They raised all the same crops we do *and* rice and flax. The biggest profits came from thousands of feet of lumber produced by the sawmills. Then the entire enterprise of Cedar Lake Place was destroyed by the War.

"Now you have Sheridan, Jesse," Lorena nodded.

"We all have Sheridan and though it may not be as big in acres as Cedar Lake one day, I expect it will be even more valuable. Are you listening, Frank? You'll be here to watch and see, young man, and to make it grow."

"Yes, sir!" said Frank lapsing into a reveries of his future, which only came to an end when the rowboat nudged into the dock and stopped.

"I have reliable information that Maud Wharton and Estelle Partier have been seen in Sioux City. That's too close," Jesse said right after dinner that evening. His voice was forceful, his manner determined.

The dessert dishes had been cleared, and coffee and cognac served to the inner circle of Sparhawk Settlers, now augmented by Simone and Randall. Jesse drew on his cigar and went on. "We are now on full alert. Each of you is to be armed at all times, either with a revolver or with a carbine repeater."

"Should I carry my bird gun?" Frank asked.

"No. It's necessary we each be able to fire three shots in quick order. That will be the alarm signal. Frank, the 22 doesn't have enough power to handle the trouble I foresee. I'll fit you out with a serious shooting piece."

"I take it that Mum and dear Aunt Estelle are not alone? Have they brought in toughs or marksmen?" asked Archie. Jesse nodded but did not elaborate. "I'll need to borrow a weapon, Colonel," Archie said, matter of factly.

"Archie, you don't have to be part of this," said Rachel.

"Oh, but I do, my dear," was the earl's reply and Rachel said no more.

That night, Lorena and Jesse sat together under the light of a harvest moon. It was a meaningful moment for them both. The situation had changed. Danger was looming and, once that was faced, there was the prospect of their separation, now that the work of the harvest was close to finished.

"Oh, look," Lorena sighed as first one shooting star then another streamed through the heavens. She and Jesse reached for each other's hands. While she studied the sky, Jesse concentrated on her moonlit face.

"I want you," he said. When she didn't answer, he brushed his lips to hers.

"I can't," she said sadly. With her hair loose and catching moonlight, Lorena stood and started for the entrance to the hotel. Before she reached it, Jesse spun her about to face him. He kissed her again seriously, hard and long, his tongue parting her lips, invading her sweet mouth to its receptive depths.

"I don't want to do this," she protested. "I mean I want to, but I *should not*. It feels wrong. I'm trying to do what seems right and this will be right when I am free to marry and to have your children. Please Jesse," she whispered. "Think of *our* future."

His embrace subsided. She broke from his arms and went over to sit on the porch rail and look pensively up at the moon. He came to her, let his fingertips travel over the delicate contours of her profile, over her smooth brow and down to the tip of her pert, pretty nose. Cupping her chin, he turned her fully to him, and his strong profile hid the moon when he kissed her lips, softly this time.

When she tried to escape, he entrapped her against the porch rail and she felt his thighs press against hers. "Lorena, you're a woman now. And we pleasure each other. We already know that." His lips moved to her ear and down long the smooth column of her throat.

"Sweet seducer," she sighed. "You're taking unfair advantage of a woman on the brink of sleep," Lorena yawned dramatically behind her hand. "Taking advantage of a woman weakened by wine, of a woman who wants you awfully, Colonel," she sighed, her eyes lit by moonlight and stirred by passion.

Jesse held himself in check. He could wait. He had an iron will. He knew he could have her now, but when the time was right and she came to him freely it would be all the more satisfying. Kissing her softly, on her eyelids, the curve of her ear, the nape of her lovely neck, he drew her wrap about her shoulders.

"Good night my love. Sweet dreams. Soon we'll be dreaming together, always."

CHAPTER 29

All the Sparhawk Settlers were on guard, most of the time. At least one of the veteran fighters—Jesse, Corbett or Luke—was on duty all the time and was occasionally concerned by the overly casual or self-assured attitudes of some of the others. Lighthearted, happy Haley, who found life to be a bowl of cherries, seemed oblivious to possible trouble. Scoffing, short-tempered Simone had to be routinely reminded to be watchful as she came and went.

Despite the level of edginess, life at Sheridan continued much as usual.

Deep into fall, with most of the harvest over, school was in session. All the children and even some adults—immigrants aspiring to improve their English—attended.

Once the wicked sisters had been recognized so close to Sheridan before dropping from sight again, Jesse persuaded Lorena, for her own safety, to stay on at the settlement for at least as long as it took him and his wily spy team to ferret out and de-fang Wharton and Partier. Lorena, who in her heart of hearts did not want to leave the land and the friends she had come to love, was willing, easy prey to Jesse's cautionary blandishments. She remained at Sheridan to give instruction in English to immigrants. Seek taught Latin of which he was an academic master, and grammatically correct High German to English speakers and to German boys and young men who had aspirations to a university education. With his natural bent for linguistics, Seek had learned German from books and from the native speakers at Sheridan.

Jesse gave a class three times a week in Greek and one every day in mathematics, both of which he had studied at West Point. Rachel gave music lessons—voice and piano— and elementary French. She had learned the language in France in her early teens.

Hamson was the expert in animal husbandry and scientific agriculture. The farmers of Sheridan—almost every one to some degree—were very receptive to learning any guidelines and techniques that would increase their crop yields and profits during the next growing seasons.

Simone, who taught household skills, also gave cooking demonstrations, which were diligently and enthusiastically attended by a good number of the German women. Many were very happy to apply the tasty devices of French cuisine, though their husbands preferred the heavier meats, wursts and potatoes, the fare of their homeland.

The unique course was conducted on many weekend afternoons at the Sheridan Stables in what Lorena christened the Lord Randall Riding Academy. Archie, who virtually commuted back and forth to Wolf, gave very precise, demanding lessons in the elegant horsemanship techniques of the Buckingham Palace Guards and of the elite Austrian Hussars. Sequoyahson, bemused by the theatricality of such riding, learned to do it with perfection but preferred the bareback freedom of the Plains Indians by whom he been taught in his youth. Lorena became adept at both styles of horsemanship and rode out with Seek every morning and evening, usually with several other companions and students.

One particularly appealing fall day, only Rachel and Lorena, dressed for a sidesaddle canter, appeared for the afternoon excursion. They waited impatiently and when it became apparent no one else would be coming, they considered what to do.

"I'm armed," Lorena said.

"Yes, and I know how well you shoot. I think we'll be fine on a quick ride particularly if we don't go too far. Ah, but here are Frank and Archie! The matter is moot."

The pair of beautiful young riders were a striking sight, one in crimson the other in blue, mounted sidesaddle, their escorts in tow. Under Archie's keen eye, they took jumps and practiced tight figure eights with bravely flaring skirts. To their devoted instructor, they were a vision of skill and vivacity. Atop their handsome blue-eyed, pale-colored Portuguese stallions, they were particularly striking. Archie, who also sat one of the exotic equines, had had the mounts delivered from Wolf just days before. He rode western style, sitting relaxed in the saddle, an indulgence he rarely allowed himself. He followed the women in a gallop when the lesson was over, scanning the horizon and occasionally looking back over his shoulder. In a holster on each saddle was a Winchester repeater. Archie warned his companions that the young horses had not yet been subjected to the sounds of gunfire.

"Archie, you worry overmuch!" Rachel scolded fondly. "There'll be no guns shooting off on this beautiful day today. Let us go on only a mile past the creek and then turn for home."

"I think we will not," Archie replied, reining in before he dismounted and flipped his rifle to the ready position. "Look there," he instructed coolly, his attention fixed on what at first appeared to be toy figures. They grew larger as they came on steadily. Soon the riders could be discerned as three distinct horsemen all well mounted, approaching at full gallop. "Guerilla outlaws from Nebraska, or worse," Archie stated.

Frank drew the single-action Colt revolver that Jesse had given him as a gift and insisted he carry. The boy cocked it and fired into the air. Then again and again, the agreed upon signal in case of possible trouble. The three inexperienced horses reared and plunged, turning in circles, brandishing their front hooves in the air. Archie was the first to get his mount under control and wheeled toward the women. He could see that Rachel was barely hanging on to her terrified horse, which had bolted into the scrub near the creek. As Rachel clutched at the reins, two more shots were heard. She called out when something fast and hot grazed her arm while her horse, now completely out of control, bolted and ran. A low hanging limb caught Rachel's shoulder full force, knocking her out of the saddle. She managed to stand up and then, holding her bleeding arm, to stagger out of the brush to see the assailants charging toward Archie and Lorena.

Lorena was just getting her terrified horse under control as Archie yanked his carbine from its holster and quick-fired three shots at the charging riders.

That did not stop their headlong rush.

"No, Lorena, don't shoot! Not now," Archie called, wheeling his horse toward her as she was leveling her carbine at the oncoming riders. "Get to the covered bridge before they come any closer. We'll have some protection and make our stand there until the others come!"

Frank, on his favorite, war-tested, gelding charged toward the line of attack. When he was almost exactly between the two groups, he made a decision that later deeply impressed Jesse and, in fact, would have been favored by any military tactician. He prepared to set up a cross fire.

After dismounting and slapping the rump of his horse to run it off, Frank slipped behind a tree, hugged it with one arm and with the other aimed his pistol at a point that he knew the outlaws would have to pass. Leading the riders as if they were flying geese, he waited until the exact, perfect moment to fire his pistol. As he cocked it, he moved his aim forward to where he calculated a rider would be. He fired. And then fired again. When the smoke cleared and the shock of the explosions passed, he saw one of the riders down, stumbling to his feet. Frank, who was wearing an ammunition belt, reloaded and fired again.

Jesse arrived on the scene riding flat out. He momentarily slowed and commanded, "Stay with the wounded outlaw, Frank. Kill him if you have to," and galloped toward the bridge.

The two other outlaws who were still mounted, pulled up

short of the bridge as bullets kicked up around them. They dismounted and with their rifles and ammunition belts scrambled for cover. For several minutes, the firing went on until Maguire noticed that the distinctive sounds of first one Winchester then the other firing from the bridge fell silent. He breathed a sigh of momentary relief. The man and woman taking cover there—Lorena and Archie—had run out of ammunition. He was no coward, but he was in a hurry, suspecting a posse might be close behind.

"George, Bud Pierce was hit," Macguire called. "He's down, but the last I saw of him he was alive. I'll draw their fire. Keep shooting. We've got plenty of bullets. The pair on the bridge doesn't."

With that, Captain Macguire stood straight up, revealing himself. There was total silence. Maguire and his partner, George Shepherd, charged the bridge, one from each end and took Lorena and Archie captive without firing another shot. Moments later the two outlaws and their captives saw Jesse, thundering toward the foot of the bridge.

"Jesse, they're well armed!" Lorena called out. He reined in and dismounted with agile speed then rolled and crouched out of shooting range. Almost at once, he saw a white bandana hanging from the end of a carbine, and he heard a voice shouting.

"I'm Andrew Maguire, not long since Captain Maguire of Mosby's Raiders. I wish to parlay!"

"Come on, then. I'm Jesse Sparhawk," Jesse replied. He strode forward toward the advancing figure who had dropped the carbine and was now waving his flag of truce in one hand.

"Colonel, I've heard much about you, all of it good," said Maguire. "I'm sorry we find ourselves on opposite sides in yet another contest. I have the girl."

"Skip the chitchat, Captain. I do not intend to waste time with a kidnapper bent on murder. Before we exchange further words, give orders that your captives not be harmed," Jesse said. Actually, he was stalling, doing the opposite of what he had said, knowing that the sergeant and the corporal would soon be joining him in the fight.

"One of my men is down back there," Maguire said. "I want him back alive. In return, I'll give up a hostage."

"Maguire, I'm a Union officer. I won't negotiate with a defeated Reb still fighting on as an outlaw, and worse—a cowardly kidnapper. Come what may, you and your cohorts will hang. How much were you paid to do this job?" asked Jesse as he glimpsed Corbett and Luke inching toward him, out of Maguire's line of sight.

"Whatever I'm getting for this maneuver is not enough, Sparhawk. Give me a few minutes to talk to my partner, see if we cannot come to some terms with you. On my honor as a one-time Southern officer and gentleman, no matter what I've now become, I give my word not to harm either hostage before you and me get to talk some more "

The implication of Maguire's last words did not escape Jesse. "I'll give you ten minutes, Maguire," he said, stepping in the direction of Luke and Corbett and, not incidentally, moving out of rifle range of Maguire's "partner" on the bridge. Standing above Luke and Corbett, who were crouching unseen in tall grass at his feet, Jesse gave orders as soon as Maguire was out of hearing.

"Go up creek," he told them. "Get under the bridge and determine the strength and position of these bastards. Then circle back to this side and if we can, we'll hit from the rear. I don't have to tell you that Lorena and Archie are in the middle of this."

The sergeant and corporal, keeping low profiles, worked in unison without words, as they had many times during the war. They slipped soundlessly under the bridge and at a sign from Corbett stopped. There were footsteps overhead and shadows. Then they heard voices.

"George, take this pretty pair on up to where the sisters are hiding. I'll wait here to keep a watch on Sparhawk," said Maguire.

"Keep on your guard, boss," was the reply and the men

under the bridge heard scuffling before Lorena and Archie, prodded by the man called George, emerged on the far side of the creek. The two soldiers, fuming with outrage, watched as the prisoners, roped together, stumbled along a dirt path toward a stand of woods. Their captor held a hunting knife at the ready close to the back of Archie's neck.

"Let my friend go, George," Lorena said. "I'm the one your employer is after."

"No, no!" said Archie. "Let the lady go, Georgie. This whole brouhaha is about me. This is a family matter and I have some very unpleasant relations."

Corbett, watching Lorena and Archie and scanning the distance in the direction they were headed, saw, nearly hidden in the shadows of a cypress grove, a four-horse carriage and two women pacing beside it.

"Luke, it's the bloody sisters," he whispered elbowing his friend in the ribs. Luke nodded, as the outlaw approached the carriage and forced the hostages to a standstill. "That is one conversation I do wish I could hear," he opined as he saw Lorena and Maud exchange words.

"Lorena, nothing will give me such satisfaction as your demise, except perhaps my son's. What Jesse Sparhawk saw in you, I could not imagine, although it just may have been the appeal of your simple innocence, feigned as it was, I'm sure. But, then again, there's no accounting for tastes, as the woman answered when asked why she kissed the cow."

"Maud Wharton, you are *mad*. It's one thing to despise a rival out of jealousy, but it's satanic to murder a son for his inheritance. As a mother, have you no sense of decency, no sense of shame?" Lorena asked.

"I lack maternal feelings for his lordship my son, always have. I am not concerned with current notions of morality, but only with what is best for me—*self-interest* is what the philosopher Hume called it, a hundred years ago. And don't delude yourself, Miss Reed, about my motivation where you are concerned. It is less jealousy that drives me than a need for self-protection. I will see to it that you are silenced forever. Otherwise, sooner or later, you well may put two and two together."

"Two and two?" mused Lorena. "I know, Maud, you're thinking of an event that occurred, or you imagine to have occurred, at Seneca Falls. What that episode may have been I have only an inkling, something to do with falsely marking a grave inscribed with Archie's name. Who, if anyone, is buried there?"

"Obviously, not the Sixth Earl of Sussex. My original plan was to have found Archie, have him disposed of in battle, shot in the back, then mourn, as a mother should before filing my claim for his estate with Parliament. When Estelle failed to unearth—pardon the pun—Lord Randall, we suspected he was already deceased, what with the armed conflict and all. We had to have proof. We may never have found a shred of it. Thus, the grave marker to substantiate my claim to the Wharton wealth and to discourage any suspicion of foul play.

"You, Lorena Reed, thwarted my plans. You just happened to be at Seneca when my sister was there also. Mere coincidence, not to be helped. Estelle nearly got rid of you in New York, but once again, she did not succeed at her mission. Estelle's competence has always left much to be desired."

"It was no fault of mine, Maud, that Jesse Sparhawk interfered and ran off the sailors I paid to take this creature away," Estelle protested. "Just another coincidence, not to be helped."

"No, it was your mistake, Estelle, but, as we shall soon see, a correctable one. As for who is buried under Arthur's stone, Lorena, it is none other than that simple backwoods lad you were nursing, your husband. His was a convenient body for the diggers to take, but another of Estelle's debacles. I mean, really, the fellow's wife—you, Miss Reed—would notice his absence. Surely, there must have been some other man alone." Maud clicked her tongue at Estelle.

"I had to give them *something* to work with, after all," Estelle sulked.

"I never could believe poor Clint would run off," Lorena said sadly, tears coursing her cheeks, "or send me that message."

"Lorena, weep for yourself while you're still able," Estelle said gloatingly, no longer content to sit in brooding pique. "If you had gone off to sea with those sailors on South Street you may have had some chance of survival. Not now." Lorena stared in outrage and disbelief at one, then the other of the women.

"You really are the wicked sisters as everyone says, but you're not as clever by half as you suppose. Don't be so sure of yourselves!" she said defiantly. "Coincidences *will* keep occurring as you well know. Keep in mind the best laid plans of mice and all."

CHAPTER 30

Jesse galloped to the rescue, splashing through the creek upstream from the covered bridge on which Maguire was trapped. Sequoyahson, Hazel and Rachel trained rifles at one end. At the other end, Robert and Frank fired at the slightest movement to let Maguire know he could not break out in that direction to rejoin his partner.

Rachel, only because of her wounded arm, had been convinced by Jesse to stay at her post and not to ride with him. Again, he repeated orders that no one was to rush the bridge.

As soon as he gained high ground along the crest of the creek, Jesse took in the situation. A carriage drawn by four horses was careening wildly back and forth, as the outlaw up on the driver's bench sawed at the reins and shouted, trying to regain control of the vehicle. Corby Nicke was on the tailgate, ready for the right moment to fling himself aboard. Luke Hamson was harassing the lead horse, trying to grab its halter to bring it under control. Both soldiers were expert horsemen but not acrobats. Both were trained to keep cool heads and not to take unnecessary chances. In combat that was the best way to stay alive and eventually prevail. Both men could see that, in their present situation, risks were high. Though George Shepherd was struggling with the reins, he used only one hand. In the other, he had a forty-five caliber revolver. He had already fired two shots that went wild. Nicke and Hamson found being fired on at such close range a most unpleasant, daunting experience and were jubilant to see

Jesse bring his tough, battle-ready war horse right up to the side of the racing carriage.

Sparhawk was within short range of the outlaw, who let go of the reins altogether to steady his revolver with both hands and point and shoot directly at Jesse.

But George Shepherd was a second too late. Jesse fired first, hitting the outlaw straight on. The impact velocity of the forty-five caliber bullet slamming into his chest propelled Shepherd forward to land on the carriage horses. Panicked even more, each horse tried to pull in a different direction and the carriage capsized, crushing the outlaw's body. It came to a skidding stop only after Hamson got control of the lead horse. When the carriage first hit the road, a door had flown open ejecting the wicked sisters onto the mossy creek bank. Lorena and Archie were not as lucky. Still tied together, they were trapped inside the battered coach, its wheels spinning, lying on its side.

"Let's GO!" Jesse shouted. "If anyone's still alive in that wreck they need help fast!" He leaped from his horse into the carriage where Archie and Lorena slumped in a corner.

Jesse slashed their bonds and lifted Lorena, unconscious, to Luke and Corbett. A dazed Lord Randall, with Jesse's help crawled out after them and all four men anxiously hovered over Lorena. Archie took her pulse.

"Weak but steady," he reported. That information sent Luke racing to the creek for cold water. Corbett folded his jacket beneath her head. Jesse, kneeling beside her, was tense and anguished. He took her small limp hand in both of his, brought it to his lips and then brushed Lorena's mouth with his. He felt her lashes flutter against his brow and sat upright to see her eyes open and a slight smile appear on her face.

"Seems I got another bump on the head, but this time, Warbird, I didn't forget one single thing that has happened to me. Jesse, I have something to tell you."

No sooner had Jesse finished saying, "Don't talk now. I love you," than shots were heard in the distance. "I'll be back. "Please get the carriage upright and turned around," he ordered the men, "get her out of the evening chill and stay with her." Only then did they remember that the sisters Maud Wharton and Estelle Partier had disappeared. "Stay with her, whatever happens!" he repeated and then he was gone.

When Jesse was in sight of the bridge, Maguire decided the moment had come to break out. With a carbine in the crook of one arm and a revolver in his other hand, he came out of cover and blazed away at the fast-approaching rider before he ducked back under the bridge. There had been nothing in combat that so drove Jesse's warrior instinct than a direct assault.

"If you want a shoot-up Maguire, you'll get it," Jesse shouted. Crouching low over the hurtling stallion's extended neck, in the true tradition of the Seventh Cavalry, he charged. He felt as if time had stopped and a thousand disparate thoughts raced through his mind, but mainly his obligation as the officer in command to those serving under him. Robert was young and Frank even younger, and neither was a professional soldier. Jesse heard his own voice, as if from far away, shout to them to keep cover. Urging his horse on, in a screamed whisper, he felt himself back at West Point where he had learned the tactic of direct assault and learned too, that almost no man can stand firm and fight before the thunderous advance of a thousand-pound stallion.

Andrew Maguire of the widely feared Mosby's Raiders had only a brief moment to be afraid. Coming at him like some satanic engine of doom, the horse, its legs stretching in full gallop at every stride, rushed toward him. The animal's ears were laid back flat, its nostrils flared large as saucers sucking wind. The mounted rider, Jesse Sparhawk, seemed to be part of the stallion, as if man and beast were one creature, when Jesse loosed an unearthly howl. The Rebel enemy Jesse saw in his path was swept aside and bowled over. One shot was fired. Maguire was dead.

Robert and Frank had rushed to the fallen man and were

standing over him. They appeared stunned, yet relieved, when Jesse joined them.

"He was the enemy. He became an outlaw. He may have been a truly brave man, once," said Jesse. The words were an epitaph of sorts, the only epitaph Captain Andrew Maguire would ever have.

"His last mistake was to mount an action with insufficient forces, the error also of Jefferson Davis and Robert E. Lee and the whole Confederate rebellion. Now—let's bring Lorena home."

That night, for the first time since they had arrived in Sheridan, Lorena and Jesse shared a bed. They went upstairs immediately after dinner. When the door clicked behind them and the bolt slid into the lock, there was a pause. A low wind whistled about the eves, and rain pelted the windows.

"I must tell you something, Jesse, now that I'm frcc of past encumbrances and we're alone together at last," Lorena said, smiling into his eyes as he leaned at the mantel looking into a leaping warm fire. She came to stand beside him.

"Don't say anything, not now." Jesse's mouth silenced hers, but she pulled away.

"Yes! I have to. Let me. Jesse Sparhawk, I really love you. You are my one true love, and were always from the instant I saw you, and will be forever."

"I know," he said huskily. " 'Whoever loved that loved not at first sight?' the poet asked, long before you and me." His open mouth found hers again, and she gently bit his lip. Her hands ruffled his hair, and she kissed his eyelids softly.

"I love you so, it nearly breaks my heart with the strength of it."

"I know," he said again. "I know you give me all of your-self every time, from the very first time." He lifted her, crossed the room and set her down before the cheval glass near the bed.

She waited impatiently for him to undo the row of buttons

down her back. He worked with a tantalizing slowness, the faintest hint of a teasing smile on his handsome face as she watched him in the glass. When he had finally undone them, she slipped her arms from the sleeves of her dress and stepped out of it. Jesse kissed her shoulder, coiled her long mane in his hand, and the peaks of her high breasts rose in dainty shadows against the long, soft-cotton shift that was all she still wore. He smiled at her sudden intake of breath, and discarded his clothes while she pulled the shift over her head. There was an instant of wonder, of surprise, as always, when they viewed each other, and then she was in his waiting arms, pressing to him hungrily. His hands held her hips locked to his while his eager mouth tasted sweetness, then his tongue teased at nipples budded to advertise her desire.

"Look how beautiful you are," he whispered hoarsely, turning her to the glass. His hands slid down between her thighs, caressing, and then her softness parted to the surge of his thrust. Hesitantly at first, then with proud wonder, Lorena watched in the glass as their lithe bodies curled and moved together, Jesse's broad shoulders and muscled arms enfolding her satin smoothness, his darker hair falling forward, swirling with hers, golden and glimmering. His tongue flicked over his lips. She met his eyes, which were almost savage, and she was fired by the pure male strength of him, by the almost brutal beauty of his chiseled face, of his lean body, the full hard-edged muscles working.

They broke apart and turned to join again, sinking onto the bed, together riding a swell, a tidal surge that crested in wave after wave of pure pleasure that dazzled their senses and left them clinging, drifting breathless in a rainbow of love.

"I used to think," Lorena whispered, drowsy and sighing in Jesse's arms, "I used to think that it couldn't be any more, or any better. And then it is."

Later, the two lovers, fully dressed and wearing heavy sweaters went down to the common room to join whomever was still sitting before the fire.

"Cold enough for you two? I'm surprised you didn't stay up there all close and comfy," said Haley jocularly.

"The thought of a good cigar, the only thing nearly as good as a good woman, brought me here," quipped Jesse.

"Not to mention a little taste of cognac," said Corby, swirling a crystal glass snifter in his hand.

"And some good company," Lorena said laughingly.

Just then, a storm, all the more menacing for being unexpected, struck with its full fury, like a predatory beast loosed on the land. Light rain became hail that was hurled against the house, striking with a sound like boulders in an avalanche. Almost instantly, the windows were thickly blanketed with snow and impossible to see through. Draughts of wind whirled into the cozy room to flutter lamp and candle flames and cause the fire on the hearth to recoil, and then spring up again.

"I think this is one of those storms that strike the plains every ten years or so," Sequoyahson said. "Winds come sweeping down from the north faster than a train can go. The temperature of the air has been known drop fifty degrees in a few hours."

"At least it's late at night now," said Hazel. Most people are tucked up safe somewhere.

"Not like the last great blizzard. That one was during the day. It caught many people out about their work," Sequoyahson said. "Lives were lost. One group of little school children froze following their teacher on a short walk of a quarter of a mile to the nearest house. Another teacher and her pupils in a neighboring town stayed put and survived the storm by burning the desks and chairs to keep warm."

"Oh, my!" Haley exclaimed. "Do you-all suppose those horrible sisters found their way to shelter? Maybe they're still out there in this." No one hazarded a guess.

"I for one don't appreciate this climate, not when it's like this," Rob announced to end the silence. "I don't like it one bit. Just think of the mercury falling so fast. Imagine a blizzard of such strength when it's still only fall!"

"We don't have to imagine. We're in the center of the storm," said Luke. " 'O, wind, if Winter comes, can Spring be far behind?' Ask yourself that, Robert. Are you sorry now you chose not to stay back there in the East?"

"I had nothing to keep me in the East. Tonight, however, I recall with fondness the man-made beauty of the city—bridges, towers, flights of pigeons from tenement roof tops on a summer's eve, forests of masts in the harbors. I think fondly now even of the slum along the river on the far east side of the Island of Manhattan. My father often took me with him on his charity calls to his impoverished patients. I was amazed by the crowded shabby rooms, fire escapes loaded with goods and furnishings, laundry fluttering across alleyways, streets lined with stalls and carts of knifesharpeners, organgrinders, ice vendors, bootblacks. What about you, Sister, do you long for the city, too?"

"I think, Rob, you're homesick, really, and missing Father. I am, too, a little, but from now on, I'll go wherever Archie goes," Rachel said smiling at her fiancé adoringly.

"And you, Jesse?" asked Corby. "Any second thoughts? Any wanderlust? There's a lot of country west of here."

"I'm committed to Sheridan," Jesse said firmly.

"And I am committed to Jesse," Lorena, curled up beside him on a horsehair sofa, said just as firmly.

"Of course, with the new railroad lines reaching out to us, and bigger, faster locomotives in the planning, we'll travel east from time to time, to New York City and farther."

"To France!" Simone said reverently. "Steamships are becoming grand and the food served aboard in the salons is splendid. Oh, I do so long in my heart to see Paris again. In springtime," she added, alert, as were all the others, to the unremitting prairie wind and drifting snow piling white against the windows of the Union Hotel.

"Work's all done. Good harvest is finished," Seek said. "There are stores enough and wood to outlast anything winter sends this way." Hazel nodded.

"Outlast it comfortably and safe, together," she added.

Again, there was a thoughtful silence. Lorena arose, added a log to the fire, watched the sparks fly and then moved to stand in back of Jesse. She placed her hands on his shoulders. He covered them with his own.

"You all know," she began, "that Jesse and I were about to say 'I do,' but we didn't. Now, we've set a new date and this time, we are not rushing into it," she laughed, radiant and beautiful, as any had ever seen her. "It is to be the first day of May in the spring of the new year."

"That'll give us all winter to *really* get to know each other," Jesse explained, laughing also.

Haley sweetly and pointedly said, "Luke?" Luke stood.

"You all know should something else. I have asked Haley for her hand in matrimony, and she has agreed. But we're not planning to hold off any longer than we have to. The first preacher, or even a ship's captain we meet up with—he's our man, right, Haley?"

"Right," she nodded. "Anytime, anyplace, any preacher man, judge or Indian chief will do for us!"

In the midst of the general rejoicing, Robert poured cognac all around and the Sparhawk Settlers celebrated—even as the weather outside grew more and more frightful. Warmed inside and out, tongues loosened and, happily cut off from the rest of the world, they gathered closer to the fire and talked on. The subject, not surprisingly, was the weather.

"This storm reminds me of a New York City blizzard some winters ago. Remember, Rob?" Rachel asked her brother.

"That one wasn't in the fall but at the very end of winter," he replied. One warm day, which had been preceded by others much like it, there was a rainbow around the sun. Temperatures were so balmy that though it was only March, trees in the park were showing buds and Long Island potato farmers were starting their spring planting."

"Then it hit us. It began with rain on a Sunday night, and by Monday morning there were ten inches of snow on the ground, and it kept falling," Rachel continued. "People went out in it thinking the worst was over, that it was about to stop. The cold was devastating and when it finally ended, a day later, the city looked as if a battle had been fought—wires were down all over, signs, shingles, hats had been blown about. I remember most clearly an overturned milk wagon."

"Didn't the government give any warning?" Corby asked.

"The U.S. Signal Service? No, I am afraid not. They predicted fair weather," noted Rob.

"Their so-called 'prophet' in the city," Rachel took up the story again, "was a fellow named Chiron. Supposedly he had telegraph contact with more than a hundred and fifty other stations which got their information from fifteen hundred weather volunteers."

"He even used a carrier pigeon for backup. The fellow closed the office for the weekend with an assurance of fair skies. Nothing was heard from him again until the storm was over," Rob said. "I am of the opinion that it's better to deal with a city storm than a plains blizzard. At least in the city you can find shelter from the cold."

"Robert, it's wind not cold alone, that's dangerous," Lorena interjected. "If you can get off high open ground and into a lowland thicket, better yet into a barn, there's a good chance of making it through. We had our share of bad storms in Seneca Falls during the time I spent there."

Sequoyahson shook his long black hair and said, "The worst storm I lived through, the coldest, was in the Dakota Territory. It was so cold my eyelashes froze stiff. It hurt to breathe. A woman or a child or anyone, can freeze in ten minutes even inside, if there's no fire to warm by."

Then Jesse, who had been silently listening to these accounts, spoke, "When Little Crow and his Sioux rose up in Minnesota, I was one of the officers to lead cavalry troops against him. We were advancing along the Republican River when a terrific snowstorm struck. You couldn't see your hand before your face. We were forced to lead our horses and some of the men refused to keep on. It's tempting to just lie down rather than trudge on through that eighteen inches of snow and vicious wind. I had to encourage, I'll say, some of the soldiers with the flat of my saber or they'd have done just that. We made it through the storm without casualties.

"On that positive note, Lorena and I will retire," Jesse announced, lighting a candle.

"Have a good night's sleep, all, that's left of it, and warm pleasant dreams. Last one to leave, bank the fire," Lorena yawned and followed Jesse from the room. The others soon sought their own beds, most supposing they would awaken to clearing skies. That was not to be.

The storm lasted through three days and nights of blowing, drifting snow. The sun, though not piercing the grayness, turned the sky an eerie yellow once or twice but it was not until the fourth day that the storm abated and the heavens began to clear.

A soft breeze blew fresh as the first breath of spring. As the sun rose higher, the settlers ventured out digging as they went and climbing the huge snowbanks, still frozen solid. By noon, the temperature had risen dramatically and by late afternoon, the snow was thawing and running rivulets. Great piles of snow slipped and roared down from the rooftops to crash below, endangering both man and beast.

By dawn of the following morning, the early risers at Sheridan were amazed to see the prairie in full flood all the way to the horizon. Much livestock was carried away and half a dozen horses drowned. Red Hat Creek washed over its banks. Great chunks of ice crashed into the covered bridge and most of the structure was swept away.

The waters receded quickly. On a morning ride, a few days later, Lorena and Jesse, Rachel and Archie, and young Frank were surveying damage along the banks of the Red Hat. Jesse dismounted where the bridge had recently spanned the creek. He walked toward what he supposed was a large section of wooden planking. As he got closer, he recognized the bodies of Maud Wharton and Estelle Partier.

* * *

On a ridge a quarter of a mile from the hotel, two graves were dug. Jesse read over them from the *Book of Common Prayer:*

> *Forasmuch as it hath pleased Almighty God of his great mercy to take unto himself the souls of our dear sisters here departed, we therefore commit their bodies to the ground; earth to earth, ashes to ashes, dust to dust . . .*

Lord Randall set two wooden markers in place. Hazel sang the *Lord's Prayer*, a cappella.

"If they were wicked and evil, why did you read and sing over those women?" Frank later asked Jesse.

"Death frees the living from judging the ones passed over. Judgment, for all eternity, is left to a higher power," Jesse explained putting an arm over the boy's shoulder. "Giving even the worst of folks a decent burial and a little reading and song eases us all of hate so we can get on with living."

EPILOGUE

May 1, 1866

"Friends, we are gathered together here in the presence of this company, to join this man and this woman in the bonds of Matrimony, which is an honorable estate . . ."

Small, lively Judge Bodner, the distinguished old jurist who had tried without success to join Lorena and Jesse in wedlock once before, was determined to complete the job on his second attempt. Judge Bodner, having been appointed to the Federal judiciary, had come west for that very purpose. Theirs would be the first of eight weddings he would perform that day and the next. The traveling minister, who served Sheridan, the Reverend Mr. Greene, visited irregularly at widely spaced intervals, and there was often a backlog of couples at the settlement eager to wed at once. Some couples had intended to be married and have their infants named at the same time. Christenings, however, were beyond the purview of the judge. They would have to wait for itinerant Reverend Greene, presently at the far end of his circuit in western Nebraska, and not expected to return until fall.

"If any person can show just cause . . . ahem," said Judge Bodner when his spectacles had slipped down his nose. While adjusting them he lost his place in the service. He searched the page before him and Lorena smiled patiently looking about at the assembled wedding guests. The entire Sheridan community was smiling with her, as were visitors who came from afar.

Granny Reed had journeyed from the Blue Ridge escorted by the mountain man Long Jack, the first time either had ever left North Carolina. Long Jack's son, Little Jack, whose height exceeded his father's by five inches and his weight by thirty pounds, had come along, too. The large young man was openly studying a group of the young, single settler girls. Dressed in their best calico, six or seven of them stood fluttering together like a mixed bouquet of flowers touched by a breeze.

Doc Ben and Molly Longworth were also at Sheridan. Jack and Jill, the lively miniature spaniels who went everywhere with Mrs. Doc, had taken a particular liking to Archie. So had Molly, herself, who would always be pleasantly stunned by her demure daughter's brilliant catch.

Ryan Q. Runion, detective, and his recent bride, the former Ethel Hope, ladies' maid at the Longworths', were in the cheerful crowd. It was Ethel who had found, under a break-front, the ring that had flown from Lorena's hand on the previous occasion that Jesse and Lorena were to be wed. Ethel had brought the jewel with her and was impatient to see Jesse put it on Lorena's finger, its destined place, at last. The pause in *this* ceremony was causing Ethel some anxiety.

"What's he doing, Q.? What's the judge waiting for this time?" Mrs. Runion whispered to her husband. Judge Bodner was patting down his fringe of white hair and wriggling his wild white eyebrows.

"It seems His Honor has lost the place in the marriage service. He's going to start over," Q. answered glancing about suspiciously, as was his habit. "Listen now, Ethel."

On his third attempt, Judge Bodner triumphed. He found his place, conducted the full service and at last magisterially intoned, "I, in accordance with the authority vested in me by the law of the United States, pronounce them husband and wife." While the new couple were still caught in their bridal kiss, he headed for the refreshments.

Linen-covered trestle tables were set out under a brilliant, windless Iowa sky. They were spread with the best provisions that could be farmed, fished, or hunted for miles around.

The feast, another triumph for Chef Simone Nicke, was followed by an open-air dance from which the newlyweds slipped away but only after several festive hours. They had said their goodbyes earlier and it was left to just one little boy to throw rice. The colonel and his bride thanked the child and then stepped into a new phaeton built at the Sheridan Carriage Works especially for the occasion. Jesse passed one arm about Lorena and flicked the reins. Their fine bay gelding hurried husband and wife off toward the railroad station in Iowa City where their luggage, sent on before, awaited them.

"Well, Jesse, we've gone and done it this time, haven't we?" Lorena said, proudly pleased.

"Sure have," Jesse nodded as they sipped champagne on the rear platform of the Continental Express, speeding east under a full moon.

"Jesse, there's something I must tell you," Lorena said when they were settled aboard the U.S. Steamship *Leviathan* departing New York Harbor.

"*Must* tell me? You've used those exact words before. Trouble followed," he faintly frowned. "Can't this something wait until the honeymoon is over?" She shook her head no, her lips curling in a smile. "Well, out with it!" he replied with a wary look and a helpless shrug.

"You, Colonel, are to become a father in October."

"Lorena!" Jesse said happily whirling her about before bringing her hand to his lips, "You've just given me the finest of all wedding gifts. I congratulate you, *mother*."

"It's your gift to me, as well. I expect many such presents from you, at least a half dozen more, father," she answered before she kissed him.

"I doubt this honeymoon will ever be over," he sighed into her ear.

The bride and groom returned to Sheridan six months later, in time for the harvest. On their first evening home, five busy rocking chairs lined the verandah of the Union Hotel. Four were occupied by women at varying degrees of expectancy— Simone, Haley, Hazel, and Lorena, who was heaviest with child. The fifth chair rocked under the feathery weight of Rachel Longworth who had always intended to marry as a virgin. With Archie's unspoken acquiescence, the couple was delaying gratification until their wedding night.

The next day Lorena gave birth to a seven-pound boy. The infant was named Jesse Sheridan Sparhawk. He was the first of seven children, six boys and a girl.

Franklin Reed, at seventeen, was selected to attend the United States Military Academy at West Point, New York. James Harlan, U.S. Senator from Iowa, made the appointment. Lieutenant Reed was graduated from West Point and wed there the same day beneath the crossed swords of his fellow officers. Brigadier General Reed retired in 1898 at the conclusion of the Spanish-American War. He and his wife were the parents of four daughters.

Chester Lincoln Sparhawk, the youngest son of Lorena and Jesse, wed the only daughter of Rachel Wharton and her husband, an English nobleman known as just plain Archie. As unpretentious as her parents, Molly Wharton, who was born and raised at Wolf on the Iowa plains, eschewed titles of nobility. Named for her maternal grandmother, she followed in her grandfather Doc's footsteps. Molly was officially Doctor Wharton-Sparhawk, but was familiarly known as Doc Molly. She and Chester had no children, but Doc Molly delivered hundreds of babies over the years, near Sheridan and beyond.

Hazel Reed, widow of Chester Reed of Marshal, North Carolina, married the educator, Sequoyahson Guess. Twins, a boy and a girl, were born to Hazel and Seek when she was forty-two and had given up hope of giving her husband progeny.

Within a generation in Sheridan, there were many Nickes, Hamsons, Wentzes, Wurtzes, and Runions—Q. and Ethel having come west. There were, however, no Longworths. Robert never married. It was rumored for many years that he was the lover of the renowned and stunning actress Caroline Tree, whom he accompanied on all her tours of the Americas and the Continent.

May 1, 1890

"It's a pretty remarkable time we're having, Lorena," Jesse said after a day celebrating their twenty-fourth wedding anniversary. They were alone at dusk on the porch of their own house, completed many years before. Lorena, who had become well known for her nature illustrations and watercolor portraits of her children, set aside her sketchbook when Jesse sat beside her. They were content as they watched a group of young people walking along the lakeshore. Their twelve-year-old daughter waved to them, before she turned her face up, and was touched by the wing shadows of a pair of fishing eagles.

"Yes, it has been and still is a remarkable time, Jesse my love," Lorena said contentedly.

BOOK YOUR PLACE ON OUR WEBSITE AND MAKE THE READING CONNECTION!

We've created a customized website just for our very special readers, where you can get the inside scoop on everything that's going on with Zebra, Pinnacle and Kensington books.

When you come online, you'll have the exciting opportunity to:

- View covers of upcoming books
- Read sample chapters
- Learn about our future publishing schedule (listed by publication month *and author*)
- Find out when your favorite authors will be visiting a city near you
- Search for and order backlist books from our online catalog
- Check out author bios and background information
- Send e-mail to your favorite authors
- Meet the Kensington staff online
- Join us in weekly chats with authors, readers and other guests
- Get writing guidelines
- AND MUCH MORE!

**Visit our website at
http://www.kensingtonbooks.com**